MAINLY FAIR THROUGHOUT THE KINGDOM

GEORGE MCBEAN

Idle George
Publications

For Fergus

CONTENTS

Prologue   1

Part One: The Start   3

Part Two: The Search   63

Part Three: The Stay   125

Part Four: The Find   175

Part Five: The Surprise   225

Part Six: The Passage   273

Part Seven: The Choice   331

Part Eight: The Return   363

About the Author   411
Acknowledgments   413

PROLOGUE

The eulogy page in my father's book is torn loose and sticks out like a bookmark. Friends who borrow it always replace the page in its rightful spot. Framed in a bold black border are words I know by heart, telling how James Munro, a scholar of yoga, was attacked and killed on a mountain trail in Nepal. Dad died in 1966 in the district of Mustang, after political tensions had been stirred with China. The district sits on the northern side of the Himalaya and although it is within the boundaries of Nepal, it shares its culture with those living on the Tibetan Plateau. This incident left me fatherless at the age of eight.

Dad's book is entitled 'An Exploration of Hatha Yoga' and it currently holds relevance for me, since he was twenty-seven, my age now, when he died. It contains his observations and instruction on a subject he seems to have loved. There are photographs too. They are printed on thin shiny paper, stitched together at the centre as they often are by Asian publishers. Black and white landscapes that capture the magnificent light of Nepal, in contrast to the greyness of Edinburgh where I now live. There are also some faded colour photographs of our small red brick house in the

Kathmandu valley where I lived as a child. Then there are pages of dad doing hatha yoga postures.

These photos are the sole visual record I have of dad as an adult. I can see his tanned body, upside down, back to front in classic yoga postures. I resemble him. I have his name, James, the same thin frame, greenish eyes and what he'd once described as our vulture-coloured hair. These pages hold for me not only the mystery of yoga but also of a father unknown.

After years of uncertainty and difficulty as a teenager, I recently completed studies in Public Health in London. I learned how the power of research and social communication tries to change people for the better. I've also recently tried some hatha yoga and grown curious as to how our thoughts influence our experiences as much as life influences thoughts.

Now some twenty years since dad died, I'm planning to take a break and return to Nepal. I want to talk to people he knew there, find his old guru and perhaps visit the place where he died. I feel that if I don't go now I may get stuck in a job rut or a new relationship or a lifestyle involving nights at the Claymore pub.

PART ONE: THE START

1

Mother first met my dad when he was a 17-year-old apprentice draughtsman in Leith's shipyards. She was a sixteen-year-old telephone operator in the drawing office. Dad's years of shipyard training became redundant, she says, when Scotland's shipbuilding industry began sinking from competition in the Far East. Mother says dad had already taken an interest in yoga before he was legally at an age for drinking. They'd saved money, stayed in at nights talking as lovers do and as a consequence been forced to marry urgently a few months before I was born. By the time dad's apprenticeship finished he'd already read every available yoga book in Edinburgh's main public library. Shortly after my sixth birthday they made the remarkable decision to take me out of school, leave Scotland and travel overland to Nepal.

It was the nineteen sixties, there was a so-called hippy trail, but mother says this had no relevance to their journey. Later in his book, dad defines the hippy translation of yoga as one of the most negative periods in its three-thousand-year history. A focus on the drug-taking habits of fakirs, wanting to escape the mind, was a false distraction from yoga's main offerings on taming a troubled mind.

Among dad's favourite books was a collection of meanderings called 'The Yogi and the Commissar', written in 1945 by Arthur Koestler. In this book two types of people are placed at opposite ends in the spectrum of human attitudes, with everyone else somewhere in-between. The Commissar at one end caring only for the state and its social policies and nothing for the self... while at the other extreme the Yogi cares for nothing but the self, showing how its job is greater in coping with everything society throws at it.

Since Koestler's book many things have changed. Few people could have predicted how widespread the global interest in yoga would become, nor how much it would help to empower women. In addition, the views of the commissar have unexpectedly spread into parts of Nepal and India like a monsoon flood. Nowadays it's even possible to find a commissar who is also a yogi, showing the fluidity of the thinking mind.

As a young boy I loved going to dad's drawing office and watching him at work. It was the only period I remember him regularly laughing. Everything in his book is so serious. I struggled to hold onto memories of when he was one of the lads and not the moral leader his tome presents.

He had a twelve-foot-long drawing-board in his office that he strode along to draw the lines of his ship plans. He and his draughtsman mates would banter and draw at the same time. They would take hours to tap in place all the pins for a French curve and then in just an instant draw the contour line of the curved deck, with one long stroke of an H8 pencil.

The most memorable occasions were on the days that ships were launched. The whole yard would stop work to come out and line the slipway. I remember men in dark grey or green overalls packed around a platform covered in bunting.

Sitting on my dad's shoulders, I recall seeing one launch vividly. It was the first time I ever saw a woman wear a sari.

National flags from the UK, Scotland and East Pakistan were hanging over the dignitaries, flapping as wild as prayer flags. Colourfully dressed people from a place called Dhaka stood, like a lost costume party, in the midst of an army of dirty men.

The yard owners, dressed in evening suits, gave their dedication speeches over a crackling public address system. Then the woman in a sari stepped forward to launch the ship with a coconut, instead of the traditional bottle of champagne. A holy man howled a religious chant.

The woman swung the coconut like a West Indian fast bowler. Once... it bounced off the hull. Twice... the same, then on the third hit it smashed and people cheered. There was a crack of timber as the ship dropped from its supports and slowly began to move down the slipway towards the water. The owners gave a 'Hip, Hip' shout on the P.A. system. 'Hooray' answered the yard. Hip, Hip – Hooray. Hip, Hip – Hooray.

As the ship ploughed slowly into the dark green waters, people realised something was wrong. The ship began to roll to one side. A silence descended on the crowd. The visiting launch party watched in horror as the ship lurched and bobbed in its wake, looking like it might capsize. People on the deck were holding on to railings. Two men at the front grabbed lifesaving rings, preparing to jump over the side. Workers poured out from doorways onto the decks, clinging onto topside railings like racing yachtsmen.

Fortunately the ship righted itself, still at an angle, but there was an audible sigh of relief. Then slowly from the bottom of the yard I heard another chant originate. One word only... followed by three loud claps of hands. Others joined in as the chorus grew louder. 'Overtime! Clap Clap Clap. OVERTIME! CLAP CLAP CLAP!' I remember my dad laughing uncontrollably while I clapped my hands in unison.

· · ·

IMMEDIATELY FOLLOWING DAD'S DEATH, MUM AND I RETURNED TO Scotland where she rented a house in rural Peebles. It must have been a sad period for her. She says I was a changed child, but she wanted to keep moving forward not go back to the city life she'd left on our travels. A familiar environment she thought would be too cruel for me.

It had long been her dream to live in the countryside. With some assistance from dad's insurance she quickly developed a business in kitchen gardening and landscaping. I quite enjoyed going back to school. It was a far cry from the sectarian battlefield I attended in Leith.

Dad's thinking is pretty clearly stated in his book, but mum's recollections add a slightly more compulsive side to his character. He was clearly not a religious man but he enjoyed the mental stimulation he gained from reading Indian philosophers, to the point of obsession. He found in yoga a completely fresh lens through which to view his life.

In dad's words, *'Religious leaders try to govern our spirituality in much the same way as politicians govern our society. They seek our vote and confidence. Yoga does not bow to religion; it is a practical discipline that brings you a more comprehensive understanding of life. Yoga focuses your thoughts and deeds and their consequences into a more united consciousness.'*

Dad clearly believed understanding him**self** through yoga was his key to a long and healthy life. Hard therefore to think that he failed, by taking a daft trek in a dangerous place.

These days the range of descriptions of yoga would likely make an old Indian yogi blush with embarrassment. The message has become personalized and diluted and as a consequence spread to more countries and more people than my dad could have imagined.

It took me some years of confusion before choosing to study Public Health. I decided to focus on a field of study where the prevention of illness was equally important as the creation of drugs to treat illness. I knew from my dad's book that the modification of certain behaviours could help save more lives than medicines. Now having qualified, I have some time to decide what to specialize in.

My professor at the London School of Hygiene and Tropical Medicine encouraged me to keep interest in the communication aspects of health. He was a great believer that across the world our beliefs should be treated as infectious and often as dangerous as any disease, because of the misery and ill health they appear to bring.

Professor Barclay, or Barkloudly as he was nicknamed, was not talking about religious belief so much as the fact that so many of us ignore proven health advice that contains scientific backing. There are many of us who believe in some fantasy cure that has no scientific proof whatsoever, while ignoring the advice we've paid to be provided with through the National Health Service. If you can answer this question he told me, why people pay taxes for advice they ignore... then there is a future for you working in public health in the UK.

2

_____

In the old-town tenement flat I've rented for the past year, I roll the air out of my sleeping bag before tying it to my rucksack. I pack walking boots and lightweight clothes, along with a six-pack of new white t-shirts. I don't need to take winter gear. I remember the area of Tamil where mum and dad shopped to buy secondhand climbers' clothing in the markets of Kathmandu.

I fit a new Toshiba T1100 portable laptop computer, into a canvas briefcase. Alongside a Dictaphone and Moleskin notebook I press dad's book into the front pocket with my passport.

The last item to pack is my lady-sized Spanish guitar, which slides neatly into its wooden case. Mum bought it in Nepal over twenty years ago, then taught herself and me the value of music to heal a bereaved heart.

I place the guitar and bags in the corner of the room and look around the flat for anything I've forgotten. The curtains are wide open, the fridge empty and its door ajar. The hall cupboards contain scores of wire coat hangers, left for the next tenants. They jingle like Nepali wind chimes as I check each wardrobe.

The ironing board has a signature pyramid burn mark, which I cover with a dishcloth. I walk on through the house to the toilet and notice water still flowing into the bowl. I quickly wrap Duct tape around the floating ball. I'll be in Kathmandu before its flushed again. I drag a black garbage bag around the living room, putting in all that's escaped my initial clean-up. I tug a small rug over the birthmark wine stain on the carpet.

The last cubbyhole provides a memory I would rather forget. A three-year relationship ended here. Not all my reasons for leaving Edinburgh are aesthetic.

On a hanger my ex-partner's old torn Californian shirt hangs, bent backwards like a young woman laughing. I open the drawer below and pause at the sight of her letter. I tear it up, throw it into the fireplace and light it, like a funeral pyre on the Ganges.

I've taken out my savings, which will give me a year or so of independence. The poorer the GDP of the country, the longer I will be able to stay. It is a journey my mother tells me will be thera-peutic. The loose ends that I leave behind seem insignificant. There are a few unused tickets for the forthcoming Edinburgh Festival and some sorry-for-me relatives and friends.

All I have to do now is to wait for the taxi.

MY PLAN IS TO FIND AND TALK TO MY DAD'S OLD GURU. MUCH OF the wisdom in his book is accredited to one man called the Moni Baba. In his quotes he describes a world still ripe for exploration, fresh interpretation, new beliefs and a degree of choice.

In one quote he states '*the recurring characteristic of all great gurus is their ability to change the way people perceive their problems.*'

I am interested in yoga, but not in submitting my mind to a diet of bumper-sticker wisdom. To do so would be akin to submission, like the nullifying rote learning of a religion.

There is a photograph that shows the Moni Baba painted like some eastern circus clown. A maroon coloured hat, eyes closed with face painted orange and a moustache and beard caked in white paste. Where western societies view our Popes and Bishops standing adorned in the robes of religious authority, this Baba wears only the earth colours of his nudity. In the photo he stands next to another yogi, with a wild hennaed beard, like the combed-out content of a coconut shell. Three white Siva strips are slashed across his brow. The caption indicates they are attending the festival of Kumbh Mela on the river Ganges, the largest religious gathering in the world. Here there are more Gods to worship than all the combined characters from Marvel and DC comic books.

The first yogic conversation I remember having with dad, took place on our roof-top in Nepal when I was eight years old, just weeks before he died.

During the kite-flying festival our neighbour's children cut my kite loose, in full flight, with one slice of their glass-coated warrior-brand string. As I stood there, near to tears, holding a slack line, my dad looked at me and said, 'James – your best friend – is your mind.' That's the bit I remember him saying loudest as if it were a commandment. Then quietly he continued, 'Your mind will be with you the rest of your life – so treat it as a friend, not as an enemy.'

Here was my dad comforting me with a philosophical outlook on life, when all I wanted was a glass-coated kite string. Wherever other kids got cuddles or chocolate in compensation for a disappointment, my father would dish out some soothing yoga.

I realize now he was trying to encourage me to understand my 'self' as a way of reducing pain, but to this day, I've never felt it was possible, since pain seems to consistently sweep away all understanding.

Over the years, I've reflected on that moment and wished I could travel back in time and repeat that conversation. To review dad's commandment with the knowledge I now have. My doorbell rings, the taxi is here, I leave the past behind.

3

——————

On-board the short flight to London, I sit next to a young woman wearing a sari. For half the journey we do not speak, then after the inflight service, I join her in waving away the cigarette smoke that is drifting above our heads from passengers behind.

I give a disapproving look to the two lads smoking, only to have one bend forward, press his face aggressively into the gap between headrests and ask, 'Whae are you lookin at?'

I don't answer.

The other takes a loud drag on his cigarette and blows a volcanic smoke spout into the cabin atmosphere. He speaks philosophically to his friend, 'A've smoked forty fags a day since a wis twelve and you know what, I've enjoyed every single one.' He then blows smoke through the gap.

I see the discomfort on the face of the women and hear her talk quietly, towards me, 'He's obviously confusing enjoyment with addiction.'

She asks me if I'm heading to, or returning to, London. I tell her I'm travelling to India, and she asks where to and for how long.

I tell her I'm travelling to Nepal. She asks me if it's a holiday or business and I tell her I'm on a search to find my father's guru.

I use the word *guru* thinking it will stimulate a cultural interest from her. She wishes me luck but does not seem interested in continuing a guru line of conversation. She has a hint of a Scottish accent in her words.

I ask where in India she comes from and she tells me that she has never been to India. She comes from East Africa and has been on a teacher training course at Edinburgh's St. Margaret's College, for two years. She says she had a Scottish teacher at school in Uganda who had helped her gain a place here. She bends forward and lifts a large bag of books. She tells me they are a farewell gift from friends in Edinburgh. They are books from the Enlightenment by David Hume, Adam Smith. Francis Hutcheson, James Hutton and Adam Ferguson.

'You'll be able to run a successful small country after you read those,' I say.

She asks me if I read books about Indian gurus.

I tell her I have difficulty pronouncing and remembering Indian names for gurus and that I tend to make up alternatives. I tell her I like some books on yoga.

She says she doesn't like books that treat people of different religions as if they are all the same.

'Why?'

'Because all religions have fundamental differences, don't they?'

'Don't you think every religion shares the same goal?' I say.

'Yes… there is much to share from different cultures without it interfering with our religious beliefs. I just hate to be told my beliefs are wrong. It's the biggest insult you can ever say to someone.'

'What do you like most about Scotland's culture?' I ask.

'Scottish Country Dancing,' she replies, smiling at her recollections.

'When I get back to Uganda I want to teach it at my school.'

'Look at us,' I say, 'you heading back to introduce Ugandans to 'Strip the Willow' and me off to Nepal with an interest in yoga.'

'I don't know anything about yoga,' she says. 'I'm an Ismaili, my guru is the the Aga Khan, a great Muslim.'

WEEKS OF SLEEPLESS ANTICIPATION FINALLY CATCH UP WITH ME. I'M unconscious most of the way to Delhi, surrounded by rows of sari-clad passengers. For the last part of the journey I snap out of sleep, wide-awake and alert. I read my now crumpled copy of *The Scotsman* newspaper. There is a science article that seems both appropriate and timely, as my alert mind likes to believe such discoveries are.

A Botany researcher claims that nature favours the seeds of trees that travel furthest from their source. Since plant-eating organisms flourish at the base of every tree, they tend to destroy most of the seedlings that fall there. On the contrary, the seeds that are carried by the wind, far from the tree, survive and flourish best. This seems proof positive that I've made the right decision to leave.

On arrival the air, smell and the night noises all confirm that this indeed is a much more exotic part of the forest. In the arrivals hall and through Immigration I find myself swept toward the luggage pickup, as if carried there by an exiting football crowd. People are speaking dozens of languages and when the conveyer starts there is an air of desperation among those ready to snatch baggage.

Any philosophical thoughts I have of returning to India are abandoned in the crushing density of people. The rickety rubber conveyor belt struggles with an assortment of heavy cloth bags and boxes. A solitary handle with a tag appears, separated from its case. My rucksack and guitar case finally glide round and I scrum to retrieve them. I have to fend off helpers whose arms are already full of other people's bags. I wrestle my belongings free, clutching them all the way to the taxi rank.

It looks as if all-out combat will be necessary for the cheaper rickshaw transport, so I hail an expensive taxi to escape the airport.

I have two nights to stay here. Mother has recommended a hotel and someone she calls the Umbrella salesman. A man I should contact about the whereabouts of the Moni Baba in Nepal.

The hotel is an old colonial building in a central part of Delhi called Three Trees and has been owned by an ex-pat family since before Independence. Outside, billboards loom over the street, proclaiming 'Mass Feeding of the Hungry on Sunday at 10am' and 'Abortion Overnight 2000 Rupees'.

Opposite the entrance there are walls full of movie posters, many torn to reveal body parts and faces of stars in previous movies underneath. The result is a collage of bearded ladies, men with breasts and one star with several arms.

Stepping inside the hotel, there is a courtyard garden of potted plants and the smell of English cooking. The interior has been painted so many times it's like cake icing has been poured from a great height to cover the walls, tables and furniture.

At the reception area there are portraits of the British Royal family, with a young Princess Diana, framed in gold plastic positioned most prominently. There is a menu that boasts nothing but the best of English food. There are glass cabinets with trophies and photos from an age when Britain's influence extended beyond the kitchen. There are sepia-coloured cricket teams, racks of tennis trophies and the odd silver polo cup dating back to 1837.

I walk past a row of white-faced hunters, brown-faced gun bearers, and sad-faced tigers. In the adjoining hall a magnificent fake marble table stands with its ornately carved lion's head legs straddling the black and white floor tiles. The table rests beneath a gilt wall mirror and on a shelf below I find a collection of neatly piled visitors' books.

As I wait for the attendant at reception to check-in, I flip through these books. They provide a glimpse into the past; names and comments by people long departed from British Raj India.

In one threadbare book is the neat handwriting of *'Captain Stephen Park-Goodman... July 17th 1929.* Address: *The Foreign Office, London.* Comments: *Impeccable service, delicious food and stunning countryside views.'*

There is the impressively small handwriting of *Julia Potts... March 12th 1942.* Address: *Granton Road, Singapore.* Comments: *How soon before we see Japanese soldiers signing in here?'*

There is a whole page with the letter **G** signed in the middle, which I take to be from some Royal's hand.

Julia Potts and the surrounding countryside are long gone, but as I flip through a more recent book, the hair on the back of my neck rises like a cobra.

On one page in a small box are the names *'Helen and James Munro'* and in brackets *(wee James).*

As with the single sweep of an archaeologist's brush, something tangible from the past is suddenly revealed. I'm looking at proof of my family's united presence here. There is a childish drawing of Oor Willie that I only now remember making, next to my father's signature.

I take the book in hand to the Reception and point out this early entry to the hotel staff. They seem amused and welcome me back. I tell them the circumstances of my return and briefly the story of my parent's last visit. I'm assigned a special room, in appreciation of my visitor loyalty.

Whenever an occurrence like this happens, its randomness makes me feel elated, briefly guided, and on the right track. I catch my breath at the coincidence of it all, even though my mother probably anticipated this or indeed set me up.

Once settled in my special room, I unpack my rucksack and set all electrical equipment on charge. I clear a space for some hatha yoga postures, and tell myself this is the moment where I should seriously begin my daily hatha yoga practice. Something I've promised myself but never found the time to do.

The Three Trees room is large, but little space is needed when you move your body into shapes and stretches that can be performed in a cave or a prison cell. I open the window at dusk to let the stale air out and the equally stale air in, along with insurgent mosquitoes.

As the sky outside darkens, I'm slowly aware of the black speckles appearing on my ceiling. I close the windows, too late and drift off to sleep as the air is filled with noise. The sound is magnified when the creatures fly past my ears. I succeed in drowning them out by humming a Neil Young ballad and slip into a sacrificial sleep.

THEY SAY IT MAKES YOU GO BLIND, BUT NEXT MORNING I TAKE ANTI-malaria pills and swallow the bitter taste of chloroquine anyway. I examine the emergence of a beard and wonder whether to go for the full yogi look. There are very few bites on my face, but the rest of my body is spotted with craters. I ask reception for advice and I'm given talcum powder, to stop the itch. My light clothes now seem too thick. My feet are swollen from bites, so I buy sandals, another step towards impending hippydom.

I scuff into the breakfast room across polished wooden floors and choose a bowl of Three Trees porridge. I eat all of my English scrambled egg on toast and put my plate on the kitchen counter. Tea bags are required to be disposed of separately in an old biscuit tin marked 're-cycling'. I can't help but think this means they'll be sun dried and re-used somewhere else as tea bags.

4

By mid-morning a heavy shower of rain cools the temperature so I decide to take a rickshaw to find the Umbrella man. As I arrive, I'm relieved his shop is still there. He seems to be doing good business with umbrellas on this wet day. The city's dust gargles down the gullies, leaving the streets shining.

Gupta, his name, is painted in red and gold above the entrance to his shop. Inside a modest box-shaped space, I introduce myself, showing him my dad's book, and inside the photos of the Moni Baba. I then tell him of my quest.

The salesman invites me to sit on the floor. He wears a neatly pressed Nehru jacket with loose pants. If he'd worn a laurel leaf around his balding grey hair, Sri Aurobhinda Gupta could easily have stood in the Roman Senate.

Aurobhinda, he tells me, is his adopted name, taken from a great Indian guru. Gupta, I'm told, is his clan name. As he speaks he pronounces the word great with a Scottish accent – I suspect for my benefit.

'Do you know what the Guptas gave the world?' he asks me in what seems a well-practiced question.

'No.'

'We gave the world... nothing.' He pauses for affect.

'Really!'

'Yes. We gave the world a zero after the decimal point.'

'Now where would we be today, without that zero after the decimal point?'

'Exactly! And more people are using it.'

'Yes.'

'It is something very special this nothing. It's a way of seeing everything. The language of mathematics will eventually dominate mankind's view of the world.'

Gupta tells me he has supplied umbrellas to all of the most important holy men on the sub-continent. Without any encouragement he speaks freely about them and randomly mentions the Moni Baba as today's most genuine living guru.

'What about other famous gurus, like – Rajnesh?' I ask, displaying my limited knowledge.

'Rajnesh? He is an influential charlatan and a devotee fucker, is that how you say it?'

'A what?'

'He rogers his followers. Western and Indian woman... no? Is my English correct?'

'Well... in some pubs, yes, that's what they'd say.'

'Good. Remember to distinguish between those who trade in ancient yoga knowledge as a commodity for personal gratification or gain – against those who have genuinely unified themselves and want to explain how they did it.'

Gupta's language ranges from sounding guru-esque, to being one of the lads.

'You mentioned the Moni Baba as genuine,' I ask. 'Why?'

'You can fill your mind with knowledge of yoga but in the end it's no different from filling your head with knowledge of British history. It has the same effect on you as being knowledgeable about the Kings and Queens of England. Yoga is not a subject you study to gain knowledge, it's a practice to gain union. It's **you** that becomes the subject and goal of yoga study.'

I see in this playful man an opportunity to play devil's advocate so I ask, 'Many people where I come from think yoga is pointless, that there is no qualification given to those who study themselves. You can't find a job by saying that you know more about yourself than anything else in the world. You need other skills to survive.'

'What has changed from ancient times is the scale of the collective knowledge that surrounds a yogi of today. Yoga has developed through the many ways it's been practiced, otherwise it would not deserve the name yoga. At the core there are however some fundamental principles and disciplines.

'What would you say is the most important discipline, Hatha or one of the other yogas?'

'No matter what discipline you adopt James, our most valued mental asset is our ability to self correct, or as you might say, to learn from our mistakes.'

'If the best guru is the Moni Baba, how can I find him?'

My question brings an unusual silence from Gupta. Asking where the Baba might be found seems to make him uncomfortable and evasive. He tells me he will first need to ask some of the Baba's friends and followers and of course he'll need to consult an astrologer for guidance.

'The Moni Baba is always on the move. His home is in the far western hills of Nepal, but before his precise location can be determined I will have to consult the position of the planets.'

'The planets? What can the planets tell you?' I blurt out, swiftly regretting my sarcastic tone.

'The Moni Baba fixes his schedule according to the planets,' the salesman says as if addressing an idiot child. 'By knowing such auspicious information as to where the planets are, I will be able to tell you which festivals the Baba will attend and at what time and place in Nepal he is likely to be there.'

Gupta suggests I give him twenty-four hours and then contact him before I leave for Nepal. He tells me he would like me to sit longer on my next visit; that I need to be prepared, that there is much I should know before I actually meet face to face with the Moni Baba.

I agree and express how grateful I am. I notice the rain outside has become heavier so I buy one of Gupta's umbrellas to join the mass of black mushroom shapes threading their way through the wet streets. Before I step out, Gupta hails me a vassal-drawn rickshaw. A thin half-naked man pulls over and waits, immune to the drenching rain.

'Can he pull me all the way back to my hotel?'

'Oh yes, God-willing,' Gupta says.

'I'm surprised these things are still legal here?'

'Oh yes very legal. Our Council tried to get rid of this de-humanising work... but one hundred and fifty thousand rickshaw wallahs protested at City Hall against the ban. It's their sole livelihood.'

Gupta slaps the side of my canvas chariot and motions for my wallah to move. It is like being inside a drum on parade day. I can hardly hear Gupta shout goodbye as my engine speeds up.

As we negotiate the bumps and holes in the road through a series of backstreets towards the Three Trees, we reach a particularly steep bridge and the rickshaw stops.

'How long have you been working on the ricksaws?' I call out.

My rickshaw driver smiles and flexes his arm muscles in reply.

I hear the wheezing of his breath as his bare feet hit the wet road and we go over the bridge hump and down the other side. I again ask how long he has been doing this work.

'Sahib. Where you from? My name is Doshi.'

5

The next day I'm back with Gupta sitting cross-legged on the linoleum floor. Pedestrians walk passed his door so quickly it gives the impression of being inside a spinning room. Gupta has assembled a pile of books, old manuscripts and charts.

'I told you yesterday that learning the history of yoga is of no more advantage to your personal yoga than learning the history of Kings and Queens in Britain. But I can tell you have an interest in hearing some of it because it might give you some insight into your father's mind and where his thoughts came from. You cannot listen only to the wisdom of men, you might just as well listen for the voice of God... for God knows where men get their ideas from.' Gupta says this with a sense of bewilderment rather than devotion. 'You will definitely recognise some of the origins of your father's quotes in the advice of those he studied, as we here already understand.'

Gupta throws me another cushion to sit on.

'Are you comfortable?'

'No, not really.'

'You asked about popularity of gurus. In India the one who is most followed is Satya Sai Baba. He has stayed most of his life here and gained a very large following. Enormous! Sai Baba is a man of miracles.' Gupta speaks with the same practiced awe in his voice as before.

'According to stories, scissors cannot cut his hair and he can cough up lingums, at any time of the day.'

'Lingums?'

'A penis... a cock? He is of course famous for other things but no followers ever mention Satya Sai Baba's name without mentioning the miracles.'

'Miracles?'

'Oh yes, Jamesji, Satya Sai Baba is a miracle worker, mainly in healing. He has also been accused of hanky panky practice by some western devotees but people ignore this because of the miracles he can perform.'

'The miracle of avoiding criminal prosecution?'

'Ah ha, the law in India – it deals poorly with crimes of the emotion. We are brought up to value getting over things rather than seeking legal action. We have far more gurus here than lawyers.'

'So who were the Moni Baba's teachers?'

'There is an entire empire of yogis who have influenced him. Beginning with Swamy Sivananda who practiced yoga in Rishakesh between the great wars. Then there is Swamy Vishnude-vananda, who became a big man in America, and I mean a big man because of his American diet. He was a disciple of Sivananda. Then there is Meher Baba who was a disciple of Upasani Maharaj. There are many books on all of these people. Your father is also respected here. Among all the people from your country who came here, the people who built the wealth of your country through trade and exploitation of other cultures, your father did not come here with that mindset. He came as someone who valued our culture differ-ently and even adopted aspects of it. Your father was influenced by a line of gurus leading up to the Moni Baba, and if you appreciate this perhaps your will even understand the architecture of your own mind, James.'

'OK. Explain the line.'

'A few gurus come to mind, but some are Bhogis and not Yogis.'

'What's a Bhogi?' I ask.

'A Bhogi is someone who sells yoga knowledge to others for financial profit.'

'You mean there's a word for the commercial teachers of yoga?'

'Oh yes. The Sanskrit language has many words for different types of people, their emotional states and their degrees of spiritual consciousness. Your language is full of words for things, machines and their parts; cars, computers, products, bits and pieces.'

'What about gurus of hatha yoga?' I ask.

'If your interest is in hatha yoga, you must include Mr. B. K. S. Iyengar, the supple practitioner of all hatha yoga postures. He is building the very first temple in India to Patanjali, and is a great documenter of the hatha yoga. He is a very flexible man and the guru to many famous people.' Gupta speaks quietly as if he's giving away a secret.

'Well. As you say, if I fill my head with this stuff it's not really yoga, it's just another history subject. I'm less interested in hearing the merits of one guru over another, I just want to know more about the Moni Baba.'

'Oh yes you are interested,' laughs Gupta, inappropriately loud. 'I can tell. Most gurus are just theatrical bhogis who crave attention. You must know if you are standing next to a real yogi and associate only with those who offer the right teaching for you at the right time.'

Gupta goes silent as if he's having second thoughts about sharing further information about the Moni Baba.

I yawn, a complete give-away as to my state of tiredness. He looks up and seems to be considering whether it is worthwhile continuing. He looks at me curiously for some time. He then claps his hands and calls out to the heavens for soft drinks.

A young boy enters the shop, carrying Fanta bottles. He puts down two and without saying anything disappears. Gupta stretches and hangs the 'Closed' sign outside on the door. He closes the folding blinds; a neon strip of light explodes into the room and stops the illusion of spinning. The salesman again sits, this time in a pensive cross-legged position while I support myself against the wall with my stiff legs stretched in front of me.

We talk a further two hours and although I have the time I do not have the muscle capacity to sit for this long, so I stretch and move restlessly between Gupta's chatter. I keep bringing the conversation around to the Moni Baba, but the salesman ignores my requests for concrete directions. My frustrations finally over-flow when I interrupt Gupta's relentless spiritual ranting.

'I'm hoping to find the Moni Baba simply because he's the one who taught my father, not so I can seek spiritual enlightenment.'

Gupta comes back with a final contribution, as if an alarm clock has gone off in his head, triggered by my impatience.

'For most children, James, seeking guidance is not something that disappears on attaining adulthood. Adults like children need to be regularly told how things work. Of course you can survive with what you know but there is also a longing to do better in most of us, especially when you find others who can help you.'

'So, tell me where the Moni Baba is now and how to find him.'

After a pause Gupta speaks as if reciting an ancient fairytale. 'He travels here and there.' I hear the lyrics of Donovan's song in my tired mind.

'He walks extensively across Nepal but it can never be guaran-teed where he will be found. He regularly visits Pashupatinath in the Kathmandu valley, during the festival of Shiva Ratri. The rest of the year, only a few people know where he lives. For three weeks around February anyone can go and meet the Baba, but unlike most other gurus the Baba does not only talk of God; he gives advice on many other matters. For the rest of the year he lives in seclusion in various remote Himalayan villages and gives audience only to those who discover his whereabouts by chance.'

'But where is he **now**?'

'No one can ever be sure where he has settled. For the past few years he has moved with a companion and sightings have become more frequent. He is always seen with a young woman who was once a Kumari, a living goddess, raised until puberty in a temple near Kathmandu. Whenever a Kumari first passes blood a new Kumari is chosen to replace her. The older Kumari is then cast out into society to fend for herself. Most have never been educated. No one dare marry such a girl for it is believed they would die if they ever have intercourse with her.

'A few years back the Moni Baba adopted the one he named Sita when she was cast out from the town of Bhaktapur. Their nomadic lifestyle together has become legendary; she dresses only in white, the colour of mourning and she has become his constant companion. He has educated her in the ways of yoga much like he did your father.

'There are many that you can talk to about the teachings of the Moni Baba, but there is no better ways of experiencing his wisdom than to find him for yourself. Now I must go home, the cricket highlights are on the television this evening and I don't want to miss them,' he concludes.

I stand and grimace as the blood flows back into my cramped legs. I stamp on the ground with my feet and Gupta laughs aloud. I ask if there are any others in Nepal who know the Moni Baba, who perhaps I should talk to when I get there. Gupta mentions a raffle-ticket salesman who is to be found outside a popular eatery on the Raj Path in Patan.

'Hemisphere jumping,' Gupta states, 'is what happens when orators begin their talks in the factual side of their brain, attracting our confidence in their knowledge and then jump to the populist part of the brain, to entertain us and keep our attention. It's why people enjoy soap operas as much as documentary film, why songs are as necessary as lectures. The raffle-ticket salesman is an expert on hemisphere jumping.'

'I can't wait to come face to face with a hemisphere jumper,' I say.

6

I consider how best to spend my last few hours in Delhi. The pace of life seems more hectic and angst-ridden than most crowded cities, but people here have been used it for centuries. I can't wait for the chance to find some peace in the Kathmandu valley that I remember living in.

I find a pile of tourist guidebooks on the bedside table. I read the punchlines describing the wonders I'm surrounded by, in the vastness of India. This is how India wants itself to be seen by the visitor. There are photos of the Red Fort, the sixteenth-century tombs of the Lodi rulers and the Taj Mahal; the world's greatest monument to love lost.

I suddenly feel exhausted. I stretch out on my bed and think what my story would sound like if I hemisphere jumped between the serious studies and the soap opera that has surrounded it so far.

I HAD A FRIEND IN PEEBLES WHEN I WAS GROWING UP. DAVE WAS ONE of the first people I met at school, after mother and I returned from Nepal. We became inseparable. I was shy and he impressed me with his ability to defend himself verbally, especially from assaults on his looks and mannerisms. We moved to Edinburgh together after school before I took up my studies in London at the London School of Hygiene and Tropical Medicine. He was like the younger brother I didn't have.

In London I worked hard for my degree and consciously avoided any serious romantic relationships. In my last year of studies I won a two-month bursary to attend a summer workshop on "Message Design" at the faculty of Communication at Stanford University in the USA. Apart from my childhood travels to Nepal, this was the only other overseas trip that I'd taken.

Down the hall from my dormitory, working in the canteen I met Fiona McRae. She was an American lass with Scottish grandparents, from Palo Alto and attracted to me, she confessed, by my accent. She let me talk for hours. She accepted the sadness in my story of a murdered father and I fell in love.

Fiona filled me with her enthusiasm to explore new places. She had a hankering to visit what she called the home country, Scotland. She was confident but abrasive and largely ignorant of any culture outside the USA. She had manufactured her beauty, the sort of appearance that takes lots of time to maintain. Big dyed blonde hair, red lips with endless changes of clothes in a day. When my course ended I invited her to come to visit me.

It must have been a bit of a shock for her, coming "home" to Edinburgh. Beautiful though it appears, it is a small town with folk not always as accepting of loud public personality as they are in California. Fiona's extrovert nature attracted plenty of gazes from people in the street.

Her culture encouraged her to share her conversations in crowded pubs, full buses, whole theatres, with potential for large stadiums of people. America she would say is built on this sort of open talk. Once she even quoted my Stanford lecturer back to me, saying, 'Free speech is a necessary component of a large multi-cultural society'. I thought at the time she was confusing meaningful speech with noise in announcing your existence. Her verbal offerings and enthusiasm were always in stark contrast to the angry whisperings of parochial Edinburgh folk.

This is where Dave came into the picture. In the circles we frequented you could get away with being verbose only if you had a quick wit as well as volume to your voice. Then everyone wanted to hear you. If you are not funny, you are immediately told so and best keep quiet.

Fiona loved it when the three of us went out together. Dave was the wit, she provided the glamour and I was the organiser. She had a cheerleader's delight for life, always positive about doing new things. Even in bad weather she would dress to be seen, turning heads with tight jeans, tank tops and aerobic clothes. Our relationship seemed full of potential and perhaps that's where it began to go wrong. Not keeping an eye on what was under our noses and always thinking about what was still to come.

Fiona grew impatient for me to open some imaginary door to the fame that awaited her. Lying in my hotel bed in Delhi I recall a moment that until now has remained buried, perhaps in the trench between my brain's hemispheres.

After a few months of living happily together back in Edinburgh, I asked Fiona jokingly if she was having an affair with someone because she'd stayed out late the night before. I caught her off-guard with the question. Her West Coast honesty flashed across her face. I knew in that space of a second that she had been seeing someone else.

With the wisdom of hindsight, I realise that our attempts to construct a relationship began to crumble from that moment on. Whether it was my questioning of her loyalty or her genuine discovery of love elsewhere, I'll never know. That night Fiona made love to me in the most memorable way. She was moody and uncharacteristically aggressive. She was passionate and inventive. She exhibited herself like never before. She teased and coaxed and screamed in conclusion, for all the wrong reasons. We lay there, naked, exhausted. We laughed uncomfortably. She was her most affectionate at the pinnacle of her betrayal.

One month later, she and Dave moved to London together. I tried to spread the blame, like water over marble, to all aspects of our relationship. All my aggressive thoughts were directed at him, not her. My last words to her were of forgiveness and best wishes. I was infected with the romantic version of Stockholm syndrome.

Just before I set off from Edinburgh, I felt totally prepared to take on this trip. As an only child, having dealt repeatedly with loss, I have no binding commitments to work or friends. I am comfortable in my own company but I fear I might suffer from doubts about doing this on my own, with no witnesses.

As I check out of the Three Trees, I sign the visitor's book once more.

James Munro,

June 1986

As usual great hospitality, a hotel that is like an old loyal friend.

7

R oyal Nepal Airlines are the only international carrier that cancels flights on days deemed inauspicious by the country's astrologers. On the day I leave for Kathmandu I'm anxious until I'm told the day is auspicious enough to fly and in a further stroke of luck I'm moved into first class. I take this as a good omen.

When you have not flown that often there is something fatalistic about air travel, unlike any other form of transport. It feels more risky, although statistics prove it is the safest form of mass transit. I have always boarded planes with a heightened degree of resignation. I convince myself that something has concluded when I board and if I arrive safely, something fresh will begin.

Flying also makes it appear there is plenty room for everyone on the planet. Asia's much talked about population explosion does not look all that bad from the air. Aside from the cities, this crowded continent seems spacious. Then all of a sudden the land is suddenly pushed up into the sky as we approach the Himalayan mountains.

I remember my dad's explaining the size of Nepal to me as a

child. He told me on a map, the Kingdom looks similar in size to England and sits like a hyphen between Pakistan and Bhutan. If you were to hammer Nepal out flat however, it would be nearly a third the size of India. Dad then tore our map of India near in half and scrunched it up to the size of England to demonstrate. That crumpled piece of paper is what I'm now looking at from the air.

What would alien creatures think of our planet if they were to find us and study it? They'd likely call it Water rather than Earth.

What if the alien equivalent of David Attenborough was sent to observe humans in the same way as we study nature and other animals? They would record all human behaviour as acceptable... simply because it exists.

Humans, in contrast, spend an enormous amount of time contemplating our mistakes. In the highest offices of the land, governments create an endless list of failures that politicians debate over before making political plans and allocating huge chunks of time to stop these things from ever happening again. We spend trillions of dollars and millions of hours essentially saying **No** to certain types of human behaviour.

From our earliest primitive cultures up to our acceptance of International Law, we have had systems in place to judge which human behaviour is acceptable or is unacceptable, from a dislike of our neighbour's habits, to efforts to end wars and conflicts, crimes, exploitation and poverty. Most of our social institutions have been designed to protect us from what we see as our own flaws.

We would be the first to confess to aliens that as individuals we lack confidence in many of our activities and that we often seek help. Many of us look to the past, to where we've come from to find help. We like to record the histories of our purpose... and not dwell on the consequences of our purpose. If we eventually disappear as a species, we will likely believe it is because we have made a very serious mistake.

As I look down towards the terraced hills sculpted from near vertical land it is hard not to admire the survival qualities of humans. We have created our own alien to guide us, something that has more power and more wisdom than ourselves. We have never seen ourselves as worthy; we are far too conscious of the impact of failure.

At the back of the plane I hear a cheer from some Nepalese men, in tracksuits. They are celebrating the crossing of an invisible border some thirty thousand feet below. We are now in Nepal airspace.

As one of the men waddles to the toilet I catch a glimpse of his arm. He has wristwatches strapped right up to his elbow. He also seems to be wearing as much as he possibly can dress up in, presumably to take back and sell. He looks like the Michelin tyre man and I wonder how long it will it take him to relieve himself in a cubicle he hardly fits into.

I fasten my seat belt as we begin to descend. Out of the window for as far as I can see, there are jagged cliffs slicing into hills dotted with homes. Some valleys are so deep the sun doesn't reach the bottom. All this land is topped with the ragged white teeth of the Himalayas biting into the blue sky, like a shark's lower jaw.

8

_____

Once landed, I clear customs and take a beat-up taxi into the city. The ride to town is an unexpected step up on the danger scale from the flight. My driver accelerates into the flow of traffic as if he has just begun his racing career. From side streets into every corner of my vision are rickshaws, bicycles, cars, trucks and overcrowded buses. The taxi's windscreen could be an Atari computer game.

As I'm sitting in the front seat, my foot repeatedly slams against the floor on imaginary breaks. I think of my relaxed voyage with Doshi's rickshaw in Delhi. It's definitely not the serene capital of Nepal I remember. The capital's initiation into traffic anarchy requires a yogic level of tolerance and skill. The taxi driver works his horn and breaks simultaneously as if he's playing a musical instrument, in an orchestra of chaotic sounds. His hands and feet compete against each other for speed.

In the city centre I see glimpses of the temples at the end of streets where this three-thousand-year-old rural culture is coming into contact with the fumes and machines of urban transport.

Rural hill people, clearly unfamiliar with roads or traffic, step out in front of us with suicidal innocence.

Faster than necessary, the taxi arrives at the Chakra Guesthouse. I pay the driver a few extra rupees for which he Namastis me gratefully then speeds off. I check in at reception with a child around twelve years old. He tells me he's the only family member who speaks English. When I ask to see a room he shows me one on the first floor. A bed, a wardrobe and an en-suite sink are squashed under a low ceiling. To see if there's running water, I turn on the tap. It's positioned in such a way it splashes on the edge of the sink and sprays me across the front of my trousers. The child looks to see how I will react then asks if I want the room. I accept, feeling this baptism may be part of a ploy to stop guests wanting to walk anywhere else with wet trousers. I'm given a padlock the size of a wall clock for the door.

My new base is nestled in the central market area of Thamel in Kathmandu. It is within walking distance of everywhere I need for inquires into the Baba's whereabouts. I unpack and succeed in taking a quick wash after allowing the tap to dribble water.

I go for a walk towards some of the sights that should feel familiar to me. I pass the Royal Palace and head towards Assan Tol, but the crowds and vehicles trying to negotiate the larger streets surprise me.

The small open-front shops are still overflowing with crafts, jewellery and clothes. Carpets hang from windows onto the ground. In this area of dusty narrow streets there is a continual background noise of cyclists ringing their bells, and weaving through the crowds. Fruit and vegetable vendors spread their baskets across the open squares. They squat selling their goods. There are still only a few butcher shops, easily identifiable by the legs of buffalo that stretch out from their doors, tripping the unobservant passer-by. Pink painted goat heads stare at customers from the walls and an assortment of beggars follow people, some with a haunting iodine deficient look on their face.

As I cross a junction into New Road, two European girls suddenly stop me. Before I know it, one is holding onto my arm, asking if I speak English and can help them. They tell me they have been accosted and followed by a man who is foaming red at the mouth.

They look genuinely concerned. The one holding onto me, points to a long fresh scratch on her upper arm and then to the red-mouthed man. She says he grabbed her outside their hotel as soon as they got out of a taxi from the airport just moments ago in a street near by.

Streams of people pass us by all mumbling in Nepali and giving us curious looks. Many of them are shouting in Nepali at the red-mouthed man, presumably telling him to go away, since within minutes he disappears.

One man in a uniform tells the girls not to worry, that the man is not well in the head, that he is a Cretin, with a harmless mental condition. He suggests we walk away in the opposite direction to feel safer. As we reach a broader cross-road, a policeman directs traffic with arms waving like a ceremonial dancer and there is no sign we're being followed. My new companions seem less tense and we formally introduce ourselves.

Gill and Alice are from England and have stopped over for a few days in Kathmandu after a gap year in Australia. They arrived only an hour ago from Bangkok. The policeman and others look over at us and a couple of motorcycles see their chance and bolt through traffic unnoticed.

Alice has blonde hair and tanned skin and looks the negative image of Gill who has jet-black hair and a pale white complexion. They seem to be drawing attention because they look dressed for the beach in Thailand, not the streets of the sub continent. Alice is wearing cut-off shorts and a silk top with spaghetti straps. Gill is wearing black denim shorts. She is clearly bra-less with nipple rings showing through a thin cotton top.

Alice tells me how she was attacked the moment they got out of their taxi. The street was very busy and she got so frightened in case the man was not alone, she ran. Gill tells me she left their luggage in the taxi and ran after Alice. They sparked a frenzy in the street with people shouting things they couldn't understand.

Alice says she doesn't know why people turned on her but she was terrified, and she could see the mad looking man chasing her.

'Aren't Hindus supposed to be like Buddhists here? We never experienced anything like this in Thailand,' remarks Alice.

I tell them their attacker looked like someone suffering from Cretinism, or more politically correct these days, someone suffering the effects of Iodine Deficiency. It is unusual for someone like him to be violent towards strangers.

'What about the foaming red mouth?' Alice asks, still troubled.

'It is the result of chewing Paan, a common stimulant here and in India. It's likely this is an isolated case. I don't believe you were really at risk from a mob in Kathamndu.'

As we all walk in the direction of their hotel, Alice is tearful because she's left her passport and money behind in her abandoned backpack. Gill has her money and passport safely zipped into the pocket of her black shorts.

I suggest they will most likely find their belonging where they left them, despite the appearance of chaos on the streets.

As we approach their hotel, Alice jumps for joy as we near the entrance and she sees the taxi driver, standing with her luggage at his feet. She is so relieved she runs over looking to give the man a hug until he steps back cautiously.

'When will she learn,' murmurs Gill.

'He will be very relieved not to have to report a couple of missing tourists to the police,' I tell her. 'You might also draw less attention to yourselves by changing out of the Bondi beachwear, if you take another stroll around town.'

'Thanks for that, guru James.' Gill says this sarcastically, without knowing anything about my background, or my quest. I smile and bow back in a guru-like manner.

I stay around until both are checked into their hotel and I invite them to have a chai tea with me once they have put their luggage into their room.

I am pleasantly distracted by this good Samaritan moment because it seems to have been successful. I am reminded of what it feels like to be that young again, at the end of your teenage years, filled with all the effervescence of adventure and potential for new relationships.

Alice and Gill return to meet me in the pokey little tearoom of their cheapest in town hotel. They have both changed their clothes. Alice is now wearing silk baggies, Gill has on slightly thicker black cotton shorts and I notice with her hair pinned up, her ear is like a curtain rail with earrings that clink when she moves. They seem comfortable pushing the boundaries of risky attire. We are at least indoors.

They tell me they are from Bristol. They've spent almost six months in Australia and are now heading home. After four weeks traveling in Thailand they've added on a three-day stopover in Kathmandu before flying home to London.

This stopover was a last minute addition and they had no idea the cultural differences between India and Thailand are so great.

'A woman should be able to wear whatever she likes,' Alice says.

'We saw plenty of photos in tourist books with half naked men in the streets of India, before we came,' Gill adds defiantly.

'Ah, but they're yogis,' I say knowingly.

The girls asked me what I'm doing in Nepal. I tell them briefly about my travel plans and the search for my father's guru. Gill laughs. I tell them I will have to leave soon to meet someone who may be able to give me more information relevant to my search. I tell them I'm going to meet up with a hemisphere jumper.

'Will he be wearing it?' asks Alice.

Alice invites me to meet up with them again later in the evening. I agree and give them my contact information at the

Chakra. I tell them to find a suitable place between our hotels to go eat food of their choosing.

I've now known Gill and Alice for one hour and twenty minutes but we each kiss on the cheek, as if we are long-time friends. They ask where I'm really going off to and I tell them, to find a raffle ticket salesman on the corner of the Raj Path who will tell me how to find my father's guru.

9

_____

Sitting on the pavement selling raffle tickets is the man whom Gupta told me makes a yearly pilgrimage to hear the Moni Baba. As he sits chanting prices, his tickets flap in the wind under paperweights that prevent them from fluttering off his cardboard box. He shouts a continual barrage of words, naming the glamorous money prizes that can be won. He appears to change accents and languages to attract different people who pass him by.

He immediately addresses me in English as I approach him. I tell him I'm interested in speaking to him about the Moni Baba. He ignores me and continues shouting, not missing a second of his sales pitch. He stands in a tattered coat but I can see glimpses of a new shirt underneath. He looks in his mid-forties, with a thick bushy moustache, waxed, like two brush handles. He has a number of deep scars on his shaven scalp.

I offer to buy a book of lottery tickets and he seems more responsive. I buy a sufficient amount of his time to answer me. His arms motion a small boy from a doorway to come and take over. Like a ventriloquist's dummy, the child begins to shout in the same voice, in the same tones, with his stance a miniature replica of the raffle man. I'm then taken down a side street to the back door of an eating-house.

After opening the door, I'm given a stool to sit on and offered a cup to tea.

'I had tea earlier,' I tell the salesman.

'Don't worry,' he tells me, 'this tea will undo the harm of your last tea.'

The raffle ticket salesman speaks in a whisper as if we are spies exchanging sensitive information. I've not to be fooled by appearances, he tells me. He owns this eating-house, but makes more money on a good day from his raffle sales than he does from his restaurant.

'When you sell luck,' he tells me, 'there are no limits to sales and no overheads.' He opens his coat and looks at his pocket watch, to illustrate his standing.

I ask when he last saw the Moni Baba and after loud sips of tea, he pulls a few dog-eared photographs out of his coat pocket and places them carefully into my lap. He blows onto his tea and sips it loudly again, as if giving it CPR. He looks at me intensely across the wide face of his cup.

I tell him about my father and his relationship with the Moni Baba; about his book on hatha yoga and my quest to find the Baba. I tell him about Gupta and what he said about hemisphere jumping.

The raffle salesman smiles and seems more relaxed.

'Hemisphere jumping,' he says, 'is something many gurus perfect.'

'Please explain.'

'You might understand it as going off on a tangent. Gurus do it all the time… some never go back to the point they started yet you find meaning in what they say.'

'And is this what the Moni Baba does?'

'Yes, he can be talking about the ancient yogi Milarepa and the meaning of the Hindu swastika and then end with how Hitler changed the meaning of that symbol forever.'

'And what is his message in that?'

'How something that was designed to symbolise good luck and prosperity in by one generation can be found by another generation to symbolise slaughter.'

'That's hardly a tangent of thought. That's pretty much straight to the point.'

'The Baba will take this guru–speak further. He might point out that people bring their own meaning to what they see and that what they bring is that which is most often ignored by the authorities empowered to teach us.'

I regret not bringing my recorder. Guru-speak indeed, ranging from religion to politics, but he also spreads out some of his photographs, as if to illustrate how quickly a subject can be changed and a tangent can be taken.

He points to one photograph showing a tiny old man, gesturing left and right. There is another photo showing a young woman with wild black hair standing beside the old man wearing a simple white dress. I look through the photos and note the Baba is speaking to a few hundred people in each.

The Baba looks older and greyer than he did in dad's photos. I flip through the collection quickly and stop at an extraordinary image of the girl in white. She has the appearance of someone in a UNICEF appeal photograph.

'Is this Sita, the living goddess the Baba adopted?' I ask.

'Yes,' he says, surprised.

Despite her wild hair and natural beauty, all eyes in the crowd are on the Moni Baba. The raffle man then hands me a small booklet with yellow weathered pages, headed in English type "The 35th Nagarkot Teachings of the Moni Baba."

I remember references to Nagarkok teachings in dad's book, but this is the first full text I've seen. 'It's from one of the yearly gatherings the Baba gives on the rim of the Kathmandu valley,' I'm told. 'Only a few copies of the Nagarkot teachings have ever been translated into English and this one is classed as one of the most influential,' the raffle-man tells me. 'It is helping to lay the seeds of democracy in Nepal.'

'I know nothing of the political situation in Nepal.'

'The King of Nepal is the paramount ruler and looked on by most to be the reincarnation of the God Vishnu. However, political change is blowing in the hills and valleys of the Himalaya.'

'Can I buy this Nagarkot booklet?' I ask the raffle salesman.

'This is my only copy,' he tells me.

'Where else can I find one?'

'Nowhere,' he says. 'This one is valuable because it is rare. There are Newaris who are on a waiting list to hold and read this copy.'

'Why don't you print more?'

'When something is common, people pay less money.'

After a moment of silence, he tells me I can read it overnight if I return it to him by six o'clock the next morning. I request it for longer but he insists I only have one night and that I should leave something I value with him as insurance.

All I have to leave him is my passport, or dad's book.

The raffle salesman sees my reluctance to hand over dad's book. He accepts it with care and gives me the Baba's manuscript with equal reverence.

I also leave him my contact address at the Chakra.

'In case I'm delayed, this is where I'm staying.'

'N'shallah!' he says, confusing me again as to his belief system.

'The Baba's words will make you, how do you say... ponder. No one is better at making you ponder than the Moni Baba.'

WHEN I RETURN TO THE HOTEL I CONSIDER PHOTOCOPYING THE manuscript. I have a serious choice to make, either to go out and have dinner with Gill and Alice or stay in and read or copy the

Nagarkot Teachings. I glance through it. It's not very long but the text is written in a dense old-English style and one sentence jumps out at me. *The animal is strong in the young – it is influenced by one's culture and education and caged only to the degree of influence these things have had.*

I ponder my animal instincts more. This Baba attracted my parents to an unknown destination on the strength of his words; they left a home I was happy in, to travel and live in a strange new culture. Why should this be such a difficult choice? I should stick to my quest and copy, yet I can't shake off the unknown potential of the evening.

The Chakra reception boy knocks on my door telling me there's a call for me at the front desk.

It is Alice. She tells me they have both moved out of their hole-in-the-wall accommodation and signed into a five-star Hotel on Durbar Marg, near me, as an end of trip treat to themselves. They have booked a table for three at the Lancer Restaurant mid-way between both our hotels. They have also been shopping in the hotel's boutique and bought more appropriate clothing. She promises me they'll both wear their brassieres so I can enjoy the food more.

Alice continues talking in a chatty voice telling me about their helpful new hotel manager Andre. He's approved their new Neru jackets as acceptable attire for Kathmandu.

I interrupt and say I'm in a bit of a dilemma and that I have only tonight to copy an important document. She suggests that I bring it to their Hotel's 24-hour business centre or record it onto a tape recorder.

'Yes,' I remind myself, 'I have a recorder. Thank you Alice, see you soon.'

I put down the phone. How often, I consider, do simple solutions seem to escape me in the company of an attractive women. I hurriedly read out the text into my tape recorder. It is dense and there is evidence of political thought from the Baba that's obviously taken root much earlier than I believed the Baba has ever referenced it. It's a speech from someone who does not babble the well-rehearsed dialog of religious speakers. It takes me thirty minutes to read, pausing occasionally to absorb the best bits.

I dress quickly for dinner with one of my new white t-shirts and khaki trousers. I'm left with five pristine t-shirts for five more special occasions.

10

At the Lancer restaurant, the girls occupy a central table in a crowded room and seem quite a few drinks ahead of me. As I join them there is an old friends' reunion feel, with hugs and kisses on the cheek.

Alice tells me that she and Gill met as Art students, and they are returning to jobs in Bristol in the film animation industry. She says she was brought up by her mother as a dancer and always liked drawing. She was attracted to film animation through her experiences of movement. Her voice is soft and I tell her she has ballerina's carriage.

'Yes quite... Prince Charming,' Gill adds.

Gill likely graduated from the punk school of art. She's now wearing her hair up, held by two drawing clips and I notice a Maori tattoo covering the back of her neck. I also notice that in the time between me entering the restaurant and taking my seat, the top two buttons on Gill's tunic have become unbuttoned.

I try to keep the conversation simple, but they are relentless with questions. I tell them I like music, play the guitar and have an interest in the use of visual art in Public Health work.

'It has a lot of uses, especially to communicate with young or non-literate adults.'

'Did you have anything to do with designing the Edinburgh tattoo?' Gill asks, leaning forward.

We are interrupted with a selection of dishes already ordered by the girls on the waiter's recommendation.

The smell of spices is so strong it clears the sinuses instantly. In this environment, Nepali food seems more delicious than I remember. Here, the vegetable korma is chieftain of the curry race, perfectly designed for this climate and atmosphere.

Alice explains that for the last seven months, she's kept an account of their travel adventures in her gap-year diary.

'You're lucky today didn't end differently,' I say, thinking of the lost luggage.

'I was so happy it didn't that once we checked into the new hotel, I actually read through all the entries. What's frightening is that I've already forgotten some of the people we met.'

'And not everyone we met got into that dairy,' says Gill.

'In order to get into that book,' Alice continues, 'we'd have to have spent at least a day or two together, sharing our life stories and then listening to theirs. Most were fellow travellers but also a few locals. We took their names and promised to get back in touch,' she says. 'Now I can't even remember what some of them look like. It's scary to have had that level of intimacy with people then forget them in such a short time.'

'Yeah,' says Gill, 'we shared more than our life stories with some of the guys.'

'I only had about twelve friends from five years of college and now I have over sixty from a few months on the road. Look at you, for example! I'm here in Kathmandu for a matter of hours, I'm attacked and you come along to save the day. You deserve at least a postcard when I get home. Where shall we send it, James?'

I confess I don't know how long it will be till I'm back in Edinburgh. But with more prodding I tell them I'm following the route

49

my folks took me on as a child. I mention my interest in yoga and suddenly Alice leans forward and Gill leans back. It is a comic reaction, both moving at the same time and they look at each other and laugh.

'OK, he's all yours,' Gill says.

'She's referring to the fact that I took yoga classes at art college,' Alice says apologetically.

'What did you learn?'

'That it was good for calming you down and removing stress.'

'And improving her orgasm,' says Gill.

'Something you don't seem to need yoga for,' counters Alice.

'I can have regular inner joy without yoga,' says Gill.

I speak more of yoga with Alice. The spicy dhal has encouraged Gill to unfasten more of the lower buttons on her tunic, exposing her belly ring. Only one button now remains between Gill's brassiere and another costume incident in the restaurant.

'There are fakirs all over India and Nepal, who go out of their way to show they can control pain. They pierce their sensitive parts and hang weights from their testicles during festivals,' I say between mouthfuls of Bhadja.

'Please please James, not at the table.' Alice speaks with a mouthful of food then looks across to Gill. 'He's all yours.'

'What music do you like?' asks Gill.

'Be very careful what you answer, Mr Munro,' says Alice. 'Realize that this one question will expose everything about yourself that's most important to us. The wrong answer and we're done as a threesome.'

'I like all music…'

'Chicken shit cop-out!' interrupts Gill.

'But particularly acoustic bands.'

'What – like folk music or yuk,' Alice sticks her finger in her throat, 'country songs?'

'Careful, we might walk out now,' warns Gill.

'Not folk music more blues, artists like Joan Armatrading? John Martyn? Richard Thomson?'

'Yes, we've heard of them. Who do you think we like?' asks Gill.

'Joy Division, The Cure, Bowie?'

'Not bad, Mr James. Alice here likes Cher but she also likes Manic Street Preachers and Neil Young.'

After the meal we move to a quieter part of the restaurant for Lassi and spiced tea. We are then offered the Nepali equivalent of Irish coffee with fruit liquors. It tastes dangerously delicious.

I am handed the restaurant bill that seems hefty and my new friends insist on paying. I walk back with them to their new hotel and they take me out back to a large garden where we sit on a swinging seat together. We continue the musical taste test with just words and nods.

Me, 'David Crosby?'

Gill, 'Ok.'

Alice, 'Fleetwood Mac?'

Me, 'So so.'

Me, 'Fisher Z?'

'Never heard of him.'

They speak of past boyfriends, their favourite bands and bad habits. For the first time, I talk about Fiona and I with a sense of detachment.

As the night comes to an end I ask Alice if she'll write it into her diary. She tells me I will be mentioned as an authority on Nepal since I had been here some eights hours longer than them.

A night guard with a lantern crosses the empty garden like a Dickensian character. He politely tells us it's late and not to giggle too loud. I offer to take them out tomorrow night to a dinner in a more economic part of town, since it's their last day.

'I know a restaurant owner on the Raj Path who has a quiet place where we can continue our conversations on travels, yoga, and rock and roll.'

11

The morning after my night out I take the Nagarkot manuscript back to the raffle ticket salesman. We sit and drink hot chai as outside his restaurant. It's well positioned just beyond the ring road at the edge of the countryside but on one of the main road arteries into Kathmandu.

The smell of fresh paratha being made along with cabbage and potato curry is mouth watering. The idea of eating Nepali food morning, noon and night is one of the easiest aspects of the culture to embrace here.

The salesman looks pleased that I have returned his precious manuscript. He tells me he read some of my father's book overnight and is impressed by my dad's respect and admiration of the Moni Baba. I ask him to tell me what it felt like to attend the Nagarkot teaching. His eyes glaze over as he begins to speak poetically as if he were still there.

'Nagarkot is a very special place. It sits on the edge of the Kathmandu valley with the holy Himal in the background. Sometimes the valley is so covered in cloud that only the Buddhist temple of Swayambunath can be seen floating, like a heavenly island.

'On the first day I heard the Moni Baba speak, a large group of Newari businessmen and their families had come dressed in their finest clothes with food and cold drinks. I remember it was bright, with clear skies. It brought the mountains even closer.

'The Baba was with his devotee Sita. He walked to the cliff edge at the very rim of the valley. He wore a faded saffron kurta and carried a staff. The girl held his arm to steady him. I remember him exploring the cliff edge carefully with his feet and the crowd falling silent. He appeared to gaze across the valley towards Swayambu temple and breathe in the air before turning to face his audience.

'He spoke to the young first, encouraging them to understand their passion for life was now at its most absorbant. They would gather experiences at their age, like crops and they should treat them as such by harvesting the best. He told them to take advantage of opportunities that came their way, knowing their youth can handle the risks. His voice spoke with gentle contentment.

'He spoke to parents suggesting that daughters should be given the same amount of food as their brothers, that girls should be valued equally and that young couples should pair with a purpose, not only to raise the status of their families but for mutual love. He suggested that love creates feelings of wellbeing and indeed that is the only way to recognise it. Don't speculate over love, just learn to recognise when it's felt in order to give it.

'I've even heard him suggest that the power that presently lies with old gurus should be tempered by new powers of decision-making given to the young. If he had said nothing more that day I would still feel I'd witnessed something special.'

'And what of the girl Sita,' I ask, 'did she talk?'

'No, she does not speak publically. I believe though that she is the source of the Baba's new teaching on youth. They say it is her that has provided him with a new incentive to discuss the rules of self-determination, but who knows really? The Baba gives audiences to the King and other rich people and yet he lives out his life in quiet isolation. He chooses to make this Nagerkot speech in public only once every few years and he glows with such encouragement for life, even at his age, it is infectious. You too must try to hear him speaking.'

'Yes. That is my intention.'

I thank the raffle ticket salesman for his time and I ask him if I can bring two other guests to his restaurant, so they can sample some of his fine Indian food.

'Can I reserve a table?' I ask.

The salesman laughs loud and longer than I believe he intends.

'Ah ha,' he continues, 'Yes... there's always a place for Baba seekers. There are no private tables in my eating house but I will oblige. I can put cushions onto the bullock cart at the back lane of the restaurant and we can serve you there.'

'Excellent. My guests are two ladies from England.'

'I am honoured,' he says. 'I have done this once before for a customer who won a prize from a raffle ticket. Her family decorated the cart to celebrate. We will clear the chickens and sweep the cow dung, it will be quite salubrious,' he says.

1 2

When I return to the Chakra I call Alice and ask her what they have been up to. Alice tells me they took a tour of Bhaktapur and Bhodnath and they enjoyed it. I tell her I will pick them up around dusk. She asks what they should wear. I can't tell if she's joking but say they should maintain their new dress code for the evening. She calls out to Gill, repeating what I say, mimicking my accent. I hear Gill reply.

'I didn't have any underwear on last night, ask him if that code still applies.'

'We'll be sitting in the back of a bullock cart. I'll leave that decision to you both.'

'A bullock cart!' I hear her groan as she hangs up.

I relax in my room, enjoying my alone time in the knowledge I will have company tonight. I wash my t-shirt in the sink. No need to break out a new one.

Dad's book has two markers that have been left inside by the Raffle ticket salesman. There is no such thing as the separation of church and state in our minds, dad writes. It is a combination of all thoughts that guide our actions. It's only within our deeds and their consequences that judgments are then affiliated.

I consider I've been trying to the forget the actions of an unfaithful lover and a bad friend and the best I've done so far is to bury them under new experiences.

I take my guitar and tune it. I play a few chords to remind my fingers what to do. I find a taxi and go pick up the girls.

They look dressed for a safari more than a dinner date. I detect some dread in their voices when they ask where the bullock cart is positioned exactly.

'I hope you are not taking us to an open field or a farm,' says Gill, 'although we've come prepared.' I congratulate her on her more farm girl than punk look this evening. She's wearing a denim shirt tucked into cargo pants that are tucked into large boots. Alice also has a long practical canvas skirt and a shirt with a high round collar.

When we arrive at the restaurant we are taken immediately around to the back lane where the bullock cart has been decorated in the style of a Maharani's carriage. It has been propped up with wooden crates and a Tibetan carpet is draped over makeshift steps running down to street level. Large cushions are positioned inside and there is a huge tray of delicious smelling snack foods in bowls in the centre. The girls' faces change from dread to excitement.

'How Bollywood is this?' says Gill.

The front pole, where the ox is harnessed to pull the cart, has been turned vertical and a mosquito net is draped over the top. A series of butter-lamps are positioned on each corner and there are small candles on each step up to the cart.

'Are you going to propose to one of us?' asks Alice.

The young boy lookalike is now dressed as a servant from the British Raj, complete with Nepali hat, black waistcoat and pantaloons. He bows and Namastis us into place. He hands us a rolled-up wash towel then offers us a cleansing Lassi drink before rushing off to the kitchen.

The girls giggle and climb aboard the cart, settling down on the cushions. They begin to feed each other with finger food.

'Who is this man, the raffle ticket salesman?' asks Gill.

'He is someone who is helping me to find my father's guru.'

'How cute is that boy, all dressed up,' says Alice.

'Sure is,' says Gill. 'I've been eying up his waistcoat.'

'What do your friends think about you making this trip, James? Is there no one who wanted to come with you?' Alice enquires.

'Most of my friends are not into travelling much. They don't have any interest in yoga, and the mere mention of the words Baba or "spiritual" is crossing the loony line to them.'

'We crossed that line a while back.'

'And burnt our bridges,' continues Gill.

'It would seem a waste of time for them to do something like this,' I say, 'whereas it's the best use of my time that I can come up with for the moment.'

'Oh and why is this not all a waste of time for you, guru James?'

'I've taken time off from following a set of plans to respond to opportunities as they crop up,' I say, elaborating somewhat on a Baba reading. 'When you have a plan you have to say no thanks to opportunities that come by chance.'

'Like buying raffle tickets. Did you get us any, by the way?' Gill asks.

'Yes, here's a book... but since you leave here tomorrow... it proves my point exactly.'

'No way!' counters Gill, 'we'll leave the tickets with you and expect full payment. Cover all bases at all times, I say.'

There is a pause while our small waiter fills our glasses with some local rice gin and tonic water.

'I know what you mean, James,' says Alice. 'I have friends who just want to stay at home. They search for employment, anything to make a living, fit in and find a mate. Giving attention to anything else **is** just a waste of time.'

'So are we your only creative friends?' asks Gill, looking at me.

'No,' I answer.

'Explain.'

'In Scotland it's like if you are given a small dose of political opinion, you can become protected for years against large amounts of it. It's all double talk designed to be vague. Everyone sees through it and yet it's hard to avoid all these social comfort blankets we are given.'

'What do you mean, social comfort blanket?'

'The NHS, help in finding work, help whenever anything in the world happens from unemployment to depression. We look to society to provide.'

'Let's hear it then from "disgruntled, Edinburgh",' Gill says.

'Not disgruntled. Just curious to spend time in a place where very little of anything like that exists. There are no social comfort blankets here. If you leave the valley here there's not even electricity.'

'Not even a paper tissue to wipe,' Gill pauses for effect, 'away your tears.'

'But they have meditation and Tantric yoga,' says Alice.

The conversation is cut as the child servant reappears with another large tray containing piles of chapatti. With a Hindu-like chant he announces the main cuisine of the evening. Rice dhal and an assortment of green curries. He takes away the finger bowl food tray and Alice move back onto her questions.

'Why leave Edinburgh to find a guru, why not stay in Scotland until you find a guru there or a least a mate to travel with?'

'Cause he's escaping fearsome Fiona's world,' Gill says.

'Not really… but it is the convenient side-effect of this trip,' I admit.

13

We can only finish half of the food we are served and before it turns cold, the child servant comes back and arranges for it to be removed.

I believe the remaining food is being taken to feed the raffle salesman's extended family in the restaurant kitchen. I am given the bill along with some milk tea and cardamom.

'It's cost less than a basket of Nans in the Lancer,' I say. I wave the bill as a triumph for creative economy.

'That's because we have not had imported alcohol,' says Alice.

Our mini manservant bows in gratitude when Alice gives him a generous tip and he gestures that we can stay as long as we like. We should however bring the tea tray into the eating-house before leaving, or the street dogs will get it.

Alice blows out three butter-lamps and lies down with her feet stretched. Gill lies alongside her, leaving me sitting upright in the small space that's left.

'You look cross with your crossed legs, Guru James from Scotland?'

'Nope, it's better for digestion to sit upright.'

'Don't you ever give up on the holy yoga talk?' says Gill.

'That's all it takes, a comment like that!' We enter a moment of awkward silence.

'I'm going to the toilet, watch out for street dogs,' I announce as I swivel off the back of the cart.

The back door of the restaurant is locked so I walk around to the front and the place is full of people eating. There's embarrassment from the raffle ticket salesman when he realises I see everyone eating from the Maharini tray of food we left. I ask where the toilet is and I'm directed towards the back of the restaurant. It's dark so I have to leave a door half open and as I stand on the two ceramic footplates to pee into a hole in the ground. I hear voices through the wall. I realise I'm only a few feet away from the bullock cart in the lane.

The girls are talking and laughing but I can't make out what they are saying. I take the full bucket of water to flush the toilet then stand nearer to the open window.

'I also see the truth in what my daddy wrote,' I hear Gill say, imitating a Scottish accent.

'I'm yogically sceptical, I want to learn more,' says Alice and they both muffle their laughter.

I laugh to myself on hearing this but I also feel hurt. They continue.

'I think that yoga's contribution towards mental health should be on the agenda of every Ministry of Health,' Gill talks in a Westminster accent.

Alice bursts out laughing. 'You're too cruel.'

'Yes... and statistics show that depression and various other forms of mental illnesses such as gayness and lesbianism can be cured with a good dose of yoga.'

There is a silence, where I suddenly imagine they are kissing. I'm also aware that whatever noise I make will be heard by them so I creep out of the toilet. I consider heading directly to the Chakra on my own, but my guitar is in the bullock cart. Whatever the evening had to offer in terms of opportunity now seems gone.

I laugh too at a recollection, thinking this is what Dave and I were like when young. We'd face the world with a friendly smile only to take the piss out of everything and everyone we encountered when we were alone. This trait was a cornerstone in our friendship.

I decide to act mature, take the girls to their hotel then say goodbye.

'How was that,' asks Alice.

'Fine,' I reply.

'You are still full of shit,' says Gill.

Alice looks straight at me, sensing my change in demeanour.

'We could hear you take a pee,' Alice says, smiling.

'We are just fucking with you, James. We could hear you piss so we know you must still be full of shit!' Gill says.

'We couldn't resist taking more of the piss out of you,' Alice says.

'It sounded like a bath tap turned on full,' Gill smiles.

'We like you Guru James Munro. We think you should write a book called *Three M Yoga*. Meditation, Masturbation and Mating... lessons in life, the male path to enlightenment.'

I resist the temptation to retaliate and join in the banter.

As we leave they point out that I've brought my guitar but not played anything. They invite me once more to come back with them, this time to their hotel room and I accept.

AFTER RAIDING THE MINI-BAR, ALICE AND GILL SING 'MEN AT WORK' in a drunken duet. I drink a small bottle of whisky and play a song by the Clash they haven't heard before.

The evening ends with us all intoxicated, talking companionship in a single bed. After some sleepy wrestling with Alice, I wake up at one point, looking at her in the dim light. She has positioned my leg between hers as a child might place a pillow. She is sound asleep, naked from the waist down, definitely a no-pants sort of girl. I can feel her heartbeat through her thighs straddling my leg.

Gill lies separately on her front at the end of the bed, still in her black bra. An eagle tattooed on her lower back holds a serpent in its claws, dangling into her butt crack.

At dawn I move out quietly while both are asleep. I pack my guitar and write a note with my address care-of mother in Scotland, two kisses and Om sign. I leave my latest friends in their luxurious air-conditioned room, knowing I may never see or hear from them again.

PART TWO: THE SEARCH

1 4

Contrary to what many people think, Kathmandu is not a cold place. Nepal is on the same line of latitude as Egypt, which puts it comfortably near to the Equator. Although the mountains stretch up into the cold atmospheres, the Kathmandu valley is only four thousand feet above sea level.

It must certainly have appeared as a Shangri-La to travellers in earlier times. There are religious monuments everywhere across the valley. One can hardly walk more than a hundred yards without encountering a statue, some stone covered in red dust, a building or a yard that is dedicated to a god. There are so many statues strewn around the three cities that it's common to see washed clothes draped over the heads or rear end of some exquisitely carved stone god. These religious artefacts are so integrated into people's lifestyle that brass foreheads and noses of statues are polished thin from the touch of hands. Sculptures we see locked in glass cases in museums are playground objects for Nepali children.

The three towns of Bhaktapur, Patan and Kathmandu make up the population centres of the Kathmandu valley. For centuries they've been credited with blending a peaceful mix of Buddhism and Hinduism. The valley has also become the frontier between ancient farming traditions and modern machinery. As fast as the Tibetans are losing their culture to modernisation imposed by China, the Newari farmers in Kathmandu are losing their land and their culture to a modernisation process that often appears equally as ruthless. The cheapest version of every machine and appliance seems to find its way here. Scooters and motorbikes, cars, busses and cheap generators are all in abundance and used to their maximum capacity. Motorbikes, with 50cc engines, strain to carry man, wife and two children through the cluttered streets. Packs of them whine like noisy hairdryers overloaded and moving at speeds that children can outrun.

Mains electricity is only available three days a week on a rotational basis. You can tell which area of the town has electricity on any given evening because generators blast out dangerous decibel levels of noise in all other areas.

Trucks and buses with wooden doors and no windows cough and stumble their way up the sides of the valley. They also move slow, at the speed of the Space Shuttle being taken out to its launch pad at NASA. Battered cars struggle to overtake them on the steep slopes, fogging the beauty of Nepal's pre-industrial countryside in fumes.

In dad's book he states, 'the lips of organized society are only recently stretching out to Nepal's rural areas and have so far had the impact of a kiss on the cheek.'

Things have changed. The arms and legs of the industrial world are now marching over land here, at least in the valley.

I try to make a weekly walk up to the rim of the Kathmandu valley. People are very different here. I realise that I will have to venture out further at some stage to find the Baba, but I'm still not sure where. Less than ten per cent of Nepal's population of sixteen million live in cities. Ninety per cent still live in rural areas. Outside the city I'm amazed at how indifferent rural Nepalese are to their country's beauty, possibly because in their lifetime they have seen nothing else.

Anything under eighteen thousand feet in Nepal is considered a hill. Only mountains higher than eighteen thousand feet are officially mountains. The Indian sub-continent, once an ancient part of Africa, broke off and is still to this day colliding into China. This slow-motion continent crash is forcing the mountain range higher every year. It leaves many parts of the region unstable with earthquakes and landslides.

One day up at Nagarkot, the place of the Baba's famous teaching, I arrive when it is shrouded in cloud. It is deserted except for farm folk. Many women on their way to work in the fields carry wing-shaped covers on their backs. These protective shades are made from sandwiching dried leaves between two flat basketwork frames and are used to protect field workers from both rain and sun. From close up, the group appears as if they are heading towards an ancient hang gliding festival. Those working in the distance look like giant grasshoppers in the fields.

While I'm in town I speak to as many people as I can about the Moni Baba, his whereabouts and his background. I hear that the Baba was once a successful businessman in India who partially lost his sight in an accident and then became a yogi. Another story suggests he was a radical lawyer tortured in an independence struggle for an ethnic minority in India. He escaped with his life, but without his sight.

For every story of the Baba's origins in India there are others suggesting the Baba is Nepali and has lived here in a forest for forty years and never left. Few people I'm told have ever had the opportunity to question the Baba on his past since he allows no time for such questions. Those who try to gain a personal insight apparently find their interest evaporate in his presence.

The Moni Baba is also described physically different to me. He is tall, presumably to shorter people, small to tall, thin to large and seen as well built by the frail. Without having the photos from dad's book I could not have imagined his appearance from the descriptions given to me.

I hear he stands out in crowds but then disappointingly that he wears the thin washed-out saffron colours of a Sanyassin, which in streets of Nepal is your basic camouflage gear.

Through the increasingly familiar streets of Kathmandu I continue a daily routine of questioning and enquiring. My curiosity about the Baba is enhanced by unsolicited descriptions of the girl Sita. She is described as the Baba's spiritual companion, but she has a role too in caring for him, acting as his eyes, constantly looking after him. I realize that she is the most unusual element in all the stories because she is mentioned in nearly every young person's account of the Baba's teaching.

It is the young who give Sita a prominent position in the Baba's legend. The accounts that include her are distinct from the ranting of older people obsessed with devotion to a god. What older devotees see in the Baba is an object to worship whatever he says. What the young see is living proof in Sita that to listen to the Baba can bring serenity to a young life.

This is the most refreshing part of the Baba's story. Some may be too young to understand all the wisdom of the Baba's words but they manage to sit for long periods listening to him because Sita is there. She appears like a celebrity, drawing attention from a growing section of the crowds to his teachings.

At his gatherings, she mixes with other women, talks to them, and occasionally administers herbal medicine. While the Baba talks, she watches and seems to have the instinctive ability to spot someone in distress. She will take a crying child or a sick woman some distance from the group and sing and chant with a small fist-sized healer's drum. I'm informed that her curative powers are superior to most Jankris, the local healers of Nepal. In return for her herbal medicines, she accepts rice or vegetable or fruit. There are no transactions in cash and there seems little in her lifestyle that requires it.

I learn the Baba often conducts informal gatherings on hill trails. They take place in small buildings or shady 'chautaras' especially constructed throughout the hills for travellers and holy men. Given no warning, people stop work and assemble to hear the Baba talk wherever he randomly appears. Oh to be on such a trail at the same time.

15

A fter nearly two months and countless interviews, I have collected several references to one person. I'm told I should talk to Tilak Gurung an ex-Gurkha who speaks English and lives in Barabase, a roadside town midway between Pokhara and Kathmandu. He is an occasional bodyguard for the Baba and protects him on his visits to crowded Kathmandu.

I'm also told that Barabase is an ideal place to catch recent news of the Baba's whereabouts. Travellers and bus drivers who commute between the two main towns often have information as to his whereabouts.

I write a letter to Tilak Gurung explaining my quest, not knowing if it will ever reach him. Surprisingly, after a week I receive a reply written neatly in English on Nepalese handmade paper.

Tilak tells me he does not know where the Baba is at present but that I'm welcome to visit. He warns I should be prepared to stay some time since he only hears occasional news. If I give him an arrival date, he can arrange for a place for me to sleep.

Meanwhile I've also made more traveller friends who arrive and go with frustrating regularity. Two Danes invite me to their farewell party, a night of music and song at the Kathmandu Guest House, which they say is famous from the 1970s as being the last stop on the hippie trail. I'm invited to perform if I wish. A new white t-shirt is unpacked, since my first is now grey with continual use and washes in Bagmati water.

The Guest House holds around sixty people in its largest room and aside from the twenty or so I recognise there is a group of locals and foreigners all resembling extras from Woodstock.

None appear to be at the end of any hippy trail. The Guest House has the ambiance of a hippie pavilion in this Himalayan Theme Park. Nuevo hippies are here to sample dope, listen to music and dance before heading back to office jobs.

The manager apologises for not having more space for our group. I also feel he does not want to lose any customers. He says it is not unusual for foreigners to sing and play music here and assures me no local will mind.

A tall man called Heinrich and his girlfriend Nani introduce themselves. He is a musician from Munich and they've been in Nepal six weeks. He's been playing here regularly with a local Nepali rock band called Elegant. He's tells me the lead guitarist Sharad will be here later tonight with an amplifier and another guitar. Heinrich asks if I'm interested in playing the most popular music for young people in Nepal.

'What music are you going to play?'

'Anything by Bob Marley.'

It turns out that Henrich's second name is Harrer and that he was named after the famous Austrian explorer and author of the same name. Henrich tells me they were in Mustang a few weeks back and trekked to the Tibetan border. He said they spoke for several minutes with the Chinese border guards. Heinrich has since written a song entitled 'Seven Minutes in Tibet'.

Nani tells me they are planning to make a trek to the Anna-purna sanctuary over the next few weeks. They ask if I want to join them on the trip.

I'm actually tempted by this offer. I tell them I will think about it since part of me wants to take advantage of any spontaneous opportunity that comes up. I also have so many questions for them about Mustang, the place where my father was killed. However, any plan that deviates me from another deviation would not be fair on Gurkha Tilak.

Henrick and I sing 'Berlin' and 'Red Skies Over Paradise' by Fisher Z. The Europeans take to the floor and dance flamboyantly with their 1970s shadows.

As the acoustic gig progresses, the local Nepalese men seem more interested in drinking beer and talking loudly.

As soon as Sharad arrives and his Fender amp is set up on a table, the room falls silent. Heinrich and I both flank Sharad and his Stratocaster centre stage. More chairs are stacked to clear a bigger dance floor. With one arm raised in a black power salute, Sharad bursts into song. Henrich and I join in behind Sharad's considerably louder Strad.

'I shot the sheriff,' he sings, and the room erupts with, 'But I didn't shoot the deputy.'

After thirty minutes of community singing and wild dancing to Bob Marley, I'm told we'll finish with Nepal's most favourite pop song. 'Hotel California' by the Eagles.

Sharad and Henrich make a fairly good improvisation, with Sharad copying Joe Walsh's lead. It brings the party to an abrupt conclusion. Everyone leaves the hotel as if it's on fire and I'm told the large crowd that gathered in the street to listen, has also disappeared.

I inform Henrich and Nani of my decision not to trek with them, explaining that I must at least try to stick to my original plan. I'll go to Barabase, spend time and sample the rural life. Hopefully this will lead to me finding Moni.

I write back to inform Tilak I will arrive on Monday's bus two weeks from now. I chant a prayer that my letter arrives before I do.

16

O n the bus ride out of Kathmandu, I appreciate the physical isolation that existed for centuries for those living in the valley. The country only opened up to the outside world in the 1950s. I look back at emerald green fields in contrast to the barren hills of the surrounding landscape. The remains of a ski lift can be seen from the road, at one time the only way to bring goods into the valley aside from foot transport or air travel. Enterprising Nepalese brought motorcycles and petrol from India. The first Italian scooters were ski-lifted into the valley, navigating the dirt roads that connected the three main towns. For years the valley operated its own internal transport system with no vehicles going in or out and parts and fuel portered in.

As the bus inches over the lip of the valley, the engine suddenly cuts and we freewheel down the road on the outer slope. It is a technique used to save petrol. The only noise is the regular screech of brakes. The road to Pokhara bends and twists, like a piece of lace piping on a Lancer's tunic. At each hairpin bend we pass workmen keeping this engineering feat from crumbing. Stunning views embrace you on each turn before your stomach catches up. The road seems impossibly narrow for two vehicles to pass.

People drive on the left as they do in India and Britain, but this is only obvious at the last minute when vehicles veer left from the centre of the road.

Two and a half hours after boarding my swerving roller-coaster ride, I arrive at Barabase. No other passengers disembark. The driver climbs onto the roof of the bus, throws my rucksack and guitar to me, wishes me good fortune then drives on. I stand at the roadside with bags in one hand, guitar in the other, alone.

Tilak, the retired Gurkha, steps forward from a crowded tea shop and introduces himself. He welcomes me with a military salute and a Namasti sign. He tells me I was easy to spot.

Tilak looks stocky for an ex-soldier and appears around forty years old. He is dressed in western clothes, with jeans and a t-shirt featuring a faded image of the actress Phoebe Kates. He apologizes for his appearance, saying he has just come from his mill. He takes my rucksack and leads me on a short trek to a small house tucked above the main street of the village.

As we stand outside what looks like an unfinished building, Tilak points to a tiny dark room that he's rented for me. It is one floor above a stable with a buffalo and three goats below. We climb a rickety wooden ladder made of logs and stripped branches. There is a single wooden bed and a yak-hair blanket. It is like a medieval prison cell. The owner of the room is a tiny old woman he calls Didi. She speaks no English and on my arrival distances herself as much as possible from me, paying more attention to the collection of animals in the yard.

Tilak points to his house a short walk further along the path. We arrange to meet there that evening after he has finished his work at the mill. Once I've settled, he tells me I should come for supper and meet his family.

I feel dazed – in a time warp. I put my bags down and sit on the wooden bed. I lift the thin hair blanket and examine the rope that's woven across the bed's side to hold it. There is no mattress. The room is like an exhibit in the Natural History Museum, from the Iron Age. It's quaint but a realization that this is my sleeping accommodation for the foreseeable future slowly sinks in.

There seems nothing for me to do here, no power to charge the Toshiba, no light to read a book, no toilet that I can see, not even a seat to sit on. I try to let the novelty of my experience take hold but a slow dread creeps in. The test will be to see how long I can survive this – so many centuries outside my comfort zone.

I pile my belongings into the corner and decide to walk around the village. It is situated near a bridge crossing on the main road to Pokhara, Nepal's second most famous town. There is one street of small shops selling clove tea and cold drinks to road travellers. If I walk straight and do not cross the bridge, there is another narrow street of shops selling cloth and an assortment of trinket goods for farming wives and families.

It seems a crossroads for both foot and road travellers, but hardly a busy one. At the back of the village there are two paths, one leading to the forest, the other to the hills. It takes me all of ten minutes to walk around the village.

There are steep hills rising behind the main road and after a little more exploration I notice the village is wedged into a valley where two rivers meet. In any other country the view of these rivers would be regarded as spectacular, but in Nepal it's average. No mountains can be seen from this spot so it's not on the tourist lists. One shopkeeper offers me a stool to sit on and gives me a free chai. He enquires if I'm Tilak's guest and tells me that tourists usually pass through very quickly. They never look closely at Barabase because their eyes are forever focused upwards, in search of the peaks. He believes he is speaking English, but for me his accent is very hard to follow and it's his skill in miming the words that gives me some understanding.

I return to my cell and think of my choice to come here. Henrich and Nani will be off on their current trek across a part of Nepal that caters well for tourists. I lie down and strangely enough doze off in sleep for a couple of hours, more soundly than I've done in weeks.

17

That night at dusk I take my torch and step gingerly along the dirt path above the village, to Tilak's house. Chickens run from under my feet and dogs bark as I pass an assortment of mud covered wooden buildings with straw and tiled roofs. I knock on Tilak's door and it is opened.

In contrast to the house's crude exterior, a young woman dressed like a Hindi movie star opens the door and greets me with an elaborate Namasti. I step through a portal as if into a different world. In the glow of oil lamps is a room furnished with western style furniture. Tilak is quick to appear, introducing the woman as his wife Maya. As I enter I meet his young daughters Subadra, a cute three-year old, and Satya who I'm told is nine. The children also give me a formal Namasti greeting and speak in accented English, saying, 'Welcome Jamesji'.

The children are well mannered and in the crude light, Maya looks absolutely stunning. She is wearing a red and gold sparkled sari, with make-up as elaborate as a traditional dancer's.

Tilak is also dressed for the occasion in a denim shirt with black cord trousers. I regret not wearing one of my three remaining white T-shirts. I did not expect this level of formality.

Maya steps forward, gesturing me to sit on one of the two couches positioned facing each other in the centre of the room. Tilak offers me tea, which I accept. He is very respectful and brings small tea glasses, placing them on a carved coffee table between the couches. I help by removing a picture frame and see it's a wedding photo of Tilak and Maya standing in front of a crudely painted Himalayan mountain scene.

'I am very honoured for you to come to my house Sir, and very sorry that we do not have enough room for you to stay here with us. Some day I will make a better space at the mill, but now Didi's place is the only spare room I can find in the village.'

'No problem Tilak, I'm happy you arranged something for me at such short notice.'

Tilak's head wobbles slightly in response. 'Sir, Didi's place is basic but very cheap.'

Maya brings in a teapot and lays it down. Matching plates are spread like the crown jewels on a tray at the side. I can hardly take my eyes off Maya. I tell myself I'm no longer an adolescent and this woman's looks should not matter to me. But I credit her presence with changing what's been a miserable trend of thought for a few hours into an upbeat state of mind.

Maya leaves and returns with a small plate of Indian sweets.

'You have lovely daughters,' I say to both of them. Tilak is the only one who answers.

'Mmn yes, thank you. My girls, but no son... yet,' he says, swallowing a mouthful of sweet.

'How long were you in the British Army?'

'Twenty years service, Sir.'

The younger of the two children runs in from a side room and Maya waves at her with outstretched arms, as if she's chasing a chicken back into a pen.

'Subadra,' Tilak says as the girl runs back out without stopping, 'go play with Satia.' Maya disappears into the small room at the back while Tilak and I talk.

'You're interested in meeting the Moni Baba?'

'Yes.'

'Sir, I will try to find out where he is, but it is not easy to know when or where the Baba will appear.'

'That's what I'm continually told.'

'It is the Baba's way.'

'Yes.'

'A wise man needs time away from his followers.'

'And the Baba seems wise indeed.'

'Do you speak any Nepali?'

'No, but I'm prepared to learn.'

'And how long will you stay here?'

'I don't know. I'll stick around for as long as it takes to meet the Baba.'

'It is so very good to speak English to you, Sir. I'm losing my English voice, being back in the village for so long.'

'You speak good English.'

'May I ask Sir, if I'm guessing your accent rightly, by thinking you are Scottish?'

'Very good Tilak, yes, I am, and not used to being called Sir. You can call me James.'

Tilak's eyes sparkle and he begins to talk fondly about a visit to Scotland he made during his service with the British Gurkhas.

'I had a Scottish officer in the Gurkhas,' he tells me, 'he was a Macdonald.'

'Yes?'

'Really,' he says, intentionally rolling his rs. 'You can easily learn some Nepali here and help Maya and my daughters understand Scottish English, Sir, James sorry! Our village has no women who can read. I hope Satya is the first.'

After a western meal of buffalo burger and chips, Tilak tells me his village has a population of around twenty families. He gives me a glass of Rakshi, a rice gin that he says is the equivalent of Scots whisky.

'Every country has developed their own brand of strong alcohol to drink, it seems.'

'Ah, but the Scots convince us to pay the most money for theirs,' Tilak says with a smile.

I remember a Billy Connolly joke, and tell Tilak 'that the Scots' contribution to the world has been staggering.' Tilak laughs aloud, repeating this joke. He tells me not to forget what Scots have done for burgers also… through Macdonalds.

18

For the next few weeks I spend most of my time around Tilak and his family as they work. Tilak and Maya are important people in this small community. He has constructed a water-powered grinding mill and with her help, they run their business on the south side of town. Throughout the year, farm families from around the neighbouring hills bring seeds for grinding. I occasionally help out with manual labour but find it absolutely exhausting. I retire to my string bed at mid-day to recover. At night I sleep as soon as I lie down and when animal noises wake me at dawn, I rise and hardly notice the bleakness of the room. I move outside immediately, bathing at the community water tap and taking in the natural beauty around Barabase.

Subadra, the younger of Tilak's daughters, is a playful independent spirit, parented by her nine-year-old sister Satya, as much as she is by her parents. On Tilak's instruction, Satya also parents me. She speaks a little English and introduces me to people. She points out dangers in the river near the mill and she gathers firewood using me to help her carry it back to the house. She is also an expert with open fires and teaches me how to keep the flame going with the minimum amount of wood.

Tilak allows me to use his prize latrine, one of three in the village he has constructed. It's positioned between a paddock for the family buffalo and woodpiles waiting to be stored on his roof. He has also diverted the river to run under the latrine to take away waste back into the river. It's a design flaw that I hope to point out soon.

Maya is considerably younger than Tilak. She comes from a lower caste family but Tilak tells me he accepted her low caste status through his exposure to international thinking in the British army. He says he arranged for Maya to be reserved for him on her eleventh birthday and married her on his retirement from the military, ten years ago, when she was just sixteen.

After ten years of retirement, Tilak has convincingly reintegrated himself into Nepali life. He lives like a local farmer with military efficiency and neatness in the workplace. He digs, constructs and drinks Rakshi like others, but polishes his boots to parade-ground standard.

The mill that Tilak owns is a simple shed in which an assortment of large cast-iron milling machines grind away noisily at rice and mustard seed. The river supplies the power by way of a small hydro-electric generator. This keeps the machines alive and active.

In movies of Dickensian Britain such a scene is always portrayed as horrific working conditions, set in the heart of a dark polluted city. Here, however, the shed is surrounded by nature, with wild flowers growing through the dusty wood cracks. Ever present is an assortment of birds that dive-bomb for the loose crumbs of grain. The mill is like a large bird feeder, set in a giant's landscaped garden.

Tilak's mill provides the only mechanized help for farmers for miles around and the community accepts it wholeheartedly as a modern and progressive business venture. Inside, thick belts and wheels spin and slap with primitive efficiency in front of a queue of chattering farmwomen. These machines are not ancient. Tilak's latest came from India only two years ago. It possesses the trendy name of 'DISCO' caste on a nameplate in front. Tilak tells me he is saving for the 'GALACTIC', an improved model, twice the size of Disco but with detachable wheels and side plates. He hopes that the Galactic will also provide electricity for his home.

With local customers taking the flowers and the birds for granted, they tend these rickety machines with love and the care. The land here is often a cruel master for subsistence farmers, with crops teased from the ground on every ledge of the steep slopes that surround us. They are regularly threatened by drought or landslide. Within Tilak's community I see humans taking mechanised control. The light bulb may not yet have arrived here but the industrial revolution has finally reached Barabase.

With no power for my Toshiba, my regular writing habits have disappeared. I've decelerated from the city buzz of Kathmandu into this biblical lifestyle in a matter of weeks. I start writing on paper but it soon runs out. I buy peanuts on sale in the market place for their wrapping paper taken from cheap school note-books. My notes from previous days are placed in my front pocket and when the front pocket is full I move them to my back pocket from where I eventually use my notes as toilet paper. I now feel no observation is worth saving more than having a clean bowel movement.

Where I once made a decision about work or leisure every few hours in Scotland, I now spend days in Barabase without having to make any serious decision about anything. This deceleration in my head throws me forward and the airbag of rural life hits me square in the face.

I spend most of my time outside, walking the hills, visiting other villages and temples or shrines; talking in a few words of Nepali and resting a lot. I only go indoors to my stark loft bedroom to sleep. The absence of any cushioned seat makes visiting Tilak's house and sitting on a chair seem like a luxury.

People pay thousands of dollars to therapists in the USA to achieve the sort of calmness and space between thoughts that I now seem to be developing, or as my dad would say, that I'm recovering here.

I wait for news to emerge of the Moni Baba's whereabouts, but there seems no urgency for this information in anyone except me. I often imagine a bird will fly in one day with a message tied to its leg and things will change. The reality is that lifestyles change here very little and you are surrounded with understanding as to why it doesn't change. At home it changes very little for people also but you are surrounded by frustration as to why not. I have to teach myself to wait my quest out patiently.

AFTER THREE MONTHS I FEEL CONDITIONED INTO THE SORT OF physical shape that's necessary for all the inhabitants of Barabase to survive. There are so few moments when there is nothing physical to do. I sense a new joy in resting when it is necessary and just not habitual.

Despite having only the worn out clothes I arrived in. I have resisted the local rough wool shirts, or Yak hair jackets because they feel rough. Tilak has lent me an old military trench coat that I prefer instead, wearing it over my now grey t-shirts. On colder days I resemble a foot soldier on retreat from the Russian front.

The fitter I become, the more I fill my days with work. My thighs and biceps increase, just as my capacity to hold a normal conversation seems to slip away. Only with Tilak, Satya and a few shopkeepers do I speak any English, so I'm barely able to keep my talking skills alive. My Nepalese is improving, but the content of my exchanges with villagers is extremely simple.

'What did you do today?' I'll say this in Nepali every day at least once to someone. My companions sit with me squat on our heels on a hillside and tell me their activities and only on rare occasions, their thoughts.

'I dug an irrigation channel.'

'Where?'

'On an upper terrace.'

'You opened up a new trench?'

'Yes.'

There's always a long silence after so many words are exchanged. We allow time for the mind to digest the conversation. I delay my next question lest I get a reputation for being too inquisitive.

'Why do trenches need to be opened up this time of year?'

'The rains come.'

'For rice planting?'

'Yes.'

Pause, for more hill gazing.

'Does everyone work together at harvest time?'

'Not together… but at the same time.'

'What do you mean?'

'People go to their fields at the same time.'

On this particular conversation, I reach the limits of my Nepali language skills. I don't understand my friend's differentiation between working together and at the same time. I ask Tilak to explain. He squats beside us and respectfully enters the silence. After a moment I continue in English.

'I hear people don't work together at harvest time, but at the same time. I don't understand the difference.'

'They go out to the fields at the same time, but from different families,' Tilak explains.

'I know, I saw them bringing in the potato harvest. It looked impressive, very well organized, with people from all around working together.'

'It's not organized, it's just that every family has their own fields.'

'So what makes you say they're not working together?'

'It's the state of readiness of the potatoes that dictates the work. Not the villagers that organizes it.'

'You mean some people could choose to stay home and not work?'

'Yes… but then someone would take their potatoes. When a crop is ready for harvest everyone comes out at the same time to make sure no one else steals their crop. People are alert more than organised at harvest time.'

19

The climate here makes it easy to exist outdoors. It's an open-air community decorated and furnished by Mother Nature. My favourite place on the Gaia estate is under a pipal tree on a trail above the village. I was raised indoors like most people in the north, moving from building to building where everything that surrounds us is constructed or manufactured. We keep potted plants or a pet to remind us of our links with nature. Northerners venture outdoors to escape the demands they have created for themselves indoors. Here, farm families are Gaia's little helpers and unable to spend time indoors because of the demands from outside. Villagers who travel to Kathmandu have mostly outdoors skills and find it hard to get indoor jobs.

A boy child is regarded as a family's most prized possession and the reasons for this are complex. Interestingly, the Infant Mortality Rate for boys in Nepal is higher than that for girls. More boys die before they are five, so there is logic to place a value on their survival. Superstitious parents dress small boys to look like girls since they believe that mischievous gods will punish a parent by taking away their most prized possessions. Young boys have their ears pierced and wear girls' clothes to fool the Gods. Cross-dressing their children is not really a solution, but it shows cultural creativity.

When I tell Tilak I'm interested in such things because of my Public Health background he tells me that most children die in the rainy season. When the rains come it washes months of faeces from the hillside into the rivers and water supply. There is a huge increase in diarrhoea and too many children die during these mid-year months. And too often, young mothers die in childbirth.

Boys are also valued here because they are every parent's pension plan. Girls leave the family at a young age to join their husband's family. More recently, the wealthier families send one son off to find work elsewhere, supporting him in the hope that one day he will return richer and support them.

The city offers the illusion of continual work. If crops or a city son fails, many families have no alternative but to seek support from moneylenders who charge extortionate interest rates. They are disliked passionately by village folk. This intricate weave of subsistence farming, animal trading, barter in marriage, plus the sibling city work is creating a new social fabric in many villages.

The average age expectancy for Nepalis is around fifty years of age. This however is very misleading because it is based on an average that is brought down by the fact that so many children die. If you get past your fifth birthday in Nepal there is a good chance you will live into your eighties, without ever having seen a doctor, without ever having taken any medicine. This is an overlooked fact that could be of use in public health campaigns in the west... that there are actually people alive today who exist without ever taking any medicinal drugs. Until recently, most people existed in this state until medicines stepped in to save those who needed it and convinced many who don't need it that they do. If you take away the iatrogenic effects, the success of medicines on people who do not need them is far less than we are made to believe. Today more and more of any health crisis is caused by what we have given ourselves rather than what we have contracted from nature.

I TAKE ADVANTAGE OF BARABASE'S CENTRAL GEOGRAPHIC POSITION and when the mood takes me I explore in every direction, sometimes walking for days. I always ask for news of the Moni Baba wherever I go, but so far nothing of his whereabouts has come up.

Across a land where distances are measured by the number of days it takes to reach your destination, I'll walk seven then take seven days to walk back. I chat to porters and traders on the trail, moving for eight to ten hours each day.

Lush terraces are carved into hills, higher than I ever believed possible. They contour down thousands of feet into deep valleys, as if a bright green cloth has been cast over a set of Lego Mountains. The scale challenges the eyes. It evokes a sense of wonder and muscle-aching appreciation for the lifestyle of the people who live here. I explore parts of the countryside where human feet are more useful than hoofs or wheeled vehicles.

When I'm in Barabase, time seems to stand still. When traders come to sell or buy things, I chat to them too. All are full of purposes that they are keen to share. Some have taken weeks to come from remoter villages.

My daily routine revolves around watching Maya prepare the early morning meal of rice and lentil – Dhal Bhat and then eating it. Masses of rice are piled high onto a steel tray with a splash of lentil sauce put into one of three indentations. If I'm lucky, twice a week Maya will make potato and curried cabbage for dinner and once a week we'll eat an egg for protein at breakfast.

Despite this compulsory vegetarian diet, there seems to be enough festival days where a chicken is sacrificed then curried and I admit loving it. Perhaps it tastes wholesome because I know how healthy the chicken is. I've already had a relationship with it. It's pecked at the rice crumbs fallen from my plate. It's scrambled squawking from under my feet. It's had a full life experiencing fear and flight from chases by children or a stray dog. It's exercised the legs I now eat, running away from villagers. It has also had its breast and wings tickled and massaged by children.

Tilak laughs at my appreciation of a chicken's life whenever he sacrifices one to the gods at festivals. He tells me that he honours their life spirit and he sounds like a Native American in a cowboy movie. I can't tell if he is serious or joking.

20

As months in Barabase pass, I discover I've been viewing everything in the village through the eyes of the friends I know from my past. In my mind I hold conversations with a whole host of auld acquaintances. Whenever I see a wooden beam I think of Paul in Peebles, a carpenter friend. I know that he'd be amazed more than I if he were here. Whenever I spot any good sewing work I think of our neighbour Mrs Kennedy. All my past friendships are like a Pavlovian trigger that responds to encounters here. There's Jimmy, my engineering friend, who would love to see Tilak's milling machines. If I see something new I usually think of someone I know who'd be amazed. Even Fiona jumps onto my mind now and again. She'd definitely like the red clothes that village women wear for special occasions.

The longer I stay here, however, the more local people I add to my consciousness. I begin to see this place through their eyes, in my thoughts and dreams. Slowly the past urgency of my life at home is beginning to fade. My computer lies unused and my walkman and camera have become paperweights. They are on display as redundant devices, unnecessary and therefore neglected.

I figure that people who visit places on short holidays, never really visit the place, they just have time to see it through the eyes of all their old friends. They never have the chance to see or live it in the same way as a local. They collect new stories but even their holiday memories are crafted for their friends at home. They'll take home observations to amuse people on their return.

Despite this length of time here, one third of my life is the same it's always been. When my head hits the goat hair pillow at night, sleep takes over. It's a sleep made sounder through physical exhaustion. On occasion I find myself waking from a dream, sitting up in bed, dodging fast cars or having western imagery in my head. I still occasionally dream of people and events in Scotland, or from TV or from Hollywood movies but I guess that's because they still represent long-held key emotions.

I've picked up most of my Nepalese-language skills from Maya. My dreams are slowly filling with Nepali words, local references and Maya. I cannot help this. She is a fascinating woman who either has absolutely no awareness that she is beautiful or places very little value on it in. On the special occasions she dresses up in her finery she looks stunning but it's the confidence she displays wearing her rough village clothes that makes her alluring. She has boundless energy and a daily routine that would floor most other women I've met. It is a physically brutal existence that keeps her in the shape you'd find in a fitness instructor. Her family training from childhood helps in this lifestyle, but perhaps it's Tilak's relationship with her that keeps them both enthusiastic about life. Other women in the village seem to have aged quickly under such exertion, but Maya seems to thrive on it.

As my Nepali improves Maya and I have more conversations, during which she seems fascinated by the fact that I've chosen to remain in Barabase. She often stares at me in my presence, as if I am the one unknown factor in a world she understands completely and labours to keep orderly.

Tilak also seems to share Maya's interest in my motives for

staying on so long and she's obviously discussed this with him. One day as we sit under the pipal tree watching the sun dip below the hills, Tilak talks to me.

'Jamesji, excuse me but why do you spend so much time looking for the Moni Baba when there are so many gurus you could follow in Britain?' Tilak seems embarrassed at his own question. He plays with one of the large leaf plates that villagers make for religious offerings and which litter the ground around us.

'I'm not looking for a guru to follow. I'm looking for the Baba because he was the guru of my father.'

'What will you ask of the Baba?'

'Since my father died in Nepal some twenty years ago, I've wanted to return to see if I can learn a bit more about him. I admit I'm pinning all my hopes on this one meeting with the Baba and not hearing anything after six months here is a bit worrying.'

'How exactly did your father die?'

'He was travelling in the hills in Mustang and some Kampa bandits attacked his group. It seems they were a desperate bunch, looking for food and money at the time. I don't really know the details but they killed him.' I swallow unusually hard after this explanation.

'Some Kampas became troublemakers near the Tibet border. They were given weapons by the CIA, to fight the Chinese.

'My mother told me most of what I know about my father. One porter who managed to survive the attack told her dad was killed for his radio and his wristwatch.'

'It is unusual for a westerner to lose his life in this way in Nepal.'

'This is why I think the Baba can help me.'

'Does this mean you are not interested in the Moni Baba's spiritual teaching?'

'I am. I feel as if I'm on a unique life changing journey and I saved enough money to stay a year or so in Nepal.'

'I was not in Nepal at the time your father died, and I don't remember hearing about it.'

'Do you think my I'm staying here longer than I should?'

'No… it's up to you, what do you want to do with your life?'

Tilak's question catches me off-guard. I believe I'm happy here now because most of my life has been spent fulfilling pre-arranged activities. Nothing in my schedule here is pre-arranged, except my desire to find the Baba. I'm enjoying things this way for the time being.

'I don't know what I want to do with my life. The lack of having an objective is the best thing that's happened. No plans, at least for a while. I'm just waiting to see what comes along from here.'

As the glow of the setting sun licks the underside of the clouds, Tilak smiles and throws the leaf plate over the edge of the hill like a Frisbee.

21

A moment later a group of women and young girls pass us carrying huge bundles of firewood. They are returning at dusk after spending most of the afternoon cutting wood higher in the hills. One young girl is carrying at least half her weight in wood. Tilak shouts to two women in the lead and they respond with laughter, shouting back something about Tilak being a Sanyassin with his pupil.

The small girl falters and stops for a rest near me. I stand and lift the load from her back and she looks bewildered. I offer to take it down later for her. She holds onto the bundle as if I might steal it. Tilak explains to her that we will deliver it and I watch as she continues running down the trail, empty handed, until she reaches the others. She is immediately given part of the load of an older woman and they continue.

Tilak tells me that people in Barabase don't have dreams for their future or plans for their lives either.

I ask what they dream about.

'They often have crazy dreams, mostly about bad spirits if things go wrong or gods helping them to make their life easier.'

'I can't imagine people here dreaming weird stuff because they all seem so balanced.'

'I remember when I was young having visions of trees that come alive and wild animals that hunt them. Where do you think our six-armed Gods and animal superstitions come from? These images can frighten sleepers awake.'

'Just wait until they are exposed to Bollywood or Hollywood's special effects and TV.'

'The majority of people here have never seen a movie or know anything of the wider world, yet when they have a fever or get really drunk, they see visions that are so scary, they do pujas to protect themselves.'

'Amazing, even with such mental purity the mind plays tricks. Most westerners have seen so many horrors on TV news and movies it's impossible to separate these images from our own creations in our dreams.'

'You say that dreams are like movies... people here when they first see a movie, says that it's like their dreams.'

'Meanwhile, I dream of meeting the Baba.'

'I know. I have some news.'

'So that's what this is all about.'

Tilak watches my expression change and takes a long village-time silence before continuing.

'I spoke to someone who was passing through yesterday, the District Chairman. He said there is a chance to see the Moni Baba in Muktinath. It involves a long walk. I can take you there if you wish. Otherwise you're welcome to stay until we hear news of him when he's closer.'

'Is there any chance of him coming closer?'

'No one really knows, but if we want to reach Muktinath in time we must leave tomorrow.'

I barely manage to conceal my excitement. I stand up immediately and agree to set off. As if prepared for my answer, Tilak gives me a list of supplies I will need on a small scrap of paper. I laugh out loud because it is an unbelievably small list – a torch, a water bottle and a roll of toilet paper.

'I think I'm still able to remember this sort of list in my head.'

'Also bring an umbrella,' Tilak tells me. 'You'll need it to protect your Scottish skin from the sun.'

As we walk back to the village I carry the child's load of firewood and it is heavier than I thought it would be. We laugh and continue talking as Tilak helps me split the load, carrying some himself. He teases me, asking if I want him to hire a child as a porter for the trek.

With departure so soon, my goal is re-established and I spend the evening in Barabase observing it with new eyes. I find a fresh incentive to write down my observations.

I've lived in Barabase for eight months and accept I might not come back. Maya is the first to be told of our departure and I feel a sudden increase in warmth between us. Our public exchanges are always proper, but in a few moments of privacy that night, I believe she is flirting with me.

We are served a trekking-size Dhal Bhat and Tarkhari meal from Maya. Afterward, Tilak opens a large Everest beer and settles into a conversation about the Moni Baba and his time as a Gurkha soldier.

'I've kept the memory of meeting the Moni Baba with me all through my years in the Gurkhas. I believe it was my prayer of devotion to the Baba that helped the British accept me into recruitment.'

'They knew of this prayer?'

'No, I was picked one of ninety, among seven hundred applicants.'

'Tell me about your recruitment,' I ask.

'Everyone goes through tests. Potential recruits have large numbers painted on their chests. I was number eighty-one, an auspicious number.'

'Obviously.'

'We were told to run for long distances up hills, sometimes against British troops who were in the country on special training. The fittest British soldiers would often beat us to the top of the hill, but all Gurkhas were the first back down. We'd all be drinking chai in the barracks before the first British soldier came in.'

'That must have pissed them off.'

'All recruits saw it as a National pride. I was given a uniform, shown how to use fork and knife. I knew nothing about the Western world. I'd only heard old soldier stories from men in the village.'

'What did you think of the UK?'

'I can never forget my first trip to London. We all accepted the new surroundings without any problems although we were shocked to see young people kissing in the street. We saw young women showing too much of their legs and thought them, how you say in English?'

'Liberated?' I add.

'No... rude.'

'In the sixties, these words had the same meaning... liberation and rudeness.'

'The first time on the tube escalators was very funny to us. Seeing a machine that takes you up steps. No one was really impressed all that much. It was just part of everything being new.'

'It's hard to believe that nothing impressed you?'

'I'm telling you the truth. Nepalese are never going to display emotion during a sightseeing trip. Although there was one thing that, how you say in Scotland – gob-smacked us all.'

'What was that?'

'We were travelling on the top deck of a bus, when we all saw a field of cows. This was on our way to the barracks, someone pointed to the herd. We had never seen such big cows. We all rushed to that side of the bus in complete disbelief. We nearly tipped the bus over. We were emotionally overcome that day.'

'A field of Holy cows.'

'Exactly,' Tilak laughs. 'Any country, that produces the mother cow to such a size, has to be special. It is a country worth fighting for. No? We had sworn a duty to the Queen... but those cows they were like the gods.'

'Huncha – absolutely!' I say.

Tilak shouts an instruction to Maya who returns to stand with a shoebox full of old photos. He shows me a photograph of his fellow soldiers on their arrival in Britain. He looks young and fresh faced and I see a resemblance to his daughter Satya, in his features.

Tilak talks more of his months in England, training, before moving on to serve the UK in the jungles of Belize and the traffic of Hong Kong. He says the Baba's teachings helped him work with many different types of people from different cultures.

'The Baba has brought you to my door, now I must take you to his door,' Tilak tells me.

'You have had a very fulfilling life Tilak and I'm grateful to share this journey with you.'

After a moment's pause he says, 'Yes, I feel fulfilled Jamesji – although I haven't yet sired a boy child.'

I look towards Maya who, on hearing this, leaves the room.

22

Tilak estimates the quickest way to reach Muktinath from where we are is to walk straight up to Manang and then cross an eighteen thousand foot pass down into Mustang. It would be easier to travel to Pokhara and head north through Baglung but time is of the essence.

We walk for five days up towards the Tibetan plateau. We sleep in small farmhouses, eating rice and lentils each day. The terrain changes from lush low valleys in the middle hills to the desolate high desert of Manang. This is a Buddhist area in a country that is ninety per cent Hindu. The hills are peppered with remote villages of stone. Each hamlet has wood piled high on the roof and where it comes from, I cannot see. There appears to be no trees so there is status attached to this display of firewood. It's stored visibly, so neighbours witness the resources of a rich family. Carbon insurance should a cold season prove particularly long.

Tilak carries a small Sony short-wave radio that he says he never travels without. He is careful to milk the energy from four batteries he's confident will last the full trip. A voice reawakens that part of my brain that's been pleasantly asleep by reciting the BBC news.

'Believe it or not... this is the only way can tell if something dramatic happens in Barabase.'

I laugh. 'You mean the BBC has a correspondent secretly embedded in Barabase?'

'No. A few years back we had a landslide near us that killed over 80 people. I heard it first from the BBC news.'

High above a raging river, a group of porters carrying huge packs wait at the opposite side of a log bridge, until we cross. Tilak's radio crackles out news headlines about the UN's slow response to global emergencies. I look around and think this whole place could be called an emergency as it is. Yet how on earth could things be done more quickly? People are all on foot, carrying essential supplies into their remote villages simply to survive.

Next up on the news is a report from the Middle East. There have been clashes between Israelis and the Palestinians. It could be a story on a loop of tape, played for the past 40 years. The following story is on an impending financial crisis and the lack of confidence in the economy. Another news headline fixed on repeat. I feel no sense of association or shock because it seems irrelevant and far away.

I look around at the weathered faces and leathered hands of rural productivity, carrying on confidently despite the hardships on the hillsides of Nepal. I then ponder this word 'confidence'. It is the only thing from the financial news that seems relevant to life here. Despite the social advances in the west and the degree of sophistication in the world's money markets; despite the continual analysis that is undertaken by pundits and investors on our economy; despite all the elaborate safety procedures to prevent markets collapsing, everything still sways or tumbles at the mention of the words 'lack of confidence'. It is perhaps the only emotive phrase left in the financial sector's vocabulary. A phrase that still strikes fear into the hearts of rich people worldwide.

'What do you think about expanding your milling business?' I ask Tilak as we walk in single file up a narrow path.

'In what way?' he shouts back as we round a cliff-side with a thousand-foot drop.

'You could set up a business making trekking foods.' We cross a deep valley on a bridge made of rope and branches.

'What's the difference between trekking foods and food?'

'The branding, I guess. You could make wholegrain muesli, and then package and supply it to some of the leading trekking agencies in Kathmandu.'

Down steps we go into another valley and over a stream on a log.

Tilak laughs but is concentrating on the trail while I'm trying to distract myself from the trail. My fertile imagination helps me take my mind off things I might not otherwise attempt. It could be the end of all thought if I put a foot wrong.

After passing the high altitude air strip outside Manang, we begin to see some signs of tourists. Little pink and white clumps of used toilet paper appear on the side of the path. I suggest to Tilak he could also manufacture Nepali camouflage toilet paper.

'That wouldn't stop this shit from washing down into our rivers during monsoon,' he shouts back.

'Yes… I'm thinking business not National health business.'

For the next two days I continue giving business ideas to Tilak. Tilak's Trekking Foods, with a fancy label and international franchise, distract me all the way to the top of the eighteen-thousand-foot pass at Thorong-la. My hands and toes freeze but with Tilak's instincts and the BBC's weather forecast we manage to get over quickly and avoid snowfall at the top of the pass.

The journey is the equivalent to two trips up and down Ben Nevis in one day, with a fair bit of time at altitude. The downward trek is a crisp knee-jarring descent on the trail to Muktinath. If the world's roads ever need re-surfacing, then the gravel required is here only a week's walk from the nearest road. As we descend through an endless stone quarry, Tilak is pacing us fast since neither of us are dressed for extreme cold, nor prepared for any long stop. We also have an appointment with a Baba we don't want to miss.

When we finally reach Muktinath, the town is crowded with people and Tilak seems pleased. We go immediately to the Temple that is a customary destination for pilgrims. The fire in my knees craves for a dip under one of the hundred and eight spouts of water beside us. Tilak seeks out the priest who keeps watch over the miraculous flame that has burned for countless years above a pool of still water.

Tilak asks the priest where the Moni Baba's puja will be performed. The priest greets us warmly, but then tells us the Baba's puja was performed yesterday. Most people who attended have gone, including the Moni Baba. We have missed him by a day. I slump to the ground with exhaustion, near the eternal flame.

23

A fter a night of disappointment, Tilak offers me the possibility of running to catch up with the Baba if we move now.

My mind says yes but my knees say no... and the knees have it. I also realize that my weakness is not just from exhaustion but possibly the after effects of high-altitude sickness. I can hardly respond to Tilak's questions, never mind move faster to catch the Baba.

After a full night's sleep in Muktinath I feel back from the brink of exhaustion and recover some strength. Tilak tells me the priest is willing to talk about the Moni Baba's visit and tell us what he taught. He's also agreed to call some devotees together to give their own accounts.

Tilak thinks we should stay and listen. This aftermath is the nearest he's been to a Baba puja in some time. There are two themes in particular he thinks are relevant to us, one being Pain and the other Desire. Tilak suggests that I should use this time to fully recover so I agree with his arrangements. He says I should record these for my collection. I tell him that if it had been a lecture on dealing with disappointment, I would be even more interested. I tell him I really just want to meet the Baba and ask about my dad. I don't tell him that I think maybe Tilak's desire for a son may cause his interest in hearing this teaching.

The priest invites us into his private room. It appears ancient and ornate, with painted walls and clouds of incense. He serves us Tibetan tea, in the finest Tibetan cups, taken from a sizable collection on display. I suggest to myself that this brew is a soup not tea, because of the butterfat floating on the surface, like an Alaskan oil spill.

After tea we are invited to sit outside at dusk. A chorus of night creatures increase their volume as it becomes darker. The bald priest begins chanting a few musical Bhajans, pronouncing his words in rhythm with his eyes closed, swaying to the sound of his own voice.

This Muktinath priest sounds similar to preachers in all other religions, detached and well practiced in the repetition of comfort words. It's like they prefer to allocate copyright responsibility for what they say to god, or in this case the many gods that are worshiped. The priest talks slowly and Tilak translates, offering opinions on what he says in English.

It strikes me that here you have the workings of every religion in a nutshell. A priest repeating words that are immune to challenge, that remain fixed like laws in the lexicon of religious language. They are not laws, but they are stories. At one time they were written for the betterment of society, now they have evolved into the battle cries of religious ideology for control in a global society. Where man has the flexibility to share and obey laws, religions cannot. They are doomed to forever differ.

The priest continues to recite teachings from his ancient books and scriptures, with their main claim to fame being they are older than any other scriptures. I sit listening, captivated more by my own questions, curiosity and exhaustion than his teaching.

I find it difficult to take this priest seriously. Any insistence that life is a mystery to all humans except a chosen few who are enlightened, his allocation of leadership to those who speak about this mystery all the time, when what's really needed are people who can help remove the mysteries. We need leaders who devote creative time to the practical challenges of improving society, not folk who keep harping on about our ignorance in comparison to a god.

I know that Tilak reads my indifference but he keeps translating anyway. I try to calm myself. I'm aware that I'm bringing global thinking to a session that will not welcome it and it is preventing me from seeing any personal value on offer here. My mind eventually wanders off elsewhere to the monotones of Tilak's voice and the priest's rant in the background.

Ahead in the distance, the Moni Baba is somewhere on the trail south, with the girl in white by his side. They might be walking slowly and maybe we could still catch them. But the hills are scarred with paths, and they need only take one turn off the main route and we would never find them.

I'm also now filled with a little dread that the Baba may turn out to be like this Muktinath priest, just another disappointing purveyor of religious jargon. Speak a language no longer useful for governance, unification or action but simply a verbal potion used to help maintain a religious person's mental health. I remind myself that the Baba's real value to me is his knowledge of my dad. I repeat this connection with my goal like a mantra, otherwise I might lose my focus.

Maybe the Baba and his female companion are camped now and looking into the same sky as we are. As the earth twists one more time from the sun, perhaps they too can see this same red beam of light touching the world's tallest mountaintops.

24

The next morning after a thin porridge breakfast, Tilak and I decide we should leave. News spreads through the village that food supplies are low because of the large gathering for the Baba. My head feels better but my knees are still painful from the fast trek over the pass.

Before we leave, Tilak tells me the priest has volunteered to discuss the teachings that the Moni Baba presented to the gathering. The talk was documented by a devotee and brought back especially for us.

Once more in the priest's private quarters with some of the Baba's followers, the priest reads aloud in English. I look around and suddenly visualize the Baba as a local health visitor, talking to hill folks about their arthritis.

'The Moni Baba's teaching on pain, which is generally associated with something that is unpleasant!' The preacher looks straight into my eyes, presumably to see if I am capable of understanding the obvious in this teaching. I can hardly disguise my cringe.

'Physical pain hurts... but so too do negative feelings and

distress; these are also painful. Pain is something most of us fear and often it is the fear that does the more damage than the pain.' I think if there's pain the damage is done.

'Some people even associate pain with evil. Anyone who wilfully or continually inflicts pain on others is regarded as evil. People in pain and people who fear are very quick to point out this evil.

'With yoga understanding there should be less fear of pain, since most of the time it occurs for a good reason.' Tilak nods with a little more approval than yesterday. I think he recognizes the Baba in this talk and I'm happy for him.

'Pain is present whenever healing is taking place. Even if healing does not succeed, it is trying to take place. Pain is simply a warning that something has gone wrong. By understanding pain, we have more chance to predict and often avoid the danger it is warning us of. If we understand pain as a warning and not the end result of something, then more serious outcomes can often be avoided. Our reaction to pain often determines whether it will spread, or be stopped within our self.'

The priest stands, sensing that he has our attention. He picks up a Tibetan teacup, into which he pours boiling water. He acts as if he is a magician on stage performing a trick. He's keen to convey this teaching in an entertaining way.

'If I were given boiling tea in a tin cup and it burned my hands, my instincts would be to drop the cup. If handed tea in this Tibetan cup however, my response is different because I know this cup is a priceless antique. Although the pain in both situations is the same, my reaction is different. If we see a reason to bear the pain we can control it to an extraordinary level of tolerance. In many a strong mind, pain can be made to disappear.'

There are nods of agreement exchanged around the room and the priest moves on to the second topic the Baba discussed, the subject of 'Desire.'

I try to associate these talks to this group of farmers but it is beyond me at the moment. Tilak, however, is keen to hear this next session.

'People are curious to know what lies ahead and are often superstitious as to what influences the future. Whatever our desires are... provides a clue as to what we might be doing in a few years' time. Our desires are created from our ability to make comparisons. The farmer who grows larger crops, has more animals, better health, more children, can become the comparative envy of others. The more comparisons we are exposed to, the more likely our envy and desires will increase. Although we seem to be surrounded by random choices, our desires are an indication of the direction we will head. Each fulfilment of a desire brings with it, not enlightenment but the sensation of relief and accomplishment. The inability to fulfil a desire brings with it frustration, and often unhappiness. These sensations of feeling fulfilled or unfulfilled play a dominant role in our future lives because by looking outward for comparisons we create our inner desires.

'What we are today can be seen as the result of a desire held some time ago. If we feel frustrated in the now, you may see some wisdom in adjusting your desires, especially if they've been expressed to others who hold you to them.

'There should be no limit to your goals, but you need to take conscious management of your desire by making sensible comparisons. Only this approach will bring you fulfilment and not frustration. Do not become the slave of your desires, and you will become better at keeping fulfilment within reach.'

Hearing such lessons in remote corners of the country seems extraordinary to me. There is a suggestion here that the old adage, you are what you eat, also applies to the mind. We are not just a product of our education or our environment, we are a product of how we process all the information we've gathered. We are in some ways... what we have talked about in the past.

I realise that appearances can be deceiving. Here illiterate farm workers and simple monks enjoy this contemplating nature of being. Despite their poverty and the despicable living conditions, they seem little interested in changing. Perhaps things will change when their children are exposed to more lifestyle comparisons than they have.

After the priest is finished, Tilak and I talk. I tell him the Baba's talk seems very intellectual for hill farmers whose desires might aspire to having more Yaks or a son. I suddenly regret saying son, but Tilak does not seem offended.

'In our language there are many words for different mental states. The Baba may not say this in quite the same way... but even in places where people use religious chanting and the repetition of words to drum their worries out of their head, the Baba's contribution can help sooth a troubled mind with clearer thinking. Our farmers may not be able to read but they require large amounts of faith to survive here. It's this type of language that helps them keep that faith. Even in a rural society there needs to be discussions on the community's collective desires.'

Essentially Tilak is telling me, so what if they have yaks on their wish list instead of a new BMW car, the Baba's advice is appropriate for both. The collective desires for a community's future is a powerful thing. Just as confidence applies to farmers and the global markets, 'desire' applies to all human endeavours. Tilak says the Baba always tailors his talk to the audience he is addressing, just as he has for me. Tilak says after yesterday when I heard the religious monolog from the priest, he thought I deserved more.

I'm left thinking that Tilak is more of a guru than I thought him to be and I thank him for arranging this session.

'It will be more interesting when you get your chance to meet the Baba face to face. To stand in front of him is to get whatever you need James, whether you are an illiterate farmer, a politician in Kathmandu or a cynic from Scotland.'

25

My desire to find the Baba is suppressed for the time being. My fear in Barabase was that the Baba might have grown old or become ill and disappeared completely, but now I know he was here two days ago. Tilak picks up on my attitude change.

After two days' rest and the healing powers of the water spouts, I feel fit enough to go on. I'm less bothered by thoughts of endurance ahead. The daily routine and exercise of the trek have disciplined me. I take joy in walking because there is no alternative. My life's comparisons are now against porters, whose strengths are considerably greater than mine and I'm inspired.

As we set off from Muktinath, we encounter many groups of porters passing us on the footpaths. In the first few days they are carrying an assortment of building materials towards us. Going up are metal sheeting for roofs, coils of plastic water pipe some six feet in diameter. Later, we meet porters on the way down carrying products from the hill farmers. There are huge bundles of the Lokta bush, used to make paper. Some carry large containers of honey, vegetables and other produce from the fields. Porters here accept long distances of foot traveling as a lifestyle... not a journey.

Down the trail from Muktinath, all travellers enter the Kaligandaki, the deepest gorge in the world. Here seasonal winds whistle up each afternoon in a rush to escape the hotter lowlands. They exhale hot air onto the lip of the Tibetan plateau and in doing so create a climate that is unique. Waterfalls that begin some thousands of feet above the trail on the slopes of the Annapurna range vaporize long before they reach the floor of the valley below. The winds are so strong the water is blown into thin air. This wind possibly robs the Kaligandaki of the world's longest waterfalls because water is but a mist when it reaches the valley floor.

I find the trail through Marpha enchanting and see why it is becoming a popular trekking highway for tourists. From the dusty paths of Jomsom, one enters lush green clearings, filled with apple trees. The children have red cheeks, like the apples they try to sell, a by-product of the persistent winds.

Tilak tells me of the small-business idea that someone reintroduced here. Not a foreigner, he says proudly, but a Nepali entrepreneur. The apple orchards are a recent enterprise facing many challenges. Growing is not a problem but exporting the apples from here is. Days of transporting the apples by porter or mule on foot trail to markets causes much wastage. Tilak tells me how some locals now turn the excess apples into a brandy that is popular, especially with the military. It can take weeks for the apples to reach markets in other towns but the brandy's appeal is strong. Tilak says military officers often arrive by helicopter to take crates of the brandy out.

As the gorge narrows, it's impossible not to appreciate the full scale of the two massive mountains above us. On one side stands Annapurna; on the other, Dhaulagiri: both over twenty-six thousand feet at their summit. These are mountains indeed.

After the gorge finally opens out, Tilak and I enter the district of Baglung. The town sits majestically on a flat hill and it's hard to believe there is no road into it. What gives Baglung its bustle is its trade and transport links. There are large groups of porters coming and going into town from the trails to Pokhara. It is a centre for commerce for surrounding villages and has its own airport, albeit four hours' walk away.

Tilak continues asking locals if they have seen or heard of the Moni Baba passing through, and up until Baglung there have been many sightings. We hear that a few nights ago he and Sita stayed in a village opposite the town with a local paper maker. In Baglung itself there have been no sightings. We seem to have lost him once more.

He is as elusive as a snow leopard and as rare as a Yeti, and as much a part of the folklore of Nepal. Tilak believes we have no alternative but to carry on walking two more days to the road head, to find transport to Pokhara. He casually mentions that in Pokhara, there is someone of interest for me to meet... the Moni Baba's daughter.

2 6

fter nearly one month of walking since we left Barabase, we sit outside a teashop just one day's walk from the road head. A group of seven porters arrive with huge Dokho baskets containing cement bags on their back, some with two strapped together. They are the pedestrian equivalent of truck drivers, with the same sort of bravado and confidence in their haulage skills. On this trail up to Baglung, these men move building materials on an industrial scale.

I am sitting on the lowest step of the teashop so my eyes are waist high to these porters. All of them have a muscle over each knee the size of a tennis ball. I've never appreciated the calves, knees and thighs of men before, and assume the women porters are much the same in build.

Many are freelance, hired by transportation companies, although others work in cooperatives or simple gangs of workers. They can deliver loads where pack animals cannot go. They walk from sunrise to dusk. They take just a few breaks besides the trail or at an established teashop like this one.

I rub my knee muscles, knowing they may soon become golfball size. I believe anyone who comes trekking in Nepal without this muscle, must at least leave with one.

As I continue with my admiration for porters I see from what's been ordered that this is not just a tea break, it's the main fuel-stop of the day. Each is served an enormous serving of white rice heaped six inches high on metal dinner plates. A little lentil sauce helps to wash the carbs down and supply the protein. This is their Himalayan-style pit stop, where the gas tank is filled and the loads adjusted before the convoy starts again.

For the next few hours, I walk behind a group of women porters carrying bales of paper wrapped flat onto their backs as if it were a fashion statement. It is handmade paper that's been used for centuries to print Tibetan prayers on. Tilak tells me that when the Chinese invaded Tibet, the paper industry in these hills nearly collapsed. A UN project helped to save the tradition and expand the industry. UNICEF Greeting cards are now made on this Nepali paper and many other products have been created from it in Kathmandu.

I think of the people around the world who have received one of these greeting cards. I cannot imagine they fully understand the physical effort that's gone into getting that greeting to them.

I carefully overtake each pack of porters on the downward trail, and find myself overtaken by them on the uphill stretches. During one steep climb behind a male porter, my face is only inches away from his bare feet. I study his slow plodding technique. His feet spread over the ground like suction pads. His toes gripping like fingers. The soles of his feet have such thick skin there are quarter-inch deep cracks in his heels. I think of the fakirs in India who walk over hot coals. No problem, really, if their feet have the same protection as these porters. It's like having thick leather boots on.

Porters have the confidence of an overlord on the trail. There is only one challenge to their occupational status, and their occupation... a road.

The few existing hill roads are often closed due to landslides and floods. It's not simply a case of laying down tarmac on flat surfaces. Tilak tells me there are plans to build a road to Baglung soon and to other places around Nepal. The unstable terrain makes this expensive, but Tilak believes that eventually it will happen.

As we approach the road head town and the end of our trek, I experience cultural shock. The atmosphere is completely different from that of the past four weeks. Crowds of people are milling around shops, talking and eating after dark. There are oil lamps burning everywhere. People in the hills do not waste fuel like this. The richer the town – the brighter the lights.

It strikes me how differently people behave in towns with roads compared to those we've just met in villages. It may have something to do with security. Here at the road head, strangers in vehicles have the capacity to make a rapid exit. In the hills, villagers feel completely safe and not at all threatened by a pedestrian stranger. Even the weirdest looking tourist does not pose a threat in the hills. Why fear anyone who is less capable of a quick getaway? Why create any mischief if you cannot easily escape?

Alternatively, towns with roads bring in strangers with such frequency that locals look like they are permanently on-guard. The bustle and excitement of the road-town raises a different sort of citizen.

When I share this observation with Tilak he answers in his guru voice, 'Never trust people who come too quickly into your life Jamesji. They have a tendency to leave the same way as they came.'

I think Tilak might be referring to me. I will eventually have to make a decision about leaving Nepal.

As we board a minibus, I watch some porters out of the window. They look different here. Not the confident athletes I've seen in the hills. Here, they are poor labourers looking for work. A group stand smoking next to a shrine with prayer wheels spinning beside them. A bored endless sweep of the hand by one sends out prayer to be hired.

These are the sort of men and women that Gupta the umbrella salesman mentioned in Calcutta. They do not need written words to guide their spiritual development. They are much more in-tune with the physical nature of their existence and they puja and walk through religious rituals and routines each and every day. It may involve spinning wheels, elaborate bowing and in some cases, dance-like prostrations. Their choice of worship over worry is physical, not intellectual.

I've heard Tilak mumble prayers on this trek. I've heard others in the close-knit homes and lodges where we stayed repeat chants of devotion late at night. No child grows up here without a high degree of physical awareness. No adult has avoided taking some sort of responsibility for a child's up bringing even if they have no children of their own. It's a society integrated in a way that we must have lived until such time as towns and cites were created, sucking people into them for a different kind of survival.

I close my eyes on the bus, exhausted, imagining pleasant images from the trek and responding to the noise of an engine for the first time in a while. It lulls me to sleep.

27

In Pokhara, I welcome the warmer weather at this lower altitude. It is a sunny day with a glorious view from the home of Sundar, another of Tilak's ex-Gurkha friends who lives by the lakeside.

I spend the day listening to retiree soldiers talk of their times in the Gurkhas. Sundar served time in the Falklands War and feels obliged to talk in English to include me. In his eyes, I'm one of the beneficiaries of his success there.

After my eighth glass of chai tea, Tilak asks Sundar if we can borrow his wooden canoe to go visit Rhumba, daughter of the Moni Baba. Sundar agrees and tells us Rhumba the hermit lives only a few hours' walk from Raj, his son. He gives us directions to Raj's farm across the lake.

Next morning at early dawn, Tilak and I carry the dugout canoe to the lake's edge. We are the only ones on the water. We paddle past a new boat made of slick fiberglass, painted bright colours for tourists, beside a hotel.

Across the mirror-calm lake, I see Machapuchhare, the fishtail mountain, reflected on the surface.

As instructed by Sundar, our timing is perfect. Raj is at the opposite shore, preparing to take some children in his own canoe to school. He meets us at the water's edge, having recognised his father's canoe approaching on our journey across. Tilak has known Sundar's son since he was a child so we have another friendly reunion. He tells us to wait for an hour at his nearby red mud-brick farmhouse, while he paddles the morning school run. I am namasti'd by five curious schoolchildren as Raj moves off down the lakeside.

Again time seems irrelevant to Tilak as we wait for Raj to return, when there is a repeat ritual of chai and endless talk. Although we have set ourselves a task, a journey to undertake, priority is given to the present moment. I know if I voice impatience, my urgency would be seen as disrespectful. This much I've learned.

Finally, Tilak asks Raj if Rhumba is at home today. Raj immediately warns us about her reputation and that sometimes she can be very *Kali,* as in fierce. The strangeness of this woman is part of her reputation. She lives alone, up and over the first slope we encounter on the hill to our left. He tells us that she is a *Jankhari,* the Nepali word for faith healer and that she has powers beyond that of the usual healer. Tilak seems to know all this already but lets Raj continue talking for my sake and because he speaks such good English. He tells us that in these parts Rhumba is a celebrity. Local villagers visit her regularly, giving her food and clothing in exchange for her chants and her cures.

Raj tells us that Rhumba has likely been out all night administering her powers to a sick community leader who lives in the next district. He has heard of the man's sickness and knows that Rhumba has been treating him. She is, after all, the local emergency health-care service. Raj tells me there are over four hundred thousand faith healers in Nepal and only six hundred doctors. It is unusual, he says, to catch Rhumba unprepared for visitors.

With my interest poked, we set off over that hill to the left, and after a three-hour walk, we reach the house of Rhumba the *Jankhari*. It is neat and tidy on the outside and has skins sewn onto the thatched roof, presumably as patches against the rain.

As soon as we approach, the door opens and a woman emerges, perfectly matched to the dainty size of her house. She is about four and a half feet tall and has a peculiar gait to her walk. I notice immediately she has a large swelling around her neck, the size of grapefruit.

She walks quickly towards a tree where she uncovers a large round two-sided drum. It is the shape of a tennis racket, supported by a solitary stick handle. She begins to slowly bang on the drum with a thin branch and on seeing me, begins to speed up, turning like a whirling dervish. She's like a figure on a Swiss clock. On the hour, the door opens and the woman comes out, twirling in time to the chimes.

To and fro she twists and stomps to the beats of her drum. She stops briefly to put on a chain of bells around her shoulder, then continues. Tilak and Raj have sat themselves on the ground but I stand mesmerized at this dance. I'm told she is singing an ancient dialect and repeating words that the crowd would usually chant back to her. As I sit, Raj translates – the Lake Pokhara Encounter.

'Women. Woman. Free. Free until fertile. Gifted. Gifted. Used until pregnant. Pregnant vessels of life. Cariers of the future.'

Rhumba whispers lines, which even with translation make no sense to me. She does not look anyone in the eye, just sings and stares into the sky or to the woods around the lake.

Raj continues to translate her words for me, adding that he may be giving meaning where there was none. He himself is confused.

'Women. Workers. Keepers. Feeders. Healers. Taught submission. And learn control. Powers.' Raj is not sure she means powers as I might.

She spits some words out in short blowing breaths. She stamps her feet between outbursts in rhythm with her drumming and the words.

'Men beware the liberator. One who comes in your form, suckled on the breast. Reincarnated many times. The oldest of our gender still in this world.'

'Ram. Ram. Beware idiot man. Rejoice. Woman mother. All things change. He is coming. I am here. Do not mock nor disbelieve. He is coming for me.'

'OM Ram Ram Ram.'

Rhumba disappears into her house in silence after this mesmerizing performance. Her song and dance appears to be making predictions. It could mean anything from the coming of a messiah to a husband in her life. Tilak and Raj are less amused than I am and I have to keep my conversations with them on the serious side. We discuss Rhumba all the way back to the boat.

'She has a high cure rate among sick people in our community,' Raj tells me. 'Her reputation as a healer is well deserved.'

'She may just be receiving credit for recoveries that healthy villagers make on their own,' I suggest. 'Illness is not often as fatal as people believed it to be.'

'No, she can definitely cure,' says Tilak authoritatively. 'Her faith healing talents were brought to attention after a Moni Baba gathering. I was there.'

'When was that?' I ask.

'About ten years ago! The Baba spoke to her and drew attention to her insights. Most people thought her a cretin with the mannerisms of madness and cursed. She was treated like the village idiot. That meeting changed her life... from being an outcast to an important person in this community. The Baba told the crowd that she was his daughter. I believe he meant spiritually rather than physically, but from that day on she has been a healer because she was recognized by the Baba.'

I point out that although Rhumba has a goitre on her neck, it does not mean that she is suffering from cretinism. She does appear to be iodine deficient, identifiable through the swelling of the thyroid gland on her neck. This does not mean that she is in any way mentally ill, but if she has children there is a high risk that they would be affected by this deficiency and be born mentally impaired.

'She could cure herself,' I add. 'She could do this easily by cooking with salt which has been iodized. It has helped to eradicate goitre and cretinism from other mountainous regions in the world.'

Raj tells me people here use rock salt mined from the hills of Nepal. Most people buy it because it's cheaper. Sea salt or iodised salt comes from India and is too expensive.

'What a character,' I remark. 'Rhumba the healer with a goitre, is worth further study.'

Rhumba has definitely found a role for herself in her community, which is a rare thing for people who are born iodine deficient. She seems to have taken this role on enthusiastically with the Baba's endorsement. The tiny amount of iodine missing in her diet has forced her thyroid to enlarge to compensate. It's a truly miracle of adaptation by the human body. Research in Western countries has dropped since its eradication in the Rockies and the Alps where people used rock salt.

The Baba has pronounced her as godlike, with a health condition worthy of adoration – yet its consequences are extremely dangerous and apparently not well known here. In return, Rhumba has managed to provide a healing incentive... through people's faith in her new status and her uncomplicated belief system. Some followers seem to have genuinely responded well to her placebo instruction.

'I guess you need to look out for a new guru called Ram,' I say to Raj.

'It is the short form of many Nepali names,' Raj tells me. 'Anyone from Ramesh to Ramananda is called Ram for short.'

'Such women as Rhumba are at risk here,' Tilak adds. 'If too many people do not get well, she will be called a witch.'

PART THREE: THE STAY

28

I n Pokhara just before we board the bus to Barabase, Tilak buys a bottle of Johnny Walker Black Label at great expense. The road journey seems incredibly short and after a few hours we are back in the familiar grip of his village.

A group of local dignitaries are invited to Tilak's mill to celebrate our return and they begin by drinking the whisky as if it were cold tea. Within minutes it's finished and they've all moved onto Marpha brandy and Raksi gin.

Tilak tells stories from the trip, how we missed the Baba, and how we met Rhumba his daughter – the healer. As the elders become increasingly drunk, there is shared disappointment at our failure. I detect this from the Nepali grunts and moans after each drink. Binge alcoholism fits in quite nicely with Hinduism here in the Himal, although thankfully it is a rare occurrence, not weekly as at home. Most of the women preparing the food do not touch any alcohol, but I spot Maya having a few sips of Tilak's drinks She seems delighted we are back.

When the food finally comes, it is the most delicious mix of potato curry and chapattis. I mention to Maya how outstanding her food is, and she says that Manang must have taught me to appreciate her food. I tell her the whole village feels like a luxury destination after returning from Manang and Mustang.

The guests who live furthest away place their last bites in their mouths, announce their departure and go. This is a tradition I'm told, to eat and leave.

I want to help Maya clear up and she allows me, but asks why I want to. She appears more attractive than ever. In my inebriated state, I explain because Tilak is now my best friend.

Tilak, having watched his expensive whisky disappear like water at a marathon finish, slurs his words and asks, 'Why is whisky so expensive?'

'Another eternal mystery… a question fit for a guru,' I answer.

There are a few people hovering around the house prepared to party so I decide to fetch my guitar, left in Barabase for the trek. I sit outside and introduce the remaining mill folk to Pete Green and early Fleetwood Mac blues. Some of the women laugh at a few drunken men who begin dancing in Nepali style.

Tilak also staggers out of his house and begins to dance with his arms waving in the air. Someone brings a drum and a small accordion keyboard. Pretty soon we are jamming R & B with Hindu bajans.

Two women sing old songs, clapping their hands in rhythm and I strum along as best I can. Maya stands with a few friends making well-practiced stationary hip movements to the familiar dances. Tilak shouts into the house and I hear him encouraging the village leader to come out and join us. The older man, who has been drinking heavily, comes out and takes off his jacket and starts to dance. Tilak picks up the jacket and puts it on back to front. He also dances around, spinning in time with the music. Tilak then suddenly walks off down toward the river and the latrines. It is a clear half moon night, dark but with still enough light to see the path.

The village leader sits down beside the clapping ladies. I

continue to play along with my two bandmates, now in a trance-like condition. As we finish playing, there is a brief silence, followed by a loud splash and curse from the river. Tilak is shouting and cursing loudly. He walks back into the yard, soaking wet. He has slipped and fallen into the river while peeing. On seeing Tilak wet, the village leader screams out in laughter, with others quickly joining in. They surround the dripping Tilak, teasing him. Maya and I smile at each other as she shakes her head. The village leader says something in Nepali I can't understand, and again he bends double with laughter at his own remarks.

Tilak also begin to laugh, and he's trying to say something that he can't quite get out. The two men hoot and holler together, Tilak still trying to say something to the elder but unable to speak for laughing. Several times Tilak begins to speak, then breaks into more laughter. Eventually, he screams through his own hysterics, 'I'm wearing... I'm wearing your jacket.' We all join Tilak in his laughter... the women are screaming loudest, covering their mouths with their hands.

29

I remember first arriving in this place. After my initial walk around, I felt there was nothing I could do here. Now I feel part of the community. I'm talked to, waved at and assigned jobs as much as anyone who lives here. I no longer hear the annoying barking dogs, or the mosquitos at this time of year. I also sense a growing impatience and frustration.

One feature of life in Barabase is the lack of privacy. There are no locks on doors. There is nowhere that I cannot be approached by people. I realise I'm being selective in friendships, memories and writing notes. I want it to appear that I can cope, so that in my mind, I can cope.

Village women in Barabase bathe in public. They walk to the local waterspout wearing only a cloth tied across the top of their chest. They then proceed to bathe as if they are posing for an Impressionist artist. The only difference is that these women are completely oblivious to anything sensual associated with this activity.

I regularly pass a stream or waterspout to find women of all ages lathering themselves through a flimsy cloth. A breast is often revealed through the wet garments. The absence of inhibition stunned me at first. Elsewhere, this image would definitely provoke sensual undertones. Here if women catch me looking, they stare back as if to say, what on earth are you looking at?

These impressionist moments are haunting. I still retain the mental residue of a Calvanist Scot. I don't hang out at waterspouts but when I pass by, I have to be aware when observation descends into voyeurism. It feels odd thinking I may be the only one stimulated by these moments.

On one particular stroll, I pass the Barabase waterspout and see Maya bathing alone. On three sides the stone wall protects the intricately carved protruding spout, its nose smooth with years of human touching. Maya's head is directly under the spout and she is drenching herself in water. She looks up and smiles. I ask about the water's temperature and she twists her long hair like a rope to get rid of the excess water. She proceeds to move her cloth garment down to her waist and soap her breasts. My head makes a spontaneous jerk to look away at clouds and distant hills. No one is around and she seems to be aware of this. In a mix of English and Nepali she asks me if I have girlfriends in Scotland and why I am not married. I mention there is still plenty of time. She lifts the cloth and scrubs at her thighs underneath. She then gestures for me to approach and hands me the soap. I lean onto the sidewall to reach it. She asks, 'Have you noticed there are very few Nepalese your age who are not married?'

'Yes. Marriage here takes place when people are very young.'

'Why do you think that is?'

'Perhaps because you have to be married before you can become intimate, but in my society that's not the case.'

She looks startled. I feel I'm in dangerous conversational territory here. She reaches over, takes back the soap and continues to wash.

'Sex is only small part thing to do with young marriages?'

At this point I am confused. If I'm reading the situation accurately, her actions are screaming sensual messages to me and yet she seems combative. I jump down beside her and Maya comes over in front of me, takes a dry cloth from the wall and begins to dry her hair. She turns her back to me then throws her hair forward and back playfully. She forces me against the wall and I find myself trapped. She reaches for a dry loose dress and proceeds to put it over her head. She turns and before the dress descends enough to cover her, she looks me straight in the eye and takes off the wet cloth revealing herself. I see in this flash of a second an invitation to assist. I step forward to help her adjust the dress to cover her. For a fraction of a second I place my hand on her hip. Her reaction takes me completely by surprise.

Maya wriggles as if to escape. I thought I'd shared a brief moment of affection, but she steps back and freezes some two feet away. She seems genuinely shocked but does not back away any further. She stands rigid in front of me and I feel paralysed… with fear.

I've obviously committed some breach of trust that I cannot undo, or guess how bad this is, nor how to proceed. In that fraction of a second, I think that my entire stay in Barabase is at risk and I feel sick. I step to the side and lean against the wall.

Strangely, after a moment of silence, it is as if the thought of things affectionate having raced out of my mind… have suddenly entered Maya's. She looks at me with sympathy, reaches out a hand to my arm. My response is to mouth an apology in Nepali and to walk away, slowly then quickly on the path home.

With my inability to read gender and cultural signals here, I rub excuses onto this relationship wound. I even explore the possibility that I may have unconsciously wanted to experience what Dave felt like in seducing a best friend's partner. I think this is my most bizarre and inventive excuse, to take a betrayal of trust and interpret it as a path towards understanding.

I cannot anticipate what Maya will make of this encounter, animal instincts or raw magnetism, but I spend the next few days terrified and mostly alone, before I find out.

30

I'm suspended on two long ropes from four bamboo poles that villagers have constructed in a single day. 'Make sure his feet are off the ground,' Tilak shouts loudly from the sidelines.

As I swing gently back and forth like a child in a nursery playground, a group of children laugh at my cowardice.

'Swing as high as you can,' Tilak shouts. They are all eager for their turn to beam this swing up to trapeze level.

It is the festival of Dashain and the swing sits above the village on the last terrace before a steep slope. It propels the children well out over the edge of a substantial drop. For the spectator it looks incredibly dangerous, especially when the rope slackens and after that moment of suspension jerks back on the down swing. Tilak explained it's a rite of passage for most children in Nepal.

Older residents of Barabase also take turns on the swing – trying, I'm sure, to relive youthful memories. The joy on everyone's face is infectious. Now that it's my turn I'm being taught how to stand and hold on by Didi and a few others.

We are joined by a group of women, including Maya, who all

begin to shout the Nepali word for 'higher' at me. I stir up the guts to beam out over the edge of the hillside. It's a leg-breaking distance to fall. I mumble a mantra to guarantee the rope's strength for my weight. One of the teenage girls rushes forward and pushes me from behind. She runs to the edge holding my bottom, then ducks and lets go. I swing back and feel the rush forward, higher than before. I'm now content to let the swing slow to a standstill, but word has spread of my initiation and there is a now a bigger crowd. Farmers look on and children are laughing. The girl who pushed me stands with her arms around Tilak's neck laughing childishly. I think maybe he encouraged her to do it.

Maya approaches me with a very serious face and stands in front of me. It is the first time I've seen her since the washing incident. She looks me in the eye and puts her hands on both ropes and places her bare foot between my legs. She steps up and begins to beam the swing high. Her back is to the valley, her face towards the village and the audience. She has an expert technique and within two swings I'm holding on for dear life. She beams us higher and higher. On the downward rush she crouches forward and looks mockingly into my face as we sweep past the ground. She then arches her body back for the push to gain speed. I feel her toes moving under my groin. Her loose skirt flaps like a flag as we launch ourselves over the hillside time and again. Thankfully, her skirt obscures my view of the drop. I feel my stomach slacken in time with the rope when we freefall from the highest point. Each time we jerk down, Maya laughs out loud and the crowd cheers.

After what seems like an age with Maya's foot wedged in my crotch, we slow down. She adjusts her windswept hair and squeals like a teenager at Tilak. Before she jumps off, she wiggles her toes deliberately. Tilak comes over and slaps me on the back. He asks if it was better than a Rollercoaster.

31

The village is transformed during the Deshain festival and there's a definite increase in the population. Younger offspring return to the village but there are also older men, dressed in Nepali shirts and pantaloons, with a suit jacket on top.

Domestic and wild animals are central to the festival. Crows and ravens are fed and dogs have garlands of flowers placed round their necks. Cows and bullocks are worshiped for their contribution to life in the community. Houses decorated with painted steps and walls suddenly make the village look fresh as well as festive. There is great enjoyment in dressing up. Children make themselves look older than their age, many wearing hand-me-down clothes too big for them.

It's the children under ten who seem to dominate the environment on such holidays. Most are already caregivers in some way, looking after their younger siblings or older grandparents. They are full of energy and free from control. They run around and play continually during Tihar. Nepal has such a hybrid mix of Asian features that a large percentage of children are strikingly good looking. There is virtually no obesity in the village, although many of the children show signs of bloated stomachs I reckon comes from intestinal worms.

I see the signs of children testing and teasing each other in their pre-pubertal relationships. The freedoms of youth activities and child-like priorities are only briefly experienced. When they reach their teens, most girls are settled into arranged marriages.

There is plenty of dancing and singing among the elderly who use such occasions to pass on the lyrics of their traditional songs. Very little of the customs are written down; they are remembered and acted out for the young. There's also some serious binge drinking and gambling among the better-off residents during the festival.

As the sun begins to set on Tihar events in Barabasi, I walk through the market past a group of children. They are chasing a stray dog to re-garland it with flowers it has shaken off. I see one child sitting alone and recognize her from the time I carried her wood from the hills with Tilak. She sits near to the bus stop dressed in a pretty new dress that is too big for her. She is unusually quiet and I detect she has been crying. I tell her not to be sad during Tihar and wipe her cheeks. It occurs to me that even the poorest of families make an extra effort to give their children newer clothes for this festivity.

I hear loud noises and shouting from the roadside tea-shop. It sounds like a pub brawl coming from a place most frequented by bus passengers. People begin to scatter from the commotion and suddenly I see a middle-aged man dressed in a Nepali suit come crashing through the door. It's like a movie scene where someone is chucked out the saloon. The man picks up his Topi hat and begins to run full pelt up the road.

Before I even stand upright I see Tilak fly out of the door. He jumps the steps in one leap and takes off after the fleeing man. He does not see me. His Gurkha eyes are obviously fixed on an enemy.

The man continues running up the road trying to flag down an oncoming minibus which drives past him full to the brim. Tilak is legging it after this man and I sprint as hard as I can to catch him, sensing something sinister is about to happen.

Just as the man begins to run again, Tilak catches up and clips his heels making him crash to the ground. Tilak then stands on the man's arm and puts his other foot on the man's neck. As I continue running, Tilak looks menacingly down at the trapped man. Any quick thrust of his foot could easily break this man's neck. His cries are choked quiet. He lies there helpless. My heart is thumping in my chest as I approach, ready to confront Tilak's crazed anger. When I reach him, I find Tilak calm and extremely controlled.

'It's OK James,' he says quietly. 'This Brahmin is just about to get on the bus back to Kathmandu and he's just relaxing before the next one comes.'

As he speaks, I see Tilak move his weight from the foot on the man's wrist to his other foot on the man's neck. His trainers are now pointing straight into the man's throat. As he manipulates his shoe, the man hardly breathes before Tilak steps off him. The man sits up and bursts into a fit of coughing.

Tilak bends down and throws a fist of Nepali banknotes onto the man's lap. He bends lower and speaks a torrent of abuse in Newari into the man's face. He repeats this outburst louder in Nepali so the crowd that has gathered can hear. All seem to nod and agree with what Tilak's saying.

I struggle to understand what this is all about. First I imagine it as a gambling debt or maybe even a cheat has been exposed. But then Tilak turns and walks away. I follow him and try talking to Tilak but he seems intent on another purpose. I ask what this commotion was about. 'Come with me,' he says. 'That man is a fucking scum trafficker... of children.'

After a few more steps absorbing what Tilak just said I ask, 'Shouldn't we get the police?'

'He's more afraid of me than the police. He won't come back here.'

'Won't he just go off and do it somewhere else?'

'I've told him to give up this business or Kali will visit him in Kathmandu. He knows I have soldier friends there and I know how to find him.'

I try to take all this on board. I'm happy Tilak has not decapitated this man in front of my eyes but concerned he's letting him go free, seemingly with a pay-off.

As we approach the little girl sitting by the side of the road she is now crying even more and looks frightened. Tilak takes her hand and walks her back to her home.

Tilak shouts more abuse at the girl's parents and throws another wad of banknotes onto the floor for them to grovel and pick up. I hear him chastise the couple for their conduct, but I see only a steely desperation in their eyes. They pick up the money and take the girl back without any sign of affection.

As we sit outside Tilak's house, he explains more. He tells me he saved that money for the annual Tihar card game with friends. Like everyone else in the village, these are a few days of indulgence once a year. But this interruption is the second time such a thing has happened.

'This is supposed to be a happy time, no?' Tilak asks me.

'Yes,' I say.

'I look forward to this every year, but now I'll be happy when it's over.'

'What just happened?'

'A few years back there was another man from Kathmandu who showed up here offering money to families for young girls. The local women chased him away, but since then some have begun talking as if it that's what they might do if desperate or have another girl child. They are poor and moneylenders have driven a few men to suicide, leaving their families destitute. What these families go through makes my blood boil.'

'Where do the traffickers take these children?'

'There is a big demand from India but bad Nepalis are also involved in the trade. They sell their children like they're livestock, boys less than girls. Some go to barren parents but traffickers also sell girls onto prostitution rings. Ex-Gurkha friends who now work with the police tell me horror stories. Some villages now believe they have been cursed by producing too many beautiful girl children and drawing the attention of these people.'

'How incredibly sad,' I think of Tilak's daughters, 'that beauty should be seen as a curse.'

A flock of small birds lands at our feet and pecks at the scraps of colourful rice seeds on the ground. It seems incongruous to be talking such horrors with Tilak, in a place like this.

3 2

For the next few months people work in the fields preparing them for the rains. They arrive early and are relentless for a few weeks. I have to abandon my favourite walk to the pipal tree on days the rain is heaviest. I begin to feel a little trapped and restless indoors. Didi encourages me to go out and help in the fields, since it is the most productive time for rice planting. I spend days knee-deep in water, pushing wet mud into broken walls in rice fields. I follow instructions because I'm in awe of the villagers' water management skills. I return to the village at night completely exhausted.

One evening I explain to Didi that her grandchildren have more strength than I have and she gives me a friendly nudge. It is such an unexpected nudge that I lose my balance and fall back over the doorstep. I lie there like a clocked boxer, down for the count. Didi blushes and I laugh, but I cannot get up. I'm at once aware that I must be seriously ill.

Tilak and Maya are called to help me into my room and during the next few days I lie completely still on my bed. My sole occupation is the visual exploration of Didi's ceiling, for I can do nothing else. I surrender myself to an unknown illness, knowing that there is little I can do and no health services to call in. I move in and out of sleep, looking up at the smoke-darkened crevices and cobwebs while I'm fed, like a child, by Didi.

Maya visits and treats me like a wounded soldier. I feel so exhausted I can't even talk to her. She accepts my silence and is completely comfortable in her role as nurse. Didi cooks a daily meal of rice and lentils, which passes through me with speed of a laxative. Maya creates a bed-pan arrangement with a pot placed strategically under the rope bed with my bottom poised in a position of deposit. When I try to occasionally sit up it is risky because I can slip through the ropes to the floor and I can become trapped.

Days pass without me knowing it. I sweat to the point of hallucination and freeze under a mountain of blankets and goatskins. Bowls of hot salty soup are poured down my throat, much of it wrenched back up. My joints ache and no one with medical knowledge is around to comfort me with explanation. After months of feeling fit and invincible, I'm reduced to a near skeleton in two weeks.

On cold wet nights Didi expertly manipulates the scarce firewood for warmth and light, while Maya towels me dry from sweating. I realise I have an alternative that no one else in the village has if my health continues to worsen... I have the money to call for an evacuation to Kathmandu and if necessary to Scotland.

Tilak tells me the problem could just be a wee touch of seasonal diarrhoea and insists I drink a homemade mix of salt and sugar water, locally known as Nun Chini Pani. It proves to be an effective oral rehydration solution.

Didi keeps saying the word *phoha* which Tilak tells me is Tibetan for stomach problems. Maya asks me if I have offended anyone recently in an effort to establish if a curse or witchcraft is behind my sickness. I deduce my curse is bacterial and comes from mother monsoon.

Up until now I have miraculously escaped any health problems.

I've eaten like a local in the unhygienic food shops of the valleys and the hills and believed I had adapted a resistance. My search for the Moni Baba is now at risk because of ill health. Didi remains upset since she thinks her push made me sick. I try to explain it was not the push. She is so superstitious she doesn't want to hear my explanation of a fever. She would rather believe it to be her fault than the result of bad karma on my part.

Maya keeps up her frequent visits, continually looking after me. I awake from my unconscious state to find Maya wiping me down with a damp cloth and talking to my groin as if in conversation with Shiva's lingam. Tilak on the other hand just makes sure I drink plenty of his miracle solution Nun Chini Pani. He tells me he has added a few prayers so a recovery might set in soon.

One night Maya is towelling me and I embarrass her by holding her hand to stop her movement because Shiva's lingum is beginning to respond. This reaction is perhaps the strongest indica-tion so far that I am getting better. Maya looks pleased. She sits up pokes at the fire and we just stare at each other, smiling.

Didi also sees a difference in my face and tells me she is very happy that I'm recovering. She tells me that since my bottom has stopped leaking she will find a foam mattress for me. I find I'm now viewed as someone who is blessed by a recovery instead of cursed by an illness.

Once again the beautiful landscapes, the friendly greetings and the faces of village children begin to charge me with a delight for life. But thoughts during my illness have opened a floodgate of ideas about my options for the future.

I observe some things differently. When I arrived, the village just contained anonymous villagers... all equal in my mind. Everyone living under the same conditions, yet now I see some are struggling for survival. It does not take much to send a family over the line from subsistence farming into abject poverty in Nepal. A misfortune, a bad debt, or a simple physical illness is enough.

I've also become wary of my affection for Maya. Sharing space, and living close with her, has made other things bearable here. I have become concerned at my growing fascination with her because now it seems to be mutual. I worry that others might notice it and fear the negative effect it would have on my relationship with Tilak.

After this length of time, I realize I've evolved to see Barabase through the eyes of the people who live here, not the friends I relate to from home. I no longer think of Jimmy or Bob, but Bahadur and Shyam. I too worry if the rains end early or late. I become frustrated when sickness and diarrhoea take another child's life needlessly. I too sense the community apprehension when government officials visit farmers or there is talk of more taxes. I share suspicions of official sounding language from people with city accents.

33

Tilak laughs one day as I crack my head for the umpteenth time entering Didi's small kitchen. We sit together and eat a porter's portion of rice while I vent my frustrations to him.

'The longer I stay in Barabase, the more hardship I see here.'

'This means you are no different to us.'

'I don't believe I have a different thinking process from people here, but our circumstances are very different.'

'What do you mean?'

'I have a life-support system that still connects me to Scotland, like an umbilical cord. I have sustenance from another place. I can leave here whenever I like. I was very near leaving to seek medical help. I don't have to accept the life here forever as people here do.'

'Have you ever considered you might live here forever?'

'No. I am very happy to be accepted, but I've a limit to my time and my status here.'

'What do you mean by status?'

'Well, it's impossible for me to develop any sort of intimate relationship here.' I smile to show Tilak I'm half joking.

'You mean you've been thinking about marrying someone here?'

'No, it was a figure of speech. To illustrate ways I'm excluded.'

'A relationship can be arranged if you would like it. In fact, Maya tells me all the time I should help arrange this for you.'

'Really?'

'Yes. She is concerned for you. There is a girl nearly of age in the next village whose parents are looking for a husband to support them all.'

'How exactly would that work, Tilak?'

'She's twelve years old and...'

'She's not a bottle of whisky,' I interrupt, 'in some raffle prize.'

'There are widows also if you prefer. There are two who are very clean.'

'Well, that's a priority. They'd have to be clean.'

'I am talking seriously.'

'I know. I'm not looking for a widow or a young bride. I came to look for the Moni Baba. My frustration grows from my failure to find him. I guess I also miss the sort of freedom I had at home to interact with women.'

'What sort of interaction?'

'In my society, women are free to make up their own minds about who they want to be with.'

'What makes you think women are not free here?'

'Here you have a bride price to be negotiated before any intimate experience can take place. I'm not even sure that intimate pleasure exists here in the same way as I understand it.'

'Do not make the mistake of imposing Christian sex values on us, Jamesji. Young people here find a way to do as they wish and it's accepted as long as they avoid making others unhappy.'

I sit for a moment and stare at Tilak.

'OK, what if I told you I have feelings for...'

Didi bursts into the room, cutting me off. She tells us that Maya wants Tilak urgently back at the mill.

146

'Jamesji is looking for a wife, Didi, what do you think of that?'
Didi laughs and asks Tilak how far away my home village is.

'Don't take her question as an outright rejection.'

'It would take about one year to walk to my home in Scotland,
Didi. It's about 5000 miles?'

Tilak turns to me and begins singing the words, 'and I would
walk five thousand miles,' then heads out the door.

I hear the commotion outside. Several people are shouting and
Maya's voice seems the loudest. I wander outside and Didi points
to two groups standing around a newly cleared piece of land
beside the river. It is amazing how sound travels in these quiet
hills. The people are a quarter mile away. I see one woman
stomping around, throwing her arms in the air at Maya. She is
waving her fist back back and forth and has what seems to be her
family around her. Maya stands alone with Satiya and several
other children from the village. I see Maya step forward and berate
this wild woman. In response, the women's family shout a chorus
of abuse back.

Tilak begins to run towards the group and once more I find
myself trying hard to catch up with him. As I get closer, I recognise
the old woman as someone familiar from the village along with
her two sons. She has a large gold nose-ring and the Mongolian
features of the high hill farmers.

As I approach, Tilak is circling the family with a menacing walk
then shouts an outburst of Nepali that I cannot understand. I
detect a serious threat in his voice. He storms off past me back
towards his house. I walk up to Maya. She gives me Satya's hand
and tells me to take the children away. Both Tilak's children seem
genuinely frightened at the antics of their parents. Maya picks up
some loose dirt from the cleared land and throws it symbolically
into the river. She turns and follows Tilak.

I ask Satiya what is going on and she explains, 'These people
have begun to build another mill on the river and daddy's just
found out.'

As I enter Tilak's house, he is looking through an old chest of tools and documents. He is more distressed than I have ever seen him. He shouts a flood of curse words in English. They are swear-words strung together in random.

'Cunt woman. Fuckshit bitch. Fucksake, troublemaker, mother-fucking bitch-demon.'

'OK,' I reply, trying to laugh this off.

'She's trying to ruin my business… slut-ass.'

I entreat him to calm down.

'Fuckinbastards,' he shouts.

Tilak throws a folder of papers onto the floor, which I think is what he's been looking for. But then he digs out a Khukuri knife and starts thrusting it into the air. Thankfully, he then puts it down and continues to search in the old chest.

'Can I help? This should not be making you so angry.'

'It's village business. Let me handle it.'

'I'm sure you can, but…'

'I have to find my business registration papers. This woman says she has permission from the district authorities to start a mill here, but it's too close to mine. They are Tamangs and I'm sure they have bribed the cuntfuck commissioner. They are trouble-makers and that woman is a mother-slut bitch.'

'Hold the rap lyrics, Tilak.'

I try to calm Tilak down but he is not listening to reason. I use the Baba's words about control and acceptance, but he ignores me. In these circumstances wisdom is just not enough, he is temporarily blinded with anger.

Tilak finds his papers and storms out the door. He looks back towards the crowd that's still gathered and for a moment I think he is going to face the family, but he turns and marches towards the hills and the district headquarters. As he paces off into the distance, I realise it will take him two days walk to confront the District Chief. I feel it's best to let him venture there on his own and allow nature to restore his tranquility.

3 4

As Tilak heads out, I walk back to the Tamangs. I find them terrified of Tilak. He's given them until the end of the week to clear out and go back to where they came from. Since they've lived two generations in Barabase, this is a frightening ultimatum for them.

The gold-nosed woman is equally hostile to me, but her two sons seem to be more reasonable. I find myself acting as peace-keeper, impressing on the Tamangs the deep spiritual values that I know Tilak holds. This is not the true face of Tilak Gurung they have witnessed.

My negotiation skills do not convince them they are out of danger. He is an ex-soldier with powerful friends who has shown his temper and given an ultimatum.

The sons stay behind as the crowd disperses and I ask them to explain their plans. They tell me they want to put up an old-fash-ioned stone water-driven mill to make a little money from those who wait too long at Tilak's mill for his grinding services. Since it is mostly 'their people' who wait, this seems a fair service to offer.

There are enough people coming into Barabase nowadays to give both mills a reasonable business.

I look at this family and think they pose very little threat to Tilak's business. They wear clothes with holes in them! I decide I'll wait until Tilak returns and try to explain their ambitions to him.

That night after my heads hits the pillow, one of the Tamang men bursts into my room. He begins waving a piece of paper in my face and shouts loudly in his own language. I'm frightened by his aggressiveness. He comes towards me menacingly and before I can react, I see Tilak step forward and swing his Khukre knife. He slices off the man's hand in front of me. It falls to the floor still clutching the paper. There are loud screams, and I wake up.

The room is dark, I am in a sweat, and no one is here.

It's ages since I felt this disturbed by a dream. I have difficulty going back to sleep. I try to relax by thinking pleasant thoughts, trying to comprehend the unusual chaos of the day.

How will Tilak interpret his experience? He definitely has the Baba's knowledge about improving one's capacity to self-correct. However, Tilak also has a set of soldier skills to call on and in this situation it's frightening to imagine him returning and using these.

It's easy to be intellectual, especially when thinking about helping another person control themselves. The Baba's theory about dealing with the aftermath of a bad experience is simply to suggest that the storage of thoughts afterwards is important. If they are stored correctly, you can reduce the emotion once you recollect later. Of course, you can't store atrocities like family violence, racism or brutality in a positive way, but Tilak is presently irate over something that should not have brought him so much anger.

35

After four days, Tilak returns and in our first encounter he is adamant the only way to deal with the Tamang's stone-age threat to his business is complete expulsion from the village. His problem, he believes, has to physically disappear. He has visited the district authorities only to be frustrated even more. He's discovered a recent breed of communist sympathisers in the hills helping the Tamangs in the district office. He's been told they have every right to start their mill. Tilak has calculated that the Tamangs will not want to stay in Barabase if life suddenly becomes unbearable for them and he knows he is in a position to make this happen. In his eyes, they have broken an unwritten village rule by not coming to him first. This, I discover, is his main case for the prosecution.

'You are a monk at heart, Jamesji. Being a soldier has been a way of life in my family for generations. Although you do not wear the robes, you seek the same answers to life as a monk.... a life of minimal disruption.'

'Is that so, honourable Samurai?'

'A soldier is trained to accept war at any moment they are called upon.'

'This is not war, Tilak... it's your neighbour's attempt at venture capitalism.'

'It is a war... in my head.'

'Can you remember what the Baba says about using your knowledge to see things positively? Not in an escapist way but in the search for an intelligent alternative to holding onto hate? There is a challenge in doing this... that's your real battlefield. No one else is at war here.'

'It only needs one side start aggression... and it wasn't me.'

'Look, I'm quoting your guru to you. Someone I've never met. You know the Baba better than I. Is this not a classic example of what he talks about? There are definitely other ways of handling this and you should try these because it will help avoid a conflict.'

'A soldier has to resist the temptation to think in certain situations and act with firm action and faith. That's what the Baba's teaching tells me... that soldiers should display the same calmness and peace of mind, which others do in their daily life, in the face of great danger or hardship. I've told the Tamangs that they must go and I was very calm when I spoke to them.'

'I don't think the Baba meant you to apply control with a cold calculating threat especially in a confrontation with a sixty-year-old woman. You're quoting the Baba out of context. I don't think that physical violence will solve this problem.'

'There need not be any violence – if they just go.'

'This is an admission that you don't have any other solutions to offer?'

'Are you saying you would never fight for what you care about? Maya has told me that you feel emotion like everyone else. Everyone must be careful of the emotions they stir in others.'

I freeze as I process Tilak's comment and suddenly think might not be the real source of Tilak's anger. This whole thing could be a complete diversion. Has Maya told him about our waterspout encounter? No, I believe he would be in *my* face were he angry with me.

I leave Tilak for a quiet walk to the pipal tree. I can tell I'm not reaching him through the right channel by trying to quote his guru back to him. He has all the confidence of a soldier's interpretation of the Baba's teachings. His present difficulties seem shaped by life before the military, perhaps from his village prejudices against Tamangs. I search for examples of how this situation could be better explained and recall a lesson from my US lectures. I decide to chance my luck and tell Tilak the gist of Communication theory.

36

I find Tilak at home drinking chai as if nothing has happened. Maya pours me a glass and I start talking. Tilak seems keen to listen, perhaps secretly wanting to open himself up to other solutions.

I tell Tilak that while studying in the United States, I learned something about the way Americans spoke about and promoted business. That America, the world's largest economy and greatest military super-power, has dragged the rest of the world struggling and kicking into the current age of communication.

'When I studied in America,' I say, 'I was amazed how advanced their communication skills and technologies are compared to other countries who still shroud information in secrecy to retain a centralised power in government. Maybe it's because there is no other nation with so many people from different countries living there, wanting to keep in touch with their families back home across the globe. The result has been an unprecedented network of global communication which is now an industry and among the largest single employers of people in the world.' I'm guessing, but I exaggerate for effect.

Tilak looks cautious, listening for the sarcasm in my voice. He has never heard me praise the United States. I've chosen my moment to give credit where it is due.

'If you think about it… it's good that with so many languages and confusion over what people say that we employ people to talk about everything that we do. Otherwise, if we were simply all employed to "make" things we'd soon use up all the earth's resources.'

'Talking is just a waste of time.'

'Exactly – it is time wasted that might be spent on more destructive activities. With more and more people on the planet, it is human activity that is now the threat to our existence and so there is a need to better manage that activity. There's room for a lot more time spent on understanding why we make all the things we do, and what the consequences are.'

'There's not much interest in talking here since there's always too much to get done.'

'Tilak, believe me. I never fully appreciated how advanced the communication thinking in the United States is, until I saw the scale and results of their outreach.'

'Very nice, but what's all this got to do with a Tamang flour mill that's not required?'

'It is inevitable,' I say, 'that change will come to Barabase. That someone will come along and try to do as well as you. You are the first innovator in the village and surely you can remember how slowly people at first began to come and see your mill and how many now use it. You are not at risk from the Tamangs, but you are at risk from your reaction to them. If you are smart you should help them set up their business. If less people wait in line for the mill service, it will draw more people to the village. You can even take some of the free time that is given by such competition and venture into other business activities. What about the trekking food ideas from the trail in Manang?' I ask him.

Tilak says he does not have the time because the mill is too busy.

'A good businessman will use their intelligence to keep adapting in a competitive business world. There is nothing the Tamangs will take away from you if you approach them creatively.'

I tell Tilak he is no longer a soldier. He is a businessman and there are plenty of examples, plenty of books and business gurus to advise him how he should act as a businessman. None in recent memory recommended the taking of a Kukhre knife and running people off their land.

For a couple of nights I do not see Tilak, but Maya tells me he is slowly changing his attitude towards the Tamangs. A solution he can live with has obviously come to mind.

Over the following weeks, Tilak offers the Tamangs the old millstone that he's replaced with his modern cast-iron technology. He helps the family cement the floor of the upstream mill and he does this all in the face of deep-rooted suspicion on the part of the Tamang woman.

The old woman appears cantankerous by nature and cannot fully accommodate this change of heart from Tilak. She continues to hound and throw insults at him as if she suspects something sinister. And if small things go wrong she is ruthless with her insults.

Tilak sees other benefits from the new arrangement and works constructively with one of the sons on a primitive business plan. Anger is now the problem of the Tamang woman; not Tilak's and he's very pleased with himself for setting an example of co-opera-tion for the village.

Maya is also relieved this matter has been resolved peacefully. She thanks me for my part in it all. I also believe that Maya is secretly delighted to have less work to do in Tilak's mill, as the Tamangs take away a sizable workload... at least for the time being.

By way of celebration I arranged a picnic with Didi, Maya,

Tilak and his girls up to my favourite hill spot. I take along my guitar.

As we eat, I ask Didi if she has ever sat in a chair before.

'Yes… I once visited a town,' she says, 'and sat on a chair. I did not like it much. My legs were just hanging there, from the knees down.' Tilak laughs as he translates for me.

'After time my legs became tired, so I tucked them up under myself where they belong.'

Tilak asks Didi something in Chepang and she produces a dusty canvas army bag. Tilak brushes the dust off the bag and passes it me. Inside is a large new envelope.

'I sent word to friends in Kathmandu before we left on our trek,' he says. 'I asked them to find copies of *The Rising Nepal* newspaper, from the time of your father's death. This arrived while you were sick.'

I open the envelope and pick out some photocopied pages and a newspaper clipping. Tilak helps me carefully open the frail newspaper and there, in the left hand lower corner, is a headline. **Western Tourist Killed in Mechi District.** There is a photograph, of a group of three men with my dad's face circled in white. I believed my father died in Mustang and I've never seen this photo before. My heart begins to race.

The story identifies a group of devotees including a westerner on a pilgrimage, attacked by bandits on a high hill trail near Ilaru. A local guide who witnessed events told the authorities my father and his companions were killed and their bodies pushed into a deep ravine. It mentions my father is 'survived' by a wife and child currently living in Patan.

It feels strange reading this. I think of my mother, who must have read the same page, long ago. I want to call her on the telephone and suddenly feel overcome with feelings of remoteness

37

I return to my ritual of walking to the bus stop around mid-day, shouting greetings at the drivers and asking for any information on the whereabouts of the Moni Baba. Tilak also joins me on occasion. The bus drivers see us coming and mostly shrug in ignorance of any news.

I tell Tilak I'm thinking of having the name Barabase inked onto my upper arm. I've been in the village for just over a year and it has become such a part of my life I feel I should never allow myself to forget the experience. Tilak tells me that Maya can easily perform this task with a thorn and some local dyes. She has done it for several women.

When I check my finances, I discover that I've earned more money in interest on my savings than I've spent living in Barabase. The kindness and support of people here has been beneficial along with the cheap cost of living. I now have all these new points of comparison – over different lifestyles. It's the one feature of my brain that has definitely expanded in consciousness.

I needed the experience of dark winters in Scotland to appre-ciate the even warm air of the lower Himalaya. After a year living in a small bare room with a rope bed, I appreciate a proper mattress. My months of sitting eating on the kitchen floor helped me appreciate how comfortable a chair can feel when I get the chance to use one. It's taken a year of washing in public to suddenly crave the seclusion of a private bathroom and the luxury of water in the home. Banging my head on Didi's low door lintel helps me appreciate high ceilings. Months of eating with my hands let me discover there is a taste of metal when using spoons and forks. I realise it has taken twelve months for the novelty of living in Barabase to wear off. A year to realise the true strengths and sacrifices needed to live here and I'm wealthier as a result.

One night a bus driver and another man who has recently heard the Moni Baba talk, knock on my door. I send word to Tilak and within a few minutes he appears and talks to the man in Newari. He explains to me that he is a find indeed, that this man is one of the very best Moni Baba impersonators.

Within a few minutes, Tilak talks this man into staying overnight and thanks the bus driver with a handful of rupees.

Sri Chitraker is a public performer from Kathmandu who makes a living as a Moni Baba tribute act. He dresses up and performs as if he is the Moni Baba. He speaks good English and tells us he makes appearances at meetings and gatherings all over the country.

So rare are the appearances of the real Moni Baba and so popular are Chitraker's talks, he says he is in constant demand and has performed at several Embassies in Kathmandu including the British.

Tilak asks if he can give an impersonation of the Moni Baba for us in English in Barabase. He agrees. Tilak goes off to round up some of the other village people who understand English and I ask Chitraker what his most popular performances are about.

For Western people, he says there is no doubt what is his most popular Moni Baba lecture... is on mediation. He tells me that

Nepalese people have to have something that lasts three hours otherwise he is mocked or chased away.

Chitraker tells me that the Baba first gave his meditation talk in Patan Dokha several years ago. He says he has performed it as accurately as he remembers and only embellishes his story with references that the Baba has added recently.

Chitraker asks if I would like the three-hour, the two-hour or the one-hour performance. I reply jokingly that I'll have to check my schedule, but he doesn't get the joke.

Tilak returns with around six people including Maya for the show. I suddenly remember my Dictaphone and leap upstairs and rummage to the bottom of my rucksack to find it, hoping the batteries still have life.

Packed into Didi's kitchen, the audience waits while Sri Chitraker retires outside for a moment. He comes back in wearing a faded saffron robe similar to that worn by the Baba. He also has a white cotton-wool beard stuck to his chin. He walks with a stoop and a large stick. Before beginning, he introduces himself as a humble vessel for the Baba's teaching.

'There is no limit to expanding one's consciousness, if one understands the careful layering of experiences… in stage after stage. The open mind is never full but the better it becomes known, the quicker it becomes whole.

'Approach this idea of making the mind whole… making it unified… as with yoga… as a lifetime labour of love.'

Chitraker speaks with what I assume are the intonations of the Baba's voice. He seems part teacher and part clown. He walks over to me and tells me that he gave this particular talk to the British Embassy club in Kathmandu some months back and there were many Europeans in smart suits who came to listen. There were even women who came to hear him. He tells me he'll speak for an hour and I ask if I can record it.

38

The Moni Baba's Teachings on **Meditation** as performed by the tribute act Sri Chitraker.

'MANY FACETS OF HUMAN BEHAVIOUR HAVE BECOME institutionalised in some way in our society. We find government and non-government institutions created to cover nearly every social concern we can imagine. Across the modern world, countries have created Ministries for Defence' – he poses like a soldier – 'for Education,' – he pretends to read a book – and for Health or Welfare and the Arts – he sketches in the air like an artist and poses as a dancer. 'But of course the main institutions are created to help governing and trade.' He takes money out of one pocket and puts it into another.

Chitraker sits down cross-legged with his hands placed on his knees like a yogi.

'Yet I tell you that one of the most important facets of our existence, our ability to meditate, has never been properly institutionalised. This facet which can mean the difference between enlightened living or enslavement to the demands of society, is still largely misunderstood or ignored.' He breathes in deep and exhales slowly.

'This word meditation is present in all the scriptures of religion and the brochures of Ashrams and Spas, but its true value to society is left unexplained. Perhaps because it was first identified and practiced by people to escape from the worry or fear or hate, that lurks in an over-active mind.

'In the English language the word meditation has a different meaning to the Sanskrit word for meditation. Today, the use of the word has become adapted for a commercially-aware trading public. It is perhaps the most misunderstood word in all the world's languages.

'Meditation is not something you learn to do, it is something you practice. To meditate falls into the same category of words as 'to laugh' or 'to cry'. Think for a moment of the word laugh and how no one really taught you how to do it. You have been able to do it naturally from birth. To laugh, cry, listen, think, eat, drink or **meditate** are all things you do naturally. It is a word that defines a response to something. Yet meditation is often listed within another family of words, with a set of skills you need to be taught, like skills you learn for sports or on the farm – to dig, to plough – or from school, to read or to write. This family of skill words represents knowledge that comes to you from an outer source, the learning of a technique, taught to you by someone else.' Chitraker stands to emphasize this point.

'You meditate by nature, you suffer when you are prevented from doing it. In such cases, you have to begin to practice it more consciously.

'You do not learn to laugh, but you are stimulated to laugh by certain events or in a natural response. You do not learn to cry, you simply do it… in certain circumstances.

'In the past, people have built Temples or Mosques or

Churches, in which to meditate... they created an environment that was designed to stimulate meditation whenever it was needed to restore balance.

'People who enjoy a laugh go to see a comedy show. People watching or listening to Madan Krishna and Hari Bunsha cannot help themselves laughing. They go to a show knowing they will be stimulated to laugh in that environment.

'In the same way as environments can stimulate you to laugh, the quiet room of an ashram or monastery can stimulate you to meditate. Where the talent of a certain comedian is needed to strike the right note of humour in you, where others do not, so too the practice of meditation depends on a teacher or a priest or an Imam that's right for you to feel the power and sanctuary of meditation.

'Before institutionalised religion, yogis knew about meditation and that it could be practiced in a cave or a forest. They knew that you did not really need the grand surroundings sold to you by religious leaders. Just as today you do not really need the Ashram or the health club to meditate. Yogis set themselves apart because they also recognized the corruption that can be practiced by religious leaders, peddling stories and rituals to keep their businesses growing. It is no surprise the first institutional structures in most cultures were devoted to a religious belief.'

Part of Chitrikar's cotton-wool beard flutters to the ground like a snow flake. He picks it up, still acting in character like a blind man. Tilak and Maya laugh. Kiran wipes the cotton wool across the sweat on his brow and reattaches it to his chin, without loss in concentration.

'Let us consider in more detail the family of words to which meditation **does** belong. The twin sister to meditation is the word "think". There are many institutions that have been built to encourage us to **think more**. We all understand what this word think means, and many of us believe that we never actually stop thinking. Well... I think therefore I am... should be rephrased to...

I think, therefore I remember. It is in this activity of thinking we find our individual identity as an accumulation of our memories and experiences. It is also here that many people find life's problems accumulating and often seek outside assistance to help them to deal with it. Many believe that they think all the time. That the mind continues to think throughout its waking state, and that even in sleep it continues to function as a thinker.

'Nothing could be further from the truth, for although the brain is always active it is not always active as a thinker. Many people are so convinced of their never-ending train of thoughts because they've been encouraged to seek out more and more to think about. Take a moment and think over what I am saying. Do you believe that you are thinking about something every minute of every waking day? Is your mind forever active in a thinking mode? Or do you recognise there is a natural break that's called meditation? Think it over.'

39

K iran moves slowly to reposition himself in the room. He remains silent as he walks, pausing, miming as if he has forgotten something.

'Ah there, now that was a fleeting moment of meditation... the space between one thought and another. Is there any proof that meditation exists naturally... yes, it's sometime called... forget-fulness?'

Then he looks at us all cautiously and says, 'With a big crowd the Baba waits longer, but I will now continue.

'Don't take this the wrong way. Everyone is born programmed to think, and we all have different capacities and skills training to do this, but it is not in our nature to think non-stop without a rest or refuge from our thoughts. Sleep and day-dreaming are as important to even the most productive mind. The biggest aid to our thinking mind comes from its twin sister, meditation. This period when the mind is not thinking... is when we are meditat-ing. It is the absence of thought. It is hard to recognize these moments, only because you do not remember them. Time still passes when we meditate but we only remember our thoughts...

not this space in between. At the end of a busy thinking day we feel exhausted, because every minute that has passed seems to have been allocated to thinking with our full attention. Yogis know that's not the case. Natural meditation will have crept into even the busiest of days and when you understand this you can add the practice of it at will.

'In same way we do anything naturally, we must first be able to recognise the value, before we practice it. Whether it is physical work, eating food or thinking a lot, or indeed meditating non stop... we only benefit from adding control over these natural urges.

'Bringing control to your thinking mind is as necessary as adding restraint to your eating habits. Without devoting specific time for mediation to help balance you, nature steps in with her own painful breakdowns.

'We still **exist** even though our capacity to think has been removed by accident or surgery, or by the ravages of illness in the brain. The individual is removed but nature still runs the show. We can easily destroy the mind or harm our body with one thought-less action. But with knowledge of meditation we can better protect our mind.'

Kiran pauses in order to emphasize the point he's about to finish.

'The heart beats, then rests before it beats again.'

He places his hand on his heart, moving it out and in with the beats.

'The time in between heartbeats is the heart's meditation.'

Chitraker begins to run on the spot. 'We know the physical feeling of what happens when we work at something for too long. We also know what happens when we don't move enough. It is the management of both these activities that gives us our health and strength or our weakness.'

Kiran then bows... finally out of character and asks Tilak if he has any Raksi. He's still the comedian and slurs his words

'You may hear people tell you they need alcohol to escape their thoughts.' Quickly sober again, he faces me.

'At the British Embassy Club when I gave this talk... at this point there was a loud chorus of people shouting *Cheers*.

'But let me finish as I did there...' and back in character he continues holding up a pretend glass.

'This is a most a harmful escape route. The mind will always want to think. That is its function. It is your problem solver and seeks out challenges everywhere it is focused. My purpose is to make the practice of meditation sound easy and available. It may require a guru to give you an explanation, but remember the meditation part can't be taught, only identified, stimulated then practiced.'

Kiran Chitraker sits and takes a drink of water.

I whisper to Tilak. 'I take it that the Baba does not act out things in this way?'

'No... Kiran's performance is unique, but he is pretty close to the Baba's message.'

'Any questions, please ask Sir?' Chitraker addresses me.

I ask him if he has seen much of the woman Sita who accompanies the Baba. He dramatically stands up and speaks in his own voice this time.

'The Moni Baba is always with the Kamari-Sita. She takes classes in meditation for children after the Baba gives this talk.'

Chitraker is still for a moment, collecting his thoughts, then he becomes Sita. He acts out her movements, like an extra from 'La Cage aux Folles'. He seems in a trance. I believe he is seeing her in his mind. He moves to lift an imaginary child and rests its weight on his hip. He makes the sound of the child crying, as a ventriloquist might. He slowly turns a full circle pointing to the distant horizon, stretching the child's imagination away from his immediate fear, to a new source of interest elsewhere in the distance. Kiran completes the circle and talks with the voice of a woman.

'This is how you can bring an upsetting thought to an end

within a child – and begin a new train of thoughts within a young mind... by simply pointing to something new. Why then is it so hard for as adults to remember this. When you understand that thoughts **naturally** end... then you can appreciate how your **obsessive** thoughts can be terminated or brought consciously under your control. This is the skill you gain from the practice of meditation.'

Chitraker looks at his watch briefly. 'I'm not sure how many succeeded in understanding meditation on that day because the Baba and Sita gave us too much to think about.'

I sit until the early hours of the morning talking to Chitraker in Didi's kitchen. I congratulate him on his performance and tell him he's definitely given me food for thought. He corrects me, saying as with food I shouldn't consume too much. Then laughs at his own joke.

'It is taken for granted among many Newari people that there will always be someone to speak out on spiritual matters, but with the rapid development of the Kathmandu valley it is now quite rare.' Chitraker ends in his best Shakespearean accent, 'When the pupil is ready, the teacher will appear.'

'I'm not a pupil, but I have been searching for over a year to find him… and the nearest I've got so far is you!' I laugh to dilute the sting of this realisation.

Chitraker informs me he must go for the dawn bus and then he casually mentions that the Moni Baba is expected in Lumbini in a few weeks' time to attend a large yoga meeting. 'If you want to see the real Moni Baba,' he says, 'you should go there to Lumbini.'

I am so completely surprised by this news, that I grab Chitraker's arm and ask him to repeat what he just said.

'Are you sure that the Moni Baba himself will be talking in Lumbini in a couple of weeks?'

'Yes!'

'Are you going?'

'Oh no. It's bad for business… I go where the Baba is not.'

I say a quick farewell to Kiran and thank him again.

Despite not having slept all night, my mind is suddenly filled with options and choices to make. I wander over to Tilak's for breakfast and tell him my news of the Baba's appearance in Lumbini. The one thing that yogis say about meditation that suddenly seems to be true, is that you cannot learn how to do it when the mind is excited or pre-occupied. It is advised that you practice when the mind is calm so it can help you when the mind is busy. To meditate at will requires this practice. It seems I've missed out on a year of potential practice.

Tilak becomes very excited at my news and tells me this must the large group of people across India who practice Hatha Yoga who meet every year in a different location. He has heard this year would be in Lumbini, but he did not hear anything about the Moni Baba taking part. It all makes sense to him.

Tilak removes any doubt in my mind and says he will get further confirmation and I should make plans to attend. He says he will talk with the next set of bus drivers and find out more. He invites me to help Maya open the mill for business.

One hour later, Tilak walks into the mill smiling. The noise of the grinding machines is so loud he gestures me outside. I step over baskets of grain and leftover husks.

'It's true,' he tells me.

'You confirmed the Baba will be in Lumbini?'

'Yes.'

'How did we not hear of this? It's the same fucking bus drivers we speak to each week?'

'The main event in Lumbini is not headlined by the Moni Baba this year. It is going to feature the girl Sita who is scheduled to demonstrate advanced Hatha Yoga postures. We never asked the drivers about Sita's whereabouts.'

'But the Baba will be there?'

'Yes. This is a sensitive issue for Brahmins and purists of the Hindu faith to accept an ex-Kumari teaching yoga in such a way. Only the Moni Baba's fame has made such a radical appointment possible for this event. He'll definitely be there.'

'It's like a gender Reformation… I love it.'

I ask Tilak how easy he thinks it will be for me to gain an audience with the Baba. He tells me it is likely to be extremely crowded, but given my father's history with the Baba I will surely find people who will get me an introduction.

41

As before, whenever I have thoughts of departure, I notice my mind make a switch from dwelling on the positive things, to suddenly identifying the more negative. It has become such an essential coping mechanism for me, it's comical to deal with. It's easier to leave if you select reasons why it's best to move on. A reason perhaps why there was never really a Shangri-La.

The night before I leave Barabase, I'm surprised by a visit from Maya to my room. It is her weight on my bed that wakens me. She puts a hand at each side of my face and kisses my forehead, then turns to leave. It is dark, with only a faint glimmer of moonlight in the room and as I sit up straight, Maya turns back. She tells me that she must go early to the fields in the morning and that she will miss my departure. She says she wanted to thank me for coming to stay in Barabase and all the help I've given to Tilak and her family.

'I will miss you all,' I say before Maya leans over me, covers my mouth with her hand and offers a cuddle in a warm seductive way. I tell her I wish her and Tilak all the very best and that I hope we can all keep in touch.

'If you speak to the Moni Baba please ask him for a blessing for us to have a boy child. The Moni Baba sent you to us. Tilak has no boy seeds and we require a boy child.'

She is wearing a thin kurta dress and as she stands to leave, I see the outline of her figure against the light of the open door. It is another encounter that leaves me with a vision that I know will remain branded in my mind. I pull at the thin sheet I have covering myself.

In that single moment, I realise how poles apart Maya and I really are. Her priorities are so different from mine that what I've been seeing as a warm relationship was perhaps for her no more than the means to an end.

If Maya took out a personal advert on some fictitious dating site it would perhaps read: 'Young married female wants man for necessary sexual backup. Only those with boy seeds need apply.'

But perhaps I'm being unfair. Perhaps I'm piling on the negative thought in order to leave this place.

My personal dating ad would read: 'Male – eagerly wants female friendship, perhaps more; likes hill walking, music, intellectual talk, seeks companionship, any nationality will do.' What Maya and I have for each other seems a few centuries apart in terms of friendship and ambitions.

The day I leave, Tilak accompanies me on my rounds through the village and helps me to translate my thanks and urgent goodbyes to Didi and numerous village friends.

When we are alone, Tilak thrusts a small piece of paper into my hand. It is a contact list of his ex-Gurkha friends around Nepal, whom he trusts should I need them.

We bow to each other in a Namaste, saluting the God in each other. I see now that Maya's friendliness and recent boldness were always dependent on him not being there. In Tilak's company, Maya has always been the subservient wife. I'm thankful I've done nothing wrong. I think how close I've come to a head-butt instead of a Namaste.

Tilak continues to shower words of affection on me.

'Maya will be working in the higher fields this morning and she wanted me to say farewell to you. She is sad that you are leaving and she wants me to thank you for all the help you have given us over the last year.'

Tilak takes my hand and massages it up and down with his thick farmworkers fingers. I tell Tilak to tell her that it is I who should be thankful for what she and his family have done for me. I add a little gratitude in Nepali for the language teaching Maya and her daughters have given to me.

As I stand at the bus stop, I feel a genuine reluctance to release Tilak's hand. He drops it, laughs and strides backward.

The residue of my feelings for Maya is replaced with the bitter taste of actually leaving Tilak. I shout that I will stay in touch.

As I wave goodbye from the bus window, I consider that a significant chapter in my life has ended, even if much of it was in my imagination.

PART FOUR: THE FIND

T he Buddha was born in Nepal. Many historians omit this information because at the time of the Buddha's birth the present-day border did not exist between Nepal and India.

Over two thousand five hundred years ago, baby Siddhartha Gautama was born in Lumbini on the low Terai areas of today's Nepal. Ironically, most of the villagers who now live in and around Lumbini follow Islam as their faith.

My first sight of the town makes me think it's under siege from a medieval army. Thousands of temporary tents are pitched around the outside of the town, all flying an assortment or orange banners. Bus passengers are forced to disembark outside the city boundary.

I make my way through the crowds without attracting attention. Now with a full beard, long hair and river-beaten clothes, I feel camouflaged. My Nepali language skills also help me to blend in. Only my guitar case brings some attention.

In the crowded marketplace, a man steps in front of me jingling what I think are a set of small brass keys. When I indicate I do not understand what he wants, he introduces himself as Nazur. He motions towards an alley and points to his ears. He then acts out a strange manipulation using one of the keys towards his ear. He dangles a larger assortment of tools; some with tiny spoons on the end and others bent like miniature hooks. Responding to my indifference, he turns away and stops a plump passer-by and offers his service free, by way of a demonstration.

Nazur and I step into the alley when the large man lifts his loose leg cloth then squats expertly. Nazur the ear-man cleans his hands on his beard, grabbing his chin and stroking downward. He has no moustache so his tongue can be seen, firmly placed on his upper lip for concentration. With great accuracy he begins to scrape clean the outer rim of his customer's ear. He manoeuvres his arms, elbow in the air and the ear pick with the skill of a barber holding an open razor. Next there is a key change and the inner ear is explored.

I watch in amazement as the tiny crooked spoon disappears into the man's head. The client's calmness shows an extraordinary trust. With his eyes closed, he exhibits an aura of delight as his ears are scraped and stroked by Nazur. Three substantial quantities of wax are produced and shown to me in swift succession before being wiped onto a cloth in Nazur's pocket. I believe there will be some bizarre further use for this raw material that I cannot imagine.

Nazur finally stands behind his customer and in a grand encore, takes hold of his head with both hands and gives a quick crick of the neck in both directions.

The man looks at me with a most satisfied head wobble, perhaps made loose by Nazur. I am then encouraged to take his place sit or squat.

Nazur appears to be someone who might provide me with local information. He seems a popular man with people walking past greeting him at every opportunity. I step forward and squat as he bids me to relax.

At first, we talk about Lumbni. I suggest the archaeological site of Buddha's birthplace must be bursting with tourist potential, yet Nazur tells me it has been left virtually untouched. He says the town contains only a few crude indicators of its links with Buddhist history. The sacred pond of Shakya Puskarini, in which Prince Siddhartha was supposed to have been bathed after his birth, lies polluted. Pilgrims do come but think twice about sampling the dark waters, now the colour of a jade Buddha. Twenty-five years of promises and planning to make the site a 'Mecca' for Buddhists have passed without much development.

Nazur proudly tells me that Muslims now look after three birthplaces of founders of great religious faiths. The Buddha, Jesus and Mohammed. He also says followers of one faith should not feel threatened by followers of another because there is no more unifying human trait than faith itself.

Nazur says many archaeologists speculate there are untold treasures still lying buried around Lumbini. He thinks it's best they remain underground until there is community interest in protecting them. Now whenever people find old treasures, he says, they just sell them off to buyers. The only really ancient building in Lumbini is the Ashokan pillar, which is under threat from the elements and vandalism.

Nazur's voice is quiet as he rummages in my ear. Suddenly his wax-mining efforts succeed and I think he's shouting. He switches to the outside of my ear. The palace walls, from which Siddhartha was forbidden to leave, are actually about twenty miles west of Lumbini at Tilaurakot in Kapilavastu. The Eastern gate from which he made his exit has already been uncovered there.

I watch Nazur wipe my ear wax into his pocket. I think if Madame Tussauds ever comes to Lumbini, Nazur and his like would score. With my second ear now clear, he asks in stereo if I would take some lemon Chai. I accept and he summons a nearby bicycle chai man.

Nazur lets me sip my tea while he continues to work on my

neck. I feel the strength of his fingers and I dare not question or disrupt him at this stage.

Given the fact that Sita is the headline act, the Moni Baba's presence here has gathered huge support. Even within a vast belief system such as Hinduism, this shows how much the role of the individual guru still plays. Hinduism regularly makes room for new religious thought and interpretation. It produces new gurus by the cartload and a few years after they pass away – if their teaching remains popular, people like the Baba become gods.

In the West, there seems religious confusion over enlightenment. Opinions offered from a different age are sacred, yet have very little to do with today's world. Enlightenment here requires that the enlightened one teaches and leaves something behind for the ages. If one's teachings are not a measure of enlightenment, then what is?

My world suddenly goes quiet, as Nazur slaps his hands over both my ears. My head is raised slowly from my shoulders and with a quick jerk I hear a crack and feel an inch taller. Nazur's voice booms in my now pristine ears.

'The Moni Baba,' Nazur projects, 'he is a Hindu... but he understands Allah!'

N azur introduces me to an assortment of the Baba's followers as they pass by. Many yogis offer tent space for rent, but luckily I find a room to stay in at a local tea-house. There appears to be no other westerners here, and I use my Nepali language skills to negotiate local rates for food and a festival stay.

Some followers have travelled from South India for this gathering. They are a surprising mix of educated lawyers and labourers; potters and politicians; monks and military personnel. They all speak with admiration of the Moni Baba but not always in a way I expected. There is a fine line between follower and flatterer.

Many have already given the Baba the status of a deity or ritual object, existing only to be worshiped and obeyed like a god. There are sycophants sprinkled across all castes. It seems no matter how often people hear the Baba's talk about 'self belief and personal responsibility,' there will always be those who prefer to pile their hopes and worries onto a god.

Early mornings on the Terai are very different to those in the hills just a few miles to the north. There are some distant storm clouds covering the mountains but here it is the coolest time of day with the air at body temperature and dawn bringing the first human activities, mass ablutions and cooking.

I sit at the tea lodge and fire up my body with a breakfast of chilli cabbage and potato curry with a roti. A bare-chested fruit seller with a three-wheeled bicycle offers me a mango as a morning delicacy. I roll a bite of the fruit around my palate to take away the sting of the curry. It brings back memories of my childhood and I squat on the pavement to savour each juicy bite. I've missed eating this fruit it in the hills.

A mango in season has to be the most delicious dessert that nature has ever designed. It comes in such an appealing oval package of green and yellow skin. When cut open by an expert, it reveals a dense orange pulse that can be fashioned with a sharp knife into any geometric shape you can craft. If folded inside out, this embroidered fruit presents itself to complete any meal. It slips down my throat as light as a sweet oyster.

As I finish eating my gourmet cubes of mango, I suddenly hear cheers and see people running up the street. I sense the excitement immediately. In a crowd scene straight from the movie 'Gandhi', I feel like an extra called into action. People are pacing towards an open corner of a large parade ground, already packed with crowds. Some begin to run. The whole place is immediately energised and I'm drawn into the hysteria as people call out that the Baba has arrived.

Before anyone can see him some fall to the ground as if their life's wish has been granted, others push toward the front of the crowd until crushed tight. I cannot reach further than some thirty yards from the front. Folks immediately pile around me and we are packed tighter than the mosh-pit at a Sex Pistols' concert.

I see an old man and a girl in white are being escorted onto the makeshift stage. The noise is deafening, possibly because of my cleared ear canals but more likely because of the yoga royalty in front of me.

After months in the isolated atmosphere of Barabase, this crush of people is both frightening and stimulating. As the Baba finally steps out of the pages in my father's book… out of my imagination and into real life, I feel goose-bumps. It is a monumental moment. I stretch onto tiptoes like all the fully-fledged devotees around me. I also see for the first time Sita beside the Baba, and she looks remarkable. It's extraordinary that this young woman stands here in what is clearly a man's world and holds such authority.

As the Moni Baba raises his arms, the crowd silences itself. The clouds in the heavens to the north have darkened and as if on cue there is a roar of distant thunder. The Baba responds to the sound and points in the direction of the noise. He stands distinctively but he is older and frailer than in photos and does not have the energy of his impersonator Chitraker. He looks styled by a Buddhist monk wearing a faded orange robe with a maroon Neru waistcoat. Only his long flowing hair and beard distinguishes him as a leader-less, self-aware yogi.

After a brief prayer is chanted over the public address system, the Baba greets the crowd in a number of languages including English. I'm reminded that throughout the subcontinent, English is a tongue that has often united people of differing cultures.

44

T he Moni Baba's talk on Hatha Yoga, Lumbini.

SITA USHERS THE BABA BY HAND TOWARDS A STAND-UP MICROPHONE and then steps off to the side.

'Thank you all for gathering at this auspicious site... today. I hear the voice of the weather in the distance. The rains speak loud from the north and we are grateful.'

The Baba stops talking for a moment and with an upturned hand looks as if he is searching for rain drops in the air. The crowd laugh.

'As you know, our weather is diverse, changes in an instant and is different over distance. We have cold blizzards in the mountains while there is desert heat here on the Terai. Our national radio station describes our weather conditions each day by saying what?'

The Baba poses the question to the crowd, puts his hand to his ear... and the crowd shout back in unison. 'Mainly fair throughout the Kingdom!'

'And what of our weather tomorrow?'

'Mainly fair throughout the Kingdom!'

'And the day after?'

'Mainly fair throughout the Kingdom!'

'*Huncha* – OK! Our national government radio station indeed can predict the future.'

This is followed by loud laughter. I notice it is mainly the Nepalese who are laughing at this statement and think it has political overtones that I and others don't understand.

'In this place over two thousand years ago, Lord Gautama wandered outside his palace and witnessed **poverty** and saw **yogis** in these streets. The teachings he left us were conceived by this encounter.

'The Buddha's teachings are fresh in my mind today, such is the lasting relevance of his thoughts.

'These two elements of life he discovered are still here in the streets... mass poverty... and for today at least, a lot of yogis.' There is a loud cheer and the Baba continues.

'People forget yoga was also conceived in the streets not only in the hills or caves. It came from a desire to seek meaning, to reconstruct the mental balance found in rural minds in a busy urban community. It may have been refined in the forests but it was traded in the streets.

'In many parts of the world, yogis and poor people are sometimes seen as the same thing!' There is a ripple of laughter across the crowd and I realize Chitraker at least got the stand-up comedian part of the Baba right.

'Yoga to a capitalist is associated with people who have no ambition, who are willing to accept unbearable social conditions and do little about it?' Loud boos.

'The Buddha's life was lived in a way Western people think was the wrong way round. He moved from a life of privilege and material wealth to a life with few possessions. His wealth of understanding came from applying creative thoughts to more situations than he had ever experienced in his sheltered Royal life. It was only after he left the palace that he began to understand the flexibility and resilience of the mind as a rare gift.

'Today we still practice the hatha yoga the Buddha witnessed, but mainly for health reasons in our community. These postures for a moment in a class are often in isolation of what else we do. Remember what else you do is as much a part of your yoga as postures.

'We can sit like yogis, eat like yogis and move like yogis but unless we do all this with awareness of all else we do, we are simply adding something new to our schedule. The Buddha made the 'enlightened mind' a goal, not the attainment of skills with postures. Your full schedule becomes the home in which you practice yoga.

'There is no escape into yoga, there is only acceptance and the strength of unification through yoga. Should you choose to make hatha yoga part of your life, know that your actions and all their consequences are the measure of your skills. In a world where your achievements are judged and valued socially, your achievements as a yogi are of value to no one but you.

'Today I have asked Sita Kumari to demonstrate her skills in hatha yoga. It is a special occasion for it is the first time a woman has been invited to this gathering and it is an honour she well deserves. She has prepared two demonstrations for you; one for beginners, showing the minimum amount of hatha yoga postures required for someone to make steady progress. Later today she will display a set of advanced postures that show what can be achieved after years of dedicated practice. Remember that yoga is not an extreme sport although it might appear that when viewing postures. If practiced regularly and patiently, the unification between the body and the mind simply grows to an extreme level.'

The Baba holds up his hands in the Namaste position. The girl

Sita moves forward and escorts him to a position just at the side of the stage, still in full view of the audience. She takes off her loose white dress and reveals a three-quarter-length Punjabi shirt on top of what looks like men's white Long John tights. She no longer looks like the young girl I'd seen in photos. Her thick crop of black hair is pleated into a ponytail and she stands with the authority of a guru.

Om, shanti, shanti, shanti.

45

The crowd repeats the chant then roars its approval as the Baba sits.

Sita throws down a thin blanket, which is all that separates her from the hard wooden stage. She also uses a thin cloth to skilfully cover her hips when she stretches her legs apart. She begins to mesmerize the crowd, moving through a graceful routine of postures; standing; stretching and bending forward to touch her toes with the ease of a circus child. She stretches backward, arching round until her hands touch the ground effortlessly as she bends forward. Sweeping up, she steps forward with one long stride in a movement that seems taken from the martial arts. Only the bow of the head at the end changes the movement into a reflective hatha yoga posture.

It is a joy to watch Sita's flexibility. She is awe-inspiring, able to balance and move with amazing suppleness and control. She demonstrates a series of asana that I'm familiar with but have never seen displayed with her level of concentration or competence. She appears completely focused throughout, looking as comfortable in an inverted posture as she does when she is standing upright.

After twenty minutes she sits, folding her legs unaided by her hands, into a full lotus position. With the crowd's eyes riveted on her, she breathes as normal without any sign of sweat or exertion.

The Moni Baba is brought to the stage-front once more, this time guided by a large man who is dressed in the same attire as Sita. The man is clearly overweight and leaves the Baba standing before proceeding to go through a similar set of postures as Sita. He can hardly reach his knees in a forward bend. The crowd seem to think this is intentional comedy and roar in laughter. The Baba signals for silence. Within minutes the man is sweating profusely, holding his arms out to the side trying to steady himself while balancing on one leg. Each time he saves himself from falling over, some in the audience can't contain their laughter and the Baba silences them with a finger on his lips. Interestingly, the man demonstrating seems to be unaffected by these interruptions and holds his concentration.

Sita then stands and takes the Baba to the microphone.

'In what you have seen so far today, know this. There is more benefit going on inside this man Prem's body, than during the demonstration of hatha from Sita. For he… it is life changing… for her it is routine. His range of movements are being expanded, the boundaries to movement are being broken; more coordination is being learned and limitations being exposed. More understanding of the self is taking place… than there is in anyone here witnessing this.

'For the young who have not yet felt the physical affects of old age there is an important lesson to take from this… it is easier to maintain something, than it is to regain it once it's lost. It is not simple going from the appearance of Prem-abundance to the look of yogini Sita.' The crowd laugh. 'But when Prem leaves here today, if he keeps up his practice of hatha yoga, then untold benefits will follow. He will find far greater choices in his life. Please show your appreciation for yogi Prem-ananda.'

The crowd cheers and the man bows, returning a Namaste sign to the Baba and his new fans. We are told there will be a short intermission for mid-morning food.

AFTER THIS FIRST DEMONSTRATION COMES TO AN END, EVERYONE begins to move sideways towards the food tents. I push my way forward towards the stage. I've been so distracted by what has unfolded I forgot to switch on my tape recorder. No matter. What was seen was more important than what was heard.

46

A few local musicians come onto the stage and give an impromptu concert with a flat accordion and drum. Given the amount of sing-along in return, I can tell they are playing a Top-of-the-Pops set of Hindi *Bhajans*.

I feel excited. I prepare myself for an actual audience with the Baba should it be possible. I do not want to lose my place near the front for the afternoon session and I can see it would be impossible to approach the Baba now because of the crowds.

As I wait, I overhear an argument in English going on between a Muslim, a Hindu and a Buddhist. It's like the joke of a Scotsman an Englishman and an Irishman walking into a bar.

The Buddhist is arguing that there is no real value for a Hindu in making offerings of food and flowers to a stone god... that in fact any stone or rock would do. The Hindu says it is the process the mind goes through when performing these deeds that provides the brain with comfort. He sounds insulted and says it is like telling a Muslim that they do not really need to face Mecca for prayers... that facing any direction will do. The Muslim then suggests whatever we describe as worship to lingum stones or

Buddha statues, is all just the babble of man. There is only one God.

'The Baba is clear on this,' the Muslim man offers. 'If we do not give our children a fresh start in life, if we stuff their minds with our cultural differences and prejudices we hold onto as our history, we have no chance.'

'You say that because Islam is not as old as Hinduism.'

'No I say this because it's clear that there is more hate and mistrust imbedded in our history than there is in our personal experiences of each other. We all come from cultures that continually refer to our history to make decisions on what we do for today and tomorrow… and herein lies our problem.'

Suddenly the Buddhist turns to me. 'Where are you from, sir? Why are you here?'

I stammer at the question. 'I'm here to make personal progress,' I say.

'You're English?' the Hindu asks.

'Sort of,' I answer, taking collective responsibility for the historic actions of the United Kingdom. 'I'm from Scotland.'

'We are discussing the self-correcting qualities of the Moni Baba's teaching on our society. Join us.'

'I overheard you talking and I apologise for all the unjustified persecution you might feel relates to my culture's history here.'

'Your culture exploited our differences, we are trying to put things right.'

'I like to think because I was not born back then… that you'll forgive me.'

The men laugh as if I've just delivered the punchline to the three men in a bar joke.

47

The crowds return but I now have a prime place from which to see. Once more the Baba is brought to the front of the stage and given the microphone by Sita.

There is a loud whining sound from the loud-speaker and people around me cringe. As the whining continues, I'm forced to cover my ears and miss the beginning of the talk.

'... it is not just exercise. Health is not the main objective of hatha yoga – although it is its most obvious side effect.

'In yoga you are being asked to expand your consciousness. In hatha you are given a physical starting point from which to do this.'

Sita then steps forward from behind the Moni Baba. She stretches out her blanket like a magician waving her cape over the floor. She begins another performance of postures, but this time she stands like a Maoiri warrior about to perform the Haka. She carefully pulls up her blouse to expose her stomach and pins it with her chin at the neck.

Then Sita stops, lets the tunic drop and walks back to the Baba and says something. The Baba announces Sita will perform *Nauli* and that people should never try this posture on a full stomach.

Sita returns to front stage, places one hand on each thigh with her fingers on the inside of her legs. She begins to roll her stomach muscles in a waltz of movement. The crowd surges forward as if the lead guitarist has just begun their solo. She isolates a central column of muscle and wiggles it from side to side on her thin frame. Sita does this for several minutes and when her breathing changes the Baba can tell she has stopped.

'If you lose sight of the muscles involved in Nauli... it is the first indication that you are eating more than you require. Keep sight of your Nauli muscles all your life as a measure of health eating.'

Sita moves into the splits and while supporting herself with both hands, effortlessly changes the position of her legs to the opposite way.

She stands and balances on one leg, whipping her other leg up behind her to touch her head as it bends behind her arm. All these movements are smooth actions, controlled with the grace of a ballerina.

It is hard to judge what sort of teaching is taking place because it is happening on so many levels. Sita appears completely self-occupied. This is not a performance of yoga. It is a demonstration we happen to be witnessing.

The crowd seem enthralled by Sita. As she performs her final postures, the Baba talks once more to the audience.

'This morning you saw the first stages of interest in hatha yoga and the postures that must be practiced. This morning's routine exposed your weaknesses in your ability to move, balance, hold a posture and relax.

'This afternoon Sita has displayed postures and movements, which can only be achieved after years of regular practice. She did not begin her yoga with this capacity... she has attained this through practice. These postures demonstrate a state of being that can benefit you in anything you undertake. It's the basic observations within your body, which guide you and show you where you need physical attention. To only practice postures that are easy is simply to maintain the status quo in areas which function perfectly well as they are. Postures that are difficult is the body's way of informing you of the areas that require extra work. Use your practice of hatha to discover your physical weak points, then devise a routine which will help you improve your overall physical state.

'Take care not to rush things and remember this type of discovery is no different for Raja yoga of self-discovery with the mind. These extreme postures are not reached by force. They are reached with the regular practice of moderate movement and posture, without any risk to the body's existing state. It is a personal choice; no one will benefit more than you. Your achievement in yoga is also a gift to all those around you who might otherwise feel obliged to nurse and care for you.'

Sita manages to integrate this talk into her demonstration and in her final headstand she lifts both her hands into a *namasti* sign while she is still inverted. It is yet further demonstration of her considerable balancing skill.

After Sita finishes, she steps back from the stage front. There is a ripple of civil clapping from the audience but no calls for an encore. People seem to accept the session is now over and begin to leave. The clouds from the north are darker and coming closer.

I see my chance. I push my way to the front of the crowd to meet the Baba. Being slightly taller than most people around me, I see where they are heading. A number of devotees have surrounded the sage and more are flocking towards him. It becomes impossible to get close to him. I also see Sita disappear into a crowd of young people, but there are less of them. With Herculean pushes, I manage to reach her. The young people who are talking to her stop when I approach. I surprise her as she folds her yoga blanket into a small cloth bag. People assume that I know her and step back. I find myself standing in front of Sita while she stares back at me, bewildered.

In a mixture of Nepali and broken English, I explain that my father was the yogi James Munro and that he knew the Moni Baba many years ago. There is a pause after I say this. She looks at me as if she understands, but says nothing. I ask her if it's possible to meet with the Baba and talk. She frowns and gestures towards the massive crowd who are now flocking around him. It seems hopeless. The Baba's admirers are seeking a blessing; a touch; a closer look, or a personal word, all the things he tells us to hold little value in, yet at this moment they are consuming the Baba's time.

As the younger audience realizes Sita does not know me, they begin also to shower her with questions, gifts of flowers and sweets. I'm left to watch as my opportunity to meet the Baba begins to disappear in a storm of admiration. Sita is bustled away towards a yogini tent where it's made clear by giggling teenagers I am not allowed to go. As she is ushered away, I shout out one last question in Nepali asking where they are heading next. She points north to the mountains and calls out something in return. A young man next to me tells me that she has said 'Thangboche' and adds that it is the famous monastery in the Everest region.

The heavens finally open and rain falls in sheets across the parade ground. Sita is under cover and the Moni Baba also disappears. This vanishing act is what he is famous for, as much as his teaching. I feel a deep sense of disappointment. The crowd becomes competitors in a formidable mud challenge, trying to reach shelter. I move through them back to my tea-shop room.

Later that evening, I feel depressed and alone. The temporary high of seeing the Baba is quickly followed by more sobering thoughts about my dad and how difficult it's been tracking his guru down.

I turn through the pages of dad's book prepared to give up the quest. I look for a reference to the weather forecast, mainly fair. I read it once more and for the first time appreciate the meaning.

It is all about our spirit's efforts in **trying** to survive and succeed. No matter what how many health failures we have, our bodies and our immune system is constantly trying to survive. No matter how often our social lives seem unsuccessful, something in our nature keeps us trying. Our mind can feel released if it begins to associate with this life flow and not become pre-occupied with the factors that hinder your life or are labelled as failures. 'As we age,' the Baba says, 'and look back through our memories, most of us will conclude that overall things have been mainly fair, because we all begin to understand how much we've enjoyed trying.'

I hardly sleep. I feel exhausted and disappointed, but I take this idea of trying to let this flow of events continue longer. I am also buoyed by the thought that Sita recognised dad's name.

By morning I resolve to make the journey to Thangboche Monastery. Although the monastery sits en-route to the world's highest mountain, I'll be pretty much guaranteed an audience with the Baba there. I've been assured there will be no crowds up in the Khumbu.

I calculate my finances are healthy enough to afford an air ticket. With an overnight bus trip to Kathmandu and a short plane ride to Lukla, my quest is resumed. This puts me ahead of the Baba. This time he will be coming to me.

48

After a brisk walk from Lukla to Namche Bazaar, I arrive without knowing the date the Baba is due to appear in Thangboche. It is one of those occasions when his appearance will determine the date, not the other way round. I stay one night in Namche, blissfully spending most of my evening alone. I hear a radio randomly playing 'Do they know its Christmas?' and write a song called 'Another project's come to town'. It's my first musical composition in a while.

Next day I pace through the Bazaar and follow the trail to Thangboche. It is a head clearing, lung freshening walk with a steady incline, around the edge of steep hills for most of the day. Eagles hover and swoop on the currents coming up from the valley. It feels cool and liberating in contrast to the heat of the Terai. I walk a little too fast and begin to feel the initial effects of altitude sickness. I find my watch a useless tool, only of use to those counting hours, not days. The timescale that now interests me, however, is how near to meeting the Baba I am.

Outside the monastery I find a room at a small lodge catering for climbers on route to the world's highest mountains. Luckily they have a tea which 'cures' altitude sickness. I also take the required rest and make inquiries at the monastery to find out when the Baba is due. Sometime in the next week or two, I'm told. I figure time will pass in a flash.

In the Kumbu the sky appears a much darker blue than it is at sea level. I remember thinking this darkness was a trick used on photographs to emphasize the whiteness of the mountains. It is, however, a staggering reality. The dark navy blue takes away the little breath most visitors have. The monastery is nestled on a plateau surrounded by classic white peaked mountains. It is quiet and serene and I anticipate it will be easy to talk personally to the Baba here.

After a few days, I acclimatize and rest. A group of Polish and Russian climbers arrive on their way down, having just climbed Everest. Two of the group take residence in my lodge. Their guides and porters camp around the valley, making the place suddenly feel crowded.

At breakfast one of the Polish climbers introduces himself as Karol. He speaks good English. He asks me what a white man is doing alone up in the Kumbu. This label and racial distinction seems as distant to me as hours in the day... to be called a white man. I feel it too obvious to be of any value, just one step more in the descriptive scale to being called human.

I tell Karol I've lived in Nepal more than a year now. I tell him why I am here and of my quest to find the Moni Baba.

He is immediately interested in my story and begins to talk animatedly about his personal yoga practice. He tells me it is very common these days to find people in extreme sports in Poland who also practice yoga. There are many who have tried to achieve great things with the help of yoga. He assumes I am a practitioner. I feel at least for this conversation I have enough vocabulary, so I say, 'Should it not be the other way round... that people are doing remarkable things while they are trying to achieve yoga!'

'Om touché.'

I talk most of the night and into the morning with Karol. He offers me some winter clothes and a warm spare sleeping bag when he sees me shivering.

49

For the next week I hear stories from Karol about his first visit to Nepal and his latest climb to the summit of Everest. He gives me vivid description of the Kumbu glacier and its large valley of jagged ice.

'At certain times of year stalagmites bristle across the landscape, pointing toward the greater universe overhead. At first I thought it a mystery for them to be without their stalactite partners,' Karol Wysocki tells me. 'Then at other times of year you see dozens of huge rocks suspended on thin columns of ice the shape of Polish wine glasses.'

Karol explains that the stalagmites are actually what is left over as summer ends.

'Winter landslides and avalanches bring many huge rocks rolling down onto the glacier, ending up on the surface between Nuptse and the west ridge of Sagarmatha. By April the glacier melts down to a lower level and the rocks are left suspended on a pillar of ice. The sun cannot reach under the shadow of the rock to melt the ice there. So as the sun melts, the surrounding floor of the valley drops, leaving these rocks supported by a pillar of ice.

'I gaze up in awe at a ceiling of rocks perched on thin stems some ten feet tall, knowing that at any time the sun's rays could melt the final millimetre of support and bring a rock crashing down on us. In their final moments these boulders appear to defy gravity, as if set in a surreal Gothic temple. It is a wondrous art show by Mother Nature, presented in her highest gallery.'

My Polish companion describes the rest of the climb with much less enthusiasm. Weeks of nights in thin tents, hearing the ice melt and crack underneath you. Occasional avalanches sounding as if they are about to sweep you away. Then the slow slog to the top, something that few would achieve without help from Sherpas.

Neither of the other Polish climbers speak English, but Karol seems keen to talk a lot. He is a full-time doctor, part-time poet and in the confines of our lodge, offers me high-altitude wisdom on his personal yoga and how he practices it to conquer these mountains.

'Since the fall of communism, young people have the chance to observe places like this. TV documentaries have been like a bird's song invitation to come here. I heard these calls in Warsaw and I come here to climb. Television has opened window on the modern world.'

Karol reaches inside his small backpack. 'I have great interest in this part of the world,' he continues. 'I read books on Yoga in English for my training I do much the Pranayama. I practice breathing techniques from this book so I can reach the summit of Everest without oxygen.'

I stop Karol's gloved hands flipping the pages with my own. I lean forward and whisper, 'This book is written by my dad.'

I watch his face change. 'And I've never met anyone else who carries a copy of it like I do.' I take my backpack and produce my copy as if playing 'snap' in a card game.

'Your father wrote this book?' Karol cannot find English words to express himself. He begins shouting in Polish to the other climbers in the lodge.

'For many climbers in Poland, this is Bible for learning breathing techniques. They used to suffer altitude sickness. They get pulmonary water in the lung and some have even died. Every climber is advised to climb only four hundred meters each day when they reach above three thousand meters.

'I now go to altitude very quickly because I use Pranayama breathing from this book. I fool my body into thinking I have slept eights hours after simple breathing for fifteen minutes. I have no altitude sickness because of your father's Pranayama lessons. Why you suffered a little on the way here?'

'Good question, I've read the book and tried the postures, but never regularly practiced any of the lessons.'

'Come let me show you – it is a very easy lesson to do.'

Karol then begins to demonstrate his yoga breathing. He pulls up his shirt to expose his bare chest, and demonstrates what he calls 'the complete breath'.

These climbers have no knowledge of the Moni Baba but are quick to pull out the vodka for a toast to my dad James Munro senior and his yoga Bible.

It is the opposite among the Sherpa guides. They have never heard of James Munro but when I tell them that the Moni Baba is about visit Thangboche, there's a buzz of excitement. They even convince the climbers to hang around.

50

It's a crisp clear morning outside the Guest House. I see her walk towards the water tap. She attracts the attention of climbers and I recognise her instantly.

In these near freezing temperatures, Sita carries a bundle of clothes and wears only a simple cloth wrapped around her. She turns on the tap and the noise of running water fills the valley. A passing yak bell plays a note then another and some distant carpenter adds a bass with hammer and nails. It's a surreal mountain opera with the star centre stage as nature's orchestra plays the opening overture. Monks begin chanting and village yak-herders whip their beasts and whistle loudly as they walk through the midst of the theatre.

Sita begins her performance. She drops her bundle of clothes under the running water and carefully separates each item with her feet. She presses down with one foot and spreads the clothes with the other, occasionally bending to rub soap onto her bundle. When finished, she arches her back, loosening her hair and dips it repeatedly under the tap. She allows the icy cold water to run through her hair and over her bare shoulders. She does not flinch although this water comes straight from the glacier a thousand feet away.

I catch a climber taking a few photographs and I'm reminded of Maya's same revealing Nepali innocence with her water-tap body language. If there ever was an image from the courtroom of gender judgements, something to confirm there is a law of attraction, here it is. All the Polish climbers are now taking photographs. To pass sentence on their conduct is dependent on the culture from which this behaviour is judged.

Karol walks over to me and says, 'It must have been like this for all of us, washing in public places, way back in the days.'

I tell him it's still common today for more than half the people on the subcontinent.

As we talk, two other older women join Sita at the tap. I catch Sita looking up at me as she continues to wash her clothes but she gives no indication that she recognises me. I detect a sadness in her eyes that was not there in Lumbini.

The older Sherpa women are now semi-naked, laughing. They look like they are wearing brown leather gloves and a dark ski-mask on their face in contrast with their pale shoulders and arms.

'Amazing,' I say, 'how the thick rug-like clothes these women wear, keeps their skin so bleached in comparison to their weather-beaten cheeks.'

Karol's eye remains pressed against his telephoto lens.

L ater that day I visit the water tap to wash also. I'm thankful the Baba remains anonymous to the climbers and a few trekkers who have arrived from Canada. I realize my only competition for his time will be the Lamas, apprentice monks and a few of the mountain guides with the Polish group.

The monks are engaged in rebuilding and repairing some areas of the monastery recently damaged by a serious fire. After hundreds of years of coping successfully with open butter-lamps, the spark from a newly installed electrical system destroyed rooms of priceless artwork.

I watch as some of the monks repaint one of the outside walls and approach them for permission to go inside and speak to the head Lama. Inside, I see two other artisans prepare a wall with a new thin layer of plaster. A third monk seems to be in a trance-like state. He gouges out an intricate pattern in the wet plaster with his fingers. His arm moves like a precision machine, weaving the design while another keeps the plastered wall wet. Line after line of the pattern appears with great accuracy. He has developed the remarkable ability to repeat the same movement time and time again as he walks along the wall. It is fascinating to watch. A mixture of paint and plaster is applied, creating intricate Buddhist designs on the wall.

A Lama approaches and without introduction tells me that he understands I have come seeking audience with the Moni Baba. He tells me the Baba knows I'm here and has agreed to see me. I am to meet him privately tomorrow after he delivers a talk to the full assembly of novice monks. Meantime I am welcome to make myself comfortable in the monastery. If I wish I can sleep in one of the side rooms on the saddle carpets and cushions on the floor. Without allowing me any chance to reply, he turns and leaves.

Sita must have recognised me from the tap and informed the Baba. Either that, or the Baba has second sight. As in Barabase, there are likely no secrets among residents of Thangboche.

I decide to take up the invitation to move into the monastery. It feels relaxed here and less fraught with a new wave of enquiring visitors. I collect all my belongings, say a temporary farewell to Karol and the climbers and move to find a corner in the monastery. I pitch a couple of saddle mattresses together to make myself as comfortable as possible.

For the first time, I feel near the completion of my goal. I also feel stimulated by the presence of Sita.

Perhaps Sita has appeared as a useful distraction because I have a slight fear of failure with this encounter with the Baba.

At dusk, I overhear people talking. I recognise the voice of the Baba. I wander to an open shuttered window and look in. The room is dark, with dust being caught in shafts of fading light from the monks' work next door. The Baba is sitting in silhouette with Sita close in front of him. They are alone. For a moment she looks around but does not see me. The Baba stares at her despite his blindness and takes her hands. She looks deeply into his face.

My instinct tells me to leave, but I'm afraid to move. Although I've heard of their togetherness, I'm witnessing the intensity of their intimacy. They sit close together for several minutes without a word. I feel guilt at watching them but I cannot leave, it is too silent and they will surely hear me. They continue sitting facing each other, exchanging something beyond words. The Baba holds Sita's hands lightly, appearing to communicate only through touch. His hand moves up her arm and she moves closer to him as if the warmth of his body compels her to be close. She bows her head and rests it on his shoulder. They continue to bask in this strange chemistry of affection that exists between them.

I wait for something to happen and suddenly it does. Sita slowly stands up. Her face catches the light and there appears to be tears in her eyes. She pulls her iconic white dress over her head and places it beside the Baba. She stands naked in front of him although he cannot see her. She takes a newly made skirt and bodice from a canvas bag and puts them on.

I have never seen any images of her in village clothes. This change makes Sita seem ordinary, more human. She bends one last time to embrace the Baba's feet with her forehead, then leaves.

I stand at the open window, wondering what will happen next.

5 2

Hardly breathing in case the Baba's yogic hearing might detect me, I tiptoe back out of the front door and into a blaze of yellow sunlight reflecting off Lotse. Half-blinded, I walk down the steps and over towards the nearest downhill path. As my eyes adjust, I see the figure of Sita walking down the hillside. It looks like this is a serious departure, not an afternoon stroll. Sita has a look of determination and permanency in her stride.

I'm tempted to run after Sita. It is as strong an urge as I've felt in a long time. To run and rescue her from whatever drama the young yogini is facing. It also seems stupid and futile. I have come all this way to see the Moni Baba. I know I must understand more of my past before I take chances for the future.

As I stand rooted in indecision, two monks run towards me. They seem anxious and ask if I know anything about medicine. I think for a moment this relates to the Moni Baba, but they tell me a monk has just fallen from a ladder.

I follow the monks back inside the monastery and find the craftsman that I admired earlier lying on the floor. It appears he's twisted his ankle and dislocated his shoulder. No one knows what to do to help him. He is Oming in pain. With all their chanting, all their knowledge obtained from meditation, these young monks have no idea how to reset a dislocated shoulder. They offer the monk tea with natural herbs and spices.

I'm sure this monk could quickly accept this as a life-changing disability with empathy and control. My public health background tells me this need not be the case. I tell a monk to run off to find Karol and bring him here.

The nearest qualified doctor is in Kathmandu. One suggestion is that we load the injured man into a basket to carry him to the health post at Lukla because he is an important artisan. It will be a four-day walk for the porter with the monk on his back. They will then see if the health assistant can help. If not, they'll take a chance trying to get on a flight from Lukla to Kathmandu. It might be a week before they reach a doctor. If not, then like others before him, he'll have to accept his disability, something he's very qualified to do.

A concerned older monk speaks to the novice monks like Captain Picard on the Starship Enterprise and says the Nepali equivalent of 'make it so.'

Karol arrives and immediately takes charge in the room. In a literal snap decision, he moves forward and asks the monks to hold the injured man's torso and head to the side. As they do this, he pulls twice on the man's arm and with only a slight yelp, be it chant or curse, I hear the monk's shoulder pop back into place.

The affected monk begins to mumble prayers and the others join in. The speed of Karol's action surprises even me. I ask if he has had much experience doing this and he tells me yes, since there a growing interest in playing rugby in Poland.

53

News of Sita's departure spreads like a spilled butter-lamp into all the crevices of this monastic community. The few monks I meet that evening do not know where Sita is heading and say that the Baba is likely to stay silent on this matter. Even the guides and porters are talking, believing it must have been Sita's choice to leave.

No one I speak to knows of any reason why Sita has left the Moni Baba. She's been the sage's constant companion for more than ten years. She's grown from a young teenager into a woman at his side. Their age difference is no explanation, in these parts, for her departure. I tell the Karol he is witnessing a drama, a celebrity break-up on the scale of Velvet Underground or indeed The Beatles. Nepal's guru pop-charts may never be the same again.

On the morning of the Baba's scheduled talk, it appears every monk in the Kumbu has turned up, along with scores of villagers trekking in. News has spread overnight to all the nearby hamlets that Sita has left the Baba. There is no longer a big enough room within the monastery to hold everyone so the head Lama moves the talk outside to the lower steps of the monastery entrance. Seats are never necessary here since everyone squats or sits on the ground.

In the fresh open air, the sun flashes off the surrounding mountain peaks as if they are capped with mirrors. The Baba's breath can be seen as he moves down towards the crowd. Some people huddle together for warmth and children run laps around the whole gathering, chasing each other. As the Baba sits, the children are immediately captured by outstretched arms from the crowd and hugged into submission to stay quiet. All wait to hear the Baba's words. With a small solar-powered PA system, he begins to talk.

'Changes,' says the Baba.

'Change comes at variable speeds. You can witness its movement in front of you or it can move so fast you don't see it come or go.

'Given a telescope the earth and planets move slowly across a night sky. Given a microscope our biology moves and changes at great speed. It is something most of us are indifferent to or like me blind to.

'Some say that all life is change,' he shouts these words, then whispers 'but change is not life... it is movement. Movement and change take place even where there is no life.

'We humans choose our **beliefs** to be something we hope will never change. We hope there is permanence to friendship, to love, as much as to rain or to sunlight. We prepare ourselves to love someone forever and with such a commitment comes a **fear** that things will change.

'So much fear surrounds "change" that most of us prefer to move through life trying to cope with things to keep them the same. With opportunity or hardships we make decisions that are not the cause of too much change. While tending our own fields of reality, we try to manage change.

'As a consequence we keep the same friends, the same interests, the same habits, the same environment and mostly the same partners because change can be a painful giving-up process; a giving up of that which has become familiar. There is no desire to give up something you cherish because you think of it as part of yourself.

'When change is inevitable, we accept this as the "will of God."

'Your mind is not only part of this change… it is constantly preparing for change. Outside of mediation, there is no time when the mind isn't preparing itself for something new, amidst that which we strive to keep the same.

'Our preparedness to change is the only thing that remains the same.'

I feel I'm witnessing one of the weirdest lectures in the Baba's life. He definitely seems pre-occupied. I sense everyone has clocked the theme of today's talk. The Baba talks in a tired voice and seems to be addressing himself and not the crowd. He sounds confused, perhaps missing Sita and trying to explain it.

'Whenever you're pressured into making decisions, you may say that you don't respond to pressure, that you can't change what you really are. Take note of this voice in yourself for this is what you say about yourself. This is a glimpse of yourself each time you are faced with change.

'You all have the ability to decide here and now to change something as small as a habit or as big as a location. Know that these moments are available to you more often than you think they are.

'We all witness the movements of planets, the stars, the consciousness of family and friends and the physical dynamics of all that surrounds us. But we are also witness the desires, addictions, the needs and the fantasies of our personally cultured minds.

'We grow our own reality from the thoughts we seed in our mind. With regular care and weeding, our reality can be as organised as any field or garden we care for. However, as in all things that grow in this world our reality is subject to unexpected natural disasters.

'We can prepare our homes for a storm but the very elements

we depend on, the sun and the rain, can cause chaos from which recovery is difficult. The key to putting things back into order lies in the way we perceive what we control and how we manage it.'

The Baba suddenly finishes with the chant Om as if that's enough for the day.

He is helped by one of the older monks and retires backs into the monastery. There is a lot of talk among the novice monks. One asks if I agree, and before I can answer, another asks me if I feel I've made the right changes in my life to come here to Nepal.

'Well, at this moment I'm not sure,' I reply.

'Most young monks are here because it was the choice of our parents,' he says, as if he's just had an epiphany.

54

I am taken aside by one of the older monks who was present when Karol healed the artisan. I'm told the Baba can see me immediately if I wish.

At long last my personal encounter with the Moni Baba finally arrives. I step indoors to a small, quiet, warm thickly carpeted room and my faith is restored. Perhaps not faith... but the feeling I am indeed in the right place at the right time. Strange how in such a country, such a sub-continent, things can appear so desperately out of control one moment and so in order the next.

The smell of incense and butter-lamps slightly disguises the musty smell of furs and un-tanned leather. The Baba sits behind a small Tibetan prayer table, the only sign of religion in the room. I speak in English. I tell the Baba I am the son of James Munro and he seems unsurprised but cautious.

'Sit young James... it's been a long time since I met you last. Tell me, how are you?'

I'm shocked the Baba remembers meeting me because I have no recollection of it at all. I tell him I am fine but that I've spent more than a year trying to find him.

'Do you know what the meaning of the name Moni Baba is?'

'No, sorry I don't.'

'It means… the teacher who does not speak much.'

I explain that I am trying to find more details of my father's death. The Moni Baba smiles and says nothing. I speak more about my own life and the long-held desire to come to Nepal to find my father's guru. I pull out dad's book and say that as a boy it was the first place I saw his photo and heard of him. I say the book is my strongest connection with my dad.

The Baba nods. 'I met you the day you arrived in Nepal with your parents. How did you find me this time?'

I explain my stopover in Delhi, my interviews with his followers and the recent photographs of him and Sita. The Baba's brow furrows as I mention Sita.

I speak more, thinking I didn't come here to tell him my life story.

The Baba finally speaks, asking me where the passion for my journey comes from. I have no immediate answer. I sense there is no hostility in the question so I reply with a fresh review of the truth.

'I have many reasons that compel me. I believe that speaking to someone my father admired and wrote about can somehow give me greater understanding.'

I ask the Baba if he has any objection to talking to me, as a non-seeker of spiritual guidance but just as someone with a few personal questions about my father's life and death.

I ask if he has any objection to me recording our conversation, and he replies that silence takes up a lot of tape.

55

My Personal Audience with the Moni Baba at Thangboche.

'DO YOU KNOW THE MEANING OF THE WORD SANYASI, YOUNG JAMES?'

'Someone who has retired from the world and gone into retreat to practise yoga?'

'Not exactly, but close. The life of a Sanyasin does involve retreat, but it is principally a retreat from speaking ungodly things or in your case let's call it unhelpful words. For thousands of years our culture has allowed Sanyassins to live among us **because** they devote their life to talking only helpful words. A Sanyasin does no harm and will only speak to you about spiritual matters. Anything mundane and of this material world is never their subject of conversation.'

'Are you saying you cannot talk to me about my father, because you are a Sanyasin?'

'No, I am hardly a Sanyasin. I've been called many things but never a Sanyasin.' The Baba chuckles.

'There is however a Sanyasin whose name is Mahindranath Avadhoot and he knows far more about your father than I do. He is definitely someone you should see before you leave these parts. He was with your father at the end. He is known more commonly as... the Avadhoot.'

It seems a difficult name to remember, so I translate it into the vernacular Scots. Have a doubt... pronounced "Av-a-dhoot". I write it in my journal and a cold wind finds the back of my neck as I sit in this now accustomed crossed-leg position.

'You must find and talk to Sita Kumari. She knows how to find the Avadhoot. He should become the goal of your quest, not me. But to get him to talk about your father may be difficult. That will be a challenge for you. That will be your yoga in these months ahead.'

'Where is Sita now?' I perk up. 'What is her full name?'

'She is Sita Joshi but better known as Sita the ex-Kumari. She has returned to Kathmandu. You will find her near the centre of Durbar Square next to the temple where she spent her childhood.'

'Can you tell me anything more about my father?'

'When I first met your father, not many western people were interested in discussing modern interpretations of yoga and this place was full of purists. But as the world changes, so too does an individual's yoga. There came a new wave of interest from the west, but many of them were also deviant. Many wanted to buy weed and fill their mind with its effects. Excess drugs have the same effect on the mind as fertilisers on crops, you know. Too much of it is not good for anyone – especially others living in the neighbourhood.

'Your father was one of the first westerners to seek me out. He became as much my guru as you believe I was his. Much of what I teach today is influenced by the ideas that James Munro shared with me. He shone a fresh light on our culture that allowed me to see it in a different way. Some people even tell me that I have a Scottish accent when I talk in English.'

'Aye – I hear it.'

'I speak of your father's desires to achieve his own perfection in yoga. He possessed a considerable intellectual armoury for his journey. It both weighed him down and protected him at the same time. He felt compassion for the people who live in these hills. I do not want to talk of his death, for it still affects me.'

The Baba sits for a moment in silence. I tell my legs to be prepared for the long sit.

'When I talk of your father, I am but a fleeting moment on the landscape of his experiences in life…

'After we talk today, you may, like he did, reinforce the conversation we are having for the rest of your life, simply because you see it as a rare occurrence. You can constantly pull this moment into your mind, examine it and replace it back as an important time, or it can fade into insignificance. It all depends on you. The real value of what I am saying to you is not in the words but in the way you will use my words and this experience afterwards.'

I force myself to relax. After all this time, I am finally conversing with the Moni Baba. I am encouraged that he is relating directly to me and not simply quoting from teachings or ancient scriptures like the monks.

'Your father chose to leave his country and go in search of something that was missing from his life. The repercussions for this action are still occurring. Your presence here today is but the latest consequence. His actions may have been provoked by love. But I also know it was his way of avoiding the hatred of other things in his life. Our egos can always justify any deed we accomplish, any thought we entertain.

'You have found me because your father wrote of me, but these were words from another time and place. I've mentioned someone else who knows more about your father than I do. The Avadhoot has received compliments from scholars in Hinduism, Buddhism,

Christianity and even Islam. He is an advocate for spirituality beyond religion but takes no responsibility to create such a tolerant society. He's been criticised by the fundamentalists in all religions. As you will have noticed, the attitudes of religious zealots rarely accommodate other faiths and offer only token invitations.

'Words are the tools we use to express our thoughts...' the Baba goes silent for a moment, then whispers more intimately to me, 'as you try to describe accurately on paper to others what I say to you here, people will seek an understanding of your motivation. People will not easily accept words without searching for a person's motives for speaking in such a way. They will be unable to see the true context in which we speak face to face. This moment, if you describe it, will always be different and have a new context.

'This moment is the alternative that yoga offers in your desire to learn. I am briefly as a mirror to you. As a guru that's my job. There are few gurus who have been able to write in a way capable of breaking through the language and cultural barriers in place when we read. Your father tried to reference the inner geography of faith and the thought processes that are similar in us all. He stressed languages are the foundations for spreading our beliefs, but it is the way we experience life that determines our faith.

'In your search to find out more about your father, let your desire lead you but not control you. Like your father, write down what you experience. Your ideas will help keep in motion the huge ocean of consciousness that meets in the collective thinking mind. It is this collective mind that is responsible for translating what we witness in our society today. We live within a world governed by natural order but increasingly we also live with the consequences of our collective thought.'

The Baba then rises slowly and shakes my hand. It is a gesture I do not expect. I see in the dim lamplight he has a tear in his eye. He says he'd like to hear the finished result of any book that I write.

He tells me to always remember Georg Fredrick Hegel's words that thesis promotes antithesis leading to synthesis.

'Whenever you speak ideas for all mankind, you will never get agreement. You will find approval from only one third of your listeners, complete opposition in another third and you will experience indifference from the remaining third! It is a formula that's repeated by all who argue over what is important.'

'And what if every single person were to agree with what you have just said?' I ask cheekily.

'Just like your dad.' The Baba leaves laughing.

56

After a restless night of dreams chasing the whereabouts of Sita, I wake late. It feels curious to be tasked with finding Sita, but I'm indifferent to spending time chasing down this Avadhoot. I try to see the Baba once more but I'm told he has departed early, escorted by a novice monk and heading to Namche. I'm told there are no shortages of young volunteers to become the Baba's new assistant.

I'm impressed by how mobile the old Baba still is. I've seen many old people wander in the villages but not many walking between them on the rougher trails.

This meeting was not what I imagined it would be like back in Scotland. I thought that gurus were supposed to be people you could stay with as long as you liked, once you found them. I feel things have been cut short.

As I think through my next move, I realise, as the Baba said, I can now decide whether to reinforce the memory of our meeting as positive or negative; it's my choice.

I say goodbye to Karol and his climbers, guides and porters. He asks me how my meeting with the Baba went and I tell him it was good in parts but overall a failed summit success. A bit like Henrick's 'Seven minutes in Tibet!'

I overnight at Namche Bazaar and eat with some fresh-faced back-backers. I join them for some alcoholic beverage and a sing-song to boost my spirits. Blues seems the appropriate genre. I play BB King's 'The Thrill Is Gone', followed by Bessie Smith's 'Nobody Knows When You're Down and Out'. Someone asks what it was like to meet the Moni Baba and what was his message. I respond with some of Guitar Shorty's 'A Little Less Conversation'.

WHEN I REACH LUKLA, THERE ARE CROWDS OF TOURISTS WAITING TO leave. Planes have been grounded and flights cancelled because of stormy weather in the south. I decide to avoid the waiting pack of people and make the walk back to Kathmandu. I pass through groups of frustrated tourists, all queuing waving tickets and pointing to watches, addicted to speed, slaves of time. I take the reverse route that Sir Edmond Hillary took on his way to Everest in 1953. Back then it took nineteen days of acclimatisation for their expeditions to reach base-camp from Kathmandu. I take seven days to walk back down. I say down, but it's the equivalent of climbing Ben Nevis, Britain's highest mountain, three times a day for a week.

On the trail I ponder my conversation with the Baba. In public health it is important to believe that all people can agree in one truth if it is proven. Immunization would not have the impact it has had if this were not so. Science and maths offer us all some imperial proofs to believe in. If everyone can agree on a single issue, then the Baba is wrong. His three-way split in responses would be false.

After a few more miles I accept that by stating there can be truths which draw agreement from all people, I am in fact disagreeing with the Moni Baba, and therefore in his second category of audience.

PART FIVE: THE SURPRISE

57

I walk into the bustling centre of Kathamandu with the same suicidal innocence I found in hill folk when I first arrived. I saunter onto main roads in a trekking daze, only to jump out the way of traffic. My meditative mind is abandoned, facing the full charge of bicycles and rickshaws.

In my new adrenaline-fuelled mode, I realise the cost of living will increase here and I'll have to be careful with my savings.

At the top of Tilak's list of ex-Gurkha friends in Kathmandu is a man called Bahadur, the man who sent the news clippings of dad to us in Barabase.

I am welcomed like an old friend and he tells me he has two rooms, within a set of houses that he owns. It is not the most salubrious area of the city but in Bahadur's words it is up and coming.

Bahadur's rickety houses have been propped up with timber since the last earthquake and would unlikely survive the next. They are located on the southern fringe of Assan Tol. Two rooms look out onto a tiny quiet central courtyard while four surrounding streets bustle with activity, eighteen hours a day.

Storekeepers, traders and shoppers come and go, like passengers at a busy bus terminal.

The area is lively and Bahadur assures me it's safe. People will be sympathetic to my presence, because I've met the Moni Baba and I'm a seeker and not a tourist. He offers me one room for a cheap rent but is delighted when I agree to pay extra rent for the remaining room so I have all the top floor. I'm happy. I have a different set of standards now for appraising accommodation.

Bahadur is a squat man older than Tilak with laughing eyes and bad breath. Two of his front teeth are missing. He is keen to hear news of Tilak, but has little attention span when I talk to him about the Moni Baba or Sita. He is forever busy doing chores, too numerous for me to identify their purpose.

I visit some of the other names on Tilak's list to see if anyone knows the whereabouts of Sita the Kumari. Most are shocked at the news of her separation from the Baba and I'm surprised this story has not spread ahead of me on the mountain trails.

Bahadur introduces me to a few locals who are kind enough to lend me odd bits of furniture including a table and chair for my room. I buy some local cloth and tack it to the ceiling and walls. This transforms my main room to look pleasantly Arabian and it collects the plaster that drops from the ceiling whenever it rains or if birds land on the roof.

Bahadur also lives in the compound, in a rehabilitated section across the courtyard. The rest is rented to an assortment of poorly paid office workers. Each evening a group of wives smash the collars, armpits and tails of their husband's shirts onto wet stones. They take a metal iron, fill it with hot charcoal and press the shirts for the next day's work. Each morning, my neighbours depart for work on motor-cycles, wearing dress shirts and wobbly crash helmets. They disappear down the road like puppets with loose heads.

Next to Bahadur's building is a large open area that is currently a squatter settlement known locally as Pipelands. It takes its name from the huge abandoned concrete sewage pipes that people live in. These pipes are all that remains of an ambitious sanitation project that lost funding through corruption. Dozens of people now live on this wasteland, half the size of a football pitch. From my window it looks like a rubbish dump. Broken pipes are topped with plastic bags to form shelters. The large unbroken pipes have become houses for whole families. These concrete condominiums are scattered across a cement obstacle course and furnished by skilful squatters. There is even a posh end for long-term residents and a poor end in the slum for newcomers.

As the weeks pass, I inquire more around town about Sita. She is not where the Baba said she would be at her old temple in Kathmandu. I also acquire an unsolicited following. People seem eager to meet me simply because I have so recently met the Moni Baba. It is not my intention to become a commentator on his teaching but I accept this responsibility as a possible way of tracing Sita.

There are rumours that the Baba's has given his last public talk in Namche Bazaar, on the subject of death. Two devotees tell me that someone from a tourist group recorded the talk and if I want, they can get me a copy of the tape. It suddenly becomes a story that I've had the last face-to-face audience with the Moni Baba and I'm not sure I can cope with this new-found fame.

The western part of me thinks it is inconceivable in this day and age that such a figure as the Baba can simply walk into the hills and never be seen again. The Barabase part of me knows this scenario is perfectly feasible.

Weeks turn to months spent mostly in hiding and helping Bahadur in his never-ending task of house repairs. I rarely speak to devotees now, although I still wander the area where the Baba said I would find Sita in Durbar Square. I've become aware of Bahadur's political views and learn that when he said his neighbourhood was up and coming, he meant there were plans to build a large retail property on Pipelands next door. It's a development he doesn't want to see happen.

After only a few enquires about the Avadhoot, I give up. People laugh when I ask how I can find him. Why would you want to interrupt him anyway, they ask.

58

There months after arriving back in Kathmandu, the Shiva Ratri celebrations at Pashupatinath bring more of the Baba's followers into the valley. There are thousands of devotees who come from India to Kathmandu each year, essentially to celebrate Hinduism's most famous orgasm. Day and night thousands of people move in through the temple gates representing the vagina of Shiva's wife Pravati, and walk passed an erect lingum (penis) of Shiva, inside the womb. The stroke of midnight on the last day, represents the actual stroke moment of orgasm. It's an event celebrated all over the Hindu world.

On reflection, you can see how these two ancient myths might work in competition for two of the world's top religions. 'What sort of sales pitch can compare to an orgasm for the Gods?' said the Christians. 'Well let's see, how about a virgin birth!'

I give up my spare room to help Bahadur accommodate some of his friends who are in town for Shivaratri. One night I decide to escape the crowd in my building and go mingle with the larger crowds at Pashupati. I decide to avoid being approached by Baba devotees I should dress the part and make myself look as much like a pilgrim as possible. I wrap a cloth around my head and cover my shoulders with a blanket.

I walk through the streets, enjoying the anonymity of my disguise. As I stop to take in the scale of the crowd, two policemen step forward and tell me sharply in Nepali to keep moving forward and not to hold up the long queues. They seem less polite to me as a local.

Squashed into the moving crowd I am carried under the great gate, like a spermatozoa, on toward the inner womb. I pass a group of street performers from an ashram in Bhaktapur moving, swaying and chanting beside the ritualistic tide of people. Many are bathing in the Bagmati river waters. They struggle and push towards their yearly appointment with Mrs Siva's bits. Some are lost in trance and display a total disregard for anything except the accomplishment of their task. I fear being crushed on the bridge approaching the temple. The crowd is so tightly packed I can lift my feet off the ground, levitating as we inch forward.

As the evening wears on, the crowd thins down enough for my feet to find walking space rather than shuffling. The troupe of street performers are still attracting an audience. They are acting out a play with a social message not a religious one – the issue of "under trial". One actor takes on the role of a youth that has been held in prison twice as long as the maximum jail sentence for his crime. Another, with the features of a European in clown make-up, is the Judge. The troupe perform this as comedy with two jailers collapsing of old age and the ever-youthful criminal scoring off his days of imprisonment on a cardboard box representing his cell. These scenes are punctuated with songs and dancing.

As I am about to leave, I lock eyes with one of the dancers. She returns the glance and holds it a moment longer. It's then that I recognise her. No longer dressed in white is that unmistakable face and posture of Sita. I am so overcome I push towards the front of the crowd. When the dance finishes I follow her, like a stalker. I am not sure how she recognized me in my disguise and I'm unsure if she did. I cast my blanket off into the street and elbow through the crowd to reach her.

When I approach, she stops and turns. I step forward and attempt a handshake.

'Do you remember me?' I say in Nepali. 'We met in Lumbini. I'm the son of James Munro. The Moni Baba was my father's guru.' She hesitates, then nods and gives me a Namaste with a respectful bow. Crowds push past, seemingly oblivious to the fact that this is Sita Kumari, companion of the Moni Baba. Here she is, standing before me in one of Hinduism's most holy sites, dressed as a traditional dancer. I feel like shouting with joy.

Sita gestures for me to follow her. We walk out towards the Ring Road where a small tuk tuk is parked full of baskets and props. She sits on the street kerb as I stand awkwardly beside her. There is a long silence as she removes her make-up with a cloth.

'I remember you,' she says in Nepali. Then to my surprise she continues, in English, 'I also heard you are looking for me.'

'I visited the temple in Assan for three months to see if I could find you. It is where the Baba told me to look for you.'

'People there do not yet know I am in the Kathmandu valley. I do not wish to return there yet. I'm staying in another town in the valley… Bhaktapur.'

'How long have you been performing street theatre?'

She doesn't seem to understand the expression street theatre. I ask once more in broken English with crude Nepali thrown in. She understands the words street circus and we continue the conversation.

Sita tells me she met the circus group in a square in Bhaktapur some months ago. They come from India and are managed by a Frenchman. 'He is the one dressed as the clown judge in the performance we just finished.' She tells me they have all been very kind to her, but they are soon moving back to India.

'Where are you staying?'

For the past month she has stayed at an Ashram run by an

American Swamy in Bhaktapur. 'They want me to teach yoga but I have enjoyed dancing and no one recognises me, wearing so much make-up.'

Sita continues, trying out her English skills more answering questions.

I ask if she has heard anything of the Baba and if she intends to return to him. She gives an answer I do not fully understand. Something about her not really having left him. That she carries him with her, now more than ever. She says she's tried to keep her identity secret but it has been difficult and now a few people in the Ashram know who she is.

Another woman performer approaches us and gives Sita a loose fitting dress. Sita stands, slips the dress over her head and skilfully removes her costume underneath. For a brief moment I see the profile of her figure, and it's very different from when she demonstrated yoga in Lumbini. The loose fitting dress suggests that Sita is pregnant.

As she gathers her belongings it seems as if the conversation is over. Sita gives me another respectful Namasti. I fumble one back. I'm so full of curiosity and desperate that our meeting will not end here. I say in haste that the Baba had mentioned a man called the Avadhoot, and that she could help me find him.

59

We sit on the street kerb and I speak of the reason I came to Nepal and how it has taken me so long to find the Moni Baba. She says that my time searching is not long compared to some.

She tells me that in her former life (as a living goddess Kumari), she could never let her feet touch the ground. She lived her whole life elevated. She could not leave the confines of her house without being carried. 'Perhaps,' she says, 'that is why I like dancing so much now.'

Sita tells me she enjoys improving her English language. That she understands more than she can speak but she has some trouble with my accent. 'I am receiving some lessons from the American Swamy at the Ashram.'

I ask if she personally knows this man who knew my father ... Mahindranath Avadhoot. She hesitates for a moment then acknowledges that she does know him. I ask if she will introduce me to him. She asks if I know he is a Sanyasin and like the Baba she warns me that he will not talk to me of ungodly things. I tell her yeah yeah yeah I understand all too well. I am supposed to meet someone who is unlikely to talk to me.

The rest of the performers all gather around looking ready to head home. Sita introduces me to JJ...Jean Jacques, the French clown judge and manager of the troupe. She introduces me as the son of James Munro.

'Ah, the famous English yogi?'

I cough out the words 'Scot's yogi,' to everyone's confusion.

Sita suggests I come to meet her at the Ashram in Bhaktapur in a few days' time. I agree and bow to them both with respect. I refit the head cloth part of my disguise and walk off.

As I cast an affectionate glance back towards Pashupitinath, I recall hearing much about the magical powers of this temple. I did not expect such a blessing as the delivery of Sita.

BHAKTAPUR TOWN, THE THIRD CITY IN THE KATHMANDU VALLEY, IS A gem of Newari art. It is preserved in its Middle-Ages glory, with the help of German aid money. The red bricks used for its construction are made directly from the land that surrounds the town. Large smoking chimneys mark where the bricks are moulded and seasonally fired in kilns. The narrow pedestrian streets are so small that porters with large loads need to stand aside to let each other pass. The layout of the town conjures up images of feudal lords and peasant farmers. But the calendars on display in these tiny street shops carry the year 2031, dated some forty-four years ahead of our 1987. On the backs of their bullock carts, people here have already comfortably rolled into the twenty-first century.

There is a cloth banner across the entrance to the Varanasi Ashram that reads in English, "Welcome All Spiritual Followers of the Vedas". There is also a small sign with the same words in plastic letters at the door, along with a painted hand pointing up the staircase. The ashram is run by a couple of young men, the

American Swamy from California and his young Indian partner from Bihar.

As I reach the top of the stairs, a western woman appears unannounced from a side door and with energetic spirituality pelts me with flowers. Another three young American women call out a chorus of Namasti's in a Texan accent. Their blonde hair is the colour of dried straw and they wear matching saris made of fine sackcloth.

As I stand outside the door of the yoga room, I hear the final moments of a talk. I glance in at a mixture of European, Indian and American pilgrims. Swamy Y, short for Yogivendranath, is asking everyone to open their inner self and let the vibrations of light enter their being.

'Open your hearts.' He gestures, with the palms of his hands facing upwards, in a Buddha pose. Some respond by shouting, 'I feel a presence!' whilst others chant the word OM.

I stand back, not wanting to be seen cringing. I watch as Swamy Y embraces the front row of men and women with strong meaningful hugs. Each devotee gazes into his eyes with admiration. One middle-aged woman does not let him go and hugs well beyond any acceptable guru-cuddle time limit. He tries to move on but succumbs with a smile until helpers peel her off him. When he finally makes it to the end of the line he looks over and acknowledges me.

Swamy Y asks everyone to hold hands and form a circle. I duck further behind the curtain for fear of being included. The group takes up its position as the back-up singers in saris begin, "Krishna ri, Krishna ri, Hari Hari Hari Krishna ri." Those who know the words sing along, others close their eyes and let their heads sway to the beat. "Subramunyan, Subramunyan, Chan Mukanatha Subramunyan."

As the crowd slowly disperses past me down the stairs into the street, I'm ushered into the herbal tea room to meet Swamy Y. He seems short for an American, with the look of a young Robert Redford, long fair hair, tied back into a ponytail.

'Hello,' I say. 'I'm James Munro.'

'Namaskar,' he says, bringing his hands up to his forehead.

'I've arranged to meet here with Sita.'

'You are the one who has been with the Moni Baba?'

As the Baba's name is mentioned the last couple to leave the yoga room suddenly turn and step back, to touch me, before disappearing, muttering in excitement down the stairs.

'Yes, that's true. Sita and I arranged to meet here, but we didn't fix an exact time. I came by on chance. I can come back if it's not convenient.'

'No, it's fine, she is just taking someone through a healing session. She will be finished shortly. Why don't you have a fresh fruit juice and I'll send her through. I heard the Baba talked about you after his last teaching?'

'Really... it was likely my father who had the same name as I have. For one famous for being undiscovered, his words sure get around here fast.'

'Oh, he's not undiscovered, he's just hard to discover. He's been a guru to the King of Nepal and many more influential people for years. Did you know he studied with the great Shivapuri Baba? We must talk sometime. I've never actually met him. You are a very lucky man to have spoken to him. We are very honoured to have Sita here with us now.'

As Swamy Y finishes talking, Sita appears at the door from a small studio room. She is dressed in the same canvas coloured sari of the Ashram. I can see a massage couch and a large mirror in the background. A well-dressed Nepali woman bows her head to the Swamy as she leaves. Sita smiles and gestures for me to join her in the herbal tea room while Swamy Y trots down the stairs after the woman.

60

Once seated facing Sita with a health juice in hand, she asks how I am. Without thinking, I say, 'I'm good, but it's interesting to see you here in this yoga fairground.' She looks back at me as if I'm complimenting the place.

Sita tells yes it's a good place to learn better English. I tell her in my best Nepali that she speaks very good English and that there are schools that specialise in teaching languages. Then I add – 'you don't need to learn English here in a school of Bhoga.'

For the first time, Sita senses my hostility towards the ashram. I see her expression change. She asks me why I have come back to Nepal if I don't like it. The word "back" takes me by surprise since I'm unaware that she knows anything about my childhood here.

'I came back to find out more about my dad. I was so young when he died here.'

'And are you now satisfied?'

I consider the question seriously for a moment, knowing how much I've learned here and not wanting to sound negative.

'I've spent more than a year living here, much of it waiting to find clues about the Moni Baba's whereabouts. I missed you both in Muktinath by one day and it took months before I found you and the Baba in Lumbini. So far I still don't know much about my dad's life here. It's hardly the detective story of the century.'

'When you spoke to the Baba, what did he say?'

'The day you left I had an audience with him at Thangboche. He told me you would know how to get in touch with this Avadhoot man. That he knew my father and that he was definitely a person I should talk to.'

Sita goes silent for a moment, breathes deep, then continues.

'And now what will you do?'

'I thought the Baba was hard to find, but even fewer people want to talk about the Avadhoot.'

'There is good reason why people are silent about the Avadhoot.'

'I know – he's a Sanyasin.'

'Yes, people here, how you say... respect that.'

'But can you help me to see him and will he actually talk to me about my father?'

'He will not talk of un-godly things. It is his vow. Ke gurne?'

'What to do? Well my dad is a pretty godly subject for me and surely he was respected as a yogi enough for this Avadhoot to give me an audience. The Baba told me that my search should become my yoga. So if I ever visit him, I can talk about the godly things dad said and leave out the ungodly loss of him and what that meant to me. Is that a way around the ban on ungodly talk?'

'Ban... what does this mean?'

'Forbidden... *nisedha!*'

When I speak fast, Sita has difficulty with my accent, but she seems to understand my meaning intuitively, if not every word.

'Maybe, it will take time to find a suitable meeting with the Avadhoot. No one's yoga is easy, it involves that most difficult of asanas... how you say, prana patience.'

As Sita speaks I find myself concentrating on every word to make sure I understand her. Her teeth are white and form the lower point of a brilliant triangle with her large gleaming eyes. Her mouth has difficulty to accommodate new English words and she displays an embarrassed smile when she struggles. I look intently at each movement her lips make. This slender strong woman I witnessed in Lumbini and the Khumbu, now sits behind a pinewood table in front of a poster of a glamorous model in a yoga pose. This is the source of my discomfort and negativity.

My image of Sita is rooted in the environment I discovered her in and I want to preserve her there, not here, in a herbal tea room in front of a Cindy Crawford power-yoga poster. She glows, like most women who are pregnant, with that confidence that something preordained is happening to them.

'How do you like living here?' I ask.

'At first I was with JJ the French performer staying at the house of Trilockia, a Newari artist who has helped the circus group a lot.'

'If it becomes too crowded I have space in my house in Assan.'

'Thank you, but the circus will travel soon and it's easier to stay close to them until they leave.' Sita pauses for a moment then continues. 'I'm expecting a child.' Sita looks at me as if she knows I already know. 'No one here knows.'

'Yes, I noticed the wee lump near your lower chakra at Pashupati.'

'I will stay here, teach yoga and learn English, until the baby is born.'

Swamy Y comes back into the herb room with another private customer for Sita. This time the lady is older and is helped out of a wheelchair by a tassel-haired girl in a dress she has long outgrown. Two young men carry the woman into the studio while the girl pushes the wheelchair under the stairs.

I quickly suggest to Sita that we meet again and she nods an approval. With her head bowed in respect to the older woman, she follows her into the studio.

61

For the next few weeks I regularly visit Sita at the Ashram. In a wave of new energy, I hardly notice what the city environment is depriving me of. I've become so emboldened by practicing the 'patience' posture I've forgotten that in places such as towns, buying time requires money.

Sita likes talking to me in English. She has begun to read English newspapers and enjoys local news from *The Rising Nepal*. I look forward to our chats in the herbal tea room about everything from what spices are best for dhal, to her knowledge of the 'psychology' of yoga.

During one encounter, I ask why she decided to leave the Moni Baba's company so abruptly.

'I'd reached a stage of control where nothing affected me emotionally. A stage the Baba had warned me about.'

'Are you saying you walked away from your guru, pregnant... without any emotion?'

'No. It is complicated but let my English try explain. The Baba has helped me for years to control all the elements in my life since he became my guru. It was he that sensed, what do you call it... a mood for self destruction in me.'

I am so interested to hear this and resist asking Sita if the Baba is the father of her child. Instead, I continue encouraging Sita to talk in Nepali as well as English to make things easier. She is beginning to pick up my Scottish accent and frankly it's a bit weird.

Sita tells me the Baba found in her a devotional flaw that he linked to the mind of a lazy religious worshiper not a yogini. He told her that the time had come to move her skills into a different environment. Only then could she truly appreciate the levels of vulnerability which exists for the others she was likely to instruct. When she learned how to share her physical presence, her feelings, her responsibilities with others, she would become a better yogini. She needed to understand at least some of the emotions that others encounter in their daily lives.

The Baba told Sita that with him she would continue to live a sheltered life. Better she learn how to live with a universal mix of feelings and to develop emotions that come from caring and sharing responsibilities with others. She should remember that no relationship should ever be taken for granted, including the one closest to her... especially with him. Sharing her skills and becoming active in other ways with people, is different from being the constant recipient of admiration and affection from a distant unknowing audience.

'If I wanted to, I could have stayed with the Baba as a giver of advice to others,' she tells me. 'I am qualified to repeat his teachings, but do not yet know how to create my own.'

'Surely everyone who chooses to be a teacher,' I say, 'needs to rely on the wisdom of those before us. Not everything you teach is newly discovered, most all of it is based on the experience of others?'

'Yes, being a spokesperson for the wisdom of other sages,

makes a teacher. But a guru relates individually and teaches only when they have accomplished their personal yoga.'

I recognise this point from dad's book... that a teacher tells you how to do it... and a guru tells you how they did it. Sita tells me the Baba gave her one last teaching before she left but it was to remain their secret.

'I guess if you tell me, you will have to kill me,' I say. There is complete confusion in Sita.

'It's a joke from spy movies,' I add.

'Spy movies?'

'I'll take you to a spy movie one day. It is an experience that will become the foundation of your new life, to help you create a lasting sanctuary for your thoughts and feelings, amidst the confusing real world of emotions and relationships.'

Sita smiles in ignorance and I immediately regret taking things too far.

AFTER SEVERAL MORE WEEKS OF TEA-SHOP MEETINGS AND LATE-night discussions, I tell Sita that I would like to include some of her anecdotes in my account of the Moni Baba's teachings. She does not object to this. She now regularly walks me to the edge of the town late at night after our chats.

One evening as the moon rises behind the mountains like a large white dinner plate, we stand at the usual departure point on the road and Sita asks me about my relationships with women.

As a language lesson this feels uncomfortable to me. Sita seems interested in how western women organize their relationships and who gives permission for couples to get together. I tell her in the West it is rare for relationships to be organised. I state that relationships are one of the only aspects of our lives that is not organized. Everything from birth registration to death certificates and most in between, is organised for us as citizens. All our education and health care is organised, all our work requirements also structured, we are subjects that submit easily to the powers of organisation. Even our days of freedom, our holidays are organized once a year and booked in advance.

Sita asks if my holiday in Nepal has been organized.

I tell her no and it's the first time in my life that there is no one else to blame if things go wrong or I perceive that I'm not succeeding.

'What makes you think you are not succeeding?'

'Something every westerner remains forever organised towards. Obtaining money. At some point I'll have to organise some income or go home.'

Out of the blue, Sita mentions there is a possibility we might be able to visit the Avadhoot soon.

I'm taken aback, and realise I've become so engrossed in Sita, I've almost forgotten my goal.

Sita says she will take me unannounced to see the Avadhoot when he gives one of his rare public appearances. It will take place in a forest clearing in the Terai. Then she says I need to prepare myself for this meeting. She looks at me intensely when she says this.

'Why?'

I'll have to accept that an actual talk with him may only be possible if he grants it. It will take a couple of days of travel together to get there and back.

As I take in this news we bow and give our usual platonic namastes. I walk back the eight miles across open fields to Assan. Taxis have become relatively expensive.

Growling dogs follow me from house to house, breaking the silence, handing over barking responsibility like a baton in a relay race. I lose them in the open fields past the potters' houses in Thimi. The idea of travelling for a couple of days with Sita puts a new spring in my step.

6 2

Having written copious notes of our conversations and the teachings of the Moni Baba, Sita surprises me one day by asking about my mother. I associate her curiosity with the fact she is getting closer to giving birth.

Sita asks me how my mother took my father's death. She asks if mum ever kept in contact with dad's friends here in Nepal, or if she had ever taken another husband.

I tell her much was unknown to my mother about how my dad died. That aside from one trip back to Nepal when I was about ten years old she's had little contact with people here, at least to my knowledge. And no, my mother had never taken another husband.

Sita then takes my hands and in an unusual gesture of affection, positions herself next to me. She tells me that she's made all the arrangements for us both to reach the Avadhoot's gathering. The sanyasin does not know we will attend. As she said before, 'You have to prepare yourself,' but then she adds 'for any anger it may provoke.'

'Anger, what do you mean by anger?'

'The Avadhoot is person… who knows most about your father's death.'

'Why should I be angry about that?'

In an emotional outburst of Nepali that I cannot fully understand, she tries to explain. I ask her to try to tell me in English.

'This sanyasin will not speak of ungodly things and will give you more questions than answers,' she continues.

'Don't worry, I won't collapse in grief if I don't get all my questions answered.' I sense her frustration with the English language.

'The Baba used to say…' she cuts herself off.

'Tell me.'

'The Moni Baba told me that the Avadhoot… is the man responsible for the death of James Munro.'

They don't come along that often, but here it is again. A short burst of words with such explosive meaning, they instantly alter priority thoughts in one's brain. For the second time in my recent life I am left to ponder the implications of a single sentence. When I ask Sita for more details, she pulls a Moni on me. She talks no more.

For days afterwards the consequences of what Sita has said sink in. If I'm truly to meet dad's murderer, I need to curb the hard-core attitude that's forming day by day. The pleasantries of yoga greetings are dropped and if I'm in the Ashram I no longer have the patience to listen to words of wisdom about how to cope with life. A growing part of me wants to be right there in front of this man to force answers about my dad… he will face my ungodly wrath.

I've always felt that everything I find out about my dad would be of help to me. I convinced myself before this trip I'd know more and therefore be happier. I now begin to imagine some darker scenarios on the horizon. A whole layer of new thoughts pile onto the surface of my freshly-constructed enlightenment.

When I was younger, I often imagined the graphic details of dad's death and these memories come back with force. I do feel a set of anger emotions, something Sita warned me against, reliving the brutality that took dad from me. I prepare myself to face someone I can finally blame for all the years of loss and hurt.

I ask Sita for more information but she has become very unco-operative, as if she's already said too much or the wrong thing. I fire questions at her and when she picks up my aggression she falls silent.

'Was the Avadhoot one of the bandits or a devotee who was with him? Was it a spontaneous act or was it planned? Was he the one who actually struck my dad down?'

Sita plays mum, except to give one Baba quote about how everyone recalls events differently – depending on how one is questioned.

Sita is clearly intimidated by my attitude. She is seeing a side of me that I don't want her to see. Her understanding of English conveniently disappears as if to block out the flood of questions. She learns several new curse words. We agree to take a few days' break from each other, then to meet and talk. This will give me personal time to think things through. She says she will gather more information about our journey, if I still choose to go.

6 3

A fter receiving a slow drip of yogic wisdom through this past year in Nepal, I am supposed to be more ready to tackle whatever life throws at me. It's frightening to feel this aggressive adrenaline rush in alongside my new fitness and strength. Both pose a potential danger to my own safety. I find myself in revenge mode, considering a number of options. I have been here long enough to form a picture of this person who may have murdered my dad. They are most likely calm and responsible and if made desperate, brutal Nepalis possess all the qualities that make good gurus and their sons the world's best soldiers.

As Chitraker the impersonator suggested... it is impossible to meditate at such times when so much is going on in the mind. It's not so much anger and hatred that's unbearable; it's the responsibility to do something about it.

As I run through imagined scenarios of dad's last moments, I must carefully consider what can be done about it after all this time. Would the authorities take action or even care about such an old case? No matter how many people this Avadhoot has helped since then, he must pay somehow.

I think announcing that I am James Munro junior, may be enough to heap guilt on this man. Then I think it through. Someone trained in the mastery of the human mind, unable to speak ungodly thoughts, having lived a lifetime in retreat and isolation; what could I really do to torment such a man?

I move on to the ridiculous. The idea of assassinating a sanyasin. I could secretly bury the body. Who will miss someone who is in retreat for years?

I go for walkabouts into Durbar Marg. I take seed to feed the doves, offerings for my forgiving side to return. I think back to my time in Barabasi, when days would fly by without any thoughts dwelling for more than a fleeting moment. Now my brain is so busy it hardly lets me sleep. I find some solace talking to Bahadur.

One night, Bahadur tells me that he served in the Gurkhas during the Falklands conflict. War suddenly seems an appropriate subject of conversation. I listen with enthusiasm to his stories as if the pupil is now ready for Sargent Bahadur to appear.

He tells me that the British army actively promoted the Gurkhas' reputation, to frighten Argentine troops into surrender. He describes in detail how the soldiers took advantage of night-vision weapons to wound as many of the enemy as possible, rather than kill them. Their plan simple, it took two fighting men to help save every injured man, depleting enemy numbers available to fight. Bahadur then tells me the gruesome story of a severed head that saved lives.

He tells me during one battle, the Gurkhas advanced trench by trench after the enemy had been shelled. Each trench contained dead enemy soldiers. The Gurkha were prepared for hand-to-hand combat if necessary but one group found a damaged corpse, with a soldier's head severed from it body. They took the head and threw it over open ground towards the next enemy trench to intimidate soldiers there.

He tells me that this one random act caused groups of inexperienced soldiers to surrender immediately. This same head was thrown into trench after trench with the same response. According to Bahadur, that head saved the lives of many young Argentinians and Gurkhas during the war. He said the dead Argentinian soldier deserved a memorial in the Falklands.

'The Argentinian soldiers believed we'd cut it off before the soldier was dead. We didn't do much fighting that day.'

Bahadur's story sounded like an honest admission rather than an exaggerated soldier's tale. I ask him a direct question.

'If someone killed your father,' I ask, 'what would you do if you found that person living a happy life, free from any punishment?'

'It could not happen here,' he says.

'What couldn't happen here?'

'No one who commits murder would be left unpunished.'

'You mean the police would arrest them?'

'The police, no, they work mostly in the city where there is more crime, but in the hills if someone kills your father, you or your family will find them and punish them. Police are not always involved.'

'Explain more. What sort of punishment are you talking about?'

'It depends. If it is a relative that kills a family member it's complicated. Husbands have killed their wives and this is not always avenged, unless there is a fully grown son. Wives have killed their husbands and children have killed a parent but that is very rare. If a father only has a daughter and is killed by a stranger, then relatives may suggest a punishment, seek compensation or take some revenge.'

'What do you mean, take revenge? Kill the murderer?'

'Not necessarily. If he was young, they might kill his father.'

'Shit, this is complicated. What has the father got to do with it? He's innocent in this, surely.'

'Ah but he's old… and the disgrace might be too much to bear. I know one such case. The father wanted to be punished instead of his son. Why are you asking me this?'

'Let me ask one more question. What if someone were to punish a well respected yogi… or a Sanyasin?'

'If a stranger kills a well respected person, they will often disappear without trace,' he laughs, 'become fertiliser for the rice paddies. If the victim is a holyman, followers might just rip the killer apart on the spot. This is a peaceful place… no one tolerates the killing of a holyman!'

64

Twenty-four hours before the Avadhoot is due to talk, Sita meets me late, on the assigned evening in Kathmandu. We board the overnight bus to Biratnager and talk for much of the journey. Sita is showing her baby bump prominently now. She talks about her life in more detail than ever, I suspect to distract my thoughts from the forthcoming meeting. Whatever the motive, she succeeds.

In the back seat of a mostly empty bus, Sita asks what age I was when I first became intimate with a woman.

I tell her I was around sixteen when I was curious enough to try but I was twenty-two when I lost my virginity. She thinks this is very very old for a man. She then asks questions about the complex set of emotions people feel afterwards.

'It was fun,' I say. 'I enjoyed the experience?'

'Why do you say this? Do you believe pleasure is the incentive for sex?'

'It has to be one of the incentives, perhaps not the objective. Whether conception takes place or not, people keep trying again and again, don't they?'

Sita says with some authority it is we who assign pleasure to the act. I'm not sure where this conversation is leading until she asks me if I have any knowledge of Tantra yoga.

'Tantra is not about sex, it simply recognises sex as another impulse suitable for the application of yoga.'

Sita describes Tantra as the ultimate exploration of intimacy. The exposure of strengths and weakness that couples make towards each other in a relationship.

I don't fully understand what she is trying to say, but it's an interesting new subject for us to discuss.

'Tantra is one of the earliest yoga disciplines,' Sita continues. 'A study of the sexual act helps people refine their perception of sex, its importance and yes the pleasure. We have religious monuments dedicated to the sexual act.'

'Yes… I've been in such a place.'

'Tantra helps people overcome shyness and fear of sex and ensures that the natural reproductive system is finely tuned for when it is needed.'

Sita tells me the superstitious beliefs surrounding her time as the Kumari and how the Baba had liberated her mind from these beliefs. One in particular haunted her as a child… that any man who has sex with an ex-kumari would die!

Hatha yoga teaching prepared her confidence for the physical act but Tantra teachings helped destroy the myths about this new level of intimacy. She confesses to having felt fearful and ordinary after sex, but the Baba explained how we must view ourselves rather than our station. She says the Baba encouraged this discovery of herself even if it resulted in motherhood. That she could now fearlessly embrace this path.

I see another opportune moment to ask who the father is, but the Tantric gods intervene. A few miles before reaching Biratnager we are at our destination.

I take Sita's hand and help the pregnant yogini off the bus. She is only a few weeks from her due date, and has calculated this from the date of conception.

It's early dawn and Sita summons a local farmer with his bullock cart to take us the remaining distance into the forest. The walk might have been easy for both of us, but because of Sita's condition we are cautious. The quiet creaking of the wheels and the gentle thump of hoofs are in pleasant contrast to the dusty, rattling old bus we've left behind. The sun is rising and time slows once more to that pleasantly familiar pedestrian pace.

As we climb off the bullock cart, Sita points to a group of people crossing a dry field into the forest. It's the rural morning rush hour, people making the maximum use of light, before it becomes too hot in the day. We give the farmer a few extra rupees since he has come a little out of his way to drop us here.

We follow the path and the air covers us both with a thin film of dust, left by the now out of sight workers. As the sun rises higher, I see lines of sweat showing on Sita's face. She smiles at me in a nervous way that is very out of character. She asks if I am prepared.

I assure her I will keep my cool with this Avadhoot and I touch my father's book in my thigh pocket for support.

As we reach the trees, two paths veer in different directions. We follow the one showing the most signs of recent usage. We find small pieces of saffron coloured cloth tied to branches, marking a direction to an even smaller path. Twenty minutes later we come to a clearing where a shelter made of twigs and newly cut foliage has been constructed.

There is a crowd of about forty people sitting. It is the same people I assumed were workers heading to their fields. I look at Sita and she gives me a supportive smile.

A queue of around ten people are standing outside the shelter. The morning sunlight now blazes horizontal strokes through the dust and devotees into the clearing. It torches the foliage of the hut with light. Sita and I sit at the back of the group in some shade.

Some people turn to look at us but I'm now covered in enough dust to blend in. Slowly, one by one people, in the queue enter the hut and I hear a muffled exchange with its occupant. On a couple of occasions, I hear a duet of voices chanting mantras in Sanskrit. It is a comical assortment of chants. One chant sounds like the popular British armed-forces song 'It's a Long Way to Tipperary'. Is the Avadhoot an ex-Gurkha?

My stomach begins to flutter further as the last person in the queue leaves the hut. Sita senses my nervous energy and leans over to take my hand just as Mr. Mahendranath Avadhoot appears from the small door.

The man is completely naked and covered in white ash with three red stripes across his forehead. He has a long flowing grey beard and hair that's matted thick in two uneven clumps on the right side of his head, like a Rasta, He is a wild-looking specimen.

He strides to the front of the crowd and looks over the seated followers before looking down at the ground. His eye sockets are blackened like an empty skull and all he carries is a large set of mala beads. I become aware that Sita is looking very closely at me.

After an introductory chant, the Avadhoot begins to talk in Nepalese, and slowly becomes more animated and louder. He talks about fulfilment never coming in a single dose. Enlightenment is a continual fight against depression, sadness and anger. It comes through a diet of actions we all have to undertake daily. It is not a vaccination from a guru.

The Avadhoot's anecdotal language is unusual as he continues on the same theme. The spirit has to be nurtured like the body, with a regular diet of healthy thought.

God is not love he says, love is like Vitamin C, it is not retained by the body but needs to be replenished. Taking guidance from chronic complainers is akin to consuming junk food, eventually you'll have health problems. If you believe that God is ever present, know that love is not, except through our actions and therefore our thoughts.

I begin to wonder how such an expression as 'junk food' can enter the vocabulary of a recluse.

He talks a little more in Nepali and asks for any questions from the group. An Indian follower asks in English about his chances of redemption after he performed a mercy killing of a holy cow that was sick at his farm. He asks as if the Gods may not forgive him.

The Avadhoot takes a stance with feet slightly apart and gives a reply about killing the cow in English that suddenly sets off a spark of recognition in me. I shake my head for clarity. I stand up. I hear Sita shout my name and I ignore her. I walk towards this man and hear Sita call a warning to the Avadhoot. He turns and faces me. I walk straight up to him.

He lowers his face to look down. I push my forehead against his, lightly, butting heads like baby rams playing.

'Dad?'

I ask again, but I know the answer. I saw it first in his stance. I heard it in the word farm, which he pronounced as 'farum'. The Scottish accent on this this one word was like a kick in the stomach. His posture had sent a chill sweeping down my spine. I look over at Sita who knows instantly I've recognised him, and she nods a confirmation. Things have suddenly fallen out of place.

65

Imagine for a moment an extraordinary occurrence in your life. A sort of John Fowles moment, like at the end of 'The French Lieutenant's Woman' when he proposes two endings to the story. The main character acts out one scenario and stays with the woman, while in another ending we explore what happens when he leaves the woman behind. Both possible endings, both believable, the consequences separated by one moment's choice.

I now face such a moment. I'm tempted to walk away but decide to confront this man who made a life-changing choice so many years ago.

He steps away from me and begs the crowd to forgive him, that he must now retire. He doesn't acknowledge me but moves off. He has no idea what is about to change for him.

I look over to Sita, who appears concerned. She set this up and I have a lot of questions for her. There is also the Moni Baba, with his selective descriptions of my dad's fate. What a pair... alongside my dad, what a trio they all are. My mind races in this new reality.

'What a fucking quartet,' I say aloud, wondering about my mother's role in all this.

I feel wave after wave of realisation wash over me. Dad speaks to some more members of the crowd as they begin to leave. He retains the aloofness of a guru, but everything I hear him say now holds an alternative if not opposite meaning.

The main crowd disperses and a few followers gather around the Avadhoot to ask questions. I push my way to the front and say, 'We have to talk.'

As soon as he looks me in the eye, the Avadoot hangs his head again. Sita approaches and tells me she will wait for me in the village where we left the bullock cart. She and the Avadhoot exchange a soft namasti, as if they know each other. She leaves in silence. The Avadhoot turns and walks into his hut. I follow, walking straight in behind him and sit on the ground opposite.

As time passes, people outside realise they are unlikely to have their audience with the Avadhoot, at least today, and leave. They don't interrupt my encounter with their guru. Within an hour everyone has gone and I'm left alone, with my ashen-faced father.

'Does Mother know that you're alive?'

'Aye!'

This is all I'm able to get out of this man. Despite my questions and outbursts, he remains silent. There is no sign of emotion whatso-ever. As darkness falls, I decide to stay. I'm not going to leave until I have an explanation... either from a Sanyassin or a father. My body language displays the hostility I feel growing towards him but my stay in Barabase trained me well. I find I can play the silent yogi game too.

It is a challenge in sleep deprivation. I am tired and annoyed, but keep it under control. My anger is poised on the tip of my tongue, ready to strike if he speaks. I sit and move and sit again in silence. He hardly moves. He uses a carved wooden stick, placed under his chin to rest his head. He's better equipped for this bout of silence. I feel like kicking the stick, from under his chin.

'Did Mother see you when she came back to Nepal?'

'Aye!'

Another day, another aye! Nothing ungodly has left his lips so far. I realise my presence is his torture. No feelings appear to disturb his demeanour. He takes an occasional drink of water and offers me dried fruit he has stored in a pot.

I realise that I've gone through life never expecting a moment like this, never imagining a reunion with my dad. He on the other hand must have known this was possible. I want to smother him with this blanket of lost time, to make him reconsider the time left. I cage him in the consequences of his actions. I am his cell and at this moment in time, he cannot escape unless he talks to me.

On day three, I find myself trying too hard to stay awake. It becomes difficult and seems ridiculous. I've hardly slept – yet I know he has. He has snored his way upright through two long evenings. I feel light-headed and catch him smiling as my head jerks forward to wake me up. I sense a mild break in the tension between us as he stands and goes outside, where I follow him, seeing he's gone out to pee. I giggle at the sustained seriousness of everything.

Just as I'm about to attempt more questioning, a well-dressed village woman comes into the hut with a small child and some rice and dhal in a bowl. She brings a large portion of rice, as if she knows the Avadhoot has company. A large clay pot of water with a lid and a ladle are then refilled and positioned in the centre of the hut.

The woman places the food bowl onto three large stones, the only furniture in the room. A brass yogi's pot containing some coins sits at the open entrance. She takes a stainless steel cup from her basket with her right hand, then respectfully touching her right elbow with her left hand, pours me a drink. The woman pushes the child, a fourish-year-old boy, forward towards the

Avahdoot. He looks at the child and then towards me with an uncomfortable quick look. He blesses the woman with some red Tika taken from his own forehead and pushes the ash, caked like raspberry mash, onto the forehead of the child. As she turns to leave with the child, I notice the boy has vulture coloured hair and green eyes, just like mine.

I shake my head as the couple leave.

'Shite, dad!'

The woman looks back and smiles as if I have just chanted a holy mantra. She vanishes as quickly as she appeared.

'I suppose the one thing about being a Sanyasin and only speaking Godly things,' I continue, 'is you'll not have much to say. Are you a devotee-fucker, dad?'

'There are mare,' he says.

'Mare what?'

'Mare children!'

'God... here you are naked in the bush.... with your willie swinging around on its day off. What are you actually doing with the people here?'

There is a pause before dad lets out a burst of laughter, loud and unrestrained.

'What's so funny?'

'I'm sorry... the thought of a lingum being called a willie and having a day off. It just got me. It's something Billy Connolly would say. Not something you'd read in the Vedas.'

'So was that... Mrs Avadhoot?'

'No,' he continues.

'Tell me more then,' I say. 'You seem to have broken your vow, unless Billy Connolly is a God you can talk about.'

'She is the wife of the local headman.'

'You've been banging the headman's wife?'

'No, no. They came as a couple to see me, together, as many couples do, when the wife appears to be barren. They ask for a blessing from the Avadhoot to help make the wife fertile.'

'So it's a blessing you gave her?'

'Society here expects help from a Sanyasin. I gave them a short puja, then a fertility thread to tie to a gate at the local temple and she paid a couple of visits at the right time of the month. It's a clinical procedure and not sexual. It's rare and it doesn't work all the time. Sometimes, however, couples do get the gift of life they both desire.'

'What if the woman is infertile and not the man?'

'When the woman truly is barren... it's a shame. There is more stigma attached to being childless here than accepting a Sanyasin's blessing. And there's little else anyone can do for such couples.'

'So you are an expert at leaving children for others to bring up?'

'Awk... in truth, others manage well, much better than me.'

'How many wee step-brothers and sisters do I have out there? Hundreds? Thousands? You've had twenty years of spreading Munro seed to the barren women of the sub-continent?'

'Don't judge these things by western Christian values.'

I sit quietly and for a change he talks.

'Rural societies and their economies here depend on procreation. It's not a leisure activity, not a selling tool for products, not something exploited by a massive entertainment industry. What large cities achieve with the regular influx of people from outside can only be achieved in villages by creating more children. New life and young energy is fundamental. Each of the families I mention have had problems with conception – not in having intercourse. These women are certainly not in love with me, they are not sex slaves of a guru, they come for a practical reason, artificial insemination. Husbands also dinnae bother, they accept lighter skin and green eyes of their child. I help the community as any a Sanyasin might.'

'Look at you,' I shout. 'Look at you. You're a manky fuck-up... living on the ground, eating gruel. You're a fucking tramp... with the emphasis on fucking.' I scream the last word.

'I don't live here... I'm not always like this.' His phrasing is slow and deliberate and he sounds submissive, no longer cocky.

I calm down after this outburst. I pull out dad's book from my pocket and slap it with my hands. 'A true mystic is someone who helps remove the mystery of life. Are these words familiar to you?' I say it again, but not as loud. 'What about removing the mystery of your death for me?'

He falls silent again.

'What could possibly have attracted you to a life like this, instead of coming home with your family?'

A tear begins to run down my cheek. It's a shock to feel I'm actually crying. I wipe my eyes before he sees it and I feel the grit on my face along with a block in my throat.

'Why did you fake your death? Why did you choose to stay here? And what is it with your fucking wife... my deceiving Mother?'

'I'm sorry. Sleep and I'll tell you.'

I lie flat on my back in death posture, and breathe deep with exhaustion.

66

My shoulders are aching with the force of sleeping in the same position on the ground overnight. The Avadhoot, in contrast, seems happy sitting up. There's no question he is winning the endurance test.

'I expected to meet you, one day, and so I have an explanation ready and rehearsed.'

'Why wait four days to tell me?'

'I sensed the early atmosphere too emotional and not conducive to an explanation.'

I find difficulty associating this man with the images and memories I have of dad. Amidst the long grey hair and the leathery sun-baked skin I see that his teeth are well kept and his physical condition is in good shape for his age. Everything but his voice fits the role he has chosen for himself. There seems little of James Munro senior left but what is there, is struggling to communicate with me.

'Ok, give me your prepared pitch.'

'There's not one day gone by that I haven't thought about you and Helen. My decision to stay here was made in haste with the complete understanding of your mother. We did not intend it to be a permanent separation. Once made, however, it could not be changed. And neither of us could afford to let regret take hold too deeply. It's brought me a sadness I live with everyday. This explanation is for your ears only. It may not answer all your questions, but it's the truth.'

'I'm all ears.'

'I have difficulty in speaking English now because I no longer use it and it's the language that holds my most painful thoughts and decisions.'

'Bear the pain.'

'It's very simple, son,' he swallows. 'We had completely run out of money and we were down to a pouch of cash that contained only the airfare home. You got sick and the doctor here said that we'd need to go to India or Bangkok to have you looked at properly. There was something wrong in your gut, you couldn't sleep, you were losing weight, but you were also bloated. It was at a time when I was just about to trek with the Moni Baba into the hills. I discussed it with your mum and we figured that if I disappeared for a bit she could claim insurance money to help settle you both back home.'

'That's it? You did it for the insurance money?'

'Yes. Aye... that's it! We did not think things through very carefully at the time and I didnae anticipate the sort of sophistication they'd now have to track down people who commit fraud. I dreamt up the scheme in a world before computers. Your mother and I thought naively that after a year or so I would be able to sneak back into Britain and we could be together again. With a new name, in a new place – you'd have your dad back. We planned to live somewhere remote in the Highlands.

'Your mother didn't come back here for two years, she told me how suspicious the insurance agents had been. Without the British Embassy's confirmation that a corpse had been found, they had been very slow to pay out. She also described how difficult it might be for me to get back into Britain. We were in despair. She was in fear of being caught and what that it might do to her and her family as well as to you and the life she had begun to build for you in Scotland. It was friends and relatives who supported you both far more than the insurance money, but the price of getting caught meant a huge lot more. The idea of prison, and the betrayal that would be felt by friends was too much for your mother. So that's it. I had no hatred of my family, just a stupid idea that seemed like a solution at the time.'

'I can't believe this or that I was never told.'

'You have to ask your mother about that. It's the truth. It was the easiest thing in the world to arrange, in fact frighteningly easy, right up to the point of my disappearance. My folks were dead. Your mother's folks still don't know or suspect anything. One of the thoughts that kept me going in the early years was the knowledge that I had provided you both with a fresh start from a pretty desperate situation. That you've had a good education and few financial worries.'

'I don't remember being sick when we went home.'

'No... and here's the cracking bit of the story. It turned you had intestinal worms. Helen told me much later that when she got you to the doctor in Scotland they gave you one dose of medicine and you passed out a toilet bowl of pin worms and were fine after that. There – but for a parasite, our lives could have been very different.'

'No one else in Scotland knows?'

'No one! When we first arrived in Nepal I was smitten by the teaching of the Moni Baba but I couldnae shake off the worry that I might not get a job back in Thatcher's Britain. Helen's parents didn't communicate with us and ironically it was them who insisted that we take out life insurance before we drove off into the wilds. We lived here watching our savings run out. One hundred thousand pounds' insurance money seemed a lot in those days. The temptation grew, the longer we stayed and the poorer we got. This idea became a solution just waiting for the right time.'

'So how did you stage your death?'

'That was the easiest part. There are many here who understand a person's wish to become a Sanyasin. It was easy to convince a few of the Baba's followers that a westerner would have to be declared dead in order to have the freedom necessary to become a Sanyasin. We thought first that an accident could happen to me, but we were sure it would be necessary to produce some sort of evidence or show remains. When a group of rogue Kampa were reported to be robbing people over in the West, it seemed that the perfect time had arrived. I put the finishing touches to my yoga book – we didn't even have a publisher at the time. Two eyewitness accounts from a remote part of Nepal were all that was necessary to report my murder. There was a sudden interest in the book. In many ways, as you can see, your dad James Munroe senior did die that day, and the few people here who knew respect that choice. That book was written with you in mind.' He leans over and touches my copy of his book.

'Well, I never got to the lesson on faking death yoga. Was the Moni Baba a part of all this?'

'The Baba is aware of what happened but he took no part in the scheme. It was entirely my invention, with Helen's approval. Only two other people plus the Baba and Helen ever knew the full story.'

'Was one of these people Sita?'

He ignored my question. There was no shutting up the silent one now.

'I sneaked once into Kathmandu to see your mother before you went back to Scotland. I came into your room while you slept. You looked poorly. That was the hardest moment in my life.' He stares at me in remembrance, fighting back emotion in his voice.

'It was hell to say a final goodbye to you, without being able to wake you up. In your room in the Dhobi Ghat, Helen and I cried like we were victims of a tragedy. Yet we were victims of a solution of our own making. There we were, all together, with the prospect of financial security at last, but with our emotions in shreds. It was a tragedy, of our own design.' He pulled back his long flowing grey hair to reveal an earring with a small cutting of vulture coloured hair attached to it. 'This is yours,' he says. James Munro senior, the Avadhoot and Sanyasin, sniffles deeply.

'I clipped this piece of hair from you that night. I realised that I would not be there when you needed me most. Not around to take you to school, watch you grow or see you play. I relinquished the most precious ambitions in my life in order to give myself the chance to study yoga so I could cope with life. What irony.

'I vowed back then and there, that if I was going to study yoga I would do it as thoroughly as any western or outsider has ever done before, as a penance.'

'And so who now judges you on your career choice!'

He stands then steps forward and helps me up. 'You are my judge and jury.' He pulls me towards him and a cloud of white ash takes to the air like talcum powder.

67

The Headman's wife returns with more food and a bag of clothes. She is again accompanied by my step-brother.

When dad sees me looking at them he says, 'There's only three others in total, not hundreds, not dozens of secret Munro children. It's a pretty limited amount of rumpy, over the years I've been here.'

'So what's sustained you all this time?'

'I don't live here. This is a temporary place that's erected each year for his visit to this village. I have a permanent home in Dhoti, in the far west of the country. You're welcome to come visit if you like.'

'Maybe, one day. I have someone waiting for me at the roadside village. Sita, the Baba's…'

'Yes. I know.'

'Sita is pregnant and is due in a few weeks. I should go find her… if she's still there.'

'Is it your child?'

'No. Maybe it's the Baba's. But that seems unlikely given his age.'

'Don't underestimate the powers of a yogi.'

'Nowadays, there's more interest in yoga than when you left Scotland.'

'Oh, so people teach yoga there?'

'Yes, but some teachers are very shallow and others claim to be gurus and succeed only in screwing up the most vulnerable portions of humanity.'

'Well, now you've found the real deal. A naked, unshaven, ash-painted Scottish yogi who chants ex-army songs in the remote forest clearings of Nepal!'

'Hey, what is it with the ex-army songs? I could have sworn I heard villagers singing the tune, 'It's a Long Way to Tipperary'.'

Dad laughs in a quick outburst. 'I'm no good at tunes for chants, so I make up the lyrics for prayers then sing them to an old tune. No one here knows the old songs my grandfather used to sing. The Avadhoot's mantras are well known for their marching beat.'

'I can picture it,' I say, 'a whole temple full of people, chanting to 'Hitler Has Only Got One Ball'!

'I should make a record of that one, shouldn't I?'

'They don't have records any more, it's cassette tapes.'

'Goodness... what next? Will you come see me?'

'Let's see,' I say. 'Will you ever come back to Scotland?'

The Avadhoot turns serious. 'James, you must say nothing to anyone of me being your father. It is a secret best kept between us, for your mother's sake.'

'Why for mother's sake?'

'It is not I who fears being caught and punished James. You think, when you look at my lifestyle that I'd fear a jail cell? Your mother is different, her lifestyle, her parents, our lies and deceit, if exposed to the authorities, would ruin her. I widnae want that to happen and neither should you. It is her who financially gained through this caper. No one else needs to ken that I am back into your life.'

'So what *are* your expectations now you've met me?'

'We're both adults now, not meeting as father and child, but as equals... with our own responsibilities. You cannot have your childhood back with me in it. We have to move on, respect each other, within our own individual challenges.'

'You think I can walk away... like this never happened? Like I can forget?'

'No, I do not wish that, but you owe me nothing. I abandoned you. You would be wise to do the same with me. My joy and my punishment are to see you here and perhaps in the near future too. You should know that I love you, but I cannot express this love by joining in your future plans or lifestyle... and you cannot join mine. I am a Sanyasin.'

'You're my... dad.'

'Yes, I fathered you... but I don't deserve the title of dad. He died on that trail in Dhoti, foolishly and mercilessly killed by the man you now see as the Avadhoot.'

'Whether you deserve the title or not, it's my right to view you as I like.'

'This is a large continent with a billion people who accept me as I am, without question. I could become very hard to find.'

'So, you'll give me nothing, except this memory of you as a selfish, unwashed holy man?'

'I'll leave something more important with you... my address. Send any correspondence you like to the Avadhoot in Silgari, Dhoti District. It will reach me at my retreat. Sita also knows the way, but she also knows no one comes uninvited. Even the Moni Baba has to give me warning otherwise he's not welcome. Sita would never bring you unannounced to my place, that's why she brought you here.'

Dad takes the cloth bag of clothes and digs out a small notebook and a pencil. He writes down his address and hands it to me. I accept the piece of paper and place it into my copy of dad's book... like a bookmark, next to his eulogy.

My father, the Avahdoot, pauses for a moment and sweeps his matted hair from his brow. Some of the red tika dust on his forehead falls across his nose. We hug a farewell. I guess he feels the need to offer a last wee bit of philosophy to weld our relationship back together after all the lost years.

'I've been studying Nepal's age-old coping strategies, and I believe they are worth preserving. You may think what I'm doing is the last thing this place needs, that it needs more business, more material development, but that's not what I do.'

'You believe in the mental equivalent of bio-diversity?'

'Aye, exactly, as part of the resistance to one narrow definition of happiness and global ambitions.'

He touches my forehead with his hand and smiles. He lifts his small brass yogi pot and leaves the hut. The woman and boy join him but he doesn't look back. The boy waves, as any step-brother might. I watch my dad's bare bum wiggle away as if it's all been a dream.

I pace off to find Sita back at the roadhead. People pass me in the opposite direction, herding buffaloes back to their homes. I consider twentieth-century rush hours around the world. At this moment in New York they'll crowding into subways going to work while in India women carry water home for meal times. People are out shopping in shorts in Australia; others shopping fully covered in Saudi Arabia. Some still spearing wild animals in rural Amazon, while others queue to buy processed food in cities. So many complex historical and geographical reasons why people are still doing things in ways that have survived or evolved until today. The jury is still out on which of these lifestyles will outlast the others.

PART SIX: THE PASSAGE

68

S ita is massaging a young baby with oils when I walk into the local teashop. I'm stunned for a moment until she stands and I see she is still pregnant. A small crowd gather around us and Sita hands the slippery child back to its mother. She takes me aside and leads me by the hand through the back door of the teashop. There on the wall is a small mirror that she poses me in front of.

Matted hair gives me a castaway look. Dust-covered clothes add to my Avadhootish appearance. Sita points to three strips of white ash across my forehead in the mark of Shiva. It seems to indicate to her that things have gone well with the Avadhoot. She smiles warmly. I have a few things to say to this woman but it's clear I should clean myself up first.

I sit under the village pump, while two children scream in torturous delight as they pump cold water over me. Cold water never felt so good. I watch my trousers being twisted into a coil and battered against a stone by the teashop owner's wife. My shirt is already out to dry in the late afternoon sun. Before long I feel refreshed and human again.

Sita leads me to the loft we have to share for the night. Two village elders bow a Namaskar towards her feet. She returns their greeting and I follow. I prepare to spend my first night sleeping with Sita on a makeshift bed of straw in what is clearly a barn. I could be in Bethlehem some 1988 years ago.

After dark, with no other lights around, the night sky becomes the heavens. Thousands of pin-head sparks of light crowd the gaping hole in the barn roof. Without the moon there seems many bright stars, a million signposts for the ancient world. I wonder how the three wise men were able to choose.

Despite my tiredness, I cannot sleep. Goats bleat beneath us and occasionally the pregnant Sita is restless. The smell of straw and drying cow dung blends with carbolic soap from my washed clothes. It's just a minor upgrade on the Avadhoot's accommodation.

I lie on the straw thinking what I can say to her about not telling me the Avadhoot was my dad. I realise that by confronting her, I'll risk this new level of comfort we've had with each other on this trip.

In the morning, Sita wakes me up with a chai and a hot paratha. She looks tired but happy. She tells me she's let me lie longer and that she spent an uncomfortable night, wrestling with the being inside her. She says she now feels the baby's impatience to enter this world.

I come straight to the point and ask why she lied to me about the true identity of the Avadhoot.

'There was no lie.'

'I see no attempt at truth.'

'Think about what I said,' Sita says defensively.

'You knowingly omitted the most important fact about the Avadhoot.'

'I helped you discover – that which was best discovered by yourself.'

She does not see her words and actions as a deception. She tells

me she used her judgement on how best to prepare me for a difficult encounter. She tells me she relied on words of the Moni Baba
for guidance.

'It was a very risky move,' I say. 'You do not know me well
enough to anticipate my reactions. What if I had violently attacked
the man before recognising him? What would I... what would you
be feeling now?'

'You are European, I trusted you would not do that.'

I suddenly sense a monumental naivety in Sita. She has not met
many male Europeans. She somehow thinks us collectively as
gentlemen. She knows little of our history... those two brutal
world wars.

'You would not be the person I believe you are, if you'd attacked
the Avadhoot. I do not know you well, you are right. But are you
saying if I get to know you better, I will not like you?' She touches
my arm as she says this.

Such a small gesture of affection and I'm won over. I put aside
my moaning and say I'm thankful to her. I am grateful to have my
father alive and somewhat available in my life, even if it still feels a
dream.

'What did he say to you?'

'He spoke a lot... mostly about the un-godly things in his life.'

'You know about the other children?' she asks.

'Yes and he explained the role he has to play as a Sanyasin, in
your culture.'

'This is something he's made up. I know of no other Sanyasin
who behaves like the Avadhoot. He's made it up in his head.'

I laugh out loud. Not only is my dad naked and promiscuous,
he's also delusional.

I tell Sita the importance my dad placed on secrecy, about the
real identity of the Avadhoot. At this suggestion she scolds me.

'If we have kept the Avadhoot's identity a secret for over twenty
years why should you worry about it now?'

I stop arguing. We are exploring new territory here. I tell Sita

I'm trying to accommodate a father I thought was dead, someone who does not particularly want me back in his life and a mother back home who has been deceptive.

'You have to consider a new relationship with your parents.' She says, while clasping the round dome of her belly.

'As soon as you left your mother's womb, you have been on your own and only in control of what you offer into every relationship, not what you get out of it. This is a time now for *you* to offer more if you wish to.'

That afternoon we wave goodbye to the villagers whom Sita has befriended and who have looked after her. We travel back to Kathmandu on the bus. I remember dad's face, the moment he recognised me. In my mouth I re-swallow the taste of anger when I think how much an actress my mother has been all these years.

69

Back in Kathmandu, I convince Sita to stay and rest at my place. I push together a makeshift bed from Tibetan cushions. I feed her some milk tea before retiring separately to sleep.

The next morning, I take a bag of coins into the doorway of a house with a single phone and a collection box. I close the door and call Edinburgh direct. I stand, listening to the call ringing at the other end. I can imagine exactly where she is, where she'll stand when she answers, what she'll look like and what's outside her window. The only thing I don't know is what she will say.

I've sent only two letters home, one from my arrival in Kathmandu, the other from Barabase. This is my first direct contact since I left, now I have news of some significance for her.

When she finally lifts the receiver, mum is very excited to hear me. She launches into a description of the present problems she's having in the garden. I can sense she'll be annoyed that she's had to come indoors with her Wellington boots on to answer the phone. I find myself hypnotised by the familiar voice, sounding on about gardening clients she's lost and accounts she's doubled. It's a different world I'm listening in to.

One of her main landscapers has recently been in a car accident but is recovering well and by the way she has a new secretary – Mary is pregnant and gone on maternity leave. There is much more news but it will just have to wait until I get back. What about me? What are my plans for returning? When is she likely to see me again? She misses me.

I can tell from her nervous energy she is either getting rid of steam or is preparing for what's coming next.

I tell her I'll let her know my plans soon. She asks if I will make it back for the coming New Year. I tell her it's unlikely. Then I start the inquisition.

'I found the Moni Baba.'

At the mention of the Baba, mother goes quiet.

'Is he still alive?' she asks.

'Yes, but he is apparently poorly.' I pause, then continue, 'you know who else is alive? Your husband, the Avadhoot ... James Munro senior, but you've known this all along, yes?'

There is an uncomfortable long silence, I push more coins into the box and think the line has been cut. I start hollering hello until mother finally chirps back.

'Good. Good it's in the open between us. Have you spoken to him?' There is a muffled noise as if she is holding her hand over the phone. I don't know if it's her crying or cursing.

'I went to one of his public talks.'

Suddenly she's back in full flow. 'What's he doing, talking in public?' She sounds concerned. 'He's not supposed to do that.'

'He does it all the time. No one knows him as James Munro. He lives disguised as a Sanyassin.' I tease her more. 'Or was he in disguise as my father?'

'Look, I'm sorry to hear the Moni Baba is sick but he's a good age and if he passes away he'll no doubt be back, reincarnated quicker than you can change a light bulb. You father is unstable, deceitful and unreliable and...' she tails off the conversation without finishing.

I sense anguish in her tone but I'm also running out of change for the call. I've rarely heard her talk like this except to people who've let their potted plants wither and die.

I give her a last desperate volley, 'I can't believe you kept this a fucking secret from me all these years. Talk about unreliable?'

'I don't know what he's told you, James, but he's been dead to me for years. At first it was tragic, our stupid plan, but you were young and I thought I would tell you when you were older. Then all this other stuff started to happen. Did he say anything about his other children? How could I possibly explain things to you? I knew there'd be a time when you'd find out, but I wasn't in a rush to tell you.'

'Don't you think I might—'

She quickly cuts me off.

'Listen, ask yourself this. In what way is he now your father? He's done absolutely nothing for you and nothing in recent years for me.'

'What about the money from the insurance policy?'

'He thought that money would support us in a life of luxury. His financial knowledge based on a rice-bowl expense account. He's no idea of today's cost of living. Things have changed in twenty-five years. That money gave us a share of a cottage in Peebles, which I've had to re-mortgage several times since to pay off the debt. Son, this is not the time to go into this but since you've now met him... you make up your own mind. Unless he has changed his selfish ways I'm guessing he's back in the hills and that you'll get more emotional support out of visiting a tombstone with his name on it.'

'I'm running out of change, mother. I'll have to call another day.'

'He's a pathetic ascetic, James, and please don't make his existence public knowledge. Take care son, I love you.'

70

For the next two weeks, Sita lives with me and it feels comfortable having her around. Because of her suppleness she has little difficulty in doing most things as normal. She teaches me how to make a nutritious spinach dish with Paneer cheese which I feed her daily. I tell her it is good for her because it contains Vitamin A. It is good because her body craves it, she tells me. This sums up our relationship. I tell Sita small bits of science and she says that science can only look where the human mind has told it to look.

Swamy Y is informed that Sita will stay with me at Bahaur's compound until the baby is born. There are two experienced midwives also in the building and should it be necessary the hospital is closer. Swamy Y accepts this maternity-leave request and tells me it's probably best since Sita's circus friends have moved on back to India. He also asks if Sita can still speak to one or two of her regular clients that are desperate to see her. Despite her advanced condition, Sita agrees.

I catch her lying on her back in our room one day demonstrating a breathing exercise to an older woman. She's told Sita she has a demon that regularly assaults her, which to me sounds like anxiety attacks. She is appreciative of Sita's advice and council. She leaves, still breathing in the recommended way, walking as if she's a bagpipe player with phantom bagpipes.

On another occasion, a man who believes he speaks to animals visits us. He is distraught at the death of a cow hit by a car, while roaming the streets of Patan. He seeks an audience with Sita to help him grieve this death.

I ask Sita later how she was able to help the man recover from his grief so quickly. Sita tells me that a foreign diplomat was driving the car that killed the cow, a crime punishable by imprisonment or eviction from Nepal. The diplomat had escaped expulsion however, much to the annoyance of the cow's owner and locals like this man. She tells me the authorities had decided the cow had committed suicide. Sita told the man that he knew better and having the knowledge that the cow did not take its own life should be of great comfort to him.

Sita has that strange power to say what is helpful even if it's not what people expect to hear. I'm convinced she would have a future as a therapist or in sales or in commercial advertising. She captivates and frustrates me at the same time. She will take my feet and massage them with the indifference of a cobbler measuring me for shoes. She will let me listen to the heartbeat of the child, and feel the movement of this small being inside her.

ONE NIGHT WHILE WE ARE PRACTICING ENGLISH CONVERSATION, WE finish by cuddling like siblings and Sita's waters break. It's eleven o'clock and Sita tells me that the baby is coming. I scream as instructed from the apartment window to summon the midwives from the houses opposite.

When they arrive, one midwife is very uncomfortable with me being there but Sita insists that I stay. The other midwife is too busy organising her birthing toolkit to bother.

Witnessing a child's birth has to be one of the most remarkable cross-gender experiences any man can have. There are so few moments left in the modern world where the organic nature of human existence takes precedence over the timetables, plans and the arrangements of people, it makes this moment more unique.

I watch the culmination of nine months of hospitality end, as the infant begins its aggressive breakout. Like a surfer trying to mount the perfect wave and stay upright, the mother feels in the straining dome for these waves of creation. She holds her breath and pushes down, balancing as long as possible, before returning to the calm in between. She then rises to the crest of the next wave and when the opportunity comes to push for the last time, she is subjected to the unrealised pain of two physical beings straining to separate forever.

The boy cries as soon as his head feels air, his body still held in the warmth of Sita. The mid-wife coaxes the tadpole remains into the world just one hour after I've called for help. With a squish and a slither the sprout emerges, the last resistance to freedom now relaxing in a slow return to normality.

Sita immediately puts the child to her breast and shares a smile with me. I am an awe-struck, helpless admirer.

Sita says the baby is to be called Ram. I tell her that's a bit of a Hindu cliché, but she doesn't understand cliché. She tells me that she insisted I be there, since she needs me as an eyewitness. Someone who can confirm that this baby is truly hers.

After initial drops of colostrum dribble into baby Ram's mouth, Sita's breasts appear to dry up. It's the first time I've witnessed a birth but I know enough to be concerned. The midwife calls out the window for backup. There are no breast pumps in Nepal, I'm told. Why would you need them, the midwife asks. The local solution is to introduce Sita to the sucking power of an older child. A month-old Tibetan boy is suddenly brought into our room from a neighbour's house and planted onto Sita's breast. The technique works instantly, and milk production resumes.

As I look at Sita, tears of joy fill her eyes and I feel and even greater bond with her. Whether she can return such feelings is still to be seen. I know she can read my feelings like an open book although I remain a cultural mystery to her. Despite my declining resources, it seems unthinkable for me to return to Britain at the moment.

71

During the weeks that follow Ram's birth, I watch Sita quickly transform herself back into shape with hatha yoga. One would never believe this young woman gave birth only a few weeks ago. Our neighbours bring her offerings and gifts for baby Ram. She takes walks around Pipelands with her child and talks to the people living there. The Buddha may have been a young man before he discovered poverty but Ram is already breathing the stench and witnessing the ingenuity associated with it, next door.

Each day I hold Ram for long periods of time. I enjoy watching this new young life grow before my eyes. My suspicions that the biological father is the Moni Baba have now faded. The initial rustic colour of Ram's skin has changed to a lighter shade of tan. I sway the boy to sleep, considering his biological heritage with new fears. Heaven forbid, we might be step-brothers.

Despite sharing the same house for over a month there remains an air of mystery to Sita, a secretive side she does not share. She will rarely speak of herself, preferring to explore my culture or my thoughts. There are times when I know she's flirting with me, teasing and baiting me. She has made no reference to the fairish skin of baby Ram. People in the neighbourhood assume that I am the father and she makes no effort to correct them. There is more than a touch of the Moni Baba in her.

We both take equal shares of handling Ram and this experience is new to us both. A newborn does not come into the world with a set of operating instructions attached.

Once after Ram took a sneezing fit, Sita and I watched as his whole body jerked in response. His little feet clenched with every sneeze and his arms waved in reaction. Neither of us knew how to respond. The absolute helplessness of a small child actually provokes you into providing its essentials. One can see the need for faith in the mind of young child, faith that food, care and attention will be provided. Surely the beginnings of all future faith are formed at this stage.

I RECEIVE A LETTER FROM MY MOTHER ASKING HOW I AM DOING AND for news of my future plans. She also includes a letter addressed to me from Fiona. My former partner writes that she left a couple of shirts at our flat and would I mail these to her.

It's a confusing time for me. I consider all my relationships with people in the past and I cannot think of two more opposites than my last two partners. I recall how often Fiona talked about herself. It was a daily therapy for her. Whatever she encountered had to be shared with others. She could not cope with keeping anything in her head for very long. Once something was experienced, her mission was to describe it. Any one of a thousand worries would become her conversational centrepiece. Friends did not particularly like this behaviour but they tolerated it because it allowed them to be the same with her. She brought out the gossip in everyone.

Sita possesses an opposite frame of mind. She does not feel the need to pass on discussions with anyone for the sake of conversation. There is always a reason for things she says and I've never once felt it was to get something off her mind.

FOR THE TIME BEING AT LEAST, SITA AND I SHARE A SIMILAR FOCUS, the wellbeing of baby Ram. She is also slowly changing in terms of how she sees herself in her community. It is not just motherhood that's bringing this change, it's also to do with her exposure to western ideas through Swamy Y, myself and recently the owner of a small shop near us selling European clothes.

Farida Tabji is a middle-aged Parsi woman who dresses in the western-style garments she sells. Each day, Farida arrives at her shop wearing different outfits and Sita has become fascinated by her. Her blouses are poorly made copies of western styles, with shoulder pads that slip out of place, giving her a lumpy look.

On blouse day, Farida walks towards the shop with her left hand stretched over and down the middle of her back, fumbling for the right shoulder pad. In full stride her right hand tries to retrieve the other pad from somewhere between her breasts. The pads are correctly lined up just as she reaches the shop door. She's like an airliner, fixing its landing gear in place just before touchdown.

On other days Farida will turn up for work dressed in a Texas cowgirl outfit, complete with boots and jeans drawn too high at the waist. She'll sometimes resemble a Russian peasant doll. In the course of a week, Farida often changes her hair from Gypsy black to Barbie blonde, with cheap wigs. She's the most theatrical character I've seen here.

I know that Sita and Farida have spoken to each other in the street. I ask Sita what she finds fascinating about Farida's shop. She tells me that since she has regained her figure, all her wrap-around cloths fit her, except her Nepali blouses, which are all too small because she's breastfeeding. She says she has never worn a bra and that she is interested in the practical aspects of a western nursing brassiere, but it's something she can't afford.

I take Sita into Farida's shop and offer to buy her any practical clothes she needs. I tell her it is coming up to one year since I first saw her in Lumbini and it will be an anniversary present.

Farida smiles in recognition of Sita and looks at me as if I should not be there. I ask if Farida can tailor Sita's blouses to better fit her and if she can show her some nursing brassieres. Farida talks to Sita in Newari and they both laugh. I hear what I believe to be Sita describing me as her husband, which in turn changes Farida's attitude.

Farida descends on Sita as if she is the dress-up doll she never had. She shows Sita the brassiere range made especially for lactating mothers. Sita is immediately keen on this first item of practical western fashion. Farida then guides Sita towards a wall of blue jeans in various shades of stone wash. Sita cannot believe the older faded looking jeans are more expensive than newly dyed ones.

Farida hands Sita a collection of fashion magazines she has lying around while she wraps up the bra. She tells Sita she can make anything in the photographs she likes. Sita flips through page after page of fashion adverts. It's like watching Didi discover how to read pictures for the first time in Barabase. I can tell another enlightenment has taken place here.

Farida encourages Sita to come by her shop whenever she wants. She gives Sita a bunch of *Vogue* magazines to take away. They have worn corners and are years old, but I guess it doesn't matter when you are trying to bridge a two-thousand-year gap.

Back in our room, Sita sorts through a small basket of her clothes to make room for her new purchase. I realise how limited her collection of clothes actually is. She has two village skirts and four chulos, the Nepalese-style blouses that for most women here are flexible enough to cover several sizes of growth.

I decide that a new bra is not enough for such a significant anniversary. I walk back to Farida's shop and buy Sita a pair of new blue jeans and two white t-shirts, one with a sparkling lotus flower on the front.

When I return, Sita is sitting in a skirt with her new bra on, nursing Ram. Since the birth, she seems completely uninhibited, perhaps she always was. I've gotten used to seeing her parade through the flat with Ram clinging to a breast.

I hand over the pair of blue jeans and t-shirt and tell Sita it's part of our anniversary present. As she takes these and immediately puts them on, I realise things are about to become weird. Sita transforms herself in front of me from someone who could have been an extra in the movie *Gandhi* to someone ready to go on stage in *Grease*. In her new bra, blue jeans and a t-shirt she need only lift up to breastfeed, she nurses Ram while flipping through magazines. She thanks me for her gift.

S wamy Y visits us more regularly since Ram's birth. I begin to wonder if he is a contender as the mystery father. He encourages Sita to resume teaching yoga. He also stays on late for English conversations with us both, to talk about what life is like in western countries.

All these years in landlocked Nepal, Sita has never seen any large expansion of water, a sea or the ocean. The largest spread of water she's ever set eyes on is the lake at Pokhara. Her visual experiences from Nepal are predominantly of undulating waves of land.

Trying to explain the cold metallic colour of the North Sea or the expanse of the Pacific is very difficult without her having any real comparative reference points for scale. To learn there is more water than land on earth seems to surprise her. The idea of land coming to an end and water stretching out to the horizon is something she can only imagine. Sita encourages Swamy Y and I to speak of such wonderful things.

Sita also likes stories of traffic and different modes of transportation that takes people long distances, like trains, planes and ocean liners. A large city containing millions of people where water is piped into a tap in every home is an incomprehensible feature of a western lifestyle for her.

When I describe how we ship containers full of bottled water across the oceans to be drunk in our homes, she is flabbergasted.

'Don't they have enough water to drink in America?' she asks.

'Yes,' says Swamy Y, 'they have more than enough. They bottle up American water and ship it to other countries like Scotland and France.' He smiles at the implications of his words.

'And,' I add, 'we ship water from Europe to America to sell there.'

Both Swamy Y and I know the lives of most Nepalese women revolve around water. They collect it; store it; use it for bathing and expertly handle it carefully in cups each day before they consume it. So much time is spent going to and from a hilltop spring, a river valley or a community pump to collect water, it becomes as valuable a commodity as any currency. The nearer it is to the home the richer one is believed to be, since one's energy and time becomes available for other activities. Most women here have lived and died devoting most of their time to the collection of water.

'How old is the water when you drink it?' asks Sita

'It is sealed so it can last a long time.'

'Which water tastes the best?'

'Well, there's a thing. Water tastes like water anywhere, especially if you have it with ice.'

'Which country does the ice come from?'

'The ice is most often just the local water frozen.'

'So people buy water from Scotland or America, then put ice from their own country into it, so it tastes like water anywhere?'

'Western people eat and drink things from many parts of the world,' I chip in.

'Some foods have travelled thousands of miles to get into our intestines,' Swamy Y adds.

'When we go to the toilet, westerners pass a stool that contains food from all over the world in it.'

'If you want to know which country creates the most international shit? I'd say it's the United States,' says Swamy Y.

73

Sita takes up teaching yoga twice a week at Swamy Y's ashram. She travels there in her blue jeans and a white t-shirt and keeps her earnings tucked into her new bra. At home she flips through Farida's magazines and marks pages. She tells me she wants to spend some of her yoga earnings on more 'western' clothes.

In the weeks that follow, the streets of Assan and the markets of Kathmandu become areas in which Sita enjoys expressing her new fashionable persona. She uses her yoga earnings to buy herself a short denim jacket to cover her shoulders in public. Her visual transformation is complete, although for my taste it is a little too country and western.

When I'm walking beside her I notice how differently people look at her now. She is charged with a new rebellious energy and seems to revel in it. She often takes my arm, in the way of a western woman. She tells me this is a pleasant advancement on walking a respectful three yards behind me. I realise it is also a consequence of her being more frequently followed by local men.

Each day the many cultural differences between Sita and I are brought out, discussed, examined, influenced, then replaced in our minds. This appears to be our chosen way of sharing. Conversations are not lengthy and recently they are punctuated by affectionate touches – a hand to the shoulder, an arm around the waist.

I still do not dare bring up the question of Ram's linage. I feel Sita is aware of my curiosity but I accept the fact she chooses to keep this to herself. She seems to have moved on entirely from the life she's lead as the Baba's companion, to becoming a modern Nepali mother.

On Swamy Y's visits to our flat, he talks about the creation of an Ashram in the Baba's name. He has his own interesting angle on the whole thing. He tells us me there are plenty of centres trying to influence people positively... but none that teach the wisdom of resisting too much influence over your life or the need to filter information more carefully. There are no Ashrams that give the Baba's insight into the practical use of silence and solitude.

I ask if he has fully considered how hard it might be to sustain such a centre. How difficult it might be to make any sort of income or profit from teaching solitude.

'After all,' I say, 'it's not the sort of thing that people will join a class, full of other people, to experience.'

The Swamy persists with his argument. 'There will come a time soon when people will gladly pay for silence,' he says with a wink. 'They already pay for water!'

ONE DAY, SITA TELLS ME THAT SHE HAS DESIGNED A DRESS AND ASKED Farida to make it for her. She points to a photograph of a full-length red dress in an old *Vogue* which has spaghetti straps and quite a flimsy top. It also has two skirts, one slightly shorter and open over the longer one below

I ask Sita what it is that she has designed for this dress. She pulls out a copy of an old tourist magazine from Farida's collection and shows me a photograph of the Living Goddess the Kumari at a window. She points to the colourful embroidered details around the neck and hem of the skirt and tells me that she has asked Farida to include these details on this red dress for her.

I think this is a great idea, very innovative, and I tell Sita that she's very clever and that the dress will look very nice. She again points to photograph, this time to the face of the Kumari and the date of the magazine. She tells me that it's her in the photograph. I'm spellbound. I stare at the face, through the layers of paint and make-up. It is indeed Sita's young face.

'Why do you want to recreate this dress?'

'It was the only part of my childhood I enjoyed. The transition made by wearing a costume from a girl into a goddess.'

Red, Sita tells me, is an auspicious colour in Nepal and does not carry the same titillation qualities it has in the west. Sita also tells me she has ordered new black lace underwear. I ask what sort of spiritual credentials black underwear has here.

FARIDA SHOWS SITA THE CUBICLE, AND USHERS HER IN TO TRY ON THE dress.

'When you have a body like hers,' Farida whispers to me, 'you don't need fashion, you just need the proper size and that's that.'

A few moments later, the curtain opens like at a Punch and Judy show.

Sita looks disappointed as the dress hangs off her, loose and baggy.

'This dress is two sizes too large,' says Farida, fetching her materials.

Sita emerges with the dress fitting like a glove. It's made of cotton, in post-box red with a double skirt and a joined bodice top. She stands staring at me, feet apart like a porter resting, trying to read my reaction.

The shock must have registered on my face, with both Sita and Farida laughing. Sita walks towards a large mirror with the curiosity of someone looking through a window at someone else. The top skirt is unbuttoned and the under skirt conceals her legs. The bodice covers her front and is supported by two thin shoulder straps. The whole dress is lined in beautiful embroidered silk details. The transition is spectacular.

Farida steps forward and pulls Sita's hair out of its ponytail grip. She makes it wild and curly. She kisses Sita on the cheek and leaves a trace of lipstick. She then takes a finger and wipes the lipstick off, placing what's left on Sita's lips. It's like a painter's final brush stoke on a masterpiece.

With bare shoulders, Sita looks as if she's stepped from the pages of the magazines she's being viewing.

'She's just moved out of your league,' Farida jokes.

I don't laugh. It's true, there does seem a transfer of power.

'Fashion is not really about what you wear, it's about the confidence you get when you wear things that suit you,' pronounces Farida. 'Young women like you have an energy that attracts attention; clothes can help you control it.'

Sita, turns and holds Farida's arms and says, 'Control does not come from clothes, Farida, they are just our disguise.'

'Sometimes, dear, you have to also control your disguise.'

'Om Farida,' I say.

Sita smiles, then asks me what I think of her new look. I don't have a chance to reply before Farida drags Sita over to the underwear section.

74

We include Bahadur more in our lives and he reveals other sides of his personality. He has, for instance, a workshop next door containing an assortment of metal tools. It's here he collects and creates things out of scrap. He makes stoves from oil drums. He knits wire fencing and makes metal signs. The city streets are a renewable energy source for Bahadur's ventures and he is not too fussy about the exact moment when items become discarded scrap. He sees what he needs for repairs in Pipelands and by chance, acquires it.

Our relationship develops further when Bahadur tells me his personal views on spiritual development. Bahadur says he is an avid reader of books written by Swamy Vivekananda about Ramakrishna, an illiterate yogi who lived in the earlier part of the twentieth century. Ramakrishna is Bahadur's guru, an example to all people who cannot read. Bahadur tells me that an illiterate yogi only reads the deeds of people, to know the ways of God.

I realise that Bahadur does not know that Sita is the girl in white that once helped the Moni Baba. He is shocked when I tell him. He knows of Sita's history but says he did not know that she had left the Baba. He tells me it's better to keep this information about my flatmate secret, otherwise Baba followers might seek her out.

I invite Bahadur to come to our flat and share more of his stories of gurus and postures with both Sita and I. He tells me he can show Sita his level of skills with hatha postures. He says this with an air of superiority as if he wants to teach Sita. Then he adds a condition. If he is going to show his yoga… Sita must show hers.

Sita agrees to Bahadur's suggestion on the condition she wants to see what level of yoga he practices. She needs to see every muscle in his body move and not just a show of postures. I note that she doesn't ask what type of yoga he practices so I assume it's to be an evening of hatha.

BEFORE FOOD ON THE ARRANGED DATE, I CLEAR A SPACE IN OUR living area. Bahadur takes his clothes off and stands naked except for a small white lingum cloth bag covering his privates. I've told him I want no naked Sanyassin appearances and it's he who reminds me that it's Sita's request to see his muscle control.

Bahadur begins his *asana* routine, somewhat slowly. I sense his confidence from his physical appearance, which is impressive for a man of his age. He also seems to take this demonstration seriously, in front of Sita. He displays a set postures, which he says are part of his daily routine. He performs each movement in a very purposeful way, with a great deal of emphasis on loud breathing. He seems to take delight in the way he breathes noisily through his nose. There is also some aggression towards his body as he huffs, pushes and slaps himself into finished postures.

I watch Sita study him carefully, as if she were a vet examining him for any sign of animal distress. Bahadur is strong and able to do the balancing postures easily. After a further set of postures all based around a lotus position, Bahadur finishes his routine by unravelling a length of bandage into what he says is a jar of salt water. To my amazement, he then swallows this long bandage, holding onto one end. Sitting in a full lotus position he leans forward and with his spine straight then pulls the bandage out of his mouth like a magician with a streamer at a kids' show.

'The salted bandage,' he remarks, 'is the yogi's equivalent of Epsom stomach salts.'

He then snorts a thinner cloth up into his nose and pulls it out from his mouth. He moves the cloth back and forth as if drying his back with a bath towel. This is working class yoga, like a coal miner back from a shift and going through his regular cleaning habits. Bahadur then sits for a moment quietly chanting, before lying prostate in a death posture.

When Bahadur finally sits up, Sita gives him her assessment in Nepali. She speaks too fast for me to understand. She occasionally slows down to include me in the conversation, with a mixture of English in which she praises him.

Bahadur looks humbled by Sita. I can tell from what little I pick up that she's reprimanded him over his treatment of certain chakras, through his aggressive approach to asanas. Bahadur sits coyly and listens while Sita heaps advice on him.

Then, with the indifference of a swimmer entering the pool for the gold medal race, Sita stands and takes off her top. She steps out of her blue jeans and looks towards Bahadur and I with her hands clasped in a Namaste sign.

She moves to where Bahadur performed, dressed only in Farida's new bra and black lace underwear. She takes a deep silent breath and begins her own set of postures.

Bahadur concentrates in total silence. I suddenly feel overdressed. We both seem seduced by the intimacy this demo. She could be on stage, in some modern punk ballet. Only the music is missing.

As she moves, I see a few details that Sita has not picked up on yet in her exploration of fashion magazines, especially in the Brazilian editions. She displays a generous overflow of black pubic hair, exposed by the briefness of her new underwear. The tufts under her arms in addition to the loose hair on her head, present a raw wildness to her movement. She, however, appears lost in her uninhibited practice.

The sight of this body, the sound of limbs and muscles moving, and the appearance of Sita's exertion are mesmerising. Her skin seems spotless, without a freckle. She continues to move and balance precisely, pointing out specific muscles to Bahadur.

My knowledge of hatha yoga is good enough to know what is difficult and what is not, but my understanding is clearly not as comprehensive as our guest's. As she progresses, it's obvious I lack the full appreciation of Sita's skill. Mozart's music, although enjoyed by common folk, requires his fellow musicians to appreciate the refinement of his genius. Bahadur is transported, watching a masterly display of physical hatha yoga postures. My only comparison is dad's book and Bahadur's previous display and it's clear that Sita outclasses both of them.

Sita has no aggression in her movements. It is a controlled display of hatha without any sort of assault on her body. Nothing she does looks as if it puts any strain on her. Even her sweat looks under her control, as if it might disappear back into her body should she command it. It is a gymnastic routine, without the theatrical posing, done in silence. I realise that Sita's entire waking state, her conversations and her actions, display this same amount of control and sensitivity. This is not another side to Sita that's presented here, there is only one. I finally see a physical manifestation of yoga in her, as a united being.

Afterwards, Bahadur asks an assortment of questions that Sita answers carefully. I understand little because she again speaks fast and directly at Bahadur. She is talking to the person and not the room and it is unimportant that I understand. I can tell Bahadur gets her meaning. He humbles himself to the point where I think he is going to crawl backwards from the room on his departure. He bows so low in appreciation he stumbles and catches his balance, over a chair. We laugh; it's lucky he has the agility of a yogi.

Once Sita and I are alone, I tell her that I could see Bahadur was trying very hard to impress her, and therein she says was his problem. He was not looking in the right place for his yoga to succeed.

Sita walks towards me, and sits on her heels facing me. I am sitting on the floor with my legs straight out in an abandoned lotus position. She stretches one hand towards me but does not touch me. The magnetism of her reach is palpable. She clenches her fist and presses it into my chest; it has the effect of a defibrillator, tingling my entire nervous system. She pushes, not forcefully, but enough to roll me onto my back. She removes her bra and I sense her arousal. She pulls my shirt over my head, and pins my upper arms to the ground. She drags down my trousers and sits astride me. My legs are placed straight between hers. She leans forward and moves slowly over me, her breasts touching my chest. Then she sits upright, taking me inside her. Her lace pants are stretched across her upper thighs, pinning my stomach down tight like a belt. Smiling, with her hands on either side of my head for support, she begins to move.

75

I did not really appreciate how much love one can feel for a tiny being or how much one senses love back unconditionally, whether a biological parent or not. Ram appears to know when he's entertaining us. He now cries very little and has the full range of facial expressions of a cartoon character.

According to Swamy Y, there's nothing better than prunes and porridge to prime a child's digestive system for solid food. He has begun eating solid food in the form of rice porridge to supplement his mother's breast milk.

In all my time in Nepal there seems little if any bottle-feeding by mothers. The reason I'm told is convenience. It's the same reason I've been told why western mothers turn quickly to formula feeding... for convenience. It seems the definition of convenience is up for cultural interpretation.

Mothers in Pipelands selling an assortment of knick-knacks or fruit always have their breasts on tap for their children. They sit on the ground, while their two year olds walk up and take a feed. I've seen older children take milk from a mother then wander to pick up a smouldering cigarette from the ground, take a few puffs and return for a top-up.

As Ram becomes more mobile, his potential playmates are a bunch of rag tag street-urchins whose education is driven by their instinct for survival.

Sita makes friends with an orphaned girl named Durga who greatly appreciates Sita's attention. She is around five years of age and Bahadur, it turns out, is the nearest thing she has to a father. Bahadur sees she never misses a meal. Some say she is his illegitimate child, but he denies this. Bahadur also helps improve the living conditions of the pipe in which Durga sleeps. He's made her a bed out of an old cupboard drawer. He also constructed a temporary gate fastened across the entrance to the pipe.

Sita, Ram and Durga roam around Pipelands each day as if it their pre-school. I observe how Sita teaches Durga how to enquire and understand. It is communication that is clearly laying some sort of foundation for the girl's learning later, even if she never attends formal school. It is also an example set for Ram

Stones from the courtyard become Sita's educational toys. She teaches the girl what is rough and round, what is heavy and sharp or hard. She will say these words in both Nepali and English, and bring Ram into the conversation. She holds things up and describes mundane objects to Durga, giving them an interesting meaning. Tomatoes are soft and red and have a smell. She will let the child sniff. Oranges roll, bananas do not. Skins are thick or thin. Water splashes and you can see through it. Durga is captivated by a set of everyday objects, given special significance by Sita, and which cost nothing to observe.

Sita also tries very hard to communicate these discoveries with Ram and he grunts and finger points in return.

I find all three regularly sitting outside on the pavement and marvels at the way Durga plays with Ram. The slum known as Pipelands has become Sita's unique Fisher-Price early learning centre.

If Sita is not around, Durga will spend most of her time with a tribe of vendors' children, all of whom are beginning to be influenced too. Durga passes on what she's learned from Sita.

My time with Ram is usually early morning when I often walk with him around Assan. The morning air is warm with the smell of incense and cow dung mingling within the narrow confines of the streets. Ram points to all the spots on our route that have been pointed to him before. At this age, he demonstrates proudly what he's been taught. He makes the effort to say names of the gods on the temple walls. He struggles to be let down to play with any other children he sees. He's just a concerned hug away from becoming a street urchin.

The irony of being in a situation similar to my father all these years ago is not lost on me. I am running low on money in a foreign country where I have a partner and a child to support. *Ke Gurne* – what to do?

No matter how hard I try to be yogic and enjoy the now with Sita, I find it difficult to halt the non-stop thinking for solutions. My logic bosses my busy brain and makes me wish I'd practiced more meditation. As the Moni Baba suggested, it's too late to start meditation when you are in a mental crisis.

My dad is alive and living here, hidden under the ash costume of a Sanyasin in the backwoods of Nepal. For most of my life he has lived in a remote area that by all accounts is fifty years behind the rest of the country in development. He has selfishly retired himself from the world I know.

I say selfishly because he has faked his death and forced others, especially me, to accept that he was dead. Not just dead, murdered. The people he lives among must know little of his origins, about his upbringing in Scotland or the family he left behind.

As much as Sita does not talk about my situation, I think we need to have a conversation about the Avadhoot.

. . .

ACCORDING TO SITA, THE AVADHOOT'S DEVOTEES ARE MORE interested in what he offers them spiritually than they are in questioning his history or his ethnicity. They look to him as a healer and a spiritual guide, as someone who has an insight into many issues of concern to them. He has become an expert about them simply because he has observed so many of them and lived among them for so long.

I tell Sita I have to make a choice soon about what to do with my future, if for no other reason than purely financial concerns. My mother, having engineered my reunion with dad, now seems paranoid over exposing his existence. She wants me to come home and is unwilling to help me further with funds, saying I should return as soon as possible.

As fate would have it, Sita hears news of the Moni Baba. She tells me he is asking to see her and the child. This message comes from people caring for him in Langtang, saying they don't think he has much more time left on this earth.

Sita and I talk and embrace the idea of visiting the Moni Baba. She tells me it might be a difficult walk to do alone with Ram. There are very few people on the Langtang trail and it would involve sleeping in the open.

I tell Sita that I know at least two others will make an excellent company for us on a trek with Ram to the mountains of Langtang.

I am grateful to have a purpose that might temporarily dissolve my confusion.

SITA TAKES TO MAYA AS IF SHE IS A LONG LOST FRIEND. WITHIN hours, she has arranged our room into two separate sleeping compartments by hanging a Tibetan carpet from a ceiling beam to make a divide. Maya is overjoyed to handle and care for Ram. At the first moment we are alone she whispers in Nepali, 'we are trying again for a boy child – like you.' It's clear she believes Ram to be my child.

Tilak is also reunited with his friend Bahadur and returns late, disappointed that Bahadur no longer drinks like before. He seems to have changed into a yogi, Tilak tells me.

While Sita and Maya chatter like friends on a hen-night, I doze off to sleep watching Ram.

BEFORE MAKING THE TREK, I DECIDE TO CALL MY MOTHER BACK. I pick a time on a Sunday when I think she will be more responsive to my financial concerns and help me cash in some items of value I own at home. I choose my words carefully.

'Yes... everything's fine but I've got only a few coins for this call. You only heard fragments of my story in Nepal, mum. I've met someone that I now have a close relationship with.'

She ignores what I'm saying and I can tell her priority is containment of the fact that dad's alive. I assure her that her secret is not out.

'Did he tell you I'm worried about this story getting out?'

'Yes.'

'Bastard. It's him who should be more worried. If I want to expose this whole charade of his, then I will. I see the *Daily Record* headline... my husband is a randy naked western yogi, fucking village women for a living. How will that look on the media here? Maybe he'll even get in *The Guinness Book of Records* with all the wee bastards he's spawned.'

'Somehow I don't think he would give a shit, Mum. He'd probably get more followers.'

'He'd get jail time... that's what he'd get.'

'So would you.'

'Well so be it. Your father has turned into a one-man sperm bank.'

I wait to hear her cool off from her tantrum. She's lived so long in fear of releasing the truth about dad.

'Speaking of banks,' I say. 'Can you send me some money?'

'Tell me more of this new relationship.'

'I need time to sort out my affairs. I have a partner and a child to consider.'

'A child?' she shouts down the phone, then I hear a muffled, 'Munro men!'

'Yes, but it's not like dad. I'm not the father but I love this woman and the child. Plus, you know when Munro men have money problems, how crazy they can act.'

My mother hangs up the phone.

T ilak and Maya take us out for a night on the town... as western couples do. With his new business wealth Tilak books a table at the town's most famous tourist restaurant in Lazimpat. Bahadur and Durga agree to babysit Ram.

Tilak lets me borrow one of his Nepali shirts. Maya wears a sari and Sita chooses to wear her red dress.

At the restaurant, Sita and Maya chatter in Nepali like they are sisters, while Tilak and I talk in English.

As I look across the table, both women look glamorous. Neither are strangers to finery, in fact it's a central part of their culture to dress up. Sita appears very comfortable in her red dress and looks like she could be from any country around the central belt of the planet.

After a few mouthfuls of Everest beer, Tilak leans forward and says, 'I was always impressed by the way you sat down in Barabase with all the different castes of people and talked to them.'

'That's because I didn't really know which caste people were from... and I had no interest in finding out.'

'But you still served a purpose. It made me think that I should visit my home village in the hills and help people as you did in Barabase. I took Maya, it was her first visit since we married.'

'I didn't know you were avoiding a return visit home?' I ask, thinking what a topical subject it was.

'For years I kept away. I was remembered only as a child, not as a man or a soldier. They also became very angry when I married Maya because she is lower caste. We settled in Barabase, where I was accepted in good status as an ex-Gurkha soldier from the British Army. After six years, my parents were very happy to see me.'

'Where is your village?'

'It's two days' walk west from Gorkha. I introduced our daughters. The family had never met them. Now I am trying again for another child. May Lord Shiva make this one a boy.'

'Wow, how does Maya feel about this?'

'Maya is going through a difficult time,' he whispers. 'I am worried about her. She has not been the same with me since we visited my home, or maybe before that, since you left.'

I drink and swallow hard.

'The family disagreement over her caste came up again. I am hoping that soon she will feel the inner contentment that women do in their pregnant state.' Tilak says this as if he's experienced an actual pregnancy.

'Are you sure this is what is troubling Maya?' I ask.

'Yes, I believe that a new child will help Maya regain her sanity.'

'Well, you would know best,' I say, smiling to confirm my sarcasm.

'While you were in Barabase, you avoided all the quarrels and politics of the village. You seemed to ignore what people were saying about you and not let it bother you.'

'I did not understand what people were saying about me.'

'Would you like to know now?' Tilak returns my sarcasm.

'I've been thinking about visiting home too,' I say. 'It's quite a decision, whether to return home or stay here longer. I have roots in two places.'

'You can't leave now, you are a father to Ram… Sita will never leave Nepal.'

Tilak's last remark hits me like a slap of common sense. The solution that's foremost in my mind is to take Sita and Ram with me to Scotland. I sit back and look sideways at Sita. I think how easily she could fit in absolutely anywhere.

'What makes you say that Sita will never leave here?'

'This is her home.'

I look again and see Sita's eyes alive, wide open, talking to Maya. Her hands gesture to illustrate some story in Nepali that's too fast for me to understand. They are laughing loudly. Both her and Maya so attentive that neither notice we are staring at them. Sita never talks to me like this.

Tilak passes me a bowl of strange fruit. He takes a small green piece and I take a larger brown portion and bite into it. My conversation stops as I realise I've eaten a hot chilli. My three friends watch as I convulse. It takes minutes before I can talk. 'That was like French-kissing an electric bulb socket,' I say. No one understands what I mean as I gasp for cool air.

Tilak tells me he is now producing electricity at the mill. He has also done well in his business by producing trekking foods.

'How are the Tamangs?' I ask, breathing fire.

The Tamangs are doing well and have bought one of his old milling machines. Even the old lady greets him now.

I turn the subject to the trek ahead to see the Moni Baba and tell Tilak of Swamy Y's plans to begin a Moni Baba centre in Baktapur.

Tilak suggests there should be no sense of doom related to the trek or in the thought of the Baba passing. He'll know it's his time and Tilak repeats the deeply held belief that this is only a transition period for the Baba – and he'll likely be very happy to be going.

I can't help but feel a sense of sadness, the side-effect of a scientific mind.

As I attempt to lighten my own attitude, I suggest to Tilak that the creation of a Moni Baba Centre would make a fantastic ending to a Hindi movie about the Moni Baba's life. All his followers showing up in a fantastic Bollywood dance finale.

To reach the Baba's hospice involves several days walk through the Langtang valley and then up to the holy lake of Gosainkund which, legend has it, was created by the god Shiva himself. Our time to reach the Baba's lodge will depend on the state of the trail and our speed while carrying all our food and Ram.

Tilak has rented what we will need and has donned his military fatigues for the trip. He has shaved the sides of his head like a monk, removing most of his grey hair and leaving the top a thick carpet of black. It's a good look for him that suits his strong face. Maya is adorned with jewellery, which Sita tells me are her fertility charms. She wears a Nepali silk blouse under a Patagonian fleece and I see a hint of a black bra. Sita has obviously taken her to Faridas. Maya also carries a modern backpack, and wears trousers and bright Nike trainers. There is an athletic look to her I've not seen before.

Sita is wearing her blue jeans and a fake North Face waist-coat over a long sleeve black t-shirt. She has Ram strapped in a small back-carrier which we will take turns in carrying. I wear a new white t-shirt, with the now well-worn trekking trousers I brought from Scotland.

Tilak arranges a four-wheel drive SUV and driver to take us to the road end. All five of us squeeze in, with me fitting in the back between Sita and Maya, holding Ram. We leave the tarmac and travel over a rough road. I hold Ram tight over the bumpy trail. Maya also takes turns holding him close to her chest, as if his proximity to her womb might influence the gender of her next child.

We are dropped off when the road ends and turns into a steep hill trail and continue walking up for the rest of the day into the valley.

It feels great to have a sense of purpose, these particular friends around me, and to be once more in the hills.

A landslide has blocked the trail but already someone has crafted an alternative foot trail, which we scamper over. This part of the walk is not difficult but it is isolated. It is a much less inhabited area of Nepal that was recently made into a National Park.

We walk through a generous garden of rhododendrons and in-between giant cliffs of granite. We march across bridges made from wire and firewood, strung over deep gorges. The crossing of bridges has to be taken with consideration for the rhythm of the person in front. Careful dance steps in case you bounce someone off. It is a beautiful path, the silence only disturbed by the giggling of Sita and Maya.

After the third day of walking, it becomes colder. Tilak and Maya make shameless carnal passes at each other, pretending it's for warmth. Both Sita and I hear a change in their speech too. There are compliments and confessions along with tender touches in their trade. The placing of a rucksack onto Maya's back becomes a sensual experience. Tilak pulls the straps over Maya's shoulders and clips the belt around her waist, his mind in a fog of desire, his hands lingering.

Meanwhile, Sita and I are changing nappies. As Maya and Tilak rub cheeks and massage each other, Sita breastfeeds and I sway the child between us to sleep.

One night sleeping in the open, under the stars, Tilak and Maya begin to make love. Sita and I waken with the noise and she cuddles up close to me. Ram is asleep and Sita gently kisses me on the lips. I feel content with her just holding me as I doze off again in fits of deep sleep.

Ram lets out a cry. The noise of an owl wakes me more and I hear a distant waterfall. I get up in the cold night and walk Ram back to sleep under the stars. I watch my breath leave my mouth and look at Maya and Tilak asleep in a single sleeping bag, the embers of love now ash and silent.

There are no sounds of anything mechanical. The billowing smoke from our yak dung fire drifts up towards the silhouette of Langtang's two sharp peaks. It's all magnificently lit by a half moon sky. I'm happy. I have few comparisons as special as this and I vow not to mark this experience ordinary or take it for granted.

79

W e first see him from a distance. It is late afternoon and we are all exhausted and as we approach the lodge where the Moni Baba sits outside. As we get closer, I see fragility in his face and frame. I believe he instinctively knows Sita is near him.

As we shout greetings he stretches out his hand. Sita takes away his staff and whispers something into his ear. She then places Ram firmly into his arms. It's as if he has suddenly been given enlightenment as a gift. In some Nirvana mind zone, he embraces Ram as if just given birth himself. He holds Ram to his cheek until his strength falters. He hands Ram back to Sita, welcomes her and us all and says he will talk to us tomorrow. He then stands smiling, turns quickly and grasping his staff for balance, walks into his lodgings.

The Moni Baba's presence in Langtang is still a secret and very few people have visited the ailing sage. We are told by a villager that we are lucky he is here... that he has been gone for over a week and only just arrived back from Gosainkund, a four-day walk away. He remained at the lakeside for days, meditating for hours.

Sita suggests it's likely he went there to die. We are indeed lucky he's returned.

'I thought if yogis wanted to die they could just do it without any problems?' I ask Sita.

'They can, unless they have something left they wish to do.'

'We may have just witnessed it, him holding Ram,' I say with authority.

'Or maybe he just forgot how to die.'

I laugh. 'You say that as if he's died before and can't remember.'

Sita doesn't laugh back and I see in her eyes a little sadness. 'We've all died before,' she says. 'But yes perhaps he's here because he felt us coming.'

Next morning I wake first in our hut, some yards from the Baba's lodge. I notice the Baba is sitting at his door wrapped in a thick blanket. Before him stretches the glorious deep valley of Langtang. He appears to be feeding some small birds with seeds.

Sita wakes and catches me staring at him and as if reading my mind, she says, 'It's wrong to think he cannot see... he has spent his life looking and seeing things others have not. It's only now in his later life his eyes do not work. He has memories and imagination and a powerful energy to lookout for the essentials of living.'

'Do you think he knows you are here with me?'

'Yes – I whispered I was now together with Munro's son. Let's go see him now.'

We both take blankets from the bed and walk the short distance towards the seer. I am still bothered that the Baba was the first to mention the Avadhoot and not tell me he was my father. I'd frankly like to know what higher order of thinking instructed him to deceive me in such a way.

The Baba welcomes us and tells us he's delighted we've come. His face is pale, his skin drawn, making his eyes stare more than nature ever intended. The questions I have for him regarding the

Avadhoot seem pointless when I see his frailty but still, I explain that I have met the man he called the Avadhoot and that the mystery surrounding my dad's disappearance has finally been cleared up.

He stretches for my hand, and says, 'I learned much from the Avadhoot... and many others still do. He's such a rich resource for this country. I would not be as knowledgeable about the West as I am, without his guidance. He is helping change some from the oppressive feudal lords into modern managers and political thinkers. It was his wish that I should never reveal his true identity. I took an oath and so I could not explain to you at the time – I hope you understand?'

I look at the Baba with his matted long grey hair and beard, his dirty fading saffron robe and say, 'You'll be pleased to know he remains as western as you are now.'

80

For two days, there is a procession of audiences, with Tilak and Maya too spending long hours with the Baba. Sita remains in his company as much as possible, breaking only to feed Ram. She tells the Baba about her work with Swamy Y. She even mentions his idea to create a Moni Baba Centre in Kathmandu. The Baba is indifferent. Tilak steps in and gives the Baba more encouragement to endorse this idea. When Sita suggests it is something that she could be involved in and might bring financial support to Ram, he gives his blessing for the venture. I wonder what this means for me and my role here.

By day three I feel even more excluded, with most conversations being conducted in private. I also speculate on whose idea it was to suggest that Ram's future be tied to an institution like the Moni Baba Centre. My feeling is that it's Tilak's idea, not Sita's, but she may well be considering this as a possibility.

I accept I am here at an especially important time in Nepal's history. These are possibly the last interviews that anyone will ever have with the Moni Baba. For the first time in a while, I take my journal and write some notes. I decide to leave speculation about my own future with Sita and Ram till later.

Very few people in the world are lucky enough to be taught by someone who is a world authority on a given subject. The Moni Baba is a world authority on yoga... yet according to his teaching there is no such thing. The only yoga that is important to me is found by me studying me, not in talking to him.

We can spend our life gathering information from people around us and depending on our environment and our education we're influenced by those saying things to our face as much as we are by reading and absorbing media. We give importance to our contact with people because without it we feel alone and our ideas more ignorant.

This information we collect helps us create our own flexible reality. We often assume whatever has worked on the micro level for us must be of some value at the macro levels of society. We have a tendency to present ourselves as gurus on whatever subject we feel we know most about. The problem with this of course is that if we all talk at once – then no one else hears what we are saying... so everyone sticks with the people they like to listen to. The Baba was my dad's guru because he liked listening to him, not because he had superpowers. Yoga is not yoga unless you know where to look for guidance... from the much clichéd self.

On the fourth night, Sita tells me that the Baba has prepared a special teaching for us both. He wants to see us alone tomorrow after Tilak and Maya are given a blessing by the Baba.

I look at Sita and make a face when she says the word blessing. I ask Sita in a moment of recklessness if the Avadhoot is the father of Ram. Sita looks at me with searching eyes.

'What an interesting thing to think,' she says, and then laughs. 'Is that what you believe?'

'Well, I know the Moni Baba is not the father.'

'Why not... there are many yogis capable of producing children the same year they die of old age.'

'Yes… that's what worries me about my dad,' I say.

Sita laughs.

'Do you remember Jean Jaques, the French street performer when we first met in Kathmandu?'

'Him?'

'Yes.'

'Does he know?'

'He was a very superstitious man and because of the Kumari curse… I did not tell him.'

This information fills me with relief. I feel so happy that I hug Sita.

'Thank you! Thanks for telling me this.'

'I don't want others to know.'

'Ok. So if I've understood this right, you lost your virginity to a French circus clown in Kathmandu? How avant-garde.'

81

What a guru chooses to say at their life's end is always significant, especially to those who have followed their teachings. It's afterwards that these words tend to be embellished by authors, decorated by sycophants and massively distributed. Books written by disciples are part of the reason that teachings last. As a guru's words spread into different languages, people with a mind to contribute to the moral and social codes that people live by, repeat them. For many centuries, these early writings offered a guide for humans to coexist peacefully.

Nowadays, we know more of these early authors of the scriptures and see the scale of their efforts to help and inadvertently control people.

There is no religion that has succeeded in its goal to make its values global, no matter how well supported and beneficial these religions have been to the individuals who practice them. None are likely to ever succeed because they are now seen as exclusive and not inclusive stories. Indeed, their aims to succeed in world domination are facing resistance.

The nearest modern-day code we have for universal behaviour is the United Nations Convention on Human Rights. It is authored by an unprecedented variety of people from difference countries. It stands as a reference for values that have been cherry-picked and polished from the world's religions and social experiences, including the unfortunate lessons we have learned when one religion masses and goes to war with another.

The protections that have been offered under human rights legislation are still not a global phenomenon, despite global participation in its creation. But as of today it's perhaps a comfort to more people on the planet than anything else in our library of guidance, because it is now international law.

I prepare to record what the Baba still has to say. I tell Sita, it's like being in an aircraft hanger full of food and then offered one meal, without a choice. Our capacity to absorb all of what the Baba might say is limited. Sita asks me what an aircraft hanger is.

We wait a whole day until the Baba calls Sita and I to his side. The mountains rise so high on the westerly side of the valley that the sun sets early in the afternoon, dipping below the rugged horizon and bringing a late-afternoon chill.

The Baba sits with his back to the light and speaks to us in English. His voice is failing him but he seems determined to communicate this message to us. Once he begins, something makes me think that Sita has heard it all before and that this teaching is really for me.

'Think about love as "mass" in science. People take it for granted and rarely look through the microscope to the particles and atoms that make up love. We are alive within this mass, we have faith in this mass yet we think of it only in general, not in specific detail.

'In Tibetan scriptures there are instructions for lovers like you. Taken from thousands of years of observation of relationships and trying to better define the element love. They have been written and re-written many times and translated by western scholars such as Orage and Gurdjief. But the power in these words is not in their language; it is in the timing of when they are spoken and how they are understood. I hope you feel their power, this day, if you can.'

Sita suggests I lean further towards the Baba with my recorder. She clearly wants me to hear this.

'Jamesji Munro junior,' in my mind I hear the words *do you take this woman*, but instead the Baba takes my hand and continues. 'People everywhere have tried to understand this mixture of inner thoughts, of empathy and desire that creates pleasant feelings. Yet as languages attempt to describe the same state, there are different kinds of love.

'Three loves you can identify clearly are emotional love; instinctive love and conscious love. There are others, but in relationships, these three are important.

'You may already be familiar with instinctive and emotional love but there are not many that truly understand conscious love. It is the most difficult to comprehend and yet the most rewarding. Those who begin to understand conscious love know yoga. Yogis love consciously.'

The Moni Baba pauses briefly for a drink of water. His hand shakes as he lifts it to his lips and he laughs at his own struggle to swallow.

'You now have a precious child called Ram to love. It is a joy beyond words for me to hold this being in my arms and to feel his young heartbeat. A moment that anyone can experience in life, I savour at the very end of my own.

'This moment is special to me, because it has not been here before and Sita is so special to me. It is in my karma to feel this now and I am exceedingly grateful for this gift. It is also an example of how with the right consciousness, one can experience joy in the midst of great physical pain. I see now a new fullness in my existence. Only those who know conscious love know fullness, for other loves can leave you feeling empty.

'Your partnership with Sita is unique. Make of it what you can, with conscious love.'

I can see his heart beat through the web of thin skin on his hands, between his forefinger and his thumb. His face is gaunt with the exertion of talking, his eyes permanently glazed. His mind is still sharp but is on automatic, driven by memories controlling his speech.

The Baba talks more of Sita and his many trips with her. He speaks of his own teachers who date well back into the last century. He speaks again of Ram, as a most precious incarnation and he laughs, causing himself to retch and cough.

Sita helps the Baba sit upright. He finds a second wind and talks to us for a further two hours before his voice weakens and the effort appears uncomfortable. He says he can no longer get up by himself because he feels 'like an old man.'

'Babaji you are an old man,' says Sita.

He laughs, as if he's just remembered, then coughs again with these two actions now intimately linked. We escort him back to the lodge and he settles lying down with a peaceful grimace. I've recorded his whole teaching on conscious love for Sita to remember him later. I think he may well die in front of our eyes.

8 2

T he next morning, I wake alone. Tilak informs me that the
Moni Baba passed on in his sleep and that Sita was there
to chant him into the next life.

I have no doubt whatsoever that the Moni Baba's ascension
into the Hindu pantheon will proceed with all the required garnish
of exaggeration. He is already rumoured to be one hundred and
twenty years old, but my guess is he was in his late eighties.

Yogis are said to die peacefully in their sleep with their bodies
showing no signs of deterioration for several days afterwards. Sita
tells me that the Baba has however requested the Langtang
Buddhists to give him a sky burial to take place the day after he
passes. She tells me that a sky burial is the Baba's wish so that no
part of him can become a religious relic, no ashes collected for
distribution and no burial site visited after his passing. His exit
doorway into the next life is to become invisible.

Tilak and Maya believe they have to perform a makeshift
Hindu blessing in the house where the Baba died. It is a simple
affair, combining rituals from both Hinduism and Buddhism, a
common practice in Nepal.

The older Buddhist villagers who have experience with sky burials are summoned. Only one family of villagers keep the necessary flock of vultures for the purpose of sky burials. These birds will literally feast on the dead.

Later that same day, the Baba's body is wrapped in a plain white cloth and carried on a single bamboo pole to the clifftop. With great respect and ceremony Sita follows, carrying Ram, and I walk behind her with Tilak and Maya. As we reach the cliff edge, a flock of large birds take to the air, circling ominously.

A village elder says a few words while another older monk prepares the Baba's body for passage. He strips off the white cloth unceremoniously and without hesitation begins to skillfully cut lines across the body into small squares, with a sharp fillet knife. Each cut marks the naked corpse like a three-dimensional image. The Baba's body lies on a flat rock as if it were a wire-framed hologram.

I'm taken aback by the graphic nature of this ceremony. I begin to see the passage the body has been prepared for, is down the gullet of a vulture. As the monk walks away from the body, things become weird. The vultures descend immediately and begin picking at what's been served them.

Sita senses my discomfort with this scene and turns to me, murmuring that pain is only part of life, not death. I believe she's also saying this to steady herself. Several villagers begin chanting through this frenzy of feeding.

I decide it's too gruesome for Ram to witness and suggest I take Ram back to the lodge. He is not too young to be harmed by this, especially when the vultures fight over bits of the Baba's corpse. Sita stays until the end of the ceremony.

That evening, I find Sita in the Baba's room, sitting with a handful of his possessions, the sum total of his material wealth. There is a small dragon-shaped metal grip, used by Tibetan carpet makers, which the Baba has apparently always carried with him. There is a ring with a large Rana diamond, given to the Baba by one of Nepal's Queens. There is one standard-issue brass yogi pot, shaped in a figure of eight. There is a white silk scarf apparently given to the Baba by the Dalai Lama, beside a crumpled copy of my dad's book.

Sita hands me the book and I notice that her eyes are swollen and red. She holds the book open at a young photo of the Moni Baba. I think to myself that this is the photo that first brought my dad to Nepal... and birds have just eaten that face.

Sita tries to tell me she will miss him, but loses her capacity to speak. I lift dad's book and notice the eulogy page is missing, it's been torn out. The Baba has also carried this book for twenty years, but knowing the true fate of James Munroe senior. I'm suddenly affected too. Sita grasps me around my neck and I hug her. We both weep helplessly for a long time, until our shared hurt dissolves.

PART SEVEN: THE CHOICE

On our return to Kathmandu, news of the Baba's death is already circulating. Sita and I lie low for a while, basking in the aftermath of the Baba's last words on love, her considering her past as I consider my future. Neither of us want to become inundated with requests to tell the story of the Baba's passing and respect his request to keep his final resting place a secret. Tilak and Maya return to Barabase.

In a development I'm overjoyed to accept, Sita begins to introduce me to people as the father of Ram. She keeps up her walks through the charcoal smoke of Pipelands and young Ram seems very happy to be reunited with Durga, his miniature nannie.

Ram is bundled joyfully onto Durga's hip and follows Sita through the vegetable stalls. The young girl takes shortcuts around the legs of vendors and under the flimsy wooden trestles displaying wares, and Sita has to keep a careful lookout not to lose them. Every evening, Sita delivers Durga home to her unusual assortment of foster parents. I rarely accompany her, because at that time of day my parental duties with Ram begin. It is always Sita who takes the orphan Durga back at night and she'll often remain there in Pipelands talking, cooking and laughing with the local women for hours.

This time on my own gives me the chance to plug in the Toshiba and type up my notes. When Ram falls asleep, I work on my collection of Baba stories, revising some, chucking out others. The scraps of typed paper that Sita has given me from the Baba's personal belongings in Langtang contain some gems. Some have potential for Baba bumper stickers. Consumed as little sugar lumps of understanding to help people sweeten their day.

Swamy Y is now fully committed to establishing an institution dedicated to the teaching of the Moni Baba. He is also helpful in arranging the English translation of some of the Baba's earlier talks. These are documents that hold some value when printed and sold and will help raise funds for the proposed Centre in Kathmandu.

I consider how much cash economies have influenced the human mind to plan into the future. In rural societies much less thought goes into the future, life goes on day to day, guided more by seasons that are constant. As soon as the mind includes cash for survival, a much more frenetic lifestyle begins. The constant need to earn, rather than gather or grow, changes everything.

When I finally have the chance to review the tapes I made of the Baba's lesson on conscious love, I find in some parts his voice is too low or interrupted by his coughing fits. I ask Sita if she can help clarify some sections. Sita takes the microphone and recites Baba's last lesson in detail, looking at me.

'Amidst all these feelings that you share with others you need to distinguish at least three different types of love. If not, you can be destroyed in the confusion over love.

'First consider instinctive love. We create it through a quick calculation. It is based on how valuable we see a potential relationship. Partners found through instinctive love are attracted to what they see as useful in each other. Instinctive love supplements a partner with what they are missing. A sense of security and comfort can be found in this newly formed love. Instinctive love is the most commonly practiced love and is valuable in the measure that one feels incomplete. By that measure, the power of instinctive love increases. Many partnerships can be arranged by society or parents or felt by individuals but through its very nature, instinctive love changes in time. As people evolve so too does the needs of the partner. Instinctive love can build powerful and necessary relationships but it is created essentially from a point of weakness. If this weakness in either partner disappears, the attractions of instinctive love fade.

'The second type of love is emotional love and unlike the other two there is little thought involved between lovers.' Sita sits closer to me with the microphone still in her hand. 'A kiss or a touch can spark the chemistry of emotional love. An emotional lover makes no analysis. Emotional lovers have no sense of control or reason to their union. Emotional lovers can spend a lifetime trying to uncover the reason for their attraction without understanding it. Emotional love is volatile, exciting and explosive; its fuse lit in the depths of desire and fulfillment. It is a chemical mixture so powerful it can on occasion damage both lovers. Beware of emotional love. Many partners grow disinterested once the fires of passion fade and they find no permanent role for each other in their relationship.'

Sita sits back. I know what's coming next but I can't wait to hear how she describes it. This is Sita speaking in rote, it's not a confession of love for me, it's an insight into what she believes love to be.

'The third and most important type of love is conscious love. You will find that conscious love is rare. It is the most selfless yet beneficial love. It is mindful love. It takes preparation in your inner world to give out. It requires knowledge of how to deliver love. All that you learn about self-awareness must be applied in the act of conscious love. All actions directed in support of your partner.

'Conscious love is mindful of a partner's desires. Conscious love requires study, knowledge and wisdom in order to manifest.'

I sing a line from the Beatles song, 'Love is all you need,' interrupting Sita.

Sita pauses, takes this in, then retorts with a smile.

'No. If love is a need, who gives it, where does it come from? It is created when a conscious lover brings out the best in their beloved.

'The Baba would say, love is not enough. *I love you* says the speaker... *then why can't I feel it,* says the listener.

'Knowing what your lover wants before they do and assisting them is the skill of a conscious lover. It's rare because most aim to be loved rather than putting effort into conscious loving. Many relationships, many friendships, which know not a physical touch, can blossom with conscious love.'

Sita puts down the microphone and walks towards me.

'Think of conscious love as a responsibility. Not everyone takes it on but when it's given, it's appreciated and is returned. Conscious love begets conscious love. Gods have been identified with love, because conscious lovers become Gods. Your yoga and thinking mind is not dependent on having a conscious lover, but on being one.'

After a long meaningful embrace, I say 'that's a take' ... and switch off the recorder.

Before Ram came into my life, I never studied children very closely. They were only there in my peripheral vision. Sita confesses much the same. Little Durga visits our house so often it feels we have adopted her. She plays with Ram in our living room. It is wonderful to watch. This beautiful child with honey coloured skin and hair as thick as a yak's tail takes charge over her adopted brother. Anyone observing these two together would see what communication skills Durga passes on to young Ram. The universal funny faces for both sadness and joy. The hide-and-seek looks, the tickles that bring Ram to laughter.

The youngsters seem well matched, and even at this young age, Sita points out the flashes of conscious love. Durga loves Ram and so Ram adores her. They regularly fall asleep in each other's arms, whether it is in the comfort of our bedroom or in her wooden drawer bed, inside her concrete pipe home.

Bahadur and I often meet and have tea in the cardboard box corner café at Piplelands. We'll talk about the political developments in Kathmandu and gossip from Pipelands.

'The police are planning to move into Pipelands very soon,' he tells me.

'What will they do with the people there?'

'Move them away.'

'How long has this plot been vacant?'

'It's never been vacant. People have lived here for as long as I remember. Half of the children were born here in Pipelands. They don't want to move, they want electricity given to them.'

'So how can we help them?'

'Make war.'

'War?'

'Yes, it's necessary in such circumstances.'

'It's necessary? You may need to embrace your feminine side.'

'It's the women stall keepers and traders who are urging us to fight. It's the surrounding shopkeepers who now want to build a shopping mall.'

'Well, I think you should choose your fights wisely.'

'If it weren't for the lack of electricity, people would still be content.'

Bahadur describes a few smaller settlements that have already been cleared from other parts of the city centre in the past few years. The authorities give in, or are bribed by rich developers and are often brutal in their resettlement procedures.

There are many poor Newari farmers who sell their land to richer Nepalis, many from outside the valley. Flat land in such an environment has now become a premium and the change that land prices are imposing on the Kathamndu valley is as serious in scale as the changes and modernisation happening in Lhasa by the Chinese.

As Bahadur predicted, a large billboard with an artist's impression of a new tourist shopping mall is posted on the corner near our apartment. Behind the hoarding, a small space is cleared and the metal skeleton of the building delivered and stored for assembly.

The residents of Pipelands are given formal warning through loudspeaker announcements and leaflets are scattered which few can read. These leaflets tell squatters they have only a few weeks to move out.

Bahadur remains resistant to the Pipeland clearances and quickly establishes himself as a community organizer against the construction of the mall. He meets with officials and is told his protests are unwanted and illegal. Bahadur suggests that if they are going to put up a multi-storey building they should leave the ground floor for the people of Pipelands, and design it to accommodate everything else on top. His naive plan marks the end of his negotiations with city leaders and begins an extraordinary chain of events.

W ith all the uncertainty surrounding Pipelands, I contemplate asking Sita if she will come to Scotland with me. I decide the best approach will be to ask her if she will marry me, so that she and Ram will have no immigration problems. An opportunity to pose this question comes sooner than I expect.

I meet Sita at the Bhaktapur Ashram one day and see her come out of a private yoga session with Swamy Y, holding his hand. I catch up with them outside the meditation room and ask if we can talk alone. I've rehearsed my speech so that it sounds as if I am offering something in a conscious love sort of way, rather than asking her for something.

I take Sita into the empty meditation room. The single window lets in the light through a circular piece of stained glass. The colour catches Sita's face, set in a look of curiosity. I stand in front of her. The room is silent and Sita suddenly looks concerned. With trepidation in my voice, I speak.

'I was wondering why you have begun to introduce me... as the father of Ram.'

'What do you mean?'

'I've been thinking about it for some time and I'm wondering if you really do see me as a father to Ram?'

'You are a very important friend for Ram. I'm sorry if I offended you by calling you his father.'

'No, no it's all right. I love the idea. That's what I want to talk to you about.'

I stream my consciousness, searching for the right words.

'Sita, since I've known you, you have been a tradition-breaking disciple of the Moni Baba; a beautiful independent yogini; a street performer; a pregnant woman; a wonderful mother, a tantric lover; and now a teacher of yoga. You are the most complex and desirable woman I've ever had the privilege of knowing. Will you marry me?'

She looks at me with laughing eyes.

'How much dowry does your family expect, James Munro?'

'Oh – thirteen highland cattle!'

'Oh, ah don't know if yer wurth that,' a Scot's accent is attempted.

'Then let's not involve any payments and make me the happiest father of Ram and your husband, Sita.'

She falls silent.

'Do I take that Moni Baba silence as a "yes"?'

'James Munro junior... what would marriage give us that we don't already have?'

'I don't know really, except that we will be together in the eyes of the authorities.'

'In my culture, marriage is a union of wealth and commitment. The women's duty is bound to the will of the man. I have no wealth and no wish to be bound in that Nepali way.'

'In my culture, it offers couples a legal protection from interference.'

'What do you mean by interference?'

'I mean that two people committing to each other and

becoming married presents a signal to others that their most important relationship is with each other.'

'This English word "committing", I have to learn when it means something good and when it means something bad.'

'Is there anything wrong?'

'James, my relationship with men has always been as a pupil to a master, from my father, to the Baba, to Jean Jaques to you.'

'Just look on me as the last clown you'll ever need!'

Sita stands up and walks over to the window. Too much has been said for me to feel comfortable now and her body language hurts me more than her words. I cannot believe I have misread this situation so badly and that she's now about to decline my offer. Perhaps it's only a moment of jealousy that's making me ask her now. A self-protective thought streaks into my mind. Perhaps she is not who I think she is.

Sita begins to talk and I believe again. She is in control and making me feel what I feel for a positive reason, not trying to hurt me.

'James, I love you and it's hard to think of any future without you. You just have to explain to me why we should marry.'

'It would give you a better chance to come to Scotland. And Ram would have a real father who will care for him in a way I never experienced as a child.'

'Move to Scotland?' she whispers.

'Moving would give you a chance to see my home and my country and time to save and decide on what you really want to do.'

'Is this your condition for a marriage?'

'No it's an opportunity if we get married. There are no conditions to my proposal.'

'I cannot even imagine myself in your world. But I understand you wanting to go back. It must be difficult for you, to be out of your culture.'

Sita takes both of my hands and rolls out my fingers from their fist position into a Namasti sign. She places my clasped hands up towards her chest. Looking straight into my face she tries to capture my gaze, shaking my hands until she succeeds.

'Let's keep to the subject,' she says. 'Your desire to go back must be something different from your desire to marry me. You are smart, but cynical. Is that the right word? You seem to respect nothing, believe in nothing. This is not lost on the people here, for although they laugh at your comments, they know they too are likely to become the focus of your laughter when they go. It is not hard to see why they suspect you, because most of them cannot compete with you.'

Stunned, I search for the helpfulness in this outburst.

'With most foreigners here, people make remarks about them in a local dialect. I'm sorry that you can't understand, otherwise you would know how foolish they consider you.'

'Do they say the same things about the Avadhoot?'

'They worship the Avadhoot. It is you who talks unkind things about the Avadhoot. It is this type of speech that draws criticism on you.'

'But they don't know the real Avadhoot, as I do.'

'He is real to them. He makes a contribution when he speaks. He is just a bad memory to you.'

'How did we get here, from *will you marry me?*'

'I don't know how much Nepali you really understand, so it's difficult to know how much you hear from the people around you.'

'What are you saying, Sita?'

'Jamesji, you smile and laugh along with people here, but sometimes they are not laughing with you.'

'I think that I fit in quite well. They do me no harm and I have a genuine affection for people I call close friends. There's Tilak and Bahadur. They are friends as close as I've ever had.'

'What about Maya, you didn't mention her.'

I look searchingly at Sita's face.

'Maya is also a close friend.'

'Maya and Tilak discussed their relationship with you with a certain amount of "curiosity" – is that the word? They told me how other villagers in Barabase viewed their dealings with you as unclean, because you look like a devil to them. You are lower than low caste. You will never get close to these people, no matter how hard you try.'

'I don't want to get close to people like that. Why are you telling me all this now?'

'I want you to understand what it would be like for both Ram and I as foreigners in Scotland. I want you to consciously think through what you are asking of us and then ask again. I promise you my answer in time.'

One morning, I hear the roar of heavy vehicles and take Ram to the top-floor stair window to look out. I see people gathering in small groups. There are shouts alerting people to the threat of bulldozers. Several groups form lines against what seems to be an army of police. I have a grandstand view over the impromptu battleground.

Residents face up to police, shouting at them. The police march forward in an organised line a few feet away from the crowd. Children cry and adults scream at each other. There is confusion everywhere as people caught behind police lines run out of their dwellings carrying as much as they can. All the police are dressed in heavy riot gear with tin helmets, bamboo shields and long clubs. Some in jeeps in side streets have guns.

The first bulldozer revs up and without any warning ploughs straight into the shelters nearest the road. There are loud cracks as pipes crumble under the weight of the machine and several dwellings are destroyed in one sweep. The crowd surges forward in protest and the thin khaki line of police holds firm, stabbing batons into the wave of residents.

Amidst the screams and noise of engines, more people come pouring in from side streets. Locals who live around Pipelands and have no love for the squatters begin scuffles.

The police, in an extra effort to protect the bulldozer, fire a few cans of tear gas into the crowd. People are forced back ten yards or so. Only a few defiant members of the residents stand in what is a no-man's land facing the police.

I move to protect Ram's eyes, but luckily the wind takes the tear gas away from us. I remain looking over the scene. I see one youth taunt the police, shouting insults and abuse. Many are holding wounds from being beaten back with police batons.

It is the red dress I see first. Through the smoke, a wave of nausea runs through me stronger than tear gas. The blood drains from my head as I stare down into the crowd. I watch Sita stand there motionless, in no man's land. She is staring at the now flattened home of Durga. I realise the bulldozer's first run at Pipeland was over Durga's home and that most likely she was inside.

A call passes through crowd as more people begin to understand this tragedy. The crowd taunt the police and suddenly the police charge. Their batons are up and I see with the clarity of a sniper's scope, a truncheon come down brutally hard on the side of Sita's head.

In an instant, I switch from my observer's role. I run down the stairs with Ram, across the yard to Bahadur's house and knock furiously on the door. My stomach is aflame. The sound of the riot is much louder here. Two women open the door and I see other refugees from Pipelands huddled inside. I hand Ram over, mumbling I have to go and help Sita.

I run out of the yard to discover a solid wall of people, mostly in panic, coming in the opposite direction. There are gunshots and screams from the crushing crowd and I'm pushed back.

Women with children are being trampled, along with the older folk who look up in terror as they tumble around in the melee. I push head down, rugby style, left leg, right leg and arm over arm through the crowd. The loudspeakers are now hailing residents to assemble in the nearby square where they will be taken by bus to temporary accommodation. It's a public safety nightmare… messages that are insufficient and too late in their arrival. Police keep urging people to disperse and return home. It is pandemonium.

When I reach the street corner, I can no longer see where Sita fell. Sirens are sounding as reinforcements arrive for the police. Trucks of soldiers throw back their tarpaulins and discharge their content like coffee beans out of a fallen bag. The place fills with uniforms and I climb onto a window ledge to look in the direction of where I last saw Sita. Adrenaline has replaced all the blood in my body. With a complete disregard for others, I plough back into the chaos.

I slam into people in the crowded spots. Some are holding wounds and head cuts. I finally reach the place where I saw Sita fall. I check my bearings against our building. I'm in the right spot but she is not here. There is space now, constantly being criss-crossed with confused people, but space. I appeal to familiar faces I see.

'Have you seen Sita?' I shout.

'She has been taken,' says a bruised vendor.

'Dragged… by her feet,' adds another quickly.

'Where?' I scream.

'There – to that cage!' he points.

I run towards a makeshift barrier guarded by police. I run straight into a row of young policemen. They are frightened boys in bulky uniforms. They refuse to move. They become the angry football supporters I confronted in my youth. The bullies I faced up to at school, the focus of all the anger I can muster. They push me and I push back. One of them falls over. Another then hits me hard in the chest with his stick. I do not feel the pain; it isn't hard enough to stop me. Their capacity to reason, like mine, has vanished.

I prepare to charge past the police when I look beyond them into the compound and see Sita sitting there. She is alive with others, holding a bleeding face, but alive. I sigh in relief and with one deep exhalation there's no need to fight anymore, no need to assault this teenager standing in my way.

Self control flows back into my being but it is still absent from my opponents. I'm manhandled and pushed back. Reason is welcomed back to my mind as if a sluice gate has been opened in gratitude. I talk to the police in Nepali.

I shout over to Sita. 'She is my wife!' I tell the police, repeating this until they understand.

Sita looks up and waves. Her red dress is torn and has been pulled up and tied over her shoulder. She's using her skirt to stop a bleeding nose. I examine her thoroughly from a distance. She holds a hand over her mouth. Although I'm still held in restraint by the young policemen, they sense I'm no longer a threat.

Sita and I exchange facial expressions. A nod says she is all right. My nod yes that Ram is safe. Her... Durga is dead. Me... yes, we have to get you out of here!

'She is under arrest,' says a more senior officer who approaches me. 'Please move along unless you wish yourself joining her.'

Sita shouts for me to go and stay with Ram. I'm parked at the tollgate of my anger, but she is right. I have to think of Ram. I wave a submissive goodbye to Sita and blow her a kiss. It is all I can think of gesturing. She signs a Namasti back, hands in front of her face.

I walk back through the carnage. Tempers still flare in pockets of violence. All the remaining protests seem spontaneous, all individual and all ending in brutal consequences.

As I reach Bahadur's, I see it is deserted. The place has been ransacked and I run once more in a panic into the courtyard. The two midwives who delivered Ram are huddled in a basement corner holding him and wailing. I think the worst for a moment till I see him smile, ignorant of events and happy to see me.

The midwives tell me the police came looking for Bahadur and raided the whole building. I thank the midwives for protecting Ram and they head off to find their own families.

When I return to our flat holding Ram, I see a broken guitar and case outside our room. Inside, the content has been turned upside down. I bed down roughly, cuddling a smiling boy until he sleeps.

8 7

B y the next day, Pipelands is a flat dusty field. The shanty houses have been harvested and stacked as rubble at one end along with the crushed pipes. Already construction workers are erecting a fence around the perimeter. People gather at the corner where the teashop once stood and conduct a small puja for three people who lost their lives in yesterday's events. Newspapers run the story saying an elderly man collapsed and died of natural causes at the scene. Natural causes brought on by the sight of Tata bulldozer. A young policeman had died from injuries after being set on by a mob. And there was the accidental death of a child, left neglected in a pipe despite warnings of the clearances.

Durga, our little beautiful friend and sister to Ram. I place a flower on the ground near the fence where Durga lived and died. She will live only in our deep memory. She will be forever telling us the colour and texture of such a flower. We will remember her delight in expressing new-found knowledge. Ram is not yet able to comprehend such a loss. He struggles with me to retrieve the flower. Death does not yet exist as a pain for Ram; he can still only see and feel life. Later he will learn what the pain of loss is… as the downside of love.

The majority of Pipelanders are systematically escorted to another settlement on the outskirts of Kathmandu valley. It is a place bigger than Pipelands, both in area and its occupancy. The new shopping mall can now be constructed as planned.

Bahadur has not been seen since Pipelands was destroyed. A few days after the event, a firebomb is thrown into a local police office causing significant damage but no fatalities. Police say the device was crude but well made. They round up some stray Pipelanders in an attempt to track down the culprits. No one is charged but rumours spread that it was Bahadur's revenge.

I consider how many Bahadurs are now out there; having lost everything that is familiar through officially sanctioned brutality? How criminal of the authorities not to spend time explaining and planning the evacuation in an orderly way? How many people are unable to return to things as they were? A growing number of people are voicing anti-government sentiments and the local communist movements are actively recruiting.

Despite offers of accommodation from Swamy Y to move to the Ashram, I decide to stay and tidy up our rooms as best I can. Returning to a normal routine with Ram is a priority and is helping me as much as him to cope. I find that along with my broken guitar case, my Toshiba computer is missing, but my floppy disks are left intact. My guitar looks like it's been through a concert with Pete Townshend and The Who!

88

Sita's nose and eye are badly bruised and she has lost one of her front teeth. Part of her hair has been shaved off in prison, to stitch a cut to her head that required eleven stitches. Ironically, this former living goddess and principal disciple of the Moni Baba was charged with disturbing the peace.

In the weeks that follow the levelling of Pipelands I feel the need to offer twenty-four-hour guardianship, although this is not in any way requested. I join in the condemnation of the violence in conversations and in articles to the press. I also recognise the confusion that still lurks in many people and fear the ease with which violence could return.

Out of the blue I hear from my dad. How he knows of my situation I don't really understand. He offers me financial help if I can make a trip to his place to see him. He provides vouchers for air tickets.

While Sita heals, she decides to cut the rest of her hair off to match the short growth around her injury. Farida tidies up Sita's hairstyle and gives her a new red dress as a gift.

Tilak and Maya arrive at our reconstructed house. He appears smart in an out-of-character official Nepali suit. Maya looks radiant and pregnant. She excitedly announces that a son is expected soon.

'Pray she's right,' says Tilak.

Tilak informs me that Bahadur escaped the Kathmandu valley and stopped over with him in Barabase while he was on the run from authorities. He had informed Tilak of the situation at Pipelands and hopes that I can continue to look after his property. He will give us a reduced rent if we send money to an address in Pokhara.

I tell Tilak my computer was stolen and that I'm short on funds. He offers to help by lending money. He asks if the computer was insured and if can claim a refund. For a moment I feel an uncomfortable affinity with my dad.

For the next few weeks, Tilak and Maya help us and many other victims around Pipelands. They are supportive to Sita and encourage her to break her silence on the matter. Tilak tackles it head on one evening

'When you were growing up, you must have been taught that the Gods could intervene at any given time and change people's lives. That if your feet touched the ground it would bring bad luck to the whole country. If such bad luck happens, is a Kumari condemned and expelled in disgrace?'

'My childhood is something James calls an encouragement towards psychosis. When I first met the Moni Baba, he gave me the gift of confidence through yoga and said only by ignoring this gift would I ever be vulnerable. I never felt frightened thereafter, until that day in Pipelands.'

Sita reaches and pulls Ram closer to her.

'Most people don't know how they will act in a crisis until the time comes,' I say. 'To fight, to flee or surrender... our three basic options.'

Maya seems less interested in this English conversation than Ram and Sita takes the boy and hands him to Maya, asking her to take him outside. I believe she is finally setting herself up for a confession.

'When I saw the bulldozer move onto Durga's pipe,' Sita says, 'I knew instantly she could not survive and that she had been killed. I felt an anger like never before swell in front of my grief. It was a rage that kept me from breaking down or weeping. I have never felt such a sensation and have been taught to avoid it because of the consequences it can bring.'

'You faced-off a row of police. That was very brave of you,' I offer.

'It was not bravery. The crowd moved back and I was frozen to the spot. It could have happened the opposite way, with the crowd swelling forward, leaving me at the back. When I found myself on my own I began to feel different. I thought of the Baba and that I might well follow him in death.'

'You were very lucky.'

'It's neither luck nor bravery. When you suddenly don't know what will come next, your faith is challenged by fear. I thought of you and Ram and I could tell people were watching me. The police were commanding me to go back; the crowd were shouting, daring me to go forward. Fear was all around on a scale I had not sensed before.

'My own death was not something I feared. It is never difficult to control fear if you are indifference to the future, but I knew Ram needed me. And I knew you would need me to be with Ram too.

'When the police charged, I looked straight into the faces of the young men. The one who struck me did not meet my eyes. He looked at me only when I was on the ground. What I saw in him was regret. I remember even smiling at him. I lay dazed, grinning. The next thing I knew I was being dragged, feet first by an older man. My dress was torn from scraping across the ground. He was a garbage collector – there to clear up a mess others had made. He continued to pull me towards the caged compound. It made me so angry to be treated like this. The blow had stunned me, but the shock of being dragged, how you say, the lack of dignity, gave me the fury of Kali. I struggled, I leant forward and grabbed the man's arm; I tore at his shirt. He began to pull me harder, pulling my hair. I kicked my legs fiercely, breaking free and standing up. I swung an arm at him and slapped him. He punched me in the face. That's when others joined in to save me by throwing me into the compound. Other Pipelanders in there helped me until you found me.

'When I saw you, again my first reaction was fear. Fear for the safety of Ram. Our exchange of looks eased the tension and it was only then I realised my tooth was gone and my nose sore. There was a lot of blood from the cut on my head. I sensed it was not life threatening to me, so I did not fight the tears that came for Durga. Control does not mean repression of grief, it applies more to its release.'

As Sita talks, I hear her struggle with her own guilty thoughts. She goes on to ask if she could have saved Durga. She is a yogini, a fully conscious observer, guided by her capacity to observe and control. She has that rare skill to take stock before acting on observations or whatever comes into her mind.

Tilak then speaks at length of the social events leading up to Pipelands, as a form of therapy for Sita. It was an inevitable conflict of interests. People were trying to solve it with Pujas when there should have been dialog with authorities. This is the gap that the communists are stepping into in this country.

'I'm not advanced enough to be aware of these social causes and therefore not "constant" in my reactions to them,' Sita answers.

Tilak suggests she will be remembered as the heroine of Pipelands. He then goes out to find Maya and leaves us alone.

I tell Sita it may also be her new responsibilities and relationships that are bringing out a degree of uncertainty in her.

Sita tells me that different people draw different personalities out of her. She tells me she will now say things she would never say in the Baba's company. She tells me that when I suddenly appeared, I provided a new way for her to see herself and that she's begun to like what she sees.

'So I'm not too judgmental?' I ask.

'You make new comparisons for me to think about... which I like.'

I pause before asking, 'Have you made any judgement on my marriage proposal?'

Sita takes a moment. It is not a thinking silence. It is more like she's waiting for my fear of her answer to disappear.

'I do not want to leave Nepal... but I know that you love Ram and I love you for that among other things. I will marry you James Munro, if you are willing to accept a toothless yogini.'

'Yes,' I chant quietly.

Then she adds, 'But no move to Scotland.'

89

In the months after Pipelands, Tilak and Maya have regular medical check-ups in Kathmandu. Sita continues to teach her yoga class. She's become the talk of the town and while the majority show her support there are a few private yoga pupils who suddenly stop their appointments. It's Swamy Y who tells me this. Sita says nothing.

I hear loud voices one afternoon while Tilak is at the door of the flat. He's shouting at an old Brahmin man that I've seen at private sessions with Sita. It's a reminder of the Tilak that faced the old lady Tamang at the battle of River Mill.

'What was that about?' I ask when he comes back into the house.

'I love my country and its culture, but sometimes old stubborn Brahmins make problems out of nothing.'

'Explain.'

'Among many Brahmins any misfortune is taken as a signal of God's judgement. That man is one who believes that the assault on Sita was most likely the result of bad karma. I was arguing with him and then I lost it when he suggested it was also punishment for Sita being intimate with foreigners.'

MAYA'S NEW CURIOSITY IN WESTERN APPEARANCES BEGINS TO manifest in purchases from Farida. Maya has already spent time trying on Sita's collection of western style clothes.

Sita assures me that it is not Farida who has encouraged Maya to dress differently nor her who taught her how to put on make-up. After all it was devotees who painted Sita's face each day as a child, not her. Sita tells me it was a single copy of the western magazine *Cosmopolitan*, with instructional make-up photos inside, that inspired Maya's new look.

Neither Sita nor Maya have ever been educated in a school but their capacity to learn is obvious almost every day. Maya dropped out after two years of primary education to care for her younger sister. Sita learned everything she knows from parents, priests and specialist tutors and mostly from imitation and intuition. Her yoga has been her university of life, giving her a doctorate under-standing of human psychology. Her legacy is surely her insights on the values, issues, problems and changes faced by Nepali villagers.

Sita points out that there are many secrets in her language and that these secrets and superstitions are used to trade power. Since learning English she can find instruction on any subject she wants. There are no longer any secrets left.

We inform Tilak and Maya that we are planning to go off to visit the Avadhoot. I tell them they're welcome to stay in our flat. Neither of them has any idea that the Avadhoot is my father and they believe our trip is connected to the Moni Baba Centre. There *are* still secrets in my world.

9 0

Arranging words on a page helps me bring thoughts to some conclusion, as meditation might. From what I've learned, Sita deserves to be the main recipient of whatever conscious love I can muster. Whenever I detect in her as a desire, I should scheme to help her fulfil it. Like a dose of micronutrients to your whole being, one has to love consciously in small doses over a long period of time, before any benefits are felt.

Being young, Ram simply soaks up as much of our conscious love as he can without seeming to realise its uniqueness or the rewards he gives us back. He is growing into a happy and inquisitive child.

If conscious love does really work, why then does the world we live in always appear chaotic to me? Is it because of how I choose to describe it to myself, or do I simply not have the capacity to see the full picture? As adults, we are exposed to the full range of opinions that people hold and it appears the same principle of promoting conscious love applies to the promotion of other things like hate, and fear. Whatever we put our collective conscious mind into promoting... so gives us that in return.

Perhaps it is a genetically passed on trait in my family, to be suspicious of what others advise as the best for you. Since my travels began, I've listened to folks lay open their beliefs. I've heard advice which seems right at the moment, only to repeat it to others later and catch it sounding patronizing or corny.

I've watched people leaving sessions with the Moni Baba filled with excitement over some sort of realisation. I've also found many unable to get past the words to the context. They leave with the Baba's words, ready to repeat them without a full under-standing of what the application of these words require. They use his words as items of trade, not instruction. They never translate a realisation into the behaviour intended. I've witnessed enough people acting in cruel or violent ways to know one cannot just ignore them and retreat. It may be our most basic instinct to flee or fight but can these adaptions still happen through conscious thinking. A thinking mind brought to a problem can surely offer several alternatives to inflicting pain or death. A mind jammed with hate often chooses violence as an escape from choice. This is especially true when misplaced fear is the result of a cultural griev-ance passed on through the generations.

There are so few people like Sita, who have such a natural ability to survive changes to their life, to see problems afresh and to confidently offer self-awareness as a solution to uncertainty. To offer faith, as understood in any language.

Adapting my own insights into a new approach to life happened unconsciously. There must have been a mental space just waiting to accommodate all these new observations. How long this vacancy existed in my brain, I don't know. It's been a process of discovery very different from the past where I absorbed from school, university, TV shows, films, books and from friends at home. I feel I've managed to accept a fuller sensation of who I am here, not just an image of myself.

At home I was part of the way things worked, integrated and too busy and too committed to perceive things differently. I realize it is not the place that offers the chance to expand one's horizons; it is the break from one's routine. Any escape from the deeds that you've created as a routine brings with it the opportunity to refresh your vision. I was excited to leave behind the security of my predetermined conduct, where necessity prevents the freedom needed to change your perceptions.

Whether you are a Nepali farmer or a Western businessman, you are prepared as a child for what's predicted for you as adults. Our brains slowly construct the world we live in and our emotions become strongly linked to what we believe. We have limited shared insight into how the world works, because each brain sees the world differently from everyone else.

Our environment in turn influences our vision. A farmer caught up in seasonal activities needs to farm; the businessman steeped in contracts and agreements needs to keep a business going. For the farmer, it's a lifestyle he sees as necessary; for the businessman, it's exactly the same. It is in defining what is necessary that there are differences.

My discoveries have been the result of exposing a committed mind in a new environment where I have had no commitments. I may not have gathered the expert observations of an academic or a social scientist, but my idle philosophizing is invaluable to me. It is a regular part of brain activity; it moulds our thoughts and influences our decisions, even if the philosophy is wrong. How else can we explain so many collective social mistakes – from tribalism to racism and religious bigotry? Finding out that our beliefs and idle philosophies are wrong or harmful can trigger change. Retreating into an echo chamber of similar thinking minds is a limiting and dangerous way to survive.

The rich cultural diversity you find in a country like Nepal seems as necessary to me as the bio-diversity required in nature's balance. Just as plant and animal lives are endangered or destroyed or controlled by the demands from one species, so too are the finite differences in our human cultures. This is especially obvious among social structures in remote regions. Languages are vanishing, as are the fashions and customs so long identified with specific ethnic groups. This is not just the sweeping influence of electricity or the new-world culture that is causing it. It has as much to do with the natural curiosity of children born in these traditional communities. Once stimulated, every young mind has the capacity to take in more than what is culturally on offer to it. It is natural then that such a young mind accommodates new ideas and adds to its own cultural knowledge. The main obstacle to this evolution comes as adults, when we lose the capacity to expand our consciousness at the same rate, we feel overwhelmed or frightened and therefore hostile to change. We are especially cautious and fearful of change in our own young. Despite the biblical look of this place, many things in Nepal have changed extremely fast.

No one represents these fast changes in Nepal more than the four people who now sit in front of me. Sita, Ram, Tilak and Maya.

Sita's experienced yogic hands are massaging Maya's feet and her stomach gently. Sita talks to the unborn child with her voice and her fingers. Tilak is speaking Nepali and English at the same time to Ram. When I look at these four, I know that I too have changed.

I sit on the seat where I first spoke to Sita about visiting dad. Another letter arrives from him. Tilak has no idea why the famous Sanyasin writes to me in English and he leaves the room out of reverence.

Inside are several hundred US dollar bills and neatly written instructions for a visit to him in Doti. He adds that if Sita is coming, she knows the way.

This jolts me because Sita has not mentioned she has visited the Avadhoot's home before. Dad continues saying he's heard of the Baba's passing and is very pleased that we were both there. He reminds me he lives in a more comfortable place than the temporary hut where we met, offers that we can stay for as long as we wish and out of respect for Sita he will put on some clothes.

PART EIGHT: THE RETURN

Sita and I decide to take the night bus to Pokhara, before boarding a flight from there to the far west. It is less expensive to break the journey this way, and we are able to pay off a few loans with dad's money before we leave.

As we pass through Barabase on the bus, I tell Sita of my time living there, waiting and searching for the Moni Baba. It is part of my story she knows little about and she seemed moved by my descriptions of living with Tilak and Maya.

It is late and most people seem to be dozing on the bus. Ram lies sound asleep next to us on the long back seat. The hum of the engine and the motion relaxes me into a meditative state. My arm brushes against Sita's, then our hands touch with a pleasant sting. I hesitate for a moment and then I kiss her. It is high risk displaying such affection in public here, but Sita responds with the same excitement as I feel.

Our fresh feelings are tested in a chemical exchange on our lips. Her eyes are closed, mine too and for a moment it feels timeless, a kiss as eternal as a mantra. As our lips part I feel an urge in Sita to say something. She opens her eyes, responding with an awkward silence. For a moment she kisses me again, this time it is a dead kiss, a farewell kiss. As our heads part I look at her with such sorrow, she laughs. She grabs my face in her hands and begins to kiss my nose. She continues with a pointed tongue searching for my eye sockets.

'My mouth is not fully healed,' she says, 'but I want you.' She moves over, sitting on my lap facing me. We are on a public bus, a child is asleep beside us and people might look round any moment. A thought flashes through my head from a fleeting tangent. We could be shamed for lewd behaviour. I accommodate this thought as I resist Sita's passion. New passengers get on so Sita moves back onto her seat. She regains control over our powerful lust and I follow her, breathlessly.

During the rest of the bus ride I believe we recover something that has been lost since we returned from the Baba's funeral... some respect for the passion that drew us together in the first place. Once more everything seems fully alive between us. If I can only learn to read when and why this passion comes and goes, I'll be better able to cope.

When we reach Pokhara, we wait at the newly refurbished airstrip where a Twin Otter with ten seats will take us to Nepalgange and then another flight the rest of the way to Silgari. We sit amusing Ram by rolling a small mandarin orange across the floor. He is now mobile enough to enjoy chasing it like a puppy fetching a ball.

We hear the flight is delayed for half an hour. It's hardly a wait at all for the passengers. Some have walked five days to get here and will walk a further three days when they land. No banging on the airline desk from delayed passengers here. There is, however, another kind of banging.

An old mountain man, possibly a Tamang, is attacking a new Coca Cola machine. He looks up and down it, as it towers over his hunched body. He walks around the side, then again to the front. He stands mesmerised. He bangs the side of the machine, then begins to press every screw and rivet that stands out from the surface of the machine. He presses the hinges, then one by one a row of plastic nameplates on the front. His coins have been put in but nothing has come out. As he kneels again and inserts his full arm into the machine, Sita walks over and presses the proper selection button and a coke clunks into the tray. The old man bows in appreciation and walks away, smugly holding his can of Coke.

Sita smiles at me and we continue our rolling game with Ram. I look back and notice the man again appears frustrated. I nudge Sita as he pulls out a large Khukri knife from his carry-on bag and plunges it into the top of the can. He doesn't know how to pull the ring opener but he does understand a Khukri's capacity to slice open a tin can. He takes a drink and puts the Khukri back in his bag. No one in this waiting room bats an eyelid at the sight of a man wielding a large knife. It is clearly a far more common sight than a can of Coke.

After the brief changeover in Nepalgunj to a smaller aircraft we swoop in to land at Silgarhi slightly late. A windsock waves like a tattered battle flag as we taxi up the grass runway. We come to a roaring stop at a wooden, windowless terminal, about the size of a garden shed.

A uniformed policeman comes running out to help open the door of the single engine aircraft. To my surprise, I see the Avadhoot standing there waiting, dressed in the saffron robes of a holy man. He looks smarter and cleaner but still passes for an ethnic Nepali, with matted hair, his caked make-up and Shiva stripes.

Three government officials on our flight are first to get out and they bow respectfully to the Avadhoot. They step forward before they are pushed aside by those waiting to get on. There seems to be more people waving return tickets than there are seats on the plane.

Sita and I exit last and are guided to the arrivals' hut by dad. He ploughs a path through the crowds with his staff and an experienced stride. The engine noise again gets loud so I shout.

'How did you know we'd be on this flight?'

Dad closes his eyes and brings his two index fingers together with his thumbs, chanting Om.

The plane behind us fills up quickly and the engines rev up once more. As the plane turns, we are all blasted with dust. It taxies back to the end of the sloping airstrip then accelerates down the grass hill and off into the air.

The noise disappears as we watch the plane become smaller and smaller. That most powerful silence of the inner Himalaya envelops us once more.

The Avadhoot welcomes us to the isolated district of Doti, his home. It's a much milder temperature than Kathmandu. Sita bends to touch his feet. He motions his hand over the scar on her head, then shakes my hand like a highlander and gives me a hug.

I pick up my backpack but dad gestures he has the services of a porter to carry everything. Sita's small bag plus mine are placed into a Dhoko basket, then Ram is strapped onto the top with a cloth tying him in. A teenage boy half my height carries the load.

'Have you no older porters – this is child labour?'

'It's an apprenticeship,' dad says.

He tells me we have a short climb towards Silgarhi. We will then stop at a tea shop where he is to meet some Tibetan monks, before taking us to his home.

As we leave the airstrip, groups of children follow us. Dad tells me that Nepal's remote airstrips are as fascinating to children as train spotting was to children at home. 'They are accustomed to aircraft yet have never seen a bus or a car, or even a bicycle in real life. They'll scream with delight at take-offs and landings. Many know the planes and pilots by name and walk for miles back to their homes after their aviation outings.'

A few plane spotters walk with us up the long trail to Silgarhi, chattering all the way.

Doti is the name of the district where dad chose to hide after faking his death – a fakir, indeed. On first sight the lifestyle seems years behind the rest of the country in terms of development.

Traditional clothes, containing subtle signs that show which caste each person is, are still prevalent here. No sports sweaters or Bollywood t-shirts to disguise one's self in here.

Dad tells me the local communities were established long ago when the Moguls first invaded India. They forced the top-tier of Brahmin families to take refuge in these hills. It is one the last bastions of old-fashioned Hinduism, with a lifestyle from the Old Testament. Until the airstrip was built a few years ago it was inaccessible and most trails led south into India.

I tell dad we found his Yoga book among the Baba's possessions and he appears genuinely touched.

'The Baba told me that you influenced him as much as he influenced you.'

'Aye... but I got the best of the deal,' he says.

I tell him the Baba's last teaching was on the subject of conscious love.

'It's one of the Baba's most influential talks. Naebody has peddled the idea of love as much as him, at least since Jesus.'

'Do you practice conscious love, dad?'

Dad looks round, recognising my sarcasm.

'Don't confuse love with sex,' he says.

He rises above the bait and continues.

'The Baba recognised there are more components to our western tax system than for love in the English language, yet love brings far better returns.'

'Did you know the Baba was given a sky burial?' I interrupt.

'No. Goodness. I didn't know that.'

'Quite a way to recycle yourself.'

'Take the Baba's advice son and put your faith into conscious love.'

'What if it doesn't seem to work, what then?'

'It may not always work in your favour but it works. Whether it is directed at a child, a spouse, a friend, a pet or a garden plant in

Peebles, what you apply properly... stimulates a predictable response.'

'Pity the Baba didn't tell you all this before you left mum and I.'

'A sky burial you say?'

'His eyes were pecked out, like...'

'Stop it.'

In the town of Silgarhi, dad leaves us and marches off to his interview with Tibetan monks. Sita and I take our time, resting and feeding Ram at a near-by teashop. Sita points out a neat row of traditional wooden-fronted shops. They look charming and idyllic but these shops also contain visual clues to the caste of the owners. One in particular bans people from the lower castes from even entering. Sita tells me the Avadhoot is doing work with local Maoists to bring awareness of this type of discrimination into the open.

We meet up with dad at the Hindu temple just as his interview is coming to an end. Sita, Ram and I walk into a small but elaborately decorated hall. Several poorly proportioned cement sculptures of Hindu Gods and Goddesses line the back wall.

To my surprise there is tension in the room so Sita takes Ram to sit outside with a group of older Tibetan monks. I stay and squat quietly on the floor near the door. I can tell dad is uncomfortable. There is an American in full monk's robes accompanying the others and he seems to be recording with a video camera. I have walked in on an argument because dad has refused to be filmed.

A Tibetan monk is translating the American's questions into Nepali for the Avadhoot to answer in Nepali. It's obviously dad's ploy to give the illusion he's a local. The American points a microphone menacingly at dad's mouth.

'So what do you say about the repression of people in Tibet? Is freedom not worth fighting for?'

The Avadhoot answers in fluent Nepali but it is laughable because he also keeps correcting the translator's English. I begin to understand what dad is saying.

'I am a Sanyasin not a monk, I only talk of matters of god and of consciousness. If you read your own Buddhist texts, true freedom does not have a geographic border... it is in the mind.'

'But how can you ignore the systematic rape and destruction of an entire culture?' The American monk spits out his question.

Dad finally gives in to an outburst in English that he badly disguises with a few Nepali words and head shakes.

'You cannot ignore social injustice. It is what you choose to do about it that is important. There is nothing whole about any of today's Nations, not in the way nature designs wholeness in its creations. All boundaries are man made, dreamed up borders. Countries are held together on fragile agreements of behaviour and even the social and ethnic mix that makes up our Nations are not all interactive supporting systems. To compare one country with another is a ridiculous measurement of the undefined against the incomplete.'

Dad waits to see a reaction on the face of his listeners. The translator seems nervously relieved his work is done. After a brief silence, dad hammers home another point.

'Tibetans are now all over the world where many have chosen to keep alive the Tibetan culture. Their strength is in their value to other cultures. People should have the freedom to be whatever they want... and not just be "Tibetan". Where is the strength or the freedom in that? It's the skills of modern governing that all Nations require... enlightened politicians... not just leaders with a god status. You harp on about the Dalai Lama, you want to reduce him to being the leader of a Nation? He is already much more than that. His teachings as a monk are an inspiration to the world. A monk's skills however are very limited for modern political leadership.'

Dad sways his head and clasps his hands. One of the monks chants Om at the mention of the Dalai Lama and the American speaks into his microphone saying *OK, that's a wrap*. I slip out and leave them to pack up. I find Sita talking with the few rough looking older Tibetan monks.

Sita also looks annoyed and I don't understand why until two of the older monks approach me and ask permission to conduct a reincarnation test on Ram. I look as Sita who rolls her eyes. When I ask why, they say they are on a mission to discover the recent reincarnation of a Tibetan Lama who died last year in the USA.

At first I think it is a joke until Sita indicates how serious these monks are. She tells me they are looking for a child born around the same time as Ram. This dead Rinpoche predicted his own reincarnation in Kathmandu and the monks have been routinely testing children.

I look across at Sita, who is waiting to see my reaction to this request. Here the monks seem to be ignoring her presence entirely.

Before I give any approval, the monks proceed to unpack a satchel of the dead Rinpoche's belongings and Ram is already looking interested in these as playthings. They've been carrying the artefacts around for more than a year. Sita tells me that Ram is the third child they have discovered that's within their required birth dates, but none of the others passed the test. They're keen to try out an assessment on Ram but I see reluctance in Sita as she plays along as the dumb mother.

The monks carry on regardless. Ram is given several puzzles to solve. The belongings of the dead Rinpoche are set among a variety of other Tibetan artefacts. Ram is observed to see which items he'll pick. Despite this assortment of objects, Ram's ratio for choosing the correct Rinpoche's belongings is high. More than half of the times he is challenged, he picks up the right object. This success rate immediately sets the monks talking among themselves and their enthusiasm is palpable.

I watch the whole thing unfold with incredulity as the Tibetans arrange and rearranged the artefacts. Ram's interest in examining the objects carefully comes from Durga, not from some past life.

The monks become more vocal and convinced that Ram has passed the test. They believe they have found their incarnate Lama and immediately offer me free education for Ram in Dharmasala. If I wish I can hand him over to them now. I feel I'm dreaming in some ancient child slave market.

Since there's a presumption I'm the father, they also offer me alternative education for Ram at a nearby Buddhist school. I'm told I can travel with the child or visit as often as I like. If I prefer, he could attend a monastery in Kathmandu.

Throughout this negotiation, the monks have completely ignored Sita. She has been silently watching to see what I might say. She waits no longer.

Sita turns on the monks and in simple Nepali, tells the Tibetans we both understand their excitement but that they cannot have her son. When it seems they are about to argue, she tells the monks that she is the ex-Kumari who travelled with the Moni Baba, at which point they bow with clasped hands. She mentions that as a child she was put through similar tests to become the Kumari. She mentions how when she was four years old, she was tested to see how afraid she was, by being locked in a room with howling noises, masks and the heads of dead animals. Sita talks as if she remembers it like it was yesterday.

'Do not confuse what you have gone through yourselves as a

child, to become a monk, as being the best path for others to follow.'

She says she's long remembered the chill of those experiences. She tells the monks their religion should see the Rinpoche in all children, that they display themselves as ignorant old men, stuck in a tradition that denies the contribution of a mother's knowledge or love to a child's upbringing.

She tells them they are as outdated as those who believe that women should throw themselves on the funeral pyre of their dead husbands, or offer children as a sacrifice to the gods when their crops fail. This practice of harvesting children for compulsory monastic life is next on the list of religious procedures to be scrapped.

'For all the good you feel you can offer people, you still insist on spreading these destructive superstitions.'

The monks look humbled although one looks insulted. They take their ancient artefacts and American sponsor and head off to catch their private plane back to Kathmandu.

Sita tells me she knows mothers who have willingly handed over their children in such circumstances mostly because they are poor and believe they cannot provide the child with anything better. When dad joins us, he says he has counselled quite a few Lamas who have moved on from monastic life. They have passed through their spiritual grooming phase and finally found another definition of themselves.

9 4

I n Silgharhi we say farewell and thanks to our young porter as dad takes the dokho basket with Ram in it and we carry our bags. We climb further on a gentle slope alone through a forest trail. Sita leads the way.

On this trail I question dad more about his political views.

'Did I hear correctly, you are against the idea of Tibetans fighting for their homeland?'

'There's a fine line between fighting for your homeland before it turns into a fight for the exclusion of everything else.'

We leave the trail near the summit of a hill and approach a derelict temple with vines and foliage covering the remains. As I approach, I notice the temple is completely hidden from the narrow trail we arrived on. At the ruins, my father proclaims we have arrived.

With a sense of drama, dad lifts up a turf trapdoor revealing a set of steps into the bowels of the earth. The whole of this hilltop is the roof of his underground retreat.

Sita, Ram and I walk down the wooden stairway into the Avadhoot's bunker. Only someone with substantial design skills and a deep paranoia of being discovered could construct this. It is dug into the ground and well disguised.

Dad disappears in the dark for a moment, then opens a series of turf shutters and the place fills with light. There appears to be two rooms. The larger has two walls full of books with a small cooking area at one end. The other is a bedroom. I ask if there's a toilet and dad points to a cloth-screened corner and a neat pit latrine.

'Well... five-star Sanyasin accommodation. How Swiss family Munro!'

'My wee But n Ben!'

Sita takes a very sleepy Ram from the dokho and in a weirdly familiar way walks into the bedroom. She waves me over as she puts Ram down on the floor and points to his hand. It is clutching a small chain from the Rinpoche that we hadn't noticed he'd kept in his fist.

'Careful,' dad says, 'it's the first sign your wee Rinpoche is an incarnated kleptomaniac.'

Dad picks up a large Kukhri knife from a woodpile and takes two smaller blades from the sheaf. He then lights a small kitchen fire by striking the two small blades together. A pile of pencil shavings turn into flames immediately and he blows them expertly into the larger woodpile. I look out the window to see where the smoke is disappearing to but I see no sign of it emerging from the house.

'I designed a ship's funnel to take the smoke to an outlet near a small stream,' dad says proudly. 'It just looks like the water is steaming.'

I browse through some thickly bound books, left on a small table. All are old and mostly in Sanskrit. I then walk to the doorway of the kitchen to watch my old man settle in at home.

'Will you take honey and goats milk in your tea?'

'What kind of tea is it?'

'It's Tetley... before Tetley ever get it. I have a number of wild bushes growing outside.'

'Any oatcakes?'

'No, but there are some rice cakes, and if I grill them, it's the nearest I have to oatcakes.'

'This is quite a place.'

'It's funny… I've seen this day many times in my mind, showing you around this house. If you ever have any doubt your life is guided by your thoughts, then remember this day as a confirmation. Your thoughts have a great influence on your path. I have willed this to happen. I have visualised meeting with you here. This moment is a manifestation of one of my most powerful prayers. I did not, however, expect to see you, that day in the Terai.'

'Caught with your pants down?'

'Yes indeed.'

95

The fire sparks to life and the slight chill in the room disappears. Dad begins to heat a blackened metal tray, placing it over three stones. He then stretches up towards a hanging basket neatly stacked with tins and brings out a handful of rice cakes. He shuffles them onto the tray like a dealer with cards. He lights two butter-lamps and offers me a crude wooden stool.

As I sit, I realise the air is becoming so smoky that the upper ceiling is now filled with clouds of CO_2. Dad lifts another latch, which allows the smoky air to be drawn out of the room. His funnel design is not as sophisticated as I first thought.

'Do many people pass this way?'

'None, that's why I chose this spot. There have been a few surprise pilgrims from India to visit the ruined temple to Saraswati. I just pop out from nowhere, like Mickey Mouse at Disney World, to check them out. I've never had any trouble all my years here. Only those I know well visit me here.'

'Like Sita?'

'Sita and the Moni Baba have often stayed here. Have you two decided what you're going to do?'

Dad's question catches me by surprise and I have no answer for it. I pause. Ram wakes with a cry and Sita seizes the opportunity to take him outside. She's heard dad's question and walks past both of us looking each in the eye, then at Ram and leaves us alone.

'Yes! We have agreed to get married but we haven't decided what we're going to do yet.'

'You must carefully think through the consequences of staying.'

'I've asked Sita if she would come back to Scotland.'

'What was her answer?'

'Well, her answer was no. I thought I'd explained the advantages of us being married to her, but it hasn't helped.'

'Have you tried explaining the advantages of Scotland to her?'

'Through her eyes, there is no advantage. She has a curiosity about life that is extraordinary and might eventually tempt her to come, but she is not fuelled by the same urge to leave her home that I was.'

'That we both were!'

'Correct. She has not grown tired of it here and she is not trying to escape anything.'

'It's clear she is interested in something new, though.'

'What's that?'

'A father for Ram.'

'Why do you say that?'

'The western concept of single parenting is almost unheard of here.'

'Well, I now know the real father was a Frenchman, but he has no idea of his child's existence.'

'I'm not surprised that Ram does not have a Nepali father.'

'What makes you say that?'

'The curse.'

'Oh yes, the curse.'

'The Moni Baba has tried for years to destroy this myth but even his powers of persuasion have not spread very far.'

I sip my tea and enjoy the fresh rice cakes. Sita returns with a sleeping Ram and curls up with him on Tibetan cushions.

We in turn walk out in silence to the edge of dad's hill, looking into a deep valley. The sunset is later than in the lower towns because of our height. A single stone seat has been fashioned, yet another indication of dad's choice to be alone. There's hardly any room for me to sit beside him.

'It's something I did not think I could ever do, retreat in such isolation for so long.'

'But did you really understand its cost to others?'

'I know it's been tough on you for a long time. But I always believed there'd be a moment when I could pay you back.'

'How can you pay for moments forever lost?'

'If you believe in the on-going expansion of people's consciousness you know there'll be an opportunity to help at all times in their life. The more aware you are of this, the more you will create and offer.'

'Do you not have to be in close proximity to someone to offer help?'

'You would be wise to consider conscious love in your present circumstance. It applies very much to your current situation. The rules are powerful. If either lover fails... then it is necessary they split up.'

'You sound like you've said this many times.'

'Yes, to myself as much as to others. A great sadness envelopes lovers who cannot let go. People fear they will not find another lover or they become jealous, or having put so much energy into a relationship they cling to each other. They are not in love but in despair and cannot see it. Jealousy can melt a conscious lover's heart like yak butter in the sun.'

'Do you think jealousy applies to me?'

'I sense it is a part of your decision to ask Sita to marry you.'

'How do you sense this?'

'Your body language, the words you say and what I've had thirty years of experience in observing. This sensing you talk of, is my job.'

'I love Sita.'

'I don't doubt it. But she also has experience in reading people and she will not accept your offer to move to Scotland if she believes it is based on jealousy or any sort of possessiveness on your part towards her.'

I'd never known a relationship without some form of jealousy. 'Is it not acceptable to show someone you care?'

'Not with Sita, she is not seeking to make a jealous lover of you. She is more likely to encourage your freedom from jealousy.'

'Is that what happened between you and mum? Do you think that you chose the right action?'

'I did not know about conscious love then. But I do now.'

A fter our first night in father's foxhole, my eyes begin to take in more of what I am surrounded by. In the room that looks full of books, I notice that one bookcase is not real but neatly painted in Trompe-l'oeil. The painting is so realistic it takes a stroke from my finger across the flat surface to confirm that it is a painted illusion. The other wall is packed, floor to ceiling, with real books.

'You have so many books, why did you paint this wall?'

'I am not a religious man James, but I'm a scholar of Hinduism with a wee touch of the Communist in me. These religious books give me the architectural framework for people's minds here. Most all of us are born into an established cultural and religious framework and live within the walls of that framework all our lives. We find comfort and familiarity in this cultural architecture. Not all of us like to live our lives within one building and those who are yogis at heart, like to explore.'

'So what exactly do you teach? How do you combine your Sanyassin… I only talk about god rule… to your sympathies with Communism, which believes there is no such thing as god?'

'Yoga frees you from these labels so you see where the source of your sympathies come from. Where religion is the agenda it can offer shelter for the lost and confused. It is not rocket science to see where it fails. Most religions encourage their followers to procreate to keep their numbers up. This is an insane policy for these times of limited resources. There is little provision of knowledge and social management to cope with increasing populations from religion.'

'You can talk, Mr bang-away-yogi.' I speak but am ignored.

'There is too much value placed on hereditary or reincarnated leadership traits here. You cannot produce the leaders required in a modern society this way. At best, most holymen are the caretakers of our fragile and often barbaric spirituality history. We need to hold them to a new social standard more than they hold us to archaic spiritual standards.'

'Sorry to be the devil's advocate, but isn't this a contradiction for you? To be critical of people who have a religious orientation? As a yogi are you not just a one-man religion?'

'You are a yogi if you practice yoga, because it becomes the prism through which you see all else. Yoga is certainly not for everyone because it takes time to train oneself. But with yogis contributing an essential element to the whole of society – including politics – we are seers who remain unseen.'

'Underground, you mean?'

'Yes, underground!' We both begin laughing.

'Do you have any success suggesting people change their faith?'

'Not their religion, but their faith. I encourage people to break the logjam of a troubled mind. Faith is the one substance that can soothe an impatient mind; on the other hand, it can be used simply to cover up outrageous mistakes. The secret is not in the promotion of faith but in knowing the right instance it needs to be applied.'

'The importance of a critical mind?'

'Who was the Buddha, if not a critical Hindu prince? Who was

Jesus, if not a critical Jew? Mohammed also saw the flaws in other religions at the time to bring home the point of Islam to a new generation. There have been many other men and women. These people are no longer alive but that critical capacity lives on in each of us. All have taken what they knew about existing religious and human governance and observed its faults then suggested changes. If taking them as an example means anything, it means following their capacity for analytical thinking more than their commandments.

'Come, I have one more thing to show you.'

He walks over to the painted wall. When he reaches the false bookcases he thumps the top right-hand corner of the wall. He lifts the heavy panel by hand, placing it to the side against an existing bookcase. Behind this panel is another room tunnelled into the darkness. He disappears inside until a burst of light shows him in silhouette opening another shuttered window.

This room is twice as big as the living room. There is a drawing board standing alone in the middle, with a T-square and set squares. It takes my eyes some time to adjust, but slowly I see the walls are covered in designs. There are shelves with what looks like thick rolls of carpets. A large Buddhist wheel of life, six foot by six foot, adorns the wall opposite.

Dad opens another window to let in more light. I realise the walls are covered in canvases all finely painted in what looks like the tradition of Newari Thanka painters. His secret room is filled with paintings, not carpets but thick rolls of paintings stacked high into neat piles. Some that hang open look unfinished but are already rich in detail. It is a palace of artwork and I gasp in astonishment as dad walks over to the wheel of life.

'This one took me almost two years to complete. It contains over a thousand figures and I use a one-haired brush to complete some of the finer detail.'

'How many do you have in here?'

'Seven hundred and fifty-eight. I sell one or two every year for

US dollars to buy supplies. I get three thousand for a small one and up to six thousand for the large ones.'

I make a quick calculation in my head and whisper, 'That means there is over three million dollars' worth of art in this room.'

'A Hindu scholar with a talent in Buddhist art… and a commercial trade, quite the multi-cultural Sanyassin, no?'

'With such Christian modesty,' I say.

'And a wee touch of working-class Scot.'

I walk around the room looking at the artwork. I'm awe-struck. I look at Sita who appears at the door. She smiles as if she has seen it all before. The work is overpowering in its detail. I look at the racks of rolled-up canvases. It is such a wealth of work I shake my head in admiration.

'You could sell this for much more in the West, with this quality.'

'So much of this type of art has been destroyed in the past fifty years. I've chosen to repaint many Tankas but also make up some compositions myself.'

'What do you mean?'

'Traditional young monk artists were often given a certain mood or teaching to convey by the high Lamas. I make up my own. I put characters together in unusual combinations, in order to convey some new meanings for people.'

Dad points to a lavish Tanka behind the fake wall. 'This character Sem Ny Negelso represents a restful mind. It can be partnered with others I choose to paint such as aggression or compassion.'

'What about combining market research with profitable arts?

'A few scholars in the West might decipher some of these messages as mere cartoons.'

Dad unfurls a three-foot by two-foot delicately painted Tanka. Among the waves of wispy clouds and traditional mountains are the usual crowds of Bodhisatva monks riding tigers or snow leopards. All this activity is being ignored by another set of finely drawn monks. On closer examination, dad's monks are all gathered in the four opposite corners of the painting huddled in front of a television set showing revolutionary images from India's communist states. It is illustrated in the perfected style of the Tanka painter.

'Tankas for the Revolution,' I say. 'You should add some Disney characters. There'd be a big market for them.'

'And a lawsuit.'

W e end up spending ten days in Silgarhi, mostly walking and talking with the artist Avadhoot my dad. Despite her toothless grin, Sita seems to blossom in the hills, away from the city. She is at her most confident in these surroundings. The area is not geared for tourists so we have to carry our own food. We stop at small houses. We hand over a bag of rice and lentils and ask the family to include us in their meal. Without question they do.

Some days, dad does not come with us and stays and works on one of his projects. He'll either be painting or reading Hindu scriptures when we return. He has a timetable for himself that is as fixed as anyone who talks of ungodly things.

The only other person we see come to the Avadhoot's door is a passing porter who makes a delivery from the nearest post office. Dad tells me he has a few subscriptions to magazines, including *Rolling Stone, National Geographic* and a newsletter from an organisation called 'Shanti Sadan' published in London. He tells me he recently received a *Newsweek* gift subscription from a Kathmandu devotee and as a result, he's also begun to receive junk mail. He shows me a pile of credit card applications addressed to The Avad-hoot, Silgari, Western Nepal. He lights his fire with these.

The western hills are far less populated than those in eastern Nepal, so it is common to find isolated communities who survive solely on their own resources. On one walk we find a field of Hemp and Ganja used for a variety of cloth products and keeping grandfathers happy with a medicinal night-time tote.

While a farmer's wife cooks us Dhal Bhat, we sit and watch as two children run through the fields clapping hands over the Cannabis flowers. They run to the house where their father scrapes it off their palms and stores it, then sends them back out on a clapping harvest. I'm told they harvest this crop two or three times in a season because they do not cut the plant.

I ask the family if they ever sell the drug to outsiders and they insist that they don't.

On returning to hobbit hill, I ask dad what he knows about the use of narcotic drugs in this part of the country. If there is any presence of drug lords and if any illicit trade has reached here.

Dad seems convinced there isn't a drug problem here, at least not yet. He tells me marijuana grows wild and has been widely used for medicinal purposes, with some recreational use by elders.

'Can you imagine these villages being napalmed by aircraft like they do in South America because someone believes that's the solution to consumer addiction?' he asks.

'Maybe you should go to the United States and sort them out.'

'In all my years here I've helped only two young people regain control after their addiction to weed,' dad says. 'Yoga would certainly be cheaper and more effective to help addicts regain control, than using incarceration or gunships.'

The morning before we leave to return to Kathmandu, Sita prepares a basket of breakfast rotis. It is the fresh smell that wakes me and after we eat she lifts a Tanka painting from the Avadhoot's shelf. She asks my dad what the painting means.

'This,' he says, 'is my interpretation of Reverend, Thomas

Robert Malthus' theory. He's the man who forecast an overpopulated gloomy end to mankind.'

'What's it about?' Sita asks.

'In its time it was popular to point out that although food supplies increase arithmetically, the human population grows geometrically, at a much faster rate.'

'What does that mean?' asks Sita.

'From the time of Buddha, the world's population has doubled only five times. And it took seventeen hundred years before we first doubled. The final doubling is taking place right now in the next sixty years. We have, if you like, always been designed to become this large in numbers, but there is also a limit to how much we will grow.'

'Are you saying human growth will end in Ram's lifetime?' Sita asks.

Dad points to his painting where he has drawn two small ducks sitting in a large pond under the Himalaya. This illustration is then repeated many times with the pond containing double the number of ducks. At the bottom of the Tanka there is a pond half full of ducks and in the last illustration the pond is full to the brim.

'Imagine this,' he says. 'A long time ago there were two ducks living on this pond. The next day there are four ducks, the next day there are eight ducks and so on.' He points down the Tanka until he reaches the second last illustration.

'Now,' he asks Sita, 'when is the pond full?'

'Now. Today.'

'Not today, but the day after it's half full!' He points to the half filled duck pond. 'This is today,' he says, 'the pond looks like there's still plenty of space. Then suddenly a day later the pond is full. This is Malthus's point that populations grow at an ever accelerated rate.'

'So, when will the earth be full of people?' Sita asks.

'Soon and in Ram's lifetime. No one has any past experience in coping with this number of people. There are six billion of us in today's pond and the UN estimates we could have as many as twelve billion by tomorrow.'

'Lord Siva!' Sita says, 'and why do we not double again?' she asks.

'There will never be 24 billion people.'

'How's that?'

'We have a limited lifespan.'

'How will it stop at twelve billion?'

'In the next seventy years the birth rates and death rates even out for humans. There will be no more growth of the human population. This is part of our design also.'

I chip in since this is something I know about in Public Health.

'It's interesting we have reached this stage in population growth at the same time as we have made advances in speaking to each other. That's why it's so important to do this talking now rather than looking back in history for guidance. No gurus of the past ever experienced the issues we face... even in this remote part of the world a Sanyassin can now read *Newsweek*.'

Dad continues, 'we need not look on this next six billion as just extra mouths to feed... we should see their future in terms of human consciousness, as the trillions of ideas and actions we can harvest to make things better. These next seventy years will be the hardest years mankind has ever experienced, because they'll bring the largest number of people into existence on earth's limited resources. It'll either provide us with the biggest gathering of fertile human minds ever assembled to meet such a challenges, or create an overwhelming number of people that need serious help to survive. Ram's generation will need to grow up, without the distractions we have created that stop us doing our job of making them aware beings. We have much to think about but we must limit the things that take people's minds off giving our full attention to young children.'

'Leave no child unattended,' I say and instantly regret speaking.

Sita picks up a sleepy Ram from under a blanket. 'We should

perhaps see Ram as an example of human consciousness in a baby,' Sita says.

Dad and I both look at each other, puzzled.

'He is learning to count just as the world around him has to and he's beginning to communicate… as you say the world is also. He's learned to feed himself but still has to learn to dispose of his own waste. If we witness his occasional tantrums and fights, we must help him. In a few years he will be fully-grown with great potential and will not grow any larger! Maybe in seventy years our world will have learned to act like the fully grown adult it will have become too.'

'I love it,' I say. 'Mankind is still currently in diapers, slowly learning how to get rid of its own crap but there's a chance it'll reach adulthood, if it survives the teenage years. Now there's an image for the centrepiece of a Tanka painting, dad.'

S ita, Ram and I return to Kathmandu with a roll of twenty paintings estimated to be worth sixty thousand dollars. I now have to find just the right buyers who will pay me without asking too many questions about the artist's origins. Like being given the medicine to cure your financial worries in a desert, then left to seek the water with which to swallow it.

Dad told me that he will send more paintings if I need them, to mum also if she will accept them. He said he always painted with us in mind. I was to view it as compensation for all these years he'd lived in isolation from us. He suggested my struggles with a decision on where to live in Nepal or Scotland, should no longer be determined by financial concerns as his were at my age.

There are three letters waiting for me in Kathmandu when we arrive. One is from Bahadur, another from my mother, which surprisingly contains a small note to me from Fiona.

Bahadur's letter is written on thin Nepalese paper postmarked Pokhara. He writes in neat English that he thinks of Sita, Ram and I often and much regrets leaving Kathmandu so quickly. He has also heard that police raided our home and prays that we are all now safe. He misses Durga terribly and many others from Pipelands. He has begun to work a little at his daughter's house in the hills of Baglung. Many people in the hills are unhappy with conditions. The Goddess Kali has taken her toll on too many poor people of Nepal.

Sita, Ram and I are ever welcome if we come near Pokhara. Om Shanti, Bahadur.

The letter from mother contains an apology for hanging up on our call, then a list of questions about my future that I still cannot answer. The short note from Fiona is postmarked eleven months earlier. She wants to know what I have done with her tennis racket. If I do not reply to her soon, it is unlikely she will ever contact me again.

The noise of the Mall's construction outside our window is much louder than before we left for Dhoti. It brings back the horror of what happened to Durga in Pipelands. Sita struggles to put Ram to sleep amidst the noise and dust. When I'm alone with Ram I think again of the anguish Sita experienced on that day. I think of how happy Durga always appeared; how she may have crouched alone in fear or been asleep and unaware, dreaming of a playtime with Ram, lying as he is now. I find tears running down my cheeks at the injustice of it all.

I dwell on what I might have done had Ram been in the shelter with Durga, or if the policeman's club had struck Sita harder, an inch to the right of her temple. It seems a very thin veil of control that covers our behaviour, when underneath lurks such primitive instincts ready to burst forth. The gurus might harp on about feelings being the consequences of attachment, but I am not yet ready to abandon my attachments. On the contrary, I feel a stronger attachment than ever to both Sita and Ram.

That night I see visions in my dreams, the cobblestones and the street views of Edinburgh, with my new family. I imagine the old ladies on the maroon buses, catching their balance at the exit when the driver hits the brakes too hard. I see the frowns on shopkeepers' faces when anyone gives them a twenty-pound note and takes all their loose change. I shudder at the thought of people calling Sita a nice oriental girl.

I see Princes Street, arguably the most beautiful street in the world, where the world's best-dressed beggars hang out and sleep rough. I imagine the pubs in Rose Street where old hard-men line up along the bar like Fakirs at Shivaratri. They have the same concrete faces, pale white scrotum-like skin pulled loosely over their skull but with holy ash falling at their feet from cigarettes, rather than from the slashes across their foreheads.

Edinburgh, whenever the wind blows away the clouds, is a sparkling stone jewel of a city. It is inclement until it is not. A place I've always called home. I decide now to make up my mind. I must stay here in Nepal and live and love my new family in Kathmandu.

I tell Sita of my decision. She looks relieved. I say I will write to my mother in the morning and tell her I must follow my heart and stay with both her and Ram. She listens and looks happy and humbled.

99

Before writing to mother, I go in search of a buyer for one of dad's paintings. I need to find out how liquid my assets are in Kathmandu. It will also give me the opportunity to send Bahadur the rent money we are due him.

Two of the local Tanka shops recognise the quality of the work I show them but tell me it is way out of their price range. I am directed to an American expert of Tanka painting who works at Phora Durbar, the American Embassy compound at Lazimpat. Without hesitation he offers me two thousand dollars in cash. I know it's worth at least three thousand. But the sight of someone waving hundreds of dollar bills in my face wins me over. I leave, passing the Embassy Dental Clinic. I instinctively pop my head into their office and ask how much they would charge to replace a front tooth.

It turns out our rent payments for the remainder of the year will cost us less than a hundred dollars but Sita's new front tooth is one half the price of dad's Tanka painting.

I know that Sita has by now accepted that she will live the rest of her life with a gap in her smile. The idea that something natural can be fixed or at least faked is not common knowledge among people here.

When I tell Sita of my arrangements to have her tooth fixed at the US dentists, she tells me there is something else we need to discuss first.

My heart sinks. I can tell she has been preoccupied with her thoughts since I announced my plan to stay. She invites me on a walk up to the edge of the valley to a hut belonging to the famed guru of the Moni Baba near the top of Shivapuri.

We walk as a family up the trail and Sita tells me that she has spoken to Swamy Y. She says his plans for the Moni Baba Centre, once complete, will contain a vegetarian restaurant; a library of Eastern philosophy books; a group of five individual meditation teaching chambers; and a hatha yoga teaching studio that can double for meetings and conferences. It will also contain a central soundproof room where people will pay money for silence.

It is now a more ambitious project than before and I feel that Sita is hinting there could be a role for her to play in its development. She tells me the Swamy is assured of help from the Immigration department for Visas for visitors and lecturers and that perhaps I would be able to stay on and work here.

Sita then goes silent. We walk up to a run-down hut where the door is open and inside sits a pair of wooden sandals next to a roped wooden bed. Sita tells me this is all that remains of the Sivapuri Baba's legacy, the Moni Baba's teacher. She suggests that the idea for a large institution in memory of the Moni Baba is an enterprise the Baba may not have welcomed. Hinduism has ordained many men and women gurus with god status for centuries. They become as Gods not as institutions. Though they've been a bit short on female Gods recently, she says.

I ask Sita what she is trying to say. She tells me that she also had a long talk with my dad while we were staying with him. It was there she realised that a different path has opened up for her. She has moved on from all the expectations of others who have guided her so far in life. She tells me that before I spoke of my decision to stay in Nepal she had considered saying that she would come to live in Scotland.

'I did not want to make that decision while I felt under pressure or while I was deeply affected by the Pipelands violence,' she tells me.

I ask Sita to explain how she came to this decision and why it took her so long.

'It did not take me too long,' she replies, 'it is a decision that came at the right time, no?'

'I suppose,' I answer.

'There is an advantage in knowing yoga, but that's all it is,' she says. 'An advantage. I'm too young to know how much lifetime value it will be, but I think I should test this advantage somewhere else rather than living off the Baba's reputation here. Your father told me I would find work easily in Scotland with my skills in yoga. I want to move there, teach yoga to Ram and all the other last ducks in the pond.'

I swallow hard. 'This is the confusing side of conscious love,' I say, 'doing what your lover requires after they've done what you require.'

'I suppose so,' Sita answers.

100

I write to mother informing her of my recent inheritance from dad's side of the family and my new plans to settle in Scotland with my Nepali wife and son. I ask if she can help find a place for us to stay. This will be quite a lot for her to take in, but I assure her we will have at least a little financial cushion to help us settle.

I also write to dad to tell him our plans to take Ram back to Scotland. I ask if he might like to attend the wedding, knowing this would be the last thing mother would want him to do.

Sita is very conscious of the ceremonial traditions of a Nepali wedding and does not want to go through all that palaver with me. I also feel it is best to keep the wedding quiet. An official marriage certificate will be comparatively simple to obtain.

'Nepali brides are usually dressed up in ornate clothes and displayed like a prize to relatives of the bride groom.'

'And therefore?'

'It's fine for big families but I've had enough of dressing up. As a Kumari, my hair was brushed and make-up put on each day just so I could look out of a window or hold audience with Panchiat leaders and visitors. Besides, my family are not paying any dowry to the Avadhoot for you.'

Sita tells me she wants to wear jeans and say, 'I do!' in a simple legal ceremony and I agree with her. We apply for all the necessary paperwork to include Ram into the Munro family. With only a few poor relatives in the valley, Sita has no reason to expect any of our friends would want an elaborate wedding. Or so we think.

After some persuasion, I book a dentist appointment for Sita and before her passport photo is taken, I accompany her to the dental clinic. Two young American dentists place headphones on Sita while they work on reconstructing her smile. They tell me the headphones are used to play music to distract her. I tell them that Sita is the least likely among their patients to require distraction while they work on her teeth. They insist on playing Talking Heads. I inform them she has not really followed pop music but is now likely to forever associate this band with drilling in her mouth.

Within a week, the dentists are finished and both Sita and I are amazed at the result. Having successfully meditated as any yogini might, through Talking Heads and the dental procedure, I see a return of confidence that I'd hardly noticed she'd lost.

I am told by Swamy Y that some of Sita's relatives have been in contact with her. They have heard of her plans and that some are planning to make an occasion of our departure. I thank the Swamy for this information and wait to see if Sita will tell me anything about these plans.

On the days leading up to the wedding, I manage to sort out the legal requirements at the British Embassy. They inform me they will accept the marriage paperwork only if someone from a recognized religious order signs it. I make arrangements through Swamy Y to have Father Martin, a Jesuit priest, conduct a small ceremony somewhere quiet. I suggest we do this at a small hotel, next to the Buddhist stupa at Boudhanath. Sita agrees to invite only a few close friends like Swamy Y, Tilak, Maya and a few Yoga Centre folks she knows.

Born into the Church of Scotland, son of a Hindu holy-man, I am marrying a Living Goddess next to a Buddhist temple in a ceremony conducted by a Catholic priest. Quite a fitting wedding plan for an expat and a yogini, I think.

101

My first hint that something strange is happening comes when I go to the Gent's toilet, just before the ceremony at the hotel. I look out of the window and I see an elephant walking past with the words *Congratulations James and Sita* written in red paint on its side. As I leave the toilet, Swamy Y drags me into a side room where Tilak is standing.

'Surprise!' he shouts, as he waves something frighteningly familiar.

'What's going on?' I say.

'Maya is here and she is with Sita helping her get her dressed up for the wedding. So you need to be dressed up also.'

'Are you sure Sita's going to get dressed up?' I ask in disbelief.

'Yes, Maya brought the woman who did Sita's make up as the Kumari.'

Tilak holds up a thick tartan kilt and smiles.

'Where did you get that thing?' I ask.

'Another Gurkha friend brought it back from a trip to Scotland. He got it at a secondhand military shop, near Stirling Castle. It's good, it's old, from the war, I'm told.'

'Which war... the Crimean?'

The article of clothing that Tilak hands me is a rough looking dress kilt. It is made of the Cameron tartan and has what looks like a bullet-hole through one of the pleats, complete with scorched edges. Tilak and Swamy Y have also assembled the accessories needed with the kilt, including a white shirt and a bow tie. A sporran has been ingeniously made from a small Tibetan carpet. Football socks and black brogue shoes with a miniature Kukhre to place in my sock for a Schian Do complete the outfit.

In the privacy of the room, I remove my newly purchased Nerhu shirt and put on the kilt. This is only the second time in my life I've worn this garment. The first time was at a church memorial service for my father in Peebles, when I was eight years old.

A thick belt with a Chinese buckle holds the kilt in place. It looks surprisingly appropriate and regal enough for a proper wedding.

As we sit and wait for the appointed time, Tilak tells me that that the main Kumari in Kathmandu is always picked as a Buddhist, born into a Newari Buddhist family. She is also considered the reincarnation of the Lord Shiva's wife Parvati, the patron deity of Hindu Royalty. The word Kumari in Nepali means virgin goddess.

As I walk into the main dining area, my soon to be wife... is surely a goddess.

A barrage of five Tibetan horns all sound at once as we enter the room. As monks blow their lungs out, others chant and clash cymbals in time. I walk towards a makeshift alter and Sita joins me. Amidst the noise and colour, we catch each other's eye in a stunned exchange at our attire.

'Nice blue jeans,' I say to Sita.

'You look good in your sari,' she says, smiling at my kilt.

I am turned to face Sita and from then on I'm transfixed. She's wearing a red and gold dress with elaborate embroidery round the collar. She is draped in gold chains around her neck and wears a tiered crown on her head. Her forehead is painted red with a simple yellow and black middle eye centred on her brow. Her eyes are rimmed in thick black make-up, with the eyebrows continuing all the way above her ears. She has thick red lipstick and the hint of a smile on her face. I feel like a Scottish country dancer who's just wandered into a Maharani's coronation.

Father Martin joins us, wearing a Nepali topi hat. He steps forward and places two scarves around our necks, then gestures for the guests to sit down. Given the number of camera flashes that continue after the horns stop, I reckon there are a fair number of hotel tourists here as well.

There are dozens of people, spilling out onto the lawn outside towards a large white canopy tent. All this secretly organised and set in place by Tilak and Swamy Y. There are a few more surprises from Tilak and Didi when I see the Tamang boys here from Barabase and Sharad with members of the rock band Elegant waving their guitars at me from the tent.

During the service, Father Martin praises the rich mix of religions in the room; he states the similarities in marriages all over the world and the universal vows that are spoken on such occasions. He mentions that all religions have tried to find a definition and a social protection for love.

He stresses the uniqueness of our particular union… introducing Sita as 'a woman confident enough to marry the man she loves.' He introduces me as a seeker and then suggests I am 'the nemesis of superstition,' which I take as a reference to defiance of the Kumari curse.

A simple vow is read out by each of us, that we will partner in parenthood and love for our life together. We both say we will and with a touch of his forehead, Father Martin pronounces us woman and husband.

There are no hymns, no prayers, no bolts of lightening to strike me down, only a Gurkha bagpiper who steps forward and plays the Flower of Scotland at the back of the room. Outside, Ram is sitting in the lap of a Mahout riding the elephant around the garden.

After enough congratulations from people to make my face feel locked in a permanent smile, we sit on rugs and cushions to enjoy a meal of Dhal Bhat. Tilak eats like a porter and Maya feeds Ram with her fingers.

After the meal, many Nepali friends leave and Sharad the guitarist asks me what song I would like to be played for the couple's first dance. I look at Sita who shrugs and says anything except Talking Heads. We agree on the Bob Marley classic, 'One Love'.

As we stand for what is our first ever dance together, the left-over guests join us and Sharad begins singing 'I don't want to wait in vain for your love.' The crowd laughs and sings along with this alternative Marley song. I stop and look at Sharad until he changes to the tune to 'One Love'. Sita does not understand the joke and we are surrounded by guests who all dance … together… and feel alright.

As the sun sinks behind the mountains, Sita and I take a walk around the stoop at Boudhanath in full marriage costumes. Locals, tourists and travelling Tibetans all stare at us. We spin the prayer wheels as we walk and Sita mumbles mantras while we circum-navigate the shrine. Swamy Y follows us with a video camera to capture the end of a memorable day. Sita and I embrace on the upper steps of the stupa, under the ever-seeing eyes on Boud-hanath's crown. A gust of wind catches my kilt.

U nsurprisingly, dad does not attend the wedding. He sends us a wedding gift marked as a Tibetan rug. It is a package that contains another fifty exquisite Tanka paintings. Dad's instructions are that half of the paintings are to be given to my mother and the other half are for Sita and I. With so many people including Embassy staff and tourists taking photographs at our wedding, dad was right to stay away.

Dad mentions in his letter he has taken on board what I said about him getting out more. He says he will visit Kathmandu and engage in some activities for the new Moni Baba Centre, 'to make sure that in the efforts to stay profitable the Centre does not dilute the Baba's teaching till its value becomes insipid.'

Sita seems excited and happy. She settles down in preparation for the unknown in Scotland, while I ramp up my arrangements to return to the all-too−familiar.

I find my mind slipping back into overdrive with thoughts of the responsibility this move has put on me. It's fine to live in a strange land where nature still rules and things that go wrong can be blamed on a host of gods. Pressure comes with the understanding of personal responsibility and for me that brings worry. I try hard to retain what I've learned from this break, so as not to slip back into old ways.

The journey my dad undertook, to study yoga through old books, seems to have shown him how a figure of speech can become a belief. How, as a society we collect these beliefs and turn them into laws. How our minds treat us or trick us, depending on how well we balance thoughts. Those ideas that require action are different from those that exist for the sake of thinking. Not all thoughts are moulded by personal experiences. Many are collected and stored like trophies. I feel that in this next phase of going home I will have to throw out some of my tarnished trophies.

As friendships often provide, a distraction from my personal challenges comes along. I'm informed by Sita that Maya has gone into labour. I hunt down Tilak in the centre of Thamel in a teashop frequently visited by ex-Kurkhas. He is eating samosa and making business deals over glasses of chai. I interrupt him to say Sita sent me to tell him that his third child is on its way.

As we leave the tea shop together, I feel the need to warn Tilak on something crucial to his future sanity.

'You know that with each of Maya's pregnancies there has always been a slightly higher percentage chance it will be a girl. It's only a fractional difference of over fifty per cent, but remember having two girls does not reduce your chances of having another daughter.'

Tilak looks at me as if I know the gender of his child already.

'Is it a girl?'

'I don't know... but if it is ... remember your reaction to this birth will have an enormous effect on Maya's mental state.' Tilak nods in reluctant agreement.

Maya's waters broke in our flat where Sita now helps her to relax. She is a few weeks early with her delivery and events happen very fast. I watch Sita as she squats next to Maya on a floor mat. Through a severe bout of contractions I think it's better to leave and take Tilak outside. Our midwife couple have come to help take care of Maya.

After a timeless period of silence we hear the cries of a baby and I hug Tilak, saying congratulations while whispering, 'show no disappointment'.

We are called in to witness Sita helping Maya nurse her new baby daughter on the floor of our room. The child seems perfectly healthy but Maya looks worried when she sees Tilak.

Tilak helps Maya to stand and move to the comfort of our bed as this tiny new girl begins her air breathing life with a feed. I'm amazed once again at the physical strength of Nepali women. Here is Maya, so soon after birth, standing and acting as if she could go out into the fields and help bring in the harvest.

If Tilak does feels any disappointment, he keeps it well hidden. I'm positive that somewhere among his superstitions, he could easily concoct an alternative belief to invest in. It's not long before I find out he already has.

'My daughter could well be the Moni Baba reincarnated,' he suggests.

'Yes,' I say, happy that Tilak has formed a useful but delusional belief to help him through this moment.

SITA, HAVING PROVED HERSELF A COMPETENT MID-WIFE, ASKS IF there might be any need for floor deliveries of babies in Edinburgh. I tell her that at present there is no such demand but who knows in the future she might be able to introduce a trendy floor-birthing clinic next door to a water birthing spa. I tell her that she will have much to offer in Scotland and that I'm sure that she helped Maya cope with the aftermath of gender disappointment. There are many cases of disappointment among parents in Scotland, that yoga would help people overcome. Sita tells me that one of the ways she helped Maya cope was to promise her we would consider her new daughter as a future bride for Ram when he grows up.

On the night of our departure, Sita takes my shoulders in her hands and once more surprises me with her maturity of thought. While she massages my neck she says, 'We are both following our individual yoga paths. You must apply your consciousness to find your own union. Do not think that I wish to go to Scotland only to teach yoga, or offer advice or that you will learn yoga from me. It is my choice to go to Scotland as a place to practice my yoga.' She then hands me my copy of dad's book, saying 'Remember this was written for you. From what you and your father have told me, there are now many people who now practice yoga in your country. The yoga pantheon has always accepted contributions made by those that practice. Today it would seem the largest contribution is coming from outside of its country of origin. I want to hear and see for myself what these contributions are. I wish to learn more from people in western cultures and I will make that my yoga.'

I think of the extraordinary journey since I left the cobbled streets of Edinburgh with this book in my hand. Tomorrow, I will walk to meet my mother there with my wife and son.

ABOUT THE AUTHOR

George McBean lived in Nepal for seven years working for UNICEF. This fictional story is influenced greatly by the author's knowledge of the country and his personal interest in yoga. He later worked as Head of Graphics and Animation at UNICEF HQ New York. His career spanned 36 years of service for UNICEF,

See www.georgemcbean.com for more about George, his writings and illustrations.

ACKNOWLEDGMENTS

I would like to thank those who have supported me in creating and finishing this book. Firstly, my oldest son Fergus who was given this story in an early draft when he left the family nest to go to University. I felt he should carry with him some inspiration from the rich culture of Nepal, a country he lived in for seven of his most formative years. To my other children Ainslie and Ramsay who were also given a draft novel when they left the nest, which served the in-all-fairness purpose of that moment.

To the people at the Scottish Arts Club who have encouraged me to take this story further since my retirement. (Hence the name Idle George Publications.) To all members of the SAC Writers Group, who recently read the draft story and gave me feedback. Especially George Wilson, Glenys Mclaren, John McLoed, Hilary Munro, Tom Gordon and Jeanette Davidson among others. To friends and readers Charlie Miller, Stewart McNab, John Olander, Rodney Hall, Don Cameron, Ariane Accardi, Tanya and Raj Dhakhwa, Heidi Larson, Biljana Labovic, Belinda Gordon, Berengere Brooks, Davina Solomon, Leilah Zahedi Alison Hampshire,

Brenda Sutherland, Sangharsha Bhatharai and Eleonore Dambre for her wisdom beyond her years. To Claire Wingfield for her editing and guidance.

Lastly my parents George and Peggy, who read the early draft and realised perhaps for the first time, that I might not return to Edinburgh for a 'real job'. Not least I'd like to thank my prize-winning novelist wife Sara Cameron McBean, whose writing skills far exceed my own and whose encouragement, along with her conscious love, inspire me.

If you enjoyed this book, please help to spread the word and consider leaving a review at Amazon, Waterstones online, Kobo, Goodreads or any other suitable site. These are an immense help to authors.

Printed in Great Britain
by Amazon